SHAKEN ALLEGIANCES
TWO DAYS FROM
THE CONTINUUM OF NONSENSE

To Adam
Enjoy this journey
across the border!

Michel Bruneau

SHAKEN ALLEGIANCES
TWO DAYS FROM
THE CONTINUUM OF NONSENSE

Michel Bruneau

CePages Press

For all those allergic to omphaloskeptics

Disclaimer

The characters in this novel are purely fictional. Any resemblance to actual people, deceased or alive, is purely coincidental.

Oddly, in spite of this standard disclaimer—inescapable legalese fodder of our modern times—some individuals will co-opt any inkling of a familiar human foible or spark of brilliance depicted in the prose they encounter as evidence serving their obsessive conviction that they have been literarily cloned. To thwart such self-aggrandizing claims and egos, beyond re-emphasizing that the characters in this novel are truly fictional, it is underscored here that any such self-association might amount to an indirect (and possibly humiliating) admission of dubious ethics and demeaning moral attitude, in some instances possibly beyond what is deemed humanly possible outside of the realm of insanity.

Still, beyond that overt qualifier and an emphasis right at the outset that "there are no heroes," some individuals will persist to recognize themselves in characters whom they deem to be intelligent, respectable, or heroic. Such individuals somehow will either have skipped the above-amended disclaimer, or will have found intelligence and heroism where there is none through some dyslexic mechanism that escapes understanding.

Thus, readers so convinced and pleased that they provided inspiration for presumably positive characters are urged to elevate themselves beyond the level of braggart by demonstrating their appreciation and conviction through a donation to the author's special retirement fund.

Note that artistic license was also taken by creating a number of fictitious agencies, institutes, and universities, to protect actual entities from prying inquiries. At the same time, for historical and political realism in this work of fiction, and to ensure that the curious public will know where to forward its relevant questions, a number of actual public agencies have been named. However, the reader should rest assured that these agencies' staff, officials, and the politicians they report to, are far more capable, knowledgeable, ethical, and intelligent than depicted here—at least, at the time of this writing.

Forewarning

The reader is forewarned that swearing in Québec, where much of the events unfold, has quite different colors than in the Anglo-Saxon world. In a society where the French-speaking population has been oppressed by religion in various creative ways for centuries up to the 1950s, but where artful frontal nudity can now be shown uncensored during the six o'clock news and where pornographic movies are broadcast uncut and unscrambled past midnight on network TV, using the Lord's name in vain—or any part of the Church's paraphernalia for that matter—has evolved to provide considerably more shock value than sexual or scatological expletives. Given the plethora of opportunities to offend by exercising creative religious taxonomy, four-letter words are too short for anyone to care in Québec.

A nun walking away from a cash-register and suddenly realizing that she was shortchanged in the transaction is liable to shout "*Maudite marde, j'me suis faite fourrer!*" (translating literally as "Damn shit, I've been fucked!") without attracting attention; although nuns are so rare in Québec nowadays—most religious orders having traded their valuable real estate for retirement annuities from a different god—they are liable to attract attention by their mere presence, without having to say a word. However, a 4-year-old boy would definitely get away with it without reprimand. However, had the same 4-year-old whispered "*Crisse, j'me me chu faite avouère*" ("Christ, I've been had"), he would likely be grounded for inappropriate abuse of Molière's language.

Now that blasphemous language has invaded prime time entertainment as the preferred technique to paint boring teleplays with a coat of realism, future generations of Québécois will be significantly challenged to create more offensive innuendoes, syntax, and constructions to distinguish themselves from their parents. But that is a different story.

January 25th

There are no heroes.

Québec City, 1:00 a.m.

"Sorry to wake you up—"

"I was up."

"Oh! You felt it in Québec, too?"

"You bet. It shook *en tabarnak*!" he said, while looking at his wife on her knees picking up pieces of a broken vase—hiding his delight to be rid of that hideous gift from the in-laws and wagging the phone receiver as the perfect excuse for not helping.

The contents of the room had vibrated, shifted or toppled as the building convulsed. Although, in reality, the structure had only swayed in relatively small, jerky movements, to Léandre, living for the first time through sudden shaking strong enough to move all frames of reference in a room was a disturbing and frightening experience. It violated his innate belief in the immovability of a strong and sturdy shelter anchored in solid, stable ground.

The unsettledness that developed when the uncontrollable foreign rhythm drove the foundations and drew the entire habitation into an infernal dance, had amplified the acuteness of his senses, distorted the perception of time and space, and trumped his ability to reliably gauge those essential dimensions. Seconds and inches became minutes and feet—or more, proportionally to the surge in adrenalin that primed every sensory receptor to an alarmed and sharpened attention level.

His wife had slept through half of the most severe shaking—inured to the nightly mattress waves generated by the constant tossing and turning of his stress-induced insomnia—only to be awakened by the crashing of her prized possession. Léandre was only half asleep, still aroused by the lure of the historical moment about to unfold under his leadership, when it all started. He felt the anguish of every long second suffered under the hand of this unwelcome intruder: the initial disturbance from the comfort of static equilibrium that foretold impending abnormalcy, the suspension of belief as the certainty of life was upturned, the fear of not knowing where the climax of the building crescendo lied, the torment of helplessly clinging to hope as the only available amulet while awaiting an undetermined end, the stunning stillness of it all when the flaring storm abated and reality returned, the relief to be a survivor escaping with minimal damage, and the emerging anxiety that followed recognizing that, while the violent trespasser had finally left, it did so only after having trampled the

sacred ground of a political process that might now be irremediably disturbed.

It dawned on him that pockets of destruction in one small
part of the province could beget irreparable damage beyond the
tangible world; if all was not fine, it risked jeopardizing their plans
for history.

"Everything's fine here," said Léandre. "Is it pretty bad
where you are?"

"It's terrible... I'm sending a chopper to *Complexe H* to pick
you up. Be there in 30 minutes. It will be ugly at sunrise, and
people will want to see that the Premier is in charge."

"How bad can it be? It just happened a minute ago, you can't
possibly have any damage report by now. Besides, there's only one
ostie de road and a couple of villages in all of Charlevoix."

A pause at the other end of the phone. The type of sudden,
lingering silence triggered when confusion emerges to shatter the
illusion that a tacit understanding exists.

Léandre had spent a few summers at a youth camp near Les
Éboulements, in Charlevoix, where he came to learn that the location owed its name to a massive landslide triggered by an earthquake in the 17th century. The Jesuit Relations reported entire
mountains swallowed by the sea, new islands emerging, rivers
disappearing, and thunder rumbling beneath the ground; powerful
imagery that captured the imagination of 20th-century kids sitting
around a campfire, but no less than a faith-enhancing experience
to Jesuit witnesses certain that the wrath of God had been unleashed for a moment—a glimpse of the Apocalypse revealed to
punish those aboriginals who harbored impure thoughts and absolute indifference to the gospel.

Kindling those camp fire memories, Léandre's grandmother
had repeatedly shared with him a similar theory on the divine
origin of earthquakes, one that she intuitively developed following
the tremor that shook Québec in the 1920s, also epicentered in
Charlevoix near LaMalbaie, and that she loved exposing in impromptu lectures intended to revive the forsaken faith of the
younger generations. However, because that earthquake only
damaged a few monumental structures in Québec, her thesis mod-
estly postulated that the earth shivers when hearts turn cold to the
Almighty, and that small quakes are calls to piety to scare the

populace and remind it that stricter punishments are awaiting unrepentant souls.

Since then, many small, inconsequential jolts were felt in Québec, years or decades apart, but all failed to summon the respect such forces of nature deserve, conspiring to melt any communal awareness of imminent danger.

"Léandre, I'm not at the ski condo at the Massif. I'm at my parents' house in Ste-Julie. The fridge is horizontal, there's broken glass in every room, and no electricity. If it's like that throughout Montréal, there won't be any voting next week. This thing will make the ice storm of '98 look like a mosquito bite."

"*Crisse!*"

The cursing did not bother the interlocutor. It was the recognized sign of acceptance into Léandre's innermost circle, as his public persona was polished and controlled, partly to mask his humble origins, but mostly because protocol dictated this demeanor—and polls confirmed it necessary.

"*Complexe H* in 30 minutes. We'll fly you to the old St-Hubert in Longueuil, along with Réal and Julien. By the time you're there, we'll hopefully have preliminary damage reports. I'll try to get in touch immediately with the *Organisation de sécurité civile du Québec* to set-up a briefing line. See you there."

Léandre hung up, and slumped on the bed.

"*Sacrament.* Just what I needed."

Solange sat next to him. Married to a politician for so long, she recognized without fail the call to duty in her husband's eyes, or rather the fire when the desire for politicking took priority over the marital vows. Kissing up to the public always came before kissing one's wife. But this time, the stakes looked high.

"Was that Florent Racine-Dostie?"

"Yep."

"It's bad? Do they already know where it hit?"

"No," he replied, while dialing, "but it looks like things in Montréal will be pretty *fucké* if what he went through is typical. He wants to fly me over in 30 minutes."

He jumped up.

"Come on, pick-up the *crisse de* phone," he shouted while pacing.

"Uh... Who's that?"

"Get call-ID *ostie d'*cheap bastard!"

"Oh..., yeah, Léandre. What happened?"

"You slept through the whole thing?" Whispering as an aside to his wife, "*Maudit* bureaucrats!"

"What thing?"

"No time to explain. Call a meeting of the policy task force. I'm sure they are not all oblivious to what happens around them, so one of them will get you up to speed. I'll call the *Complexe H* office in a few hours on the secure line. We might need some serious damage control and policy strategies, so get their *viarge de* brains storming."

Léandre slammed the phone, as he always did after talking to one he considered inferior or incompetent. He felt an oppressive rush of stress overpowering him and, aware of the prognosis for skyrocketing blood pressure, he took deep breaths to regain his composure and reassure his wife that he wouldn't let any attack shorten their life together.

She pulled out some clothes for him—a set of matching casual pants and shirt, a three piece suit, a few ties—assuming he might be gone for a couple of days.

Admiring her slender, shapely body in a see-through nightdress as she bent to pull his travel case from the closet, he felt a surge of lust for his lifelong companion. He surmised that making passionate love to her at this juncture, in the most explicitly and sensual manner, as typically done in the opening pages of many novels according to a proven recipe to turn flaccid stories into best sellers, would definitely be the thing to do. But duty called.

Waiting for the chauffeured limousine, he grabbed the remote and channel-surfed while dressing up.

Gloucester (Ottawa), still 1:00 a.m.

While Canadian television has its aficionados and detractors, both groups agree that it is generally not worth watching in the middle of the night. James, usually not up at that time, had just reached the same conclusion.

He found channel-surfing to be a futile exercise—not an amazing discovery as he expected no less—but he had hoped that the news stations would not still be re-running yesterday's evening broadcasts. After all, he wondered, how much time can it take for the news bureaus to wake up, plaster make-up on a news anchor, and plant him or her there just to acknowledge the event and create a war-room tension and the appearance of news?

Yet, he found valuable information where it was lacking: from the disturbing fact that all the Montréal-based stations were out. The snowy image on the monitor drenched the room in a blue glow reminiscent of the Poltergeist movie—minus cute kid. The utter absence of broadcasting from Montréal confirmed his suspicions.

His calculations were simple. The time lag between the sharp seismic P-waves that had hit the house like a truck and woke him up, and the horizontally swaying S-waves that had followed, pointed to an epicenter maybe at most 150 miles away. Seismic vibrations felt at a single geographical location do not provide enough information to reliably identify the location of an epicenter—three different points where such vibrations are recorded are necessary for this purpose. Failing the availability of such triangulation, James had mentally drawn a circle of 150 miles radius around Ottawa. It intersected two possible culprits: the Northern Québec or the St-Lawrence River seismic zones. A quick assessment of the severity and duration of the vibrations he felt during the event (akin to using a poorly calibrated "biological seismograph," he thought in jest), factoring the epicentral distance into the equation, suggested a rather strong earthquake magnitude—6.5, maybe more. That ruled out west of Ottawa, leaving only north or east as possible sources.

Reliable predictions were obviously not possible using this empirical technique, but given that he had long preached that Montréal was an underestimated seismic risk, almost dormant since the 18th century, he envisioned that the worst had happened. This time, the epicenter of a large Canadian earthquake would not be located in the middle of an ocean, the arctic, the tundra, or a national park, but possibly in a crowded urban center. Unfortunately, he dreaded, his professional guesses were often accurate.

He went upstairs to his office and logged on to the computer. This is the internet era after all, he thought, and television is so "twentieth century." As usual, instead of impatiently watching the stream of meaningless messages on the dumb computer screen while the sluggish Operating System ran its bloated spaghetti code and loaded all of its drivers to boot up, he contemplated the inspiring winter view from his frosted window. Mortgaged to the bone for the pleasure of an unobstructed view of the Rideau Canal, the peacefulness of the thin ribbon of ice was a balm for his sore life.

The public gardens and mature trees lining the peaceful linear urban oasis betrayed its original purpose and excruciating birth. He knew that the canal was built in the 19th century at the cost of a thousand lives by the hands of Irish and French Canadian laborers working in insalubrious conditions, under the supervision of the British Royal Engineers. He knew that it was built to connect the mighty St. Lawrence River to the also imposing Ottawa River, stringing together lakes up to the Rideau River, to provide an alternate waterway to Montréal in the event of further attempts by the Americans to invade Canada. He was also aware of the checkered past of the last segment of the canal—a waterway narrower than a football field that cut Ottawa in half, built to bypass the falls where the Rideau River dives into the Ottawa River. And that the coveted luxurious real estate on both sides of the canal concealed its past role as an effective divider between the neighborhoods of the wealthy, educated, self-righteous Protestant ruling class on its west bank, and the shanties of their arch-rivals, the disenfranchised Roman Catholic working class. Fully aware that the canal had provided a buffer between simmering animosities periodically revived through harsh economic times—even aware that when a riot erupted out of a passionate and irresolvable political conflict in a distant past, the opposing political factions eventually faced each other with arms and cannons on a bridge over the canal.

Yet, in the night, the ribbon of blue ice, reflecting a bright moon, was a soothing vista that made him forget his professional frustrations. A lone skater glided by, as sometimes happened at such odd hours. He wondered if the earthquake had opened cracks in the world's largest skating rink.

He loaded the internet browser to visit the Earthquakes Canada website of Natural Resources Canada, more specifically the online automated reports of recent seismological activity. Automated maybe, but not immediate, as no information on this earthquake was yet posted.

Strange, he thought. Triangulation and magnitude estimates should not take so long.

Returning to archaic but reliable technology, he grabbed the radio. One hand on the radio dialing stations in succession, the other on the personal computer's keyboard still teasing cyberspace for a meaningful response, he flipped through the AM stations, searching for news.

"Music, boring music, Muzak, punk noise, crappy pop, mindless music," he deplored, condemning all channels as endless tombstones of the intelligent radio of days past.

"Bingo."

At last, a voice on the radio, freed from music, connected to the entirety of an intelligent being, and ready to express or channel opinions, thoughts, and possibly news.

"You are listening to CHOK-AM, choc-radio."

Vaudreuil-Dorion, 1:05 a.m.

"You are listening to CHOK-AM, choc-radio. It is 1:05 a.m., -30°F, and I am wondering if any of you can hear me."

Richard Turcotte, alias Dick Nightrock in his quest for stardom, felt that this gift from the gods of fortune might just be his long-awaited chance to break out of his dead-end night shift disk jockey assignment, and make it in the "big leagues" of the media world. To leave once and for all the crummy little station crammed into the "most ugly concrete-box equipment shed on earth," in the middle of a cow field west of Montréal, and join a real one, smack-dab on the island, with all the designer furniture, sparkling floor-to-ceiling windows, perks and privileges—and prestige—that came with the position.

"Folks, I just took a shower of CDs that are now piled up on the floor. There's nothing left on the fixed shelves, and the tall bookcases have toppled on the chairs in front of me. I am fine, but the Nightrock won't be playing music anymore tonight. This thing is a serious matter. It looked like the end of the world was here, but since I'm alive, I guess that it must have been either a huge explosion, or a plane crash, or an earthquake. There are no windows in this studio, so call me. Tell us all what happened."

While his phone had a dial tone, Richard worried that it didn't prove anything. All other phones might be dead. Or their owners for that matter, he feared. What if—beyond comprehension—he was the lone survivor of a nuclear holocaust?

"Call us at 555-CHOK, and let us know what the hell happened where you are. 555-CHOK, 555-CHOK. Cell-phones at *-CHOK. Is there anybody out there who can hear me at all?"

The sudden glow of a light on the switchboard brought hope to his aspirations for fame.

"Caller on line 1, the Nightrock welcomes you. Tell us what you know."

"Am I on?"

"Yes, it's your turn to enlighten us. Go ahead."

"Hey man, this was hell. I thought I was going to die! All the furniture shifted left and right, up and down, even the piano moved 10 feet."

"Ten feet. You're sure?"

"At least, man. I mean, the lamps swayed so hard they hit the ceiling and broke."

"Where are you?"

"I'm in Laval, man. It felt like a giant took the house and shook it like a piggy bank to get spare change out of it. Everything is upside down. It's a huge mess, man."

"Are you calling on a cell phone?"

"No, no, regular phone, man. But we have no electricity, I'm using a flashlight now."

The phone console lit up. The public was on all lines, waiting to share its nightmarish experience. This is going to be a very good night, mulled Richard with satisfaction.

"Thanks for your call. Caller on line 2, you're on."

"Hello?"

"Yes, hello, hello. The previous caller told us his piano moved 12 feet. What happened to you?"

Pointe-aux-Trembles, 1:10 a.m.

A mountain of engine blocks intermingled with debris from their crushed crates arose from the otherwise flat topography of the warehouse floor. An indistinct warehouse on the east end of Montréal Island among many in which the same scenario played out, where shelves spilled their fraction of the gross domestic product onto hard concrete slabs. With the difference that, in this warehouse, a monotonic excerpt from Wagner's "The Ride of the Valkyries" started to play repeatedly from one particular pile of debris.

This musical call from his cell phone brought Jules Letarte back to consciousness. Pinned under a couple of 6-cylinder SUV engine blocks, a sizeable number of bones pulverized, and bleeding to death, Jules woke up dazed and confused. His first hallucinatory thought was that he had been crushed, dried, ground, and recycled into top-grade fertilizer, and that he was tied by the entangling roots of various vegetables sucking the life out of him. His future was actually less promising.

Unable to move a limb, reduced to suffer the annoying chirping of his cell phone and powerless to answer, he was drifting slowly into unconsciousness, returning via delirium to this way-station refuge where the mind disconnected from the excruciating suffering endured before deliverance by death. The incessantly repeating incantation reminded him of a parliamentary bell calling all to vote, as he'd heard on TV during a filibuster by the opposition party boycotting the session to prevent the vote on a question.

The question!

An impulse to vote invaded his whole being, rekindling his will to live. He could not die without expressing his support for the question.

"*Oui, oui, oui, oui...*" emanated from the heap of metal and wood, loudly at first, with each positive endorsement slightly fainter than the previous one. Whispers, followed by a few unintelligible gasps, and then silence, as the Valkyries died at the same time.

Rivière-des-Prairies, 1:15 a.m.

Lise's husband did not like to stay idle in the watchmen's office. Not much typically happened during his night shift, so he liked to walk the aisles, amazed at the diversity of goods produced by the global economy and in transit via the huge distribution center under his surveillance.

This passion for strolling the aisles had once created somewhat of a problem, as Lise wanted him to be always reachable, at any time, in case of emergencies, or for whatever purpose pleased her fancy. She liked to control people, and her husband was no exception; of all people, she particularly wanted to keep him on a tight leash. As, she believed, any good dictator, priest, or dominatrix knew, implementation of total control required tools. She henceforth had felt fully justified to "loan" him her office-paid cell phone during the nights, taking it back in the mornings before she left for work. This scheme had worked well given that her office had never called her on that cell phone before, but her belief that the device was merely a prestigious but useless toy had just been shattered.

She wanted the phone back, and fast, but her worries compounded significantly as her husband failed to answer. She dialed repeatedly, unaware that each time, in the Pointe-aux-Trembles warehouse, her call launched a few bars of the bastardized rendition of Wagner's epic from under the mass of debris from which the *Oui's* had died earlier.

Lise Letarte, director of the *Organisation de sécurité civile du Québec*, was a political appointee, obviously endorsed by partial supporters, but blasted by others as being unable to grasp the level of her own incompetence. Not irremediably stupid, she recognized the current situation to be an emergency that would require her to report to work—as a civil servant who clearly differentiated work from duty. Copies of detailed emergency response plans that she would need lied neatly stowed somewhere in file cabinets at the office—at work, not at home—and it dawned on her that she had better get there at once.

A fair commute to downtown from the north-east end of Montréal Island. But first, she planned a detour via the warehouse where her husband worked.

Ottawa, 1:15 a.m.

"Where are my highly paid responsible officials when I need them?" muttered the Premier.

The RCMP officer at the front door knew better than any citizen how to read the man, and was not about to be misled by his monotonic, near-somnolent speech. Next to the Premier, Droopy Dog might have looked like an over-caffeinated, agitated mutt, but nobody could be as insidiously politically lethal as the Premier. Behind his back, his own Party members called him the Stealth Executioner. Under a stern calmness was a resolve that could fatally slice and dice the political career of any subordinate.

Whereas the media remained puzzled about how such a colorless persona could become Chief of the Democratic Canadian Rightist Alliance Party of Canada, bewitch the electorate into a near-hypnotic comatose state, and get elected by sweeping all the seats west of the Rideau Canal up to the Pacific Ocean, they knew that behind the mask of compassion and smooth aura of calm, poise, and tolerance was a political barbarian who left a trail of blood on his road to the top.

Brendon Decker now occupied 24 Sussex Drive, the official residence of the Prime Minister of Canada, as if he had paid the mortgage and had no intention to sell. Yet, he found the property unfit to his ego.

First, the lot was squeezed between two brash neighbors, being adjacent to the French embassy and a stone's throw from the official residence of the Governor General of Canada across the street, equal in size to the former but only a fraction of the latter domain. Brendon begrudged that prestigious acres were wasted to provide a foreign foothold to France—an historical archrival of the Commonwealth—but he more deeply resented the disproportionate estate bestowed to the official representative of the Crown, mostly owing to the Governor's privileged constitutional status, and partly ensuing from the poor excuse of it being the place of residence of the Canadian Monarch when that personage deigned visit Ottawa once every decade or so. While he had pledged allegiance to the Crown, as a legal necessity, he was foremost a Canadian, proud of his English heritage, but prouder of having built Canada following the trail of hard work blazed by his ancestors and without help from the distant motherland of bygone times. At best, he saw the monarchy as serving the single purpose of being a convenient symbolic reminder, not of where sovereign power lied per the Constitution, but rather of where within the multicultural mosaic of the nation lied ownership of the country—a parliamentary democracy owned, and to remain owned, by Caucasians of Anglo-Saxon ancestry.

Second, while located within the narrow park of manicured lawns and gardens that hugged the southern shore of the Ottawa river, the mansion's riverside panorama spanned the bland northern shore, a ribbon of modest waterfront bungalows interrupted by parks at the mouth of the Gatineau River that provided an uninspiring foreground to the skyline of government office buildings and pulp and paper mills' chimneys towering in the distance. What irritated Brendon was not the dullness of the view, but rather that after extenuating daily fights working on securing the nation's constitutional future, his desire to immerse himself in the appeasing contemplation of peacefully flowing waters was frustrated by the unavoidable coupling of the river view with that of its Québec shore, the province at the root of all his problems. All because of another monarch.

Brendon's resentment toward the Monarchy was partly rooted in the dissymmetric love between a motherland and its colony; a flawed relationship in which insatiable parents had sucked the natural resources and blood of its dependent, but had abandoned the colony to its own key battles when bold political support was needed. He resented that so much Canadian territory was yielded to the United States without a shot fired, by the majority decision of international panels in which British members sided with the Americans for political considerations. He resented that the British sacrificed Canadian troops instead of their own, as a result of selfish unmitigated tactical disasters during World War II. He resented that the Queen of England, when asked to arbitrate the dispute between Canadians who advocated that either Toronto or Québec City be selected as permanent seat of the Canadian's Parliament to end two decades of unpopular perambulation of government between the two cities, didn't favor the English interests and selected instead an unruly logging village in the hinterland at the tail end of the Rideau Canal, sitting on the border between the country's then two provinces of Québec and Ontario, and equidistant to the proponents' suggested capitals. He resented that the Crown, after the Conquest of 1759, allowed the French habitants to keep their French schools, their French civil law, their Catholic religion, and their land, instead of being assimilated or returned to Europe. Even though this was done for pragmatic reasons, partly to avoid insurrections and other rebellions that would have compounded the British's problems in America at the time, Brendon blamed a spineless monarch's lack of authoritarian resolve then for his problems today.

The RCMP officer was still standing guard at the front door, never to interrupt the Premier's musing, awaiting further inquiries or instructions.

"Where is our precious lobotomized brain trust when the Country needs it?" iced the Chief in his maple leaf-covered pyjamas.

"I have called each one of them sir, but only reached answering machines," he replied, not hesitating one moment to deliver the bad news, knowing that the Premier never crucified messengers, rather keeping his venom for the culprits, patiently waiting for the ideal opportunity to deliver a sly malignant sting.

"Send them cars. Drag each one of these clowns out of bed. I want them on the Hill by..." looking at his watch, "2:30. Tell them that the anal retentive son of a bitch from Alberta is in a bad mood."

That went without saying. Four weeks of bad news in the polls with the vote in Québec one week away had not left much to rejoice about around Parliament Hill lately. Brendon wasn't quite sure yet what had just happened 15 minutes ago, but, like everything else in life as far as he was concerned, it was political. And as political events went, in his mind, the steps of the process were always the same: Assess the situation, identify the stakes, set priorities, establish strategies, forge alliances, destroy the opposition, and rapidly capitalize on the gains. And this might just have been the event he had been waiting for.

Québec City, 1:40 a.m.

Alone, waiting on the top floor of *Complexe H* for his colleagues and the promised helicopter, Léandre stood at the window surveying the great expanse of the *Plaines d'Abraham*, a 270-acre park owned by the Government of Canada in the middle of the Provincial Capital, once a primeval forest explored by his North American ancestors at the dawn of the 17th century. He always enjoyed the superb view of the peaceful oasis, bordered on the north by the *Grande Allée*, uptown's largest artery, through which tourists and civil servants reached the heart of town, itself sheltered by fortification walls and only accessible through a few narrow stone portals. An "alley" that had grown into a living and civilized artery, rather than a highway, abundantly flanked by *cafés-terrasses* where civil servants and tourists alike could relax and share the *joie de vivre*, hearts at a slow pace, free of stress—a small slice of the promised Utopia that the New World's abundance had failed to deliver.

The oasis of intersecting woodland and manicured lawns was bordered on the south by steep cliffs that defined its historical purpose, rising on the shores of the majestic St-Lawrence river, the long-coveted channel of commerce into North America along which Québec was strategically founded in 1608. The outstanding view from atop the cliffs allowed one to monitor all maritime traffic, but given that the river remained two-thirds of a mile wide at Québec's narrows—an order of magnitude wider than the conquerors' European rivers—prevailing 17th- and 18th-century technology made it hard to blockade all navigation. The tactical topographical advantage was particularly ineffective against a British fleet of 30 warships, 90 transport vessels, and 60 small ships and schooners that anchored in sight of the French in late June 1759, which maneuvered freely up and down the river throughout the summer, played a war of position with its 30,000 soldiers, and at times bombed Québec City from a distance. However, although unable to restrict all these movements from their elevated position, the 3,000 French soldiers, 13,000 militia and a few allied aboriginals were able to frustrate British invasion attempts all summer long.

Beyond the numbers and the small tactical details of those unfruitful maneuvers, forgotten by most, all those living in the Great White North knew—having learned it from at least one of two biased historical perspectives—that by fall, English General Wolfe, in a final attempt to assault the French fortifications, sailed past Québec City undetected in a dark night, anchored to the west, dispatched troops on landing barges, and ordered his soldiers to climb up the 300-foot cliff and be ready to fight on the *Plaines d'Abraham* at sunrise. The cliff was undefended as it was believed unscalable. Yet, Wolfe exploited a fundamental rule of war games in which, given equally competent artillery and tactical skills, the number of men available to sacrifice need only exceed that of the opponent, and was confident of winning on those terms even if only a fraction of his army could reach the open fields on the plateau.

Although the biased English and French high-school curricula both spared the schoolchildren needless gory details, it was understood that lowly ranked soldiers having joined the military as destitute men seeking shelter and food, always aware that desertion was punishable by death, and ordered to climb in absolute silence, clung to branches and roots up the slippery cliff with the same desperation they clung to life, also holding the forlorn hope that battles would be few and far between, and that when they occurred, chance alone would spare them from the fatality of a bullet, as they knew this to be a godless world from battlefield experience. It was a tacit expectation of nonsensical wars, that in spite of their determination to survive a perilous climb for the privilege to line up as targets in yet another decisive battle—to tempt fate anew once at the summit—many soldiers fell off the cliff to their death, from various heights, in perfect silence, hoping to survive with only crippling injuries, understanding that all those who compromised the success of the operation by breaking the silence would be killed at once. The other infantrymen pulled their weight, guns, cannons, and officers to the top, and set the stage for another long day, planning to spill gallons of anonymous blood to save theirs and to quench the thirst of generals, kings and nobles who need enemies to bolster their power.

The *Complexe H's* window also afforded Léandre a clear view of the *Citadelle*, the historic military fort anchoring the city walls on the eastern end of the *Plaines*, built by the English more or less atop the foundations of the earlier fortifications from which the French garrisons woke up at dawn on that September 13th, 1759, alarmed by sentinels that a sea of 5,000 Red Coats was in formation ready to attack. General Montcalm was compelled by training to answer the challenge by the sacrifice of his battalions. That morning, in the plains of Abraham Martin, where Champlain's cows used to graze a hundred years earlier, another kind of cattle stampeded to butchery. After a short, gory engagement, the forces in the field judged that ample blood had been spilled for the day and that further fighting was futile. Military maneuvering, skirmishes and ransacking continued outside the besieged city until it surrendered after a few days. Neither Wolfe nor Montcalm survived the battle, as an omen of French and English relations for centuries to come, symbolizing the pain—and claims for the same land—to emerge from a difficult co-existence born that day.

As time passed at the pace of that century in Léandre's history books, as fighting continued from Québec City to Montréal until the French forces on the continent capitulated a year later, as Kings and Queens of Europe capriciously swapped jurisdiction over colonies like kids trade hockey cards, returning to a vanquished foe land that could be easily retaken in a subsequent war; as thousands of Acadians families were split and deported to dozens of foreign destinations around the Atlantic ocean, as English merchants landed as conquerors despising the habitants, as the past was full of horror and the future uncertain, the French civilians anchored themselves on a tract of country and stood steady with an undefeated resolve. Their forefathers had cleared the trees, worked the fields, and built the foundations of a civilization, and they became solid links in that chain of history—their allegiance to the land was an unbreakable bond. This country was their home, so they learned to live with the unwelcome guests.

However, the modern reality transcended the lessons of dusty history books. As most Québécois, Léandre never though of the *Plaines* as a green memorial to the clashes for supremacy of the French and British Empires, nor as a blunt reminder, by the victorious invaders to the vanquished, of a battle that changed the fate of North America. Rather, far from exposing a repository of collective memory dwelling on a dark humiliating past, the pristine view from Léandre's window provided him with a kaleidoscopic vision of a brilliant future. For this was a park that politics could never reclaim.

This was a park where families played and loved, picnicking in the summer, strolling amidst colorful trees in autumn, and sliding on fancy toboggans or improvised cardboard luges throughout an eternal winter. This was a park that hosted from time immemorial the traditional bonfire of Québec's *St-Jean Baptiste*—the de facto National Holiday on June 24th—and the main stages of countless national and international festivals and celebrations, such as the *Super Franco-Fête*, the *Chant'Août*, the *Festival d'été*, and many more. This was a park where artists and poets composed and sang hymns to the *Québécité* and anthems to a country that remained to be understood, to be proclaimed, and to be built. This was a park that belonged to the people and to the nation, not to Wolfe and Montcalm whose statues strategically located by the park custodians, were only visited—and painted white—by pigeons.

Léandre saw all this and more when contemplating the park. His scrutiny of the land always reached the magnificent river, following its eastward flow, up to where it split into two wide and independent rivers at the tip of *Île d'Orléans*, separated from their destiny by this imposing obstacle but reunited ever more impressively after having circumvented it, near La Malbaie where its shores were by then tens of miles apart; the shores of one river expanding for a few more hundred miles before reaching the ocean, as an inspiring metaphor to the destiny of a country yet to merge into the international community. Léandre's vision was always emboldened by the unfolding landscape in his sight.

This landscape provided an additional personal connection, the two rocky cliffs constricting the river reminding Léandre of his father, a construction worker stationed in the remote camps of Northern Québec, building dams to bathe the province in renewable energy and generate prosperity through exports to neighboring states. Rarely home, more a paycheck than a husband, definitely a part-time father, he once described to his 8-year-old son how a dam engineered to span between Québec City and Lévis, coupled with another one at Cap Rouge to prevent Québec City from becoming an island—mammoth infrastructures that would at best resemble the smallest dams on which he was working—could create a reservoir of abundance from an inexhaustible natural resource. Although it was a silly idea that would have generated hydro-electricity at the expense of flooding one of the most scenic regions of North America, Léandre grew to understand the image for the power of its analogy rather than as an actual project without merit. Yet, when admiring the beauty of the landscape, Léandre always envisioned that immense dam, raising the water to the top of the cliffs, creating a beautiful lake at the edge of the *Plaines d'Abraham* for boating and swimming, skating and ice-fishing. A huge concrete dam erected in his imagination as a memorial to a father crushed by heavy machinery in a minute of distraction, inattentive at the wrong moment, possibly day-dreaming or preoccupied about his family, at a time when social nets barely existed and when his family tumbled from middle class into hardship.

His father built the country with concrete. Léandre, as a politician, wanted to build a country with ideas and ideals.

Réal and Julien's arrival put an abrupt end to Léandre's random historical and societal contemplations. They entered the room dragging their feet, slumped forward as if slightly crushed by the oppressive pressure of a dreadful task ahead.

"If your wives bitched for leaving them alone to pick up the broken china," Léandre greeted them by saying, "let me know and I'll have flowers shipped to them with a note reminding them they didn't marry accountants."

"The place is a bit of a mess but she's fine," stated Réal, to emphasize that some true compassionate concerns would have been appreciated. "Shaken but fine."

"Actually, not much broken at our place," said Julien, some-what surprised at the suggestion that the damage should have been worse.

"Can't you afford better than plastic plates?"

"Seriously. Nothing moved around at all. Maybe it has to do with the fact we're built on rock or that we're in one of those century-old uptown buildings, with foot-thick stone masonry walls? I don't know."

"Anyhow. This thing might be dead serious," said Léandre. "We don't have any tangible information yet, but Florent suspects Montréal could be so deep in *l'ostie d'marde* that we may have to postpone the referendum."

"*Câlice*, timing could not be worse," said Réal, running his hand over his head, as if to comb the two hairs remaining an-chored there against all odds. The rest of his hair had fallen victim to the travails of a quarter-century-long political life working with his friend Léandre for the *Cause*. Réal Chaput-Vigneault was proud of the fact that not a single *"d'ostie d'enfant de chienne d'anglais"* could pronounce his last name correctly. Minister of Transportation for the *Parti National* government, Cabinet Minister, an absolute and unconditional friend of Léandre, he had devoted his life to helping him invest the National Assembly in Québec with the political structure to legitimize its name.

For decades, as an expression of its emerging nationalistic aspirations, based on the historical and sociological conviction that Québécois are a people and a political nation that should have democratic control over its affairs and its destiny—which Réal held as self-evident truths—the Québec government had liberally christened as "National" most of its assets and provincial initiatives; the provincial capital became the National Capital, the provincial legislature became the National Assembly, the Québec flag became the National Emblem, and Québec's declaration that the Saint-Jean-Baptiste holiday would become its official National Holiday shamed Canada into renaming its own imperial-consonant Dominion Day into Canada Day. Archives, libraries, museums, institutes, agencies, centers, programs, fictitious hockey teams, awards and honors, all sporting the "National" label, all masking the political reality of belonging to Canada, all milestones toward a vision indifferently leading to either an estranged relationship with the rest of the country or an equal partnership in trade.

Yet, while the polls consistently showed that a distinct majority of the province's residents felt first allegiance to Québec and described themselves as Québécois before Canadians, they also showed for many years that most were reluctant to part with their Canadian passports. Québécois, in an ultimately pragmatic way, wanted to belong to two countries.

Réal never knew how to overcome this dichotomy, and had resigned himself to the fact that the *Cause* seemed a lost one after all.

Until recently.

With his *Parti National* government under the leadership of Léandre Laliberté, elected in a landslide victory shortly after a federal government harboring unsubtle hostility toward Québec took over in Ottawa, all the right stars seemed to align in the most unbelievable confluence of events. Never before had the ultimate goal seemed so near, so possible, so tangible. As such, a major disturbance one week before a plebiscite set to determine the political future of the nation could not be less timely.

"I've also called a meeting of the policy task force for 5 a.m. on the secure line," said Léandre. "They're supposed to be in the *Complexe* by then."

"I'm not sure about this," suggested Julien.

"Why?"

"If this is going to be as much heavy-duty stuff as you think it is, I think you should talk to the task force face to face. You know how I feel about *les osties d'*conference calls."

Léandre had picked Julien Léveillé as his political adviser for two reasons. First, he was impressed by the freshly graduated non-assuming young Ph.D. in political sciences, a Québécois who'd gone to the best institutions in Europe to learn his Machiavellian trade. Second, Julien was a most sincere and convinced nationalist who happened to be the son of a still influential and highly pro-federalist former Premier of Québec. Hence, enlisting the son was also an attempt to neutralize the father. Overall, Julien was often passive, hard to engage, almost distant, definitely a pessimist, but when passionate about a cause, he wasn't shy to express his opinions—using the vernacular of his colleagues if needed to underscore disagreement.

Léandre also valued Julien's instinctive flair for grass-roots sensibilities and the marketing of populist ideology. In the electoral campaign that brought the party to power, Julien was the one who'd coined the catchy slogan *"Donnez deux L's au Québec"* (give two L's to Québec) that indirectly evoked both an inspiring nationalist dream and an empowering mandate, substituting Léandre's initials to the homophone *"Donnez deux ailes au Québec"* (give two wings to Québec).

"What do you propose then?"

"Visual signals speak as much as words. Your presence in the meeting is essential. Either you go to the task force or bring the task force to you. Don't give them the freedom to huddle, whisper, and maneuver unseen and beyond your reach."

"I know you think that they are a rather thick bunch that should never be trusted to make the right strategic critical decisions," said Léandre. "On the other hand, at 5 a.m., there's a risk that they'll just be a bunch of zombies, so a conference call will probably be good enough just to get them started."

"You're the boss."

Léandre paused. This was typically Julien's cue to insinuate a major mistake was about to be made, and that he would enjoy ribbing him about it in the future.

"Ok, *crisse*, you're right! Fly them all to Longueuil!"

The outside door suddenly opened, drowning the room with the noise of the helicopter's engine. The captain's voice was inaudible, but they all understood it was time to board.

Ottawa, 2:30 a.m.

Four sleep-deprived cabinet ministers were clustered around the small mahogany table of the Prime Minister's office in the Parliament Building, waiting for the Premier to stop gazing through the window into the night, to turn around and start the meeting. Wayne Greenbriar, Minister of National Defence, Graham Murdoch, Minister of Resources, Kaylee Carling, Minister of Finance, and Shirley Coulthard, Minister of External Affairs, all appointed by Brendon, all serving at his pleasure, all waiting for the chief to break the silence.

Brendon Decker always carefully planned his words, to the public for sure, but more importantly to all his political colleagues, friends or foes, as individuals often moved between the two groups, both ways, with surprising frequency, depending on which way the winds blew. Having brokered the most potent union of politically disparate groups in recent Canadian history, he saw allegiance as volatile and cheap within the Canadian political community.

He had learned early on how to reconcile contradictory ideas. Born in a small rural community hundreds of miles north of Edmonton, where televisions were useless and life was a punishment that consisted of long, brutally cold winters interrupted by brief interludes of buggy summers, this son of a minister-Minister—a protestant pastor who'd served as Minister of National Defence in a past government—rapidly absorbed the unchallenged paternal dogma. Beyond the usual fare of Puritanism and religious teachings, his father was exceptionally qualified to train his son in the cold, dispassionate realities of life, filtered through the tenets of his particular dual expertise. As such, his entire philosophy was founded on the basic premise that killing can be good if approved and blessed by God. From there, all Good and Evil is simply a matter of relativity.

Brendon's political career grew in leaps and bounds, through carefully selected moves, alliances, and allegiances. He mastered the art of political illusion, his preferred tactic consisting of making strong and clear promises in the one-liner format that so strongly appealed to the mass-media, while subsequently drowning the listener in endlessly detailed and complex tutorials structured to bewilder and deflect any possible attempts at in-depth scrutiny. Decker's "Hit-Fog-Spin Strategy": Hit hard with the vote-grabbing appealing concept, fog the political analysts with tons of irrelevant information delivered in a slow, media-adverse and boring tone, and spin the infinite details—that nobody could find the time or resources to verify—to create the illusion of a level of mastery on the issues.

Shielded from media deconstruction, his snowballing popularity propelled him to the top of his Party, and simultaneously to chief of the Official Opposition in Parliament. From there, he concluded that the dynamics of the multi-party political landscape in Canada would condemn him to remain in the opposition forever unless that landscape was fundamentally altered, which provided him impetus to conceptualize and create the Democratic Canadian Rightist Alliance Party.

Recognizing that the Country was in a political stalemate, Brendon was convinced that he could cajole the electorate into supporting his restructured party, one that projected the illusion that the four major opposition political parties had set aside their differences and united to defeat a government that reigned by capitalizing on the prior political division, having never needed more than 30% of the electoral vote to seize power.

Brendon achieved his objective by stealing the most popular politicians from the three other major opposition parties, renaming his own party to create the illusion of unity (and unification), ignoring the other atrophied opposition parties, and promising what the electorate wanted to hear. To capture British Columbia, he showed compassion and painted enticing pictures of a workforce benefiting from government-blessed labor unions. To sweep the Prairies, which he embodied by his birthright, he showed compassion and pledged to redress years of neglect and disinterest from past federal governments. To take Ontario, he showed compassion and trumpeted the virtues of industrial entrepreneurship as the engine for Canada's future. To win votes in the Maritimes, he did nothing, because he considered them to be a bunch of welfare addicts and government-sucking liberals, although these thoughts were never expressed verbally to anyone. And to attenuate the contradictions between these glowing promises, he used his calm and unassuming demeanor to give demagogy a semblance of legitimacy and unite the country to oppose Québec's aspirations to uniqueness and—worse—nationhood, capitalizing on the fact that no Canadian wanted that province to secede. Not that they frankly cared much for that rogue, trouble-making province, Brendon thought, but rather because he believed that Canadians couldn't stand the notion of an imposed divorce that would split the country in half.

As illusions, they were most effective. They allowed him to seize absolute power, getting his party representatives elected in nearly all conscriptions, losing seats in the Maritimes, but making up the difference by winning in the English-speaking conscriptions of Québec, the only places in that province where the party fielded candidates. The absolute absence of any French-speaking representative in his majority government did not perturb him; on the contrary. Never explicitly even suggesting it in public, his political colleagues knew that his strategy to get elected would dare the Québec government into launching another referendum.

And it did.

Nonetheless, banking on the Québécois' attachment to the unique inalienable rights and freedoms intrinsic to Canadian citizenship, they anticipated a most positive outcome from this process, one in which, given forces so hostile to the province on the federal side, a referendum loss for the Québec government would be the kiss of death to the secession forces for at least a century, if not forever. Unfortunately, counter to those idealistic expectations, the latest polls indicated, slightly more than a week before the vote, that the referendum would pass in favor of separation, by a 55-45 margin.

All the ministers leaning on the mahogany table, fighting to keep their eyes open, knew the dire reality of those poll results. They knew that although only those in the province of Québec were eligible to vote, they had the power and duty to steer the debate, to taint the facts, to infiltrate the media, to hinder and obstruct the process, so as to achieve the desired outcome. As rowdy spectators trying to affect the outcome of a hockey game in favor of the home team, they had a duty to interfere by any possible means, taunting, screaming profanities, even sending a few extra players on the ice in connivance with the referees if necessary.

Yet, they also knew that this emergency nocturnal summons was not just another strategic meeting to conspire on how to defeat the referendum. At least, not in a conventional sense. For that reason, they were most anxious for the Premier to share his thoughts.

Wayne Greenbriar, appropriately assigned as Minister of National Defence, was a true Saskatchewan redneck whose political acumen made up for his lack of a high school diploma. Always trigger-happy, pleased to shower the woods with bullets to indiscriminately terrorize roaming creatures of all sizes, and just as pleased to aggress intellectual analysis with belligerent and misguided verbal salvos, it helped that the Canadian forces did not have much firepower might after all. A used-car salesman in his former life, prior to becoming a born-again politician, he provided Brendon with the "pulse of the prairies," a grass-roots understanding of the population scattered in the countless hamlets of rural Canada where the roads are forever straight and the summers as harsh as winters. He could connect with the electorate—the local folks—in a way that the son of a minister could not, even a son with a foot in the northwestern-most corner of the prairies.

Graham Murdoch, to Brendon, was beneath contempt, and yet valuable. Sporting an irritating preppie look he seemed to have never outgrown—possibly on purpose, to disarm those he was about to smoothly rob, speculated Brendon—the political sciences graduate from Queens University had extensive linkages to the establishment and old money that kept the wheels of the party well oiled. Minister of Resources was neither a demanding nor a strategically important assignment to Graham, but it carried the perks and privileges required to keep him happy, and the symbolic access to the ear of the Premier required to keep the tap of party contributions solidly running. Besides, he could connect with the electorate—the social climbers engrossed by their aristocratic ambitions—in a way that the son of a minister could not, even a son catering to a rightist agenda.

Kaylee Carling, Minister of Finance, was undeniably the most qualified member of Brendon's team. With decades of political experience, she was the only dissenting voice that had survived Brendon's ascension. She had an uncanny ability to sense emerging threats before they had a chance to bloom, and usually had the wherewithal to develop elegant solutions to expediently squash those thorny issues. Her aspirations to Brendon's job were unclear, as she maintained a composed demeanor and kept in check her few tightlipped confidants. But she could connect with the electorate—the intelligentsia—in a way that the son of a minister could not, even a son unchained from the homestead by the strength of his intellect.

Shirley Coulthard's assignment as Minister of External Affairs was the price paid to attract to his coalition this star politician from another party. Her strong people skills compensated for her dismal intellectual abilities. She could also connect with the electorate—the urbanites with cosmopolitan aspirations—in a way that the son of a minister could not, particularly a son with no patience for confabulation.

Kaylee and Shirley were also specially picked by Brendon to project an image of diversity and inclusiveness in his government and cabinet, thus distracting media attention from the fact that the elected party was dominantly a WASP, male cohort.

All four mastered political gamesmanship and perfectly understood their respective motivations for accepting to suffer Brendon's sulking, and multiple other shortcomings. As different individuals, different reasons sustained their willingness to participate in the brutal process of a governing Decker, but as a united team, they recognized and valued that Brendon's zeal to squash foes was only surpassed by his unwavering resolve to defend his allies, a highly prized quality in the modern politics of evanescent allegiances.

Brendon turned away from the window and slipped into the chair at the end of the conference table, slowly, almost ceremonially, as if hovering and landing into a throne, but failing to adopt a dignified posture, rather slumping in it, as he usually did. He broke the silence.

"Graham, did your eggheads confirm?"

"Yes, the Canadian Hazard Information Service informed us that it was a Magnitude 7 earthquake, epicentered right in the middle of Montreal."

"Isn't that stuff only supposed to happen in Vancouver or California?"

"I asked the same question. To use their exact words, they said a Magnitude 7 there was a low-probability event, but most definitely a probable one."

Seeing Brendon scowl, he volunteered additional information: "They indicated that earthquakes at least that strong are expected to occur every seventy years or so near Quebec City, and that one is overdue there by the way, but with respect to Montreal it was less clear."

Remembering that Brendon hated uncertainty, Graham clarified, "They were categorically clear that the whole St-Lawrence Valley is capable of generating such large events, but that it is not possible to reliably predict how often. In fact, from their historical records and reports, the largest earthquake known to have occurred in Montreal is a Magnitude 6 in the 18th century."

"That's almost 7 right there," said Brendon.

"I thought the same thing, but they explained to me that they measure these things using some sort of scale such that a 6 is actually ten times less severe than a 7."

Brendon's thoughts wandered for a moment on the potential of such a scale for political purposes, to massage data and distort communications—announcing that the budget deficit "only" increased by one unit on the "magic scale" would shrink the perception of a distressing crisis into that of a mild inconvenience—but the distraction was brief. He sighed, and pulled himself straight in his chair.

"Well it happened. So talking about probabilities and historical records is not going to help. If Joe and Jane Public understood or cared about probabilities, casinos and lotteries wouldn't make obscene profits. The real issue is how bad it is going to be. Wayne, any reports?"

"Nothing on the DOD side. I have guys checking the media but all the core Montreal stations are down at this time."

"Down?"

"No feed. Television or radio. Suburban radio stations are live, but at this time of night, they are mostly playing pre-programmed music streamed from unmanned digital servers. A few have late-night lunatics and agitators running hotlines, but they are only speculating on what is happening so far."

"My guys say that we should expect massive damage," noted Graham. "They rated the earthquake as identical in power to the one that hit Los Angeles in 1994 and caused $30US billion in damage."

Brendon paused. As ice thawing, the deep frowning wrinkles engraved in his forehead progressively melted and one could almost discern a smile emerging from the serious, pensive face—tentative colors attempting to disturb a gray canvas of sustained anger and frustration. The fighting emotions engaged to a draw, and while a full smile did not bloom, the resulting rictus revealed that Brendon was at least somewhat enthused by visions of great possibilities.

"Guys, God has just kicked in, and the pendulum is swinging back to our side. The *Parti National* could be completely fucked up if we play it well. I think we can give these assholes a run for their money."

If most people talked like Brendon, exclamation marks would have become an endangered species in the world of punctuation. Although his use of foul language was absolutely inexpressive, he never hesitated to pepper his message with obscenities to emphasize his feelings. Brendon used vulgar expletives as proxy to the display of emotions, but did so only within the trusted confines of his most private inner circle. The privilege of hearing Brendon swear was one's reassurance of membership in that prestigious group.

"Wayne, get your troops on stand-by for a humanitarian assistance mission, but nobody moves before we authorize it. Shirley, get our embassies on the scoop, tell our U.S. friends that we will also keep them posted on a nation-to-nation basis. And remind them that we are talking about the Canadian nation here. Kaylee, start spinning the story that the government will take all measures to ensure that this event will have no impact on our national economy, and whatever it takes to reassure investors. Graham, have your friends in high places mobilize their media staff, and get our departments ready to feed them our gospel over the next few days. Get started with a message of public interest explaining to the public the tremendous risk for destructive earthquakes in Quebec, and get them ready to fly out as soon as reports of major damage come in."

Brendon, fists on the table, smiled—for the first time in weeks.

"This is going to be a lot of fun."

Vaudreuil-Dorion, 2:45 a.m.

"You are listening to CHOK-AM, choc-radio. It is 2:45 a.m., -33°F. This would be the time of our usual news break, but frankly folks, YOU are making the news as we speak, as you have been for almost two hours since we were struck by what appears to have been a major earthquake.

"So let's continue taking your calls. All circuits are busy but keep calling, please, keep calling.

"Your vibrant testimonies so far have enlightened our listeners, providing all of us with an understanding of the reality of what appears to be a major disaster. The valuable information you are providing is helping us better grasp the magnitude of what has happened. The terrible experiences you have willingly shared with us have painted a vivid image of what Montréal may look like tonight.

"Yet, we have not received a single call from the center core of the island itself. No communication from anyone between Highways 13 and 25."

Richard impressed himself with his ability to elevate the communications above the mumbo jumbo he despised but had to dish out nightly to the station's target demographic. He was pleased that callers from all walks of life had found him in their serendipitous search for news, fully embracing this up-scaling of audience quality above that of the outcasts usually tuned to his broadcast of dreadful music. He believed the process of establishing himself as a credible, professional-sounding news anchor was successful—christened by an earthquake as the new voice in live reporting, empowered to be more assertive and aggressive in the process to satisfy the population's thirst for information.

"If you have been with us since 1:00 a.m., you have heard of pianos in Laval that have moved 15 feet, of apartment houses in Brossard that have shed their masonry cladding, of broken glassware piled on floors throughout the *Rive Sud*, of shattered windows in Longueuil, of alarms ringing everywhere, and many more. But not a single call from the big island! This information vacuum worries us. Please, if you are from Montréal, call us now!"

Richard pushed one of the red flashing buttons on the switchboard, as if randomly awarding lottery prizes.

"Caller on Line 3, tell us your story."

"Is it my turn?"

"Yes. Are you calling us from Montréal?"

"No... uh, sorry. But I was on my way to it. I'm calling from my cell, you know."

Richard was disappointed, but, if anything, it confirmed his suspicions that a telephone black-out afflicted the metropolis.

"Where are you now? Can you keep us posted as you approach the city?"

"Well, that's what I wanted to do, you know, but I'm pretty much parked on the 20 south of the tunnel. Nothing moved for over an hour, so, you know, I got out of the car, and walked to check it out. Damn, it's cold! I mean, you guys have been saying minus 30 all night, so you know how bad it is, but you forgot to mention the wind chill factor. You know, it is bloody damn cold here."

"Yes yes yes, we know. But what did you see?"

"I couldn't walk all the way to see it for myself, 'cause you know, the police are not letting anybody close anymore. But the story here is that the tunnel is blocked."

"You mean closed?"

"No, no, blocked. Out of service, you know, full of water apparently."

"Full of water?"

"Yeah, water! You know, with cars and bodies floating in it a few feet down from the entrance. Apparently."

Richard had to contain his jubilation upon discovery of this golden nugget of information. He elected to disregard the mention of floating bodies, concerned that offending the sensibilities of the audience could chase some to another station, but was otherwise delighted to report this shattering news, consistently to the tone of his newfound professional delivery.

"Incredible! Dear listeners! You heard it on CHOK first, the Louis-Hippolite Lafontaine tunnel has been destroyed by the earthquake! It has been fractured by the forces of nature and is now out of commission for an undetermined amount of time, maybe forever. This confirms our worst fears. Nobody knows the extent of destruction in the city, but this new information attests that we are indeed in the midst of a major disaster."

Richard was unsure whether he was inflating the story for impact, or whether the story would indeed overwhelm beyond imagination. For sure, though, as the severity of reported damage escalated from broken china to destroyed infrastructure, the four walls of the small windowless studio slowly morphed into a closing noose. A story of this magnitude would rapidly awaken the media giants who would rush to the fore, leaving tiny and resourceless broadcasters—such as CHOK-AM—in the dust, brutally trampling Richard's hopes of fame and recognition. All the lights on his phone glowed red, pregnant with testimonies, but he was anxious they would turn dark as soon as the giants unleash their infinite resources and real reporters to assault the field. It was crucial, at this juncture, to assess what the competition knew.

An earphone tethering his left ear to a portable radio, he gave callers lots of air time to express their poorly articulated thoughts while he scanned the airwaves searching for competition. He was delighted to discover that, no matter the airwave, except for distant stations, only noise was heard through the small earphone. The almighty CBC and other private network giants, all located in downtown Montréal: silent.

Richard realized that, in the middle of that dark, post-disaster night, he owned the airwaves—he was the information. There simply was no alternative. Reflecting on that sobering thought—the awesome ability in hand to reach an absolute audience—he felt it within his power to connect the current compendium of anecdotal testimonies with substantive and official information sources. From the entire spectrum of approaches to proceed towards that goal, spanning from sophisticated enticement to gritty challenge, Richard instinctively followed a familiar road of modern talk radio.

"Dear listeners, citizens of Montréal, we are living through what now appears to be a major catastrophe, and yet, no news from our public authorities. Where are our elected officials in these critical times? When are we going to hear from those who hold power in this country?

"I hereby urge government officials to contact CHOK-AM as soon as possible to inform us of their actions and of the measures they will take to assist the population of the metropolitan area in this most critical situation. Key officials from every government agency should know how to reach us on our special direct line, or could just call us at 555-CHOK. Whatever's more convenient. Call us now!"

Gloucester (Ottawa), 2:47 a.m.

The packsack seemed too small to contain all the hardware assembled on the kitchen table. Hard hat, gloves, flashlight (with extra bulbs and batteries), pocket knife, tape measure, compass, clipboard, pens, survey book, small calculator, cell phone with extra batteries, a digital camera with five high-capacity memory cards and four sets of batteries, a 35mm camera with wide-angle and telephoto lenses, flash, 20 blank films, road maps, bottles of water, chocolate bars, dried fruits, energy bars, surgical masks, iodine pills, Imodium, miscellaneous basic toilet articles, sleeping bag, and clothes for four days. Warm clothes.

James sacrificed the laptop as he could not rely on the availability of external power. Besides, the benefit-to-weight ratio for that device was too low, particularly given that it would turn into a dead-weight liability beyond the first battery charge. Packsack space was too precious to waste.

He elected to forgo half of the water bottles that would be desirable for such an operation, relying on the abundance of snow to refill empties, hoping to find relatively clean deposits under the cruddy crust of urban snow banks. Theoretically, body heat should melt the content of refilled bottles stashed in the inside pockets of his parka, but he had never field-tested this strategy to replenish resources. Never before had he conducted earthquake reconnaissance activities in such bitter cold. He wondered whether periodically sharing the protected warmth inside his parka with cylinders of ice would turn out to be more unbearable than suffering from dehydration.

He considered ditching one of the cameras, but this redundancy was deemed crucial given the high risk of a camera freeze. The primary camera would be kept along the warmer bottles of already melted water, on the pack side closer to body heat. The back-up cameras would be kept wrapped in clothes and in the middle of the bag.

The extra items that did not fit in the backpack would be carried in the car, as a precaution. Unable to predict how often and how far he would have to venture by foot, he anticipated the worst-case scenario of an extended excursion beyond the reach and comfort of his car, carrying all key equipment and vital supplies on his back. Stowed in the trunk of a car abandoned to freeze during his expeditions would be battery chargers and their car adapters, filled portable gas containers, a box of extra water bottles—hopefully resistant to the pressure of water expanding into ice—and a partly torn-up sleeping bag.

James dumped the sleeping bag in the trunk, for safety more than with any intent of actually using it, convincing himself that his winter suit would do fine to house him continuously for a few days, unable to envision where sleep could be had in what promised to be challenging working conditions. In the best of worlds, James would have owned a lightweight sleeping bag of high-tech synthetic insulation materials that folded into a small loaf, but he abhorred camping. His, a bulky sleeping bag of bygone era, was low-tech, heavy, and one that his wife had forgotten in the basement when she moved out.

Their last conversation was precisely on the eve of another such reconnaissance visit, as he was planning his departure. He was methodically packing, going through his check-lists, and sharing with her his enthusiasm for what lied to be discovered ahead. She was half-listening, half asleep, but fully worried and tired of seeing her earthquake-chaser leave again. She envied her friends, married to men of more sedentary, safe occupations, such as bureaucrats, or night-watchmen. He remembered her last words.

"Why don't you wait a few days before going there?" she had pled.

Oblivious to her fears, he had answered as an academic, addressing the words rather than her underlying concerns.

"You know the importance of a first immediate visit within hours of the event. Who knows what will get removed or destroyed in the next few days as they try to restore traffic? Or save face."

"It's a very big disaster. They won't be able to do that much, you know."

"Maybe. Maybe not. This is a once-in-a-lifetime event, and I am not ready to take this chance."

She had heard it all before. All earthquakes were once-in-a-lifetime events.

"Do you really need to go? What do you expect to find there that you have not found anywhere else, anyhow?"

"Ah, some of the usual for sure, but probably much new, too. You know how earthquakes are: a new surprise every time!"

Then, in a rare moment of lucidity, he had sensed her distress, an unusual distress, something askew. He had taken her in his arms and pressed her warmly in a tender hug. Her hold was limp.

"Don't worry, I've done this often enough that I know not to do stupid things. Safety first, always."

She knew there was no way to stop him. She had held to him as long as she could, without strength, collapsed in his arms.

When he came back from his expedition, she was gone. She had left a short, factual note, unambiguous as to her decision, without motive or justification, knowing that he would look for a rational explanation when none could be articulated. She ultimately settled for a peaceful life with a bureaucrat whose most perilous activity during his 32.5 hours workweek was to carry a cup of boiling water from the coffee machine back to his cubicle.

"You know how earthquakes are: a new surprise every time!" he remembered, as he closed the trunk after pushing the sleeping bag to the back, behind the gas containers.

James checked his emails one last time before leaving. As expected, nothing but junk mail had piled up during the night as the unshaken parts of North America were sound asleep and news of the earthquake had not yet traveled the globe. Soon, the worldwide earthquake engineering community, a group of experts from all disciplines—engineers and non-engineers alike—sharing the goal of making communities less vulnerable to earthquakes, would learn of the event. Being one of the community's points of contact closest to the epicenter, beyond those directly within the disaster stricken area and obviously incapacitated, he anticipated that many would seek to enlist his assistance as the local disaster tour guide, and that such requests would start to gather in his electronic mailbox over the next hours. He did not object to eventually providing such a courtesy, but first needed to assess first-hand the extent of the disaster and the professional lessons to be learned from it. One such anticipated lesson was whether the seismic design requirements that had been mandatory for years in the province were understood and applied correctly. The unanticipated lessons that remained to be uncovered would likely be more interesting, as always.

He drafted an email message strongly discouraging everybody else from planning a reconnaissance visit, particularly in light of the brutally cold conditions, advising them to stay home at least until the mayhem of it all abated and a better assessment of current conditions was possible. For lack of time to create a distribution list of hand-picked relevant recipients, he spammed his electronic message worldwide to all email addresses in his unsorted list of contacts—close friends, colleagues, and professional acquaintances alike, as well as forgotten encounters whose business cards were collected out of professional etiquette and run through the card scanner "just in case." He also configured his email account to automatically forward a similar message in response to all communications received in his absence.

As he enabled this feature in the software, he wondered whether the perfidious systems that automatically generate junk mail would lift key words from his message to generate creative email headers mixing earthquake disasters and mercantile activities of dubious merit. More importantly, he wondered who was likely to contact him over the next few days.

He thought, "*Shit-head* won't. He'll go on his own and make a fool of himself as usual."

To be safe, he reminded himself not to answer his cell-phone during the next few days, using the vocal mailbox as a filter to avoid unpleasant encounters, although aware that it was unlikely to happen given that the only radio station that broadcasted news out of Montréal since the earthquake struck had not yet received a single call from the downtown core, suggesting that cellular mobile communications there were inoperative.

Japan, 4:00 p.m., (3:00 a.m. EST)

Professor Momoyama Nomiya, armed with his English-Japanese dictionary, carefully read the email from his good friend from the National Research Council of Canada.

The message on his screen stated: "Dear All. As you may know or will soon learn, Montréal, Canada, was just hit by a severe earthquake. The magnitude is not known yet, but it is possibly sufficiently severe that significant damage will be recorded. However, it is highly recommended that you DO NOT attempt to visit Montréal at this time. All of eastern Canada is currently under a brutal cold spell, and this would create unusually harsh conditions for an earthquake reconnaissance visit. Furthermore, given that Montréal was most unprepared for an event of this magnitude, the response and recovery activities will be slow and difficult. Authorities will not appreciate the benefits that typically could ensue from post-earthquake technical reconnaissance visits, and are expected to be uncooperative, if not outright hostile. Should you insist in coming to Montréal in spite of this stern warning, prepare to be fully autonomous for the duration of your trip."

Professor Nomiya immediately called his secretary, instructing her to purchase plane tickets for Montréal.

Nomiya was enamored with a songstress from Canada and, as an offshoot of that enthusiastic devotion to her music, he adamantly fantasized that such a fine artist could only emerge from the most modern country in the world, consequently a country with infrastructure and buildings designed and constructed in compliance with stringent state-of-the-art codes. Just as he refused to acknowledge the detractors of his esteemed singer—those fools who compared her angelic soprano voice to the screeching of forks grating on a plate—he dismissed James's cautions as alarmist and over-protective. A case of well-intentioned, self-deprecating Canadian humility that should be overlooked. He was confident that much could be learned to enhance the practice of earthquake engineering in Japan by studying at once the successful seismic performance of engineered constructions in the epicentral region, and contrasting this to the damage suffered by Japanese constructions affected by similar earthquakes in the past.

At the same time, as an ulterior motive, he saw the rapid deployment of a small delegation of 20 engineers from the South Hokkaido Institute of Technology as a strategic initiative that could help enhance the academic and professional reputation of his institution among his peers. An immediate one-week visit would allow them to collect sufficient first-hand data that an army of assistant professors and post-doctoral students would rapidly digest to generate the first reconnaissance report on this earthquake distributed throughout Japan.

He felt so fortunate to have met this Canadian researcher from the National Research Council of Canada at the last World Conference on Earthquake Engineering. Overwhelmed with emotions at the thought of visiting the native home of his beloved diva, blessed by the rewards and privileges of academic freedom—and the liberty to squander research grants wherever scholarly merit could be asserted—basking in the spirit of international scientific collaboration and global collegial friendship, he typed with two fingers a long and tedious email seeking to enlist James's assistance to the Japanese delegation from the South Hokkaido Institute of Technology in a tour of the most impressive structures throughout the earthquake-stricken area.

The warm missive of "japanglish," only partly comprehensible in spite of the author's best intentions, was greeted by an automated standard reply effectively repeating the message Momoyama had received earlier.

Undeterred, he proceeded to assemble his delegation, optimistic that communications would become possible upon his arrival to Canada. Worst-case scenario, his team would undertake the reconnaissance effort unassisted, still a worthy endeavor sure to be successful.

Pointe-aux-Trembles, 3:05 a.m.

The roads, avenues, boulevards and, particularly, the highways of Montréal have never catered well to those seeking the pleasures and privileges of car ownership. Every year, potholes the size of craters randomly erupt across the city's paved surfaces, as an uncontrollable acne reaction to spring thaw, abundantly providing for the prosperity of repair shops always ready to fleece hapless customers. Every year, crews adorned with fluorescent orange jackets set camps atop the busiest roadways to repair or replace those parts of the infrastructure that fail to reach their promised service life, for lack of maintenance or poor conception, ripping asphalt, crushing concrete, cutting steel and digging dirt, for the pleasure of creating multiple choke points and delays across the transportation network, assaulting residents and tourists alike with the deadly sluggishness of unionized work. Every year, squadrons of salt trucks rove across town answering the sightings of snow and ice, spreading the toxins that transform pure white flakes of crystallized water into gray briny slush pummeled and splashed onto begrimed banks, and simultaneously soaking the infrastructure into the corrosive agents that accelerate its gangrenous decay, nurturing the growth of malignant tumors that mutate steel and concrete into rust and dust. And year-round, while urban density and hostile bylaws conspire to make street-side parking on the roads, avenues and boulevards of the city scarce and unmanageable—and sometimes prohibitively expensive—the expressways readily become linear parking lots during rush hours, frustrating hordes of commuting suburbanites.

However, while clogged highways provided a clientele and incentives for urban core renewal and a successful public transportation system, the city had not yet fallen victim to insufferable system-wide perpetual—around the clock—traffic deadlock. As such, Lise was wondering what could possibly have caused the traffic jam that imprisoned her in the middle of the night.

The last few miles took more than one hour to drive, the last minutes mostly at a standstill. The possibility of a major car collision blocking all lanes would not explain why the opposite lanes had been free of cars all that time. Automobiles crashing and piling-up in the east bound lanes would have been most unlikely to cross over the Jersey barrier onto the westbound lanes.

An orange glow ahead suggested that something was ablaze, and thus that immobility was likely to persist for quite some time. She suspected that those at the tail end of the long pack of cars behind her would eventually carefully navigate in reverse the few miles back to the last exit; provided a Good Samaritan volunteered to steer all oncoming cars toward the exit, preventing a continual replenishment of the queue, her turn to back-out from this dead-end would come, at some unpredictable time. Eventually.

From her car, she could see the distribution center where her husband worked, across the field of oil storage tanks that bordered the highway. She fumed that the unfortunate blockage, whatever it was, occurred before this exit ramp, instead of after. Chronically impatient, she contemplated walking the distance. Only the bitter cold and wind chill made her hesitate. Leaving home in a rush, she had not planned for more than a hop from the parking lot to the warehouse, and had grabbed her favorite winter coat and boots, clothing emphasizing fashion over warmth. Nonetheless, impatience won over hesitation. She pulled onto the side of the road and parked the car there, intending to walk up to the exit, and then to the warehouse. She realized the futility of that plan as she stood alongside the car.

She had driven hundreds of times under the inconspicuous bridge that crossed the highway, a dark rusted utilitarian truss that carried pipes from a tank field on one side of the highway to the refinery on the other. No more memorable a structure than a telephone pole, the once-invisible but sound structure was now an inescapable, disturbing failure. From a distance, she could see segments of large broken pipes spread across the highway, some cars crushed under their weight. Additional vehicles had crashed into those cars or hit other scattered debris that blocked the entire width of the expressway, creating a pile-up of twisted steel and maimed bodies. Flames were twirling out from the segment of pipe embedded at the high south bridge abutment, where the pipeline would have normally connected with the pipe-bridge. The violent fire, fueled by the refined products of the petrochemical plant, danced with the wind, caressing all things within a 30-foot radius, seeking ignitable footings, threatening to spread. The road was impassable.

No fireman in sight.

With resolve, she elected to cut through the field, determined to walk a straight path to the warehouse, a shorter distance, but over more arduous terrain. She straddled across the divider barriers, crossed the opposing lanes, and proceeded across the field, each step sinking knee-deep in soft snow. In the darkness, trekking close to the stubby cylindrical oil tanks shaped like oversized above-ground swimming pools, she noticed that oil was escaping from under large unnatural bulges at their bases. Other, taller silo-like liquid storage tanks had buckled inward, like juice boxes with the air sucked out of them. Foul-smelling liquids also surrounded the base of these tanks. Some spills were contained in small circular pools demarcated by raised mounds of soil, others slowly streaming through the snow and toward the highway. She strayed from the most direct course to avoid the contaminated snow.

The distribution center was adjacent to the plant, east of its property line. Relieved to reach the firm ground of its parking lot, she rushed to empty the accumulated snow scooped in each step by the shaft of her stylish boots, never designed for the rigor of deep snow-wading expeditions. The instant sting of sub-zero air was painful, but less than walking atop the moist ice blocks that had packed solid at the bottom of her boots.

Eager to escape the glacial ordeal, she was undeterred by the locked front door of the warehouse and ready to break a window, when she noticed the already shattered bay windows of the low-rise main office appended to the taller storehouse. She hesitated a moment, on the thought that thugs might have broken that glass—thugs that might still be inside the building—but all caution was dissolved by the wind chill from a sudden gust of cold air. Through the window frame, after taking a moment to survey the content and layout of the rather plain small office, she followed fresh dirty tracks on the carpet that led straight to the warehouse, determined that it was preferable to catch up to the intruders than be first discovered by them. Besides, the tracks progressively led to the warmth of the warehouse, as far as possible from the arctic air near the broken window.

She exited the main office from its inside door to the depot, stepping a few paces into the large enclosed space before stopping, amazed by the sight. The large, brightly lit storage facility where she sometimes met her husband had been vandalized beyond recognition. The disheveled content of the dark warehouse bathed

in the glow of a few battery-operated emergency lights. Where
formerly stood wide, immaculate rows of stacked crates now lied
a formidable chaos. Automotive parts buried in heaps of clothes,
food, and other unidentifiable goods, lined the entire floor. Looking at the scale of the disorder, unable to make sense of the horrible, overwhelming mess, Lise felt as if she had entered the bedroom of some giant teenager. She corrected her first impression,
remembering the clean, infinite rows of lined-up boxes that used
to span floor to ceiling to rather resemble the obsessive, rational
tidiness of a sick young adult oppressed by an abusive mother,
imagining the crushing burst of violence unleashed by this fero-
cious mother nature. She loved the peacefulness of tidy rooms,
the Zen of orderly spaces, the sense of security and control that
emanated from clean aligned structures. The destruction ahead
saddened her for so many reasons.

"Hey you!" shouted a voice from behind her.

Her heart jumped. A gush of adrenaline seized her. She
froze.

"What are you doing here?" barked the man.

Turning around to face the thug, ready to fight for her life,
she noticed on the shoulder of the shadowy figure a shiny badge
reflecting the light from behind. The standard embroidered
golden piping revealed the menacing wrestler to be only a short,
overweight security officer hiding his own fear behind assertive
commands.

"Lise Letarte, head of the *Organisation de sécurité civile du Québec*," she replied to the nakedness of his authority.

His face remained in shadow, but she interpreted his silence
as incredulity. After all, ordinary warehouses did not receive many
visitors, and certainly deserve none of such stature. She volunteered identification, slowly pulling from her purse an official-
looking government card adorned by the obligatory horrible
photo. As the guard moved into the light to inspect the card, she
could at last see his face and assessed from his dull response that
she had gained control of the situation. Actually, in spite of his
failed attempts at reconciling the mug shot buried in heavy layers
of make-up and the shaggier version in his presence, the guard
accepted the evidence as satisfactory only because he concluded
that someone determined to create a false identity would not pick
such an unimpressive one.

"Have you seen the night watchman?" She refrained from adding "He is my husband," to preserve the prestige of her status and maintain command.

"No."

"How long have you been here?"

"About an hour. I got dispatched in answer to an alarm. Because of the broken windows, I have to stay to prevent looting. Company rules."

She thought only an old bachelor would have nothing better to do than stick around in such a crisis, and believed he fitted the description.

"Did you check out the entire warehouse?"

"There's no way to walk around in there."

"You didn't try hard. There's a watchman in there. Give me your cell phone?"

She grabbed it and dialed. The Valkyries started chiming from the second row.

"That way!"

Guided by the music, they climbed the piles of broken goods, advancing through the debris, eventually reaching a heap of mangled metal sitting in a bloody puddle.

"Shit! I'll never get it out."

Unsure what "it" was, the officer faked sympathy: "Uh…, yeah, pretty terrible. Is this why you're here?"

She raised her right eyebrow in a telling disdain. She had no time or interest to pretend friendliness to a security officer she'd never see again. She kneeled on top of the pile, and sank her arm in shoulder-deep, searching for what was once hers, blindly confident in the stability of the randomly interlocked steel pieces. The rummaging lasted a few minutes. Then, in surprise and absolute satisfaction, a mile-wide smile stretched her face as she proudly pulled a singing bloody cell-phone from the heap of debris—the kind of broad smile from which beauty is usually conceived, but a sterile smile for her. Oblivious to the dumbfounded guard, having regained what she sought, she left in a heartbeat.

It didn't cross her mind to fake the afflicted widow part or even acknowledge her relationship to the shattered, dead body she abandoned. This would have required something she didn't possess. Far from bereaved, she had long since stopped caring about her husband—like one tires of the latest gadget that has ceased to amuse. It had been a marriage of convenience to leverage what had once been two identical salaries, which became a lopsided deal when one of the two career ladders ran out of rungs. The companionship struck on the attributes of a temporary compromise served its purpose for a while—much like a starter home—but as her prospects further brightened, she had been ready to trade for a more upscale model compatible with her standing, only held back by her secret struggle to figure out how to ditch her matrimonial partner without losing half of a common estate she felt to be legitimately hers. The convenient earthquake provided her with a brutal but effective solution that would allow her to keep it all—an omen of good things to come, in Lise's mind.

Outside the warehouse, the stinging cold was gone. The air was a mixture of fresh, cold ambient winter purity disturbed by swirls of hot, foul smoky vapors. The entire tank farm was ablaze. Flames raised along the stretches of oozing fuels that connected the puddles surrounding each ruptured tank. The intense heat had melted the snow along wide bands delimiting the fire. On the windward side of the inferno, smoke blown away, it was possible to walk in bearable heat on wet ground along the edge of the melting snow bank. She followed this alternative, longer path to return to her car, trudging across muddy flats and contaminated streams that spoiled the environment beyond the confines of the refinery.

"This is going to be a long day," she thought, severely underestimating the length of all present and future pains.

Longueuil, 3:15 a.m.

The helicopter touched down just long enough for Florent to hop aboard. He sat next to Léandre, nodding to Réal and Julien in the back-seat. As he slipped the muffling full-ear cups of his headphones, he stared at the two squeezed partners, wondering how long they would last jammed in their uncomfortable restrained space.

"Don't worry for us. We've been backbenchers long enough in our youth to feel right at home here," volunteered Réal in a sizzling, distorted pitch atop the hiss of the cockpit radio.

"Good, 'cause you may not feel so comfortable after our little city tour. I have drafted an itinerary based on the preliminary information we could collect. If it checks out, it will give us a pretty good idea of just how bad it could be overall."

As they gained altitude, Montréal revealed itself as a huge black hole, a pitch black core surrounded by a dim halo of sparkling lights. The entire island was blacked out. The usual landmarks were imperceptible. The usually bright cross atop Mont Royal, a tall steel tower framed with spheres of light suggesting a rosary, erected in memory of the wooden cross planted there in the early days of the colony: dark. The rotating beacon on the roof of *Place Ville-Marie* that lit up at night, illuminating the surrounding sky and marking the central point of downtown: dark. The high-rise towers, the stadiums, the busy roads: dark. The second largest French-speaking city in the world was dark.

Nonetheless, through the darkness, Léandre still could see the island. When he saw the outline of Mont-Royal cut through the halo of suburban lights and fade into the darkness as the helicopter gained elevation, he apperceived the lone mountain emerging from the island's flat plains as the city's dividing landmark, with Anglophones established in the prestigious mansions of its western-flank enclaves and Francophones settled in its eastern-flank districts, spreading to fill the island in their respective directions. He saw the outline of the island faintly etched in the snow by the moonlight, its southern tip wrapped by the broad elbow of the St-Lawrence river, bent ninety degrees, the islands at the upper tip of the bend only leaps from the downtown core.

More intense than mere geographical features, he also saw the balcony of City Hall where France's own General DeGaulle proclaimed "*Vive le Québec libre*" in a passionate breach of diplomatic protocol on a warm summer evening in support for Québec's sovereignty. He saw the old Forum, the arena where, a decade before DeGaulle, a subdued nationalism was revived by the riots that erupted when the nation's star Francophone hockey player was unjustly suspended for fighting back in response to the abuse of Anglophones who acted on the widely held belief that a conquered people were undeserving of any favors. He saw all those and many more shining lights in the darkness of Montréal, because these were brighter than what eyes could see and no natural or man-made event could ever extinguish those beacons.

Instead of going toward the island, the helicopter veered east, towards two distant strings of white and red lights lined up a few miles apart, straddling the boundary between darkness and suburban lights. As they approached, Florent commented.

"This is Highway 25 leading into the Louis Hippolyte Lafontaine tunnel. It has turned into a three-mile-long parking lot on each side. Apparently, water infiltrated and filled the tunnel."

The seasoned politicians pressed their faces to the glass, trying to absorb as much of the scene as possible, with the gravity of kids spying through the window of unsuspecting neighbors caught in some forbidden act.

After hovering above the tunnel entrances for a moment, the pilot drove off north, heading toward a bright orange sky. What looked at first like a gorgeous, dense cluster of sunset clouds at dusk from afar, revealed itself up close as a cluster of turbulent smoke plumes spewed from burning reservoirs. The pilot kept the group at a safe distance from the intimidating artificial volcanoes.

"The refineries have encountered some problems," said Florent, purposely understating it as he pointed to the large flames visible a few miles to the northeast. "The 40 is blocked at a few points there and elsewhere, as some older overpasses have collapsed. A number of fuel tanks have presumably fractured and spilled; a few are burning. Sporadic fires have been reported inside the facilities themselves, but we don't know more."

"Can this spread out of control?" asked Léandre.

"Hard to tell. We don't have enough information on this yet. There is sizeable separation between the plants and the surrounding neighborhoods, so that should help, but the major concern is whether the fumes could be toxic. The police have decided to evacuate a 2-mile radius for now. They can't pragmatically do more eastward as the bridges out of the island are apparently impassable. They will reassess when they can find somebody to conduct toxicity readings."

After observing the inferno for a few minutes, silenced in awe by the dark specter of a combined conflagration and widespread toxic death, the team resumed his westward flight above the invisible city.

"Are there plans in action to set up emergency shelters?" inquired Léandre, snapping back from his torpidity, latching on to the realization that evacuation was already underway, and pondering what would be the political ramifications of such a civic disturbance. "Will they gather people in surrounding schools?"

"Such plans likely exist, but we have not been able to establish contact yet with the leadership of the *Organization de sécurité civile du Québec*. However, gathering people anywhere will be of mitigated benefit unless they can be provided with food, electricity, and, most importantly, heat."

Léandre looked at the cockpit panel an instant, as a reflex, as if a gauge could show the ground-level temperature.

Florent instructed the pilot: "Turn on the spotlights, and circle down and around the stadium."

Those words brought a dreaded thought. They had not yet conceived the inconceivable. They all implicitly accepted that boats sometimes sank, planes sometimes crashed, and buildings sometimes collapsed, standard tragedies of the technological folio germane to each era of innovation. But they also harbored the archetypal fear that when the Titanic sinks, the Concorde crashes, and the World Trade Center collapses, when monumental technological landmarks that symbolize the best that humankind could engineer disappear forever, humanity is brutally confronted with the impermanency of its creation, the limits of its ambition, and the sinking, crashing and collapsing of its confidence—painful reminders that hurt, in so many ways, at so many levels.

As they approached the billion-dollar structure, the powerful light beams projected from the underside of the helicopter reflected on the white concrete structure that once housed the Olympic games. The elegant stadium tower, a five-hundred-foot-tall sculpture that once projected from the ground at a 45-degrees angle, cables fanning from its tip supporting a fabric roof that enclosed the stadium by covering the oval opening above center field, once the tallest leaning building in the world, was now a horizontal wreck of massive broken segments. Through its collapse, it crushed the slender cantilevering ribs that met at the oval opening and supported the stadium's bowl-shaped concrete portion of the roof, turning an architectural marvel into a snapped burrito shell of intertwined concrete, fabric, steel bars, tendons and cables. The white elephant laid down forever.

Nobody commented. While an architecturally pleasing design envelope from a distance, the ascetic, poorly finished concrete stadium lacked warmth, suffered from poor ergonomics, never achieved profitability, and, like a curse, tarnished the political aura of those embroiled in the endless, messy quest for solutions to those problems. Yet, the loss inspired a deep sadness, like the sudden death of an imperfect spouse that one could never quite decide to divorce—robbed of the hope that a once-great love could be rekindled and familiar failings someday rectified.

The helicopter approached the downtown core, leaving the stadium far behind. The spotlights were not as effective in revealing the extent of damage there, but, in the shadow of September 11, 2001, all on board were relieved that, on prime assessment, the high-rises that defined the city skyline were still standing. There was debris in the streets, water flowing from broken water mains, and evidence of damage in the surrounding lower buildings, but apparently no tower had suffered a fate similar to the World Trade Center collapse. As a terrorist, Mother Nature had effectively crippled the city, but she had spared the jewels of the downtown core, to the relief of Léandre and his cohort. The odd solace in seeing the high-rises stand was in reaction to the fear of known tragedies—in opposition to the dejection induced by knowledge of the forthcoming hardships and horrors of a familiar history about to be repeated. Unknown futures, tragedies that remain to be played without a script, can be approached with the blind faith of optimism, with the hope that in spite of bleak first impressions, the future is only an approximate forecast that could still unfold better than expected.

In spite of the uplifting satisfaction of having witnessed survivor buildings, the team was drained by the emotional grind of the short tour, and orders were given to return to the St-Hubert base. The incremental benefits of extending this visual survey were deemed to be marginal at best, given that damage to the more common low-rise buildings could barely be detected in total darkness from the height of a helicopter.

Instead of flying a direct route, the pilot took the initiative to loop over to the Champlain bridge, and followed the river by the Victoria and Jacques Cartier bridges on the way back, mostly out of curiosity since these were the bridges most directly linking his daughter on the island to his home in Brossard. All bridges were eerily free of traffic, for reasons that could not be detected at the onset. Disappointed that his exhausted passengers had collapsed in their seats captive to their thoughts, he did not dare bring attention to the detour to the first two bridges, but planted the helicopter mid-air in front of the Jacques Cartier Bridge, and, steadfast in his resolve to have the highest authorities inspect it, captured their attention by commanding the chopper to simulate the abrupt shaking of rough turbulence.

Flood lights beaming anew, the helicopter scanned the entire length of the bridge. All eyes were fixed on the long, century-old landmark truss structure, which seemed intact, yet strangely free of traffic. The explanation for this unusual condition was found at each of the bridge's ends, where some of the approach spans had collapsed. A few cars had piled up in the open gaps, others stopped at the edge to prevent further casualties.

"*Calvaire,*" sighed Léandre.

"Is there any known operational access route to the island or are they all cut like this?" asked Julien.

"Preliminary information indicates that all transportation infrastructures to the island are cut in one way or another."

"What about the airport?" asked Léandre.

"We don't know yet about the buildings there, but it appears that the runways are out of commission. The grounds sank and heaved locally, while batches of sand apparently oozed out of the ground and accumulated on the runways at various locations."

"*Calvaire Calvaire Calvaire!*" said Léandre, with a crescendo in emphasis.

The implications of the disaster were startlingly clear to this select group of politically savvy representatives of the *Parti National* government. They understood that "spinning" of an empty message would be ineffective, and that some actions would be required. Some tough actions, in a tough political arena, where the gladiators would trample much blood-soaked sand. For in the end, one of the warriors would be met by another disaster, of another type, with a clear finality and no possible recovery. Léandre had no intention of losing that battle.

Ottawa, 4:00 a.m.

The four Cabinet Ministers had reconvened in the Premier's office to review drafts of contributions to a press release. A somewhat nervous Kaylee read first to a stoic Brendon.

"At 12:57 a.m., Eastern Standard Time, a Magnitude 7 earthquake struck Montreal."

Brendon stopped her right there. "Not good. For Christ's sake, this goddamn press release is meant to drive into everybody's skull that this is a Canadian disaster that will be met with a Canadian response. I want 'Canada' to be in almost every fucking sentence. Got it?"

"Uh, yes, yes," said Kaylee. Although used to percussive obscenities uttered in Brendon's usual expressionless tone, it always took her off guard when mixed with personal criticisms. Fully confident in her political sagacity, she did not believe it mattered to be so picky, but she was discountenanced by her failure to have anticipated Brendon's childish fussiness. "So, let's say: 'At 12:57 a.m., Eastern Standard Time, a Magnitude 7 earthquake struck the Canadian city of—' "

"Metropolis. There are more than goddamn French Canadians in Montreal."

"The Canadian metropolis of Montreal. OK!" Although she felt like saying "the fucking Canadian metropolis of Montreal" to deride Brendon, she possessed neither the assertiveness nor the power to risk such aggravation.

Trying to regain her composure following this dreadful start, Kaylee paused to red-mark her copy with the appropriate changes. Although she thought she had carefully "Brendon-proofed" her document, she undertook to edit it on the fly to avoid further outbursts from her grumpy Premier, attempting to anticipate as best as possible what else might cross him.

"Preliminary reports indicate that significant damage has been suffered, although..." she struck out the words "although the exact nature of this damage remains to be determined at this time," and improvised. "Uh... and the Government of Canada will undertake everything under its power to ascertain with more precision the extent of this damage."

"Do we know for sure there will be significant damage?" snapped Brendon.

"'Significant' is for sure!" volunteered Graham. "'Significant' is the perfect non-descriptive, imprecise word we need in this case. In any event, our eggheads at Earthquakes Canada briefed us that a Magnitude 7 will wreak havoc in any city not prepared for an earthquake of that magnitude."

In the long pause that followed that sentence, he could read the natural follow-up question from the stare of those around the table, and clarified: "And Montreal is definitely not considered to be prepared for an earthquake."

Graham could have sworn he saw a gleam of satisfaction wipe a wrinkle of worry from the Premier's face.

"What is 'everything possible in its power' supposed to mean?" queried Wayne. "Does it mean we will send our troops in now?"

"No, no, that's the stroke of genius in this sentence." corrected Brendon.

Kaylee felt relived by her boss's compliment, although she did not have a clue what he was talking about.

"The Government of Canada will not send any troops, unless the Quebec government requests it."

Brendon paused a moment to savor the thought. His perusal of the blank faces around him re-affirmed his cynical conviction that his brain trust had a propensity to freeze at critical times, suffering from occasional deficiencies in Machiavellian thoughts or similar strategic thinking, as if they were the quadruplet victims of some rare congenital disease.

He clarified: "It is the prerogative of a provincial Premier to declare a region a 'disaster area.' Doing so triggers a shower of federal dollars dispatched, per some goddamn generous pre-established formula, as post-disaster financial assistance to offset the disaster response expenses and the cost of rebuilding infrastructure and personal property. These bums practically declare every windstorm or rainfall a 'state of emergency' just to get their hands on that relief money."

While quiet, they could see where his argumentation was leading.

"Now, if a disaster is big enough to get our money, it's big enough to need our resources—it's just like some huge fucking package deal that delivers the full-blown mighty resources of all relevant federal departments and agencies throughout the crisis.

If they call it a disaster, they get our dollars, and we are compelled as a responsible federal government to kick in and deliver to the province-in-need the full assistance it needs."

Brendon slammed his open hand on the table with great delight, concluding, "I just can't wait to see that son of a bitch pushed by the media into calling us to send in the army. They could kiss their claims to sovereignty on the ass goodbye."

Kaylee rapidly absorbed the lesson into a closing statement for the press release: "The Government of Canada is prepared to take all measures to ensure this tragic event will have no impact on our national economy, and stands ready to offer the population of Montreal and the Province of Quebec all the assistance it may request."

Convinced that his own contributions to the press release would be torn into shreds, lacking much of the political finesse Brendon was seeking, Graham said, "Hey, this gives me a couple of additional ideas to feed the media. Let me spend another hour to work on my part of the draft."

Brendon's ancestors did not include any *coureur des bois*, the Anglo-Saxon nobility at the roots of his family tree having been more interested in the commerce and trading of furs than in generating the goods themselves. He was nonetheless busy spreading traps, starting from a few well-positioned ones along the main trail he expected his prey to follow, and thinking about how to strategically widen coverage to span all possible alternative routes. Hence, while his brain trust was still digesting his prior lecture, he was trying to anticipate his adversary's other possible moves. This was crucial, since the first trap, although difficult to circumvent, was too obvious.

Vaudreuil-Dorion, 4:45 a.m.

The drive down Highway 417 linking Ottawa to Montréal (called Highway 40 past the Québec border) had been almost uneventful. Among the many long ribbons of asphalt unfolding straight through a flat, featureless agricultural land, Highway 417/40 was a strong contender for the title of "most boring road to drive in Canada." Daytime or nighttime, its only dangerous feature was a propensity to put drivers to sleep, boring them to death—a symbolic peculiarity when approaching the national capital. The magnet of Montréal, with its nightlife, professional sports teams, arts, and cultural events, kept the road well traveled by frequent users who could—fortunately—drive it with eyes closed.

Countless times, James cruised the 417/40 daydreaming or mulling over professional concerns, never paying attention to the features of an infrastructure that inexorably aged. Now, for the first time, James was paying attention, wondering which cracks in the road and damages to the bridges were signatures from the ravages of successive Nordic winters, and which were new. On his way to downtown Montréal, keeping his eyes on the prize, he would not stop to investigate anything—much less damage that could not at once conclusively be attributed to the earthquake. Nonetheless, in the black of night hours after a major earthquake, special caution was warranted, and he slowed down to the pace of a jogger when approaching each bridge, assessing whether it was safe to proceed before crossing. He was particularly afraid of settled approaches.

He knew the weakest link in any structural system to be the first to fail during an earthquake. For most short bridges without columns and piers, he believed that this weakness lied either in the small metallic or elastomeric devices—known as bearings—that support a span on its abutments, or in the earth-fill approaches leading to the span. He was fully aware that the most mundane overpass could become a lethal hazard when the man-made earth mound created to raise the road up to a bridge settled during strong ground-shaking. He was particularly leery of any bridge's span supported by piles or other competent foundations, which would not settle like its approaches, resulting in a lowered roadway leading straight onto the riser of a concrete step, with the potential to wreck the car's suspension, or worse, depending on the height of the resulting riser. Unsuspecting drivers had splattered on bridge abutments, as flies on windshields, during the 1994 Northridge earthquake in Los Angeles, when some bridge approaches settled more than five feet, leaving exposed the equivalent of road-wide concrete barrier walls. James had no intention of experiencing this phenomenon first hand.

The brutally cold night ensured a clean windshield, but James did not need squashed bugs to remember the vivid Northridge images. At each crossing or overpass, when he slowed down, he guesstimated the size of the step, if any, and logged it in a notebook kept open on the passenger's seat. At first, when leaving Ottawa, he'd observed some "bumps," mostly driving over bridges in that part of the valley known to lie on top of thick soft clay deposits, a type of soil well known to strongly amplify the ground shaking from distant earthquakes. Then, nothing, up to the Ontario-Québec border, from which point onward bumps reappeared and became progressively larger from one overpass to the other. At the 40-540 interchange, approaching Montréal, a few cars lied on the side of the road, a few wheels and metallic debris scattered across the field. James estimated the steep quake-made vertical ramp to the first bridge of this interchange to be at least six inches tall, substantially more than observed previously, and he speculated that the unsuspecting drivers had lost control, possibly airborne, as they ran at full speed into the obstacle.

With appropriate circumspection, James's progress toward his goal was slow, but not impeded, until a mile prior to reaching the *Ile aux Tourtes* bridge, where the highway was clogged. The long row of immobilized cars had obviously not been assembled by an army of early birds seized by a sudden desire to await a beautiful Nordic sunrise. He understood that this unscheduled stop was to be the starting point of his first expedition. He parked the car on the shoulder, wrapped himself in his winter gear, and grabbed a camera, ready to document the damage to the infrastructure ahead.

As he opened the door, the heat of the protected enclosure was sucked out by the Siberian cold. Comfortable beneath layers of thermal clothes, James walked onto the bridge up to where the road dropped into the bay. Successive spans had been toppled by the earthquake and lied propped on a bridge pier at one end, nose in the water at the other, as if all had been pulled off their supports in the same direction. James recognized this as a classic case of unrestrained simple bridge spans, each supported on fixed bearings tied to a pier at one of their ends and on roller bearings allowing free movement at the other end—spans so constructed to accommodate the lengthening and shortening resulting from the natural property of materials to expand and contract as temperature rises or falls. James guessed that as the bridge shook longitudinally during the earthquake, the roller bearings on a number of spans visibly slipped off their supporting pier; highly predictable failures, in his opinion, given that he could not identify any measure implemented to prevent such undesirable motions. James nonetheless chose to document this unique case in which the individual bridge segments were likely contracted to their shortest length at the cold temperature that existed at the time of the earthquake, further facilitating this type of collapse.

After taking a dozen snapshots of the fallen spans at different zoom lengths and framing, earnestly hoping that the miracles of modern digital photography post-processing combined with the ambient moonlight would help compensate for the flash and film ISO deficiencies, James pondered how to cross to the island of Montréal. Curious onlookers came and left, standing incredulous at the edge of the disjointed bridge, taking a picture, trying to make sense of it all. A few came in pairs or small groups, having met as they parked, sharing their concerns, exchanging stories, all seeking information on how to reach the island. One described similar span failures at the *Taschereau* bridge. Another claimed witnessing a train derailing during the earthquake. A barn collapse, cracks in the ground, walls overturning, thunder and lightning, waves at ground surface, animals howling before the quake, sulfur taste in well water—part testimonies, part entertainment; stories at liberty to confuse fiction and reality.

The mile-long walk back to his car afforded him time to contemplate various options. Given that the *Île aux Tourtes* and *Taschereau* bridges, at the edge of the *Lac des Deux Montagnes*, were the island's crossings farthest from downtown Montréal—where he remained convinced the epicenter had to be located—the fatal damage at such a distance from the city center suggested that most other highway bridges were probably also closed. James wondered whether the two railroad bridges further south might have fared better, given that such light bridges are typically designed to resist the lateral forces induced by the front of locomotives wiggling left and right between the rails, but then remembered that railroad bridges are often supported on unreinforced masonry stone piers that are known to be most vulnerable to earthquakes. He did not pursue this thought further, given that crossing a railroad bridge by car was not sensible, and that walking the 30 miles to downtown was also out of the question.

The distant buzzing noise of a familiar engine echoing in the cold winter night gave him an idea. A possible solution that might warrant further consideration.

Back in his car, after starting the engine to feed the heater, he tuned to CHOK-AM.

Vaudreuil-Dorion, 5:00 a.m.

"...amazing story. We wish you the best of luck, buddy. So folks, that brings us to six major crossings to the island closed. And frankly, I'd be surprised if any are open at this point.

"It is now 5:00 a.m., and -38°F. You are listening to CHOK-AM, the only station in Montréal that has been broadcasting continuously since a catastrophic earthquake struck four hours ago."

He had periodically checked, scanning the airwaves to verify whether this remained true, but true or not, he felt this was a most effective approach to kill any listeners' temptation to tune to a competing station. He felt that major media never hesitated to inflate facts to aggrandize their self-perceived importance and ability to shape history, and his goal was to emulate them in this crisis.

"Ladies and gentlemen, dear public, if you have been with us throughout our coverage, you know the news is grim. If you are just joining us, allow me to briefly recap the events of the night. Thanks to all those who have called us to provide factual, precise information, we know that none of the bridges to Montréal have collapsed completely, but they all have suffered sufficient damage to be closed, including the *tunnel Lafontaine*, which is filled with water. Wired telephone service appears to be down on the entire island. Cell-phone communication seems slightly better, but is not working in the center districts of the island, roughly defined north to south as from river to river, and west to east as from Highway 13 in Dorval to Highway 25 in Anjou.

"There is no electric power available on the island. Some residences also have no water or gas. We have no word from Hydro Québec, Bell, or others as to when any of these services will be restored. In fact, we have received no information from any of the responsible governments or authorities with regard to this catastrophe. None have called us.

"Ladies and gentlemen, considering that we have just experienced a major earthquake, an earthquake strong enough to move pianos from living rooms to kitchens, an earthquake that has destroyed the fundamental utility services on the island, where are our leaders? Where are our fat, overpaid politicians when we need them? When it comes to whether or not we should separate from Canada, they manage to find ways to shower us day and night with unwanted information, but when it comes to the basic survival of this city after a national catastrophe, where is our leadership? Their silence is disturbing, and telling.

"I am hopeful that Jim Sunshine, your DJ for what would have been the usual morning drive, will soon walk into the studio, and take over the show. Jim lives nearby and I am most confident he will anchor CHOK-AM's continuous coverage of this disaster through the morning for you, taking more of your calls. In the meantime, allow me to replay the first 15 minutes of our broadcast that immediately followed the earthquake, to give you a sense of the confusion and concerns that prevailed at the time, and a recap of how the news slowly trickled to us on the state of damage throughout the stricken area. As this plays back, I invite our government officials and their fat bureaucrats, or any responsible public agency, to call us and inform us, the public, us, the taxpayers, of what they will do at once to respond to this emergency.

"If you have a message of critical public interest, or any other important information that you would like to provide off the air, please call 555-CHOX, instead of 555-CHOK. The CHOX is a direct line that will allow us to talk off the air during this re-broadcast of the critical first 15 minutes after time zero."

Richard had no illusions. Even in this time of crisis, no government agency or politician in their right mind would waste their time with a small private radio station known best for broadcasting apathetic elevator music by day and abrasive neo-punk and post-grunge by night. Therefore, to stir up some interest and generate some appeal, he had determined to move his operation on-site. He needed two things for that purpose. First, the new portable dish recently acquired by the station for the purpose of broadcasting live from the premises of any sponsor, an investment made for mercantile purposes but that could be used by Richard in his attempt to enter the world of live news. Equipped with automatic satellite locator tuning, this proved to be the best toy on the market for such an endeavor. Second, he needed Jim Sunshine, the station's only DJ trained to operate the gadget and link its feed to the studio broadcast. He needed Jim for a crash course on how to operate the portable dish from the field, but also for his technical studio-operator expertise to air his live broadcasts. His repeated calls over the past hour for Jim to "walk into the studio any minute now" were incantations indirectly imploring him to report to work for those two purposes.

Beyond the technical aspects, Richard was still lacking a plan. Once "live in the field," then what? Information has to be dug up. Being in the studio was being far from the action, but information rang off the phone, in a continuous stream, coming free and easy. Leaving the secure confines of the studio, the initial appeal of "live" could fizzle to nothing unless he could unearth the stories and the story-tellers linked to the debris on the ground. In a television-centric century, stories could still stand on their own without images, but a radio journalist relying merely on expanded description of damage to capture an audience would not survive the fickle attention span of today's channel surfers. There was no point going into the field to collect the same anecdotal evidence and nescient, uninformed opinions he had been gathering for the past four hours from a random sample of well-intentioned, passive observers. The field had to spotlight key players and knowledge-able statements anchored in ground truth. The field had to beam to the satellite facts and statements that could potentially impact the lives of the listeners, not the incoherent or ignorant rambling of feckless bystanders preaching from atop snow banks. Richard fully recognized this challenge, but was still lacking a plan to make the broadcasts interesting without access to any key officials or politicians.

A ring from the CHOX line on the switchboard cut his reflection. Could it be?

"CHOK-speaking. What can you do for the population of Montréal in this time of crisis?"

That seemed like an aggressive but appropriate greeting. Unfortunately, the answer was "nothing." Only an engineer on the line, with a convenient offer.

"Yeah, I think that's a good idea... That's easy to arrange because I happen to own one... I'd definitely like to do that... That would be a reasonable deal... No, I'm waiting for someone to set up some equipment in the studio before I can leave the studio."

At that very moment, Jim Sunshine walked into the studio. The wide smile on his face confirmed that he had been riveted to the morning broadcasts and was anxious to take over the open-line format and further agitate the population.

"Listen, you've got a deal! I'll see you there in 45 minutes. Maybe sooner, but definitely in 45 minutes," he said, just before hanging up.

The stars had aligned perfectly.

Longueuil, 5:15 a.m.

The five-member policy task force landed in Longueuil late, sleepy and disheveled, yet flustered that the simpler option of a conference call had been discarded. Conference calls were the blessed buffers of schedules stacked with meetings—hardened bureaucrats mastered the art of hiding behind a speaker-phone while checking emails or typing reports, at best paying cursory attention to the discussion, skillfully contributing well-timed general remarks to suggest otherwise. At 5:00 a.m., it might even have been possible to participate in such a call with eyes closed, mind partially engaged. Instead, they were forced to attend an in-person meeting, out-of-town, at an unsightly hour, for the only marginal benefit that nobody would be asleep during the meeting.

Léandre, Réal, Julien and Florent had taken advantage of the delayed start of the meeting to rest and recover from their stressful sightseeing tour. Time that could have been used to prepare for the meeting was instead invested into reflective silence, as a balm on minds numbed by the surreal damage to familiar sights. In that shared limbering mood, they awaited the arrival of the task force, coffee turning cold. This musing persisted undisturbed by the noise of landing helicopters, footsteps, and doors opening.

When the late team entered the meeting room, at the sight of its somber leaders, all resentment for being dragged to Longueuil vanished. The hazy painting of reality, drawn by the large brush strokes of succinct briefings on the possible state of affairs, suddenly took on life, connected to the unstated gloomy message of those who had been there to see. They sat quietly around the conference table, as if entering a sacred temple, not even daring to whisper.

Léandre first broke out of his thoughts with a long and deep sigh. He stood up and described in vivid detail their observations while pacing across the room, only stopping to draw their itinerary on a large map of Montréal pinned to the wall. All through his exposé, he emphasized the primordial need for this government to be realistic yet breathe optimism, to coldly assess the situation yet exude compassion, to be assertive and decisive yet considerate of dissenting opinion—in other words, to act now and discuss later, unilaterally under the guise of an inclusive process. The task force's instructions were to oversee all official press releases, to ensure compliance to this philosophy while sustaining the vision of a successful, soon-to-be-recovering Québec. Consistency in message and frequently reiterated content, starting with an early morning communique at once, a press conference by Léandre at 10:00 a.m. for whomever from all the invited news media could make it to Longueuil on such a short notice, and subsequent deployment of whatever bold communication strategies could be imagined with more time in hand.

Drained of energy, Léandre sat back in his chair and invited the group to brainstorm, to anticipate how groups hostile to the separatist agenda could use this disaster to discredit the nationalist aspirations of his government.

Immediately, one task force member volunteered: "I wouldn't be surprised if the number of casualties were constantly brought up as way to insinuate incompetence, with estimates rising everyday. Imagine the *Toronto Star* headlines heralding '1000 Deaths in Montreal Quake' on Monday, 'Death Toll Could Reach 2000' by Tuesday, 'Government Hiding True Numbers of Dead' on Wednesday, and 'Largest Mass Murder in Canadian History' by the weekend."

"I heard a specialist the other day," said another. "Some British academic from Vancouver making cold, calculated statements to the media to the effect that on a planet with a population of six billion people, if everybody lived to be one hundred years old, then, mathematically, sixty million persons would die every year, presumably replaced by sixty million births. That's two hundred thousands per day, about one thousand per minute. Of course, he was presenting that information in a different context, apparently to emphasize the amazing capacity of adaptation of humanity, but I'm sure he'd be pleased to be on television again."

"What for?" asked Florent.

"To minimize the psychological impact of the numbers."

"That's the view from 30,000 feet, looking out the window of an airplane," countered Florent. "When you are in a cylindrical steel cage sharing space with other prisoners unknown to you and that you'll never see again, the insignificance of human life is brutally clear. From that high, individuals can't be seen—they do not exist. In fact, as you fly further north, as traces of civilization disappear from the view and the landscape becomes peaceful, unblemished by the scars of society, it becomes so clear that humanity is a burden for the globe. It's a nice philosophical reality, but that does not really help us."

"Agreed," added a fourth. "Complex adaptive systems are great concepts for academics, but that's theoretical rhetoric that will fly above everybody's heads. Nobody really cares if one thousand people die per minute, or even per second. It doesn't matter at all, as long as you're not one of the thousands, as long as your loved ones are not part of the thousands."

"Ouch, that's blunt," countered Florent.

"Facts are facts," responded the team member.

"But of no value, even if packaged nicely," answered Julien.

"The key lies at the other end of the spectrum," said a senior member of the task force. "Every time numbers will be brought up, emphasize the individual. Take the high ground. Each individual matters, numbers don't. In spite of our absolute insignificance at the global scale, we have an essential significance at a personal level, a unique flame of life. This thirst for life is our cherished essence, our fundamental gift. It is all we own. This flame can be weakened, assailed by the hardships of life, or nourished and strengthen by love, by a resolve to fully realize our potential. As long as it burns, the privilege of presence exists. When that conscience is crushed, this freedom dies, this beauty is extinguished. There is no solace to be found in knowing that many flames die simultaneously, and those who focus on numbers for the sake of sensationalism profane the value of life and the memory of the departed."

Nods. This would be the adopted strategy.

"What about a possible exodus?" asked the blunt team member.

This caught the attention of the group.

"If the city is unserviceable for too long, many who leave may never come back," he clarified.

All wondered.

In silence, they all realized that Montréal wasn't built against nature below water level and awaiting to be submerged like a modern Atlantis, on the slopes of a volcano at risk of being buried under thick lava deposits like a contemporary Pompeii, or surrounded by obsolescent nuclear power plants about to melt-down Chernobyl-style. They knew that cities destroyed by fire or earthquakes had been rebuilt before, and they figured that it would be the same this time. Too much infrastructure existed for the city to become a ghost town. However, they ignored whether a substantial population shift could threaten rapid economic recovery.

"There could also be a political exodus," suggested the same person, to break the long silence. "If Francophones leave Montréal, they'll remain in the province, but Anglophones will likely leave the province, and they never do that silently."

All remembered the symbolic staged parade of empty Brinks trucks leaving Montréal for Toronto days before the 1980 referendum on sovereignty, to create the illusion of fleeing capital as a consequence of a possible victory of the separatist agenda. All remembered that many Anglophones also moved out of Montréal around the same time, in fear of becoming a minority in a new country to which they felt no allegiance, or pretending such a fear as opportunists blaming the political climate for moves that were purely business-driven, routine transfers to headquarter offices in Toronto.

"If many of the Anglos leave Montréal, maybe this could help the vote," suggested Réal. "Considering that the Canadian government is rubber-stamping the Canadian citizenship applications of all immigrants living in Québec to buy as many 'no' votes as possible for the referendum, maybe some level of exodus of the Anglos will counter-balance this gross abuse of the system."

Another member of the task force chipped in, reminding them, "All those who have been official residents in the province at any time of the year prior to the referendum are eligible voters. So, technically, if we reschedule the vote more than one year from now, all those who left the province after the earthquake would be ineligible to vote. Allowing some time for the emigrants to sell their houses, and for us to be able to establish their termination of residency, it might be better to wait 18 months. Within that time frame, there would also be one income tax cycle for which one must declare residency. Announcing a special disaster recovery income surtax might even help a few undecideds to declare residency in Ontario before the end of the fiscal year."

Léandre was uncomfortable with such extreme tactics. Even though he harbored a grudge toward English Canadian politicians—particularly those throughout Canadian history who never blushed at asserting their perceived supremacy—he believed bully politics to be fraught with risk. Ugly politics could be effective to achieve immediate desired results, but would fail to fulfill his aspirations to leave a positive mark. The judgment of history is not kind to the self-righteous moralist agitator or to the executioner of sordid plans hatched through some contraption of twisted logic and hate.

In Léandre's assessment, one such shameful Canadian moment had occurred in Montréal itself in the mid-19th century, after an election that brought Reformers to power on the strength of French Canadian support and representatives, when the Anglophone Tories—staunch supporters of British supremacy, yet relegated to the opposition and unable to prevent passage of a bill to indemnify the largely French Canadians victims of the Rebellions of 1837—led an inflamed mob to burn down the Parliament building and attack the residences of several Reform leaders. Shortly thereafter, the seat of government was moved from Montréal to Toronto, on the excuse that the "Queen City" was less susceptible to "ethnic tensions."

However, that paled in comparison to the deeds of Governor Lawrence, the wretched Canadian historical figure Léandre most despised. All the essays, books, and dissertations in Léandre's collection concurred. In the mid-18th century, concerned over a possible rebellion, and dissatisfied of the reluctance by which the conquered French pledged an unconditional oath of allegiance to the British crown, Lawrence undertook to deport the French Acadian population. Tens of thousands of Acadians, having committed no crime, were dispossessed and scattered across more than a dozen English colonies along the eastern seaboard, deliberately separating husband, wife, and children by shipping them to different destinations. As a result of this callous, genocidal decision, and victims of abuse wherever they landed, many perished from hunger, disease and misery—when they didn't outright drown in ships that sank before reaching the foreign shores. For the few that remained or returned, the wounds never healed, transmitting the pain through generations.

Léandre, determined to win the referendum on the merit of ideas and ideals, would not support the discriminatory strategies of ethnic biases of his colleague. He refused to burden his descendants with a tarnished name. He aspired to build history on the pride of a nation's self-determination and inclusiveness. In his view, freedom was foremost a self-assuming choice, a rebirth of conscience of the self, an acknowledgment of one's value, happiness, love and responsibilities. A faith in the ability of each person to discover, love, assume, nurture, and guard his or her flame of life, to altruistically and compassionately spread that inner peace, free of calculations, expectations, deceptions, full of honesty, generosity, liberty, and purity. Freedom was choosing that course, in full recognition that entirely opposite choices were also possible. Freedom was thriving to create optimists instead of catering to the fears of pessimists. These ideals drove Léandre. Pragmatism and politics were the means to an end, like unavoidable interference in the signal of an immature technology called mankind.

Léandre cut short the discussion.

"Exodus is a moot point until we can get an assessment of the time it will take for the city to recover. What are the assessments of the *Organization de sécurité civile du Québec* in this regard?"

"We have not yet been able to establish contact with the Montréal headquarters," answered Florent.

"*Tabarnak!* What are these *ciboire de crisse* doing?"

Montréal, 5:30 a.m.

The challenging slalom course between crater-size pot-holes, also known as the venerable *Boulevard Métropolitain* expressway, could only be threaded in slow motion. No longer were the tired workers, the daredevils, the road-raged, the inebriated, and the heavy-footed drivers able to navigate the city at open throttle in the dead of night, punishing their cars' suspension with carefree disregard to the speed limit.

At first, the drive back towards downtown had been hassle-free—not surprising, given that the collapsed pipeline-bridge blocked highway 40 in Pointe-aux-Trembles, leaving the bare multi-lane ribbon of asphalt wide open to the few cars trickling from each access ramp along the way—and Lise covered most of her usual commute distance in record time. But traffic volume grew fast and driving conditions worsened as she approached the city center, degenerating into severe congestion. She had expected deserted roads all the way through, except for the odd emergency vehicle. Instead, moving at a snail's pace, a perplexing mass of "crazies" rushing to town in the wee hours of the morning for unknown reasons turned the last few miles of her commute into a nightmare.

The collapsed spans of otherwise insignificant bridges, by impeding the usual flow of taxpayers through their invaluable infrastructure, had spontaneously generated a rush hour at a time when Montréal usually still slept.

The crawling expressway traffic funneled as best it could through exits and scattered itself over whatever local streets seemed passable, oozing through those as an excruciatingly viscous flow of metal-wrapped humans—a flow unpredictably slowed and stopped by random debris blocking streets or accidents created by annoyed, impatient motorists seeking alternative routes to their destinations and fighting for every inch of roadway.

Oblivious to the turmoil, stuck in that gridlock, Lise Letarte's mind wandered. She pondered, wondered, and planned.

"A commanding and assertive stance will be in order; perception matters, reality is flexible, truth is relative, as always.

"Spending a few weeks in Myrtle Beach this summer might be preferable to the usual Hampton Beach vacation.

"There were emergency response plans for chemical spills, floods, ice storms, and even one for terrorist attacks, so there has to be one for earthquakes. Somewhere.

"Definitely a closed-coffin ceremony for whatever will be pulled out from the pile of debris. In any event, the demands of the job over the next few weeks will justify delegating the burden of arranging the funeral—maybe to one of his kids, or possibly even his ex-wife.

"The staff must locate the response plan, and outline the recipe to follow. That's what staff is all about.

"This may provide the perfect opportunity for getting a promotion, or at least a salary adjustment. Meeting the Premier would not hurt.

"An hour, door locked, to read the response plan and memorize the jargon, enough to reassure the authorities and keep them at bay for a while.

"Not having internet access for the next few days will make it impossible to check the on-line reviews for the newest convertible BMW model—the dealer will most certainly agree to extend the deadline for the quote.

"All response and recovery information shall be centralized and controlled by the *Organisation de sécurité civile du Québec* headquarters, and nothing shall be released without my explicit approval, to ensure smooth and coordinated operations.

"The ski trip scheduled for next weekend is shot, unless there is a way to exit the island."

Lise's mind, not accustomed to being interrupted by work-related matters, was working in overdrive to harmonize her key preoccupations with some level of civic duty. Her neurons and synapses, normally woven into a stable, intermingled network committed to the pursuit of selfish pleasures, were irritated and tortured by the omnipresent turmoil, in some way mimicking the distress of the transportation infrastructure.

Trial-and-error navigation through the urban obstacle course of debris and blocked passageways was laborious, but would be the only alternative for quite some time.

Vaudreuil-Dorion, 6:00 a.m.

James was curled behind Richard Turcotte, imperfectly shielded from the gale of freezing cold air, as the snowmobile zoomed across the frozen river towards Montréal. He was disappointed that the disc jockey wasn't wider bodied, wondering how lifting compact discs all day at a desk in front of a microphone as the sole occupational aerobic activity can burn calories, before remembering that bureaucrats like himself also come in all shapes and sizes.

He did not remember the equation to calculate the wind chill factor effect, but felt in his bones that any physical phenomena magnifying the torture already inflicted by still air at -40°F was positive evidence that there may be no God after all. It was usually when immersed in those moments of self-inflicted pain that he questioned whether the concepts of professionalism and sanity were mutually exclusive, and whether dedicating one's life to chasing butterflies in tropical climates would have been a more laudable goal than chasing earthquakes wherever and whenever they chose to occur.

Cold. A temperature uncomfortably low for humans. A relative concept. In Panama, cold is the iced piña colada one drinks sitting in front of the air conditioning unit. In southern Florida, cold is a day without swimsuits. In Washington, cold is when thin ice has formed on the pond. In Québec, cold is when the purest air penetrates multiple layers of clothes and kills—definitely uncomfortable.

Cold country. The insanity of building homes where winters are longer than summers. The foolhardy dream of building a country where crops rush from seed to harvest within a narrow window of warmth squeezed between walls of frost, vulnerable to the vagaries of climate, teetering at the edge of famine. The absurd legacy of a misguided navigator seeking gold in the new world and a northern passage to Asia, instead of Caribbean beaches or Polynesian archipelagoes, who failed to grasp the hostility of winters that repeatedly decimated three quarters of his crew. The persistence of imprisoned explorers, praying for spring to free the hull of their vessels clutched by an infinite river of ice. The fervor of militia and revolutionaries, adapted and bound by blood to their native snow-covered land, defending their enclave of dignity, fighting for freedom and ownership of a bequeathed winter, never tamed, with extreme cold that lashed.

Extreme cold that sucked the heat and life from exposed flesh. Extreme cold that iced the senses and seized the soul, as the assaulting pain eased into the numbness of the forever winter. Extreme cold that killed.

James found himself wishing to accelerate global warming, imagining some national policy encouraging all citizens to leave their cars revving at full throttle all night, a brick on the gas pedal, or better still a grand master plan to corral all Canadian engines in special plants designed for the specific purpose of pumping the maximum possible amount of greenhouse gases into the atmosphere, in a willingness to boil and drown half the world to restore some justice in sharing the warmth of the sun.

Yet, at the same time, James was grateful for the past few days of sudden polar climate that enabled an expedient crossing to the island, bypassing the logistic complexities of securing a vehicle after an airlift or after a speedboat ferry in milder temperatures. If anything, the winter had been uncharacteristically benign until then and, in hindsight, he wished there had been a longer freezing spell prior to the earthquake, just to reassure him. The disturbingly thin ice bridge was covered by cracks that James was sure could be seen and heard propagating if not for the high speed and deafening noise of the engine. It was clear to him, even if he was ignorant of the engineering equation to quantify the bearing capacity of an ice sheet, that they would have punched through to their death had they been a few pounds heavier—an occupational hazard he had never imagined before.

The snowmobile slowed to climb onshore, reducing the artificial wind speed and providing some temporary relief. Near still air at -40°F felt bearable, as they circuitously navigated between the built environment seeking to reconnect with Highway 40. They had agreed to drive nonstop along highways straight to the city core, unless overwhelming instances of major significant damage that warranted a pause for close scrutiny were encountered. Unseated tombstones and toppled chimneys were neither of engineering interest or newsworthy items considering the Klondike-like possibilities awaiting them downtown.

They rapidly reached the embankments of the highway, and rode down into the sunrise, passing the long string of westbound cars at cross-purposes unable to escape the island through the *Île aux Tourtes* bridge.

Ottawa, 6:30 a.m.

Communique from the Government of Canada.

At 12:57 a.m., Eastern Standard Time, a Magnitude 7 earthquake struck the Canadian Metropolis of Montreal. The shallow hypocenter of this earthquake was located 10 miles directly below the downtown area. Such earthquakes have been recognized as likely to occur at that location by Earthquakes Canada, and their probability of occurrence has been factored into the development of the Canadian seismic maps that are an integral part of the National Building Code of Canada, the Canadian Highway Bridge Design Code, and similar design standards pertaining to other kinds of structures. These maps and corresponding design requirements are used in conjunction with the special seismic provisions mandated for various construction materials (such as steel, reinforced concrete, and others) as specified in documents published by the Canadian Standards Association.

Modern buildings designed in compliance with these Canadian codes and standards benefit from the latest knowledge on how to design structures to survive earthquakes without endangering the lives of occupants. However, there exists many buildings that have been designed or constructed at a time when knowledge on how to achieve earthquake-resistance did not exist, and such buildings would not provide the same level of seismic performance and protection as modern Canadian constructions. The decision on whether or not to upgrade such existing seismically-deficient buildings prior to an earthquake, to enhance their safety levels to comply with the latest code and standards, is the prerogative of individual local jurisdictions or regulatory authorities. The same can be said for bridges and other structures.

Preliminary reports indicate that significant damage has been suffered in the regions in proximity to the earthquake's epicenter. The Government of Canada will undertake everything under its power to ascertain with more precision the extent of this damage. The Government Operations Centre (GOC) is already mobilized as the country's strategic-level operations centre to coordinate the activities under the jurisdiction of the federal departments and agencies during this national emergency, as well as to provide national communications and geomatics teams of specialists. Satellite-based photography will be provided by the Canadian

Aerospace Agency as a tool to help identify areas of significant damage.

In collaboration with the Royal Canadian Mounted Police, Defence Research and Development Canada, the Public Health Agency of Canada, and other agencies, the Canadian Emergency Management College has trained the country's finest first-responders and emergency response managers to be abreast of the state-of-practice and be well-versed in the state-of-the-art knowledge in this field, and these highly qualified professionals are in place in their provinces of origin to ensure the most efficient recovery activities. As requested, the Government of Canada has the ability to deploy complementary highly trained teams of experts to assist in various emergency response and recovery activities. The Government of Canada can also exercise international cooperative agreements to welcome special teams of experts in the search and extrication of victims from debris, if necessary.

The Government of Canada continues to monitor the situation, and will deploy, enact, or legislate the measures necessary to ensure prompt recovery of the affected population. The Disaster Financial Assistance Arrangements agreement already commits the Government of Canada to provide financial relief to its citizens to help them bear the cost of this disaster. Existing income tax legislation also forgives penalties and interest in fairness to victims of disasters.

The Government of Canada is prepared to take all measures to ensure that this tragic event will have no impact on our national economy, and stands ready to offer the population of Montreal and the Province of Quebec all the assistance it may request.

End of communique.

Montréal, 7:00 a.m.

After a bumpy ride on the embankments of highways 40, 13, and 20, dashing to reach the city core without detours into residential, commercial, or industrial neighborhoods, Richard had parked the snowmobile alongside one of the collapsed spans of the *Turcotte* interchange, next to a long, twisted steel bar protruding from the ripped side of the massive concrete structure. The bridge girders once perched atop the tall, slender concrete piers had been half-driven into the frozen ground upon impact. Originally conceived by Cartesian aesthetic canons as an elegant cluster of intersecting curves and sweeping spirals, like a three-dimensional calligraphic symbol for the gods of modernity, but definitely built lacking in resilience against both the pernicious wear of aging and the brutal demands of extreme events, the tarnished and ruptured segments of elevated roadway lied crisscrossing atop each other, limp, dug in snow like beached gray whales.

James was not surprised. Before the earthquake, the tangled mess of overpasses, connectors, and access ramps, woven over ground-level roads and railroads, exhibited the gangrenous scars of its neglect: cracks opened by expanding reinforcing bars bursting out of the concrete from the indignity of corroding salts; rust stains streaking down exposed surfaces, across the black patina etched by the perpetual blasts of diesel grit and soot; sagging spans injured at birth by the premature removal of formwork and creeping concrete mixes; honeycombs of macules and tumors delineated by networks of cracks penetrating a concrete attacked by the leprosy of alkali-aggregate reaction—a condition created by the inadvertent use of concrete aggregates having a propensity to adversely react with the concrete cement, slowly expanding over the years, distorting lines that were once straight and surfaces once flush.

In James' harsh judgment, in rancor to the ignominy of a monument to engineering ignorance, that interchange should have been torn down years ago and replaced by a proper landmark, instead of being patched and fixed piecemeal as if trying to cure cancer by enwrapping the sick organs in band-aids. The earthquake executed what nobody had the guts to do, amputating a lifeline to downtown Montréal from its disgraceful appendages, oblivious to the wrath of the city's motorists who would be caught in the morass of traffic jams for years to come. Like many other earthquakes across the world had before, it acted as an impressive and brutal agent of urban renewal, remodeling the city and its infrastructure by weeding out the inadequate and obsolete, without concerns about re-election, not bothered by planning to accommodate affected users and owners.

Richard saw the concentration of collapsed infrastructure as an awesome train wreck, a majestic expanse of destruction where each chunk of fallen concrete, each fracture in the fabric of the built infrastructure, each car perched at the edge of a precipice where once lied a ribbon of urban decay, was newsworthy. Although he shared a last name with the deceased interchange, a distant tie to a common ancestor of centuries past, Richard wasn't overburdened by grief or mourning—he was exalted to live the news. Tangible news. In the field.

He set-up the transmitter and provided a brief tutorial to James on how to address the general public: avoid technical terms, focus on general descriptions that someone at the level of a 6th grader could understand, and "Don't worry, I'll direct you by my questions to focus on the things that really matter."

Unnecessary familiar generalities, as James was experienced feeding the media the light science and engineering knowledge they had sought following past earthquakes, and bored by their shallow single-minded obsession to reduce all world events through the lens of national or regional significance. The sensationalism of a disaster that indiscriminately kills hundreds of thousands in one swoop; the fascination with images of widespread destruction; the complacent uplifting stories of Canadian cargo planes bursting with generously donated goods often unrelated to actual needs; the brief episodes of self-assessment through the journalistic hunt (under the guise of scientific investigation) for experts who could point to shortcomings or violations of local standards, lax code enforcement, failures in engineering judgment, and poor leadership that could lead to similar disasters at home, to assuage the population's self-righteous hunger for scandals and fickle interest in accountability; the overwhelming resources needed to probe in-depth beyond superficial claims; the rapid disinterest; the inescapable and erroneous implied conclusion that such disasters are unlikely to occur at home; and the return to the usual fare of politicking, sports, infotainment and other distractions. A cycle most familiar to James.

"You are listening to Dick Nightrock on CHOK-AM choc-radio, providing you with direct coverage, *live*, on-site, near downtown Montréal where it all happened this morning."

In his earbud, Richard heard an exalted Jim Sunshine confirm that the feed was loud and clear, successfully broadcasted to the world, and captured on tape for the nation's posterity.

"It is 7:00 a.m., and close to -40°F and I am at the *Turcotte* interchange with Dr. James Laroque of the National Research Council of Canada, an earthquake engineering expert who has visited many cities worldwide destroyed by earthquakes in the past, and who is exclusively attached to CHOK-AM this morning to describe for us the terrible destruction wrought by our own Montréal earthquake.

"Dr. Laroque, we are looking here at what remains of the *Turcotte* interchange, a vital link of the Montréal infrastructure, a series of bridges that all our citizens have crossed at one point or another, and that our incompetent politicians have consistently refused to replace for years. Many of us in the past have worried that these bridges were slowly falling apart and dangerous. Well we don't need to worry about that anymore; they're completely gone now and it happened very fast. Dr. Laroque, tell us, why did these spans collapse?"

James knew how to remain professional and not fall into such a trap, but this initial outburst revealed that among all the sensation-seeking journalists he had met before, Richard was in a class of his own, with blunt delivery and a politically charged agenda. This relationship would be like dancing with a bear in a minefield.

"Well, Mr. Nightrock, it is not possible to provide great certainty in any forensic analysis that is based only on visual observations. To provide a reliable scenario of why a particular structure has collapsed, an engineer needs to collect the structural drawings and soil borings data, look for compliance or non-compliance with the existing codes and other documents that embody the latest knowledge, develop simple models as well as complex computer-based analytical models, and simulate how the structure responded in a dynamic manner to the earthquake. All of this to be able to identify the points of excessive demands or structural weaknesses and to understand how the collapse mechanism progressively developed."

James knew Richard would not like the answer, but undertook to elevate the discussion to the highest possible level to appropriately counter the outrageous opening statements. As in any haggling ritual, the second party to disclose its hand has the luxury of setting the target middle ground and to disproportionately position its first offering such as to optimize the chances of converging to that desirable target, the number of iterations needed to reach it being only a function of the aggressiveness and patience of the sparring parties. Hence, to Richard's low first blow and apparent axe to grind, James countered with a strictly highbrow stance to ensure an acceptable symmetry on the political spectrum.

Richard also knew how to play the game.

"Surely Dr. Laroque, with your extensive experience in this field, you must have some preliminary opinions. Bridge spans that collapse must certainly have been observed in past earthquakes, and the reasons behind such common failures must be known with some degree of certainty by the expert community."

James elected to respond with generalities, throwing bits of insight on the known seismic behavior of bridges as bait to cautiously steer the interview towards a neutral territory, directing the path of inquiry by planting small chunks of technical meat along a suggested intellectual trail.

"Indeed, Mr. Nightrock, it is possible to speculate, but one must be very careful not to confuse speculation with reality. Bridge spans may collapse for a number of reasons, and a common one is lack of adequate bearing support. It is well known that many bridges are constructed with expansion joints, to allow the free elongation and contraction of spans that occurs when temperature increases or decreases. In fact, I believe that during the past century, a span of the Trois-Rivières Bridge over the St-Lawrence River did collapse as a result of such thermal effects. The common practice in bridge engineering has been to fix one end of a simply supported span, and allow the other end to slide longitudinally, in a guided way. During earthquakes, as the whole structure vibrates, it is sometimes possible for the sliding span to actually displace beyond the length of its support and therefore drop off its piers. In fact, to prevent such occurrences, bridge design codes typically specify the minimum support length required at these bearing locations."

James needed no further evidence than the leaning piers and scrape marks left on them by the fallen spans to be near certain that it was the phenomenon he had just generically described that had led to the collapses in the case at hand, but judged that some reservations were appropriate given his interviewer's propensity for political belligerence. Barely concealing his intentions, Richard attacked:

"Dr. Laroque! This seems to me to be a very diplomatic way to confirm what we suspected all along: our government does not have a clue on how to design bridges to survive earthquakes. The pride of our Ministry of Transportation, and some of its largest modern engineering accomplishments—the spans of our urban infrastructure, no less—are now roads to nowhere, reduced to a heap of crushed concrete and twisted reinforcing bars."

"Allow me to provide some nuances, Mr. Nightrock. It is fair to assume that seismic design requirements had not been enacted in any North American bridge codes at the time this interchange was constructed. Much has been learned on how to design bridges to resist earthquakes since the 1970s, but it is a long and laborious process to conduct research and translate the resulting findings into design concepts and recommendations that can be adopted into legal documents. In fact, the first prescribed seismic design specifications appeared in the 1980s editions of Canadian bridge codes, but, as enlightened by continued further research over time, some would even argue that the first truly effective seismic design and detailing requirements have only appeared in Canadian bridge codes in the late 1990s."

Nightrock, taken aback for a moment, frustrated in his initial efforts to find unambiguous fault in the system, reloaded his venom reservoir, and charged again.

"This is disgraceful! We have a government that knew fully well that its bridges were wholly inadequate to resist earthquakes, and it never bothered to fix them! Our leaders never bothered to tell us, the public, the taxpayers they bleed to sustain their fat salaries, that we have been driving on bridges precariously hanging at the edge of incipient collapse, awaiting for the first small vibration to brutally drop and possibly kill. Why this cavalier attitude and blatant disregard for public safety from our elected officials? Why have these constructions fit for Third-World countries not been fixed? Why have these time bombs not been replaced by structures that meet the latest design codes?"

Unaware of Richard's inexperience, James was stunned by this vicious mood swing. The traditional, respectful haggling ritual was derailed, replaced by an unpredictable and unprofessional process. James's first reaction to Nightrock's excited rants was to terminate the interview—he was familiar with the debate tactics of skillful journalists (even the unethical ones) and could navigate the flow of their questioning by carefully crafting the kind of informative yet noncommittal answers that kept lawyers at bay, but he wasn't sure how to dodge the machine-gun fire of an enraged lunatic.

At the same time, he felt challenged, intrigued by the opportunity to reach beyond the sparse audience of popular science programs, and enthused about being freed from the masters of sound-bites that excel at truncating hour-long interviews into 10 controversial seconds of out-of-context citations. Emerging from this brief pause, James jumped on the opportunity to educate, and possibly embarrass the agitator in the process.

"Considering that approximately 99% of the existing infrastructure has been designed either prior to the existence of codes, or at a time when codes did not have seismic design requirements judged adequate by today's standards, replacing this entire inventory of structures or retrofitting it to achieve compliance with the latest code requirements would be prohibitively expensive, and in fact, might be fiscally irresponsible and impossible. At best, at the cost of substantial tax dollars, a program to upgrade the key public infrastructures could be initiated, and implemented over the best part of a decade, and investments in that economic activity would be typically done at the expense of other programs that would have to be sacrificed, or special taxes would have to be levied."

Another few seconds of mutual silence. A twinkle in Richard's eye. The delight of a good argument, the pleasure of confrontation, the enjoyment of exchanges with a partner capable of repartee.

"You are so right, Dr. Laroque. Our elected officials and top bureaucrats would have to sacrifice their special interest trips to the Carribean, their chauffeured limousines, their plush offices overstaffed with secretaries who spend the day knitting, their 30-hour work weeks and 6-week vacations, and early retirements at 50 with deluxe compensation packages. We wouldn't want to deprive any of them of the meager benefits of civil servility just to keep a few concrete chunks hanging on to their piers during an earthquake."

James tired of the sterile debate. Having completed his public service duties for the time being, he walked away from the demagogue who was entangled in his own rhetoric. From his bag on the snowmobile, he collected his equipment for a few measurements and photos of the damage in the light of sunrise, devoting precious time to his professional endeavors. As impressive as they might have appeared to the novice, these collapses were far from surprising, for all the reasons he'd outlined in response to Richard's questions. James already had, in his collection from prior earthquakes, hundreds of photos of similarly collapsed spans. Nonetheless, all the evidence in plain sight had to be rigorously documented.

Québec City, 7:15 a.m.

Communique from the Government of Québec.

At approximately 1 a.m. today, for the first time in recorded history, a severe and damaging Magnitude 7 earthquake has struck the economic heart of our nation. All transportation routes to the island of Montréal are cut due to infrastructure failures. Telecommunications services are down in the center core of the island. Reliable damage reconnaissance has not been conducted yet, and no official report of financial losses is available at this time. Estimates of losses substantiated by credible projections from actual data will be released as soon as available.

Without speculating on the outcome of this particular event, it is recognized that past earthquakes of this magnitude have inevitably resulted in hardships to the impacted populations, and that recovery depends on community resilience and extent of infrastructure damage.

Within hours of the earthquake, Premier Laliberté, together with the Minister of Transportation Chaput-Vigneault, toured the damaged areas from the air, to get a first-hand appraisal of the situation. As a result of this preliminary assessment, Premier Laliberté has committed to deploy all the government's available resources to assist the population through these infelicitous circumstances, to provide all Québec citizens with the utmost personal care they deserve, and to ensure the fastest recovery with minimal impact on the nation's economic activities. To protect the freedom and richness brought upon our collective conscience by the unique beauty of each life, the government will undertake all in its power to aid those weakened and assailed by the hardships resulting from this earthquake.

Emergency response activities are already underway, under the stewardship of the *Organisation de sécurité civile du Québec* tasked to coordinate the efforts of all government agencies during the response and recovery period, and who will issue updates on activities underway as well as specific notices detailing specific actions and services to the population in need.

Premier Léandre Laliberté will hold a press conference today at 10 a.m. at the St-Hubert airport in Longueuil to inform the nation of the situation.

End of communique.

The public announcement purposely avoided labeling the event a disaster, far less a catastrophe, nor did it acknowledge possible casualties, but the media would generously pepper those words all over the news as often as needed for weeks to come, avoiding the propagandist traps of the party in power, but also as indiscriminate peddlers of information obsessed with captivating the public's attention.

Montréal, 7:45 a.m.

Lise Letarte slammed the doors of the file cabinets that lined the walls of her office. Her chronic impatience had been worn thin by the successive annoyances that challenged her determination to report to work, particularly through the last leg of her journey which started at the foot of the high-rise where the interminable obstacle course veered from horizontal to vertical.

She had arrived at that bifurcation point half an hour earlier, stressed by the ordeal of having driven the last few horrendous miles of her commute along a messy, tortuous path on roads that would otherwise have been straight if not for the endless debris and groups of frost-bitten citizens that either wandered around in disbelief like zombies, ran around hysterically without obvious purpose, or endeavored to move rubble along human chains in futile attempts to rescue victims trapped in collapsed buildings—a crowd that in her opinion would have been better advised to seek shelter from the cold, but that fortunately dwindled to nothing as she entered the business district.

Upon arriving to the building that housed the headquarters of the *Organisation de sécurité civile du Québec,* still at ground level, it didn't impress her that it seemed to have weathered the earthquake without visible distress—it had never crossed her mind that it wouldn't, and she was too impassive to be moved by such a discovery. However, her apathy vanished at the first obstacle; she exploded when the door to the underground parking garage steadfastly refused to open, ignoring the repeated violent swiping of her access card. The green and red bulbs on the card-reader remained dark, acknowledging neither rejection nor acceptance. Their refusal to light up hinted that the building's emergency power back-up had failed, for unknown reasons. Lise, ungrateful that the building had neither collapsed nor been severely damaged and rendered unserviceable, was fuming at being snubbed by technological junk.

Entirely focused on this minor frustration, she was unaware of her overall good fortune. A few weeks after she had assumed directorship of the agency, she embarked on a personal crusade to fight a cost-cutting plan by the Minister of *Sécurité Publique* to move the *Organisation's* head office from its executive floor in the newest and most prestigious high-rise in town, to an inconspicuous unreinforced masonry building. Unknown to her, as a result of the earthquake, the guts of that unreinforced masonry building were entirely exposed to the elements, wood floors precariously sagging between wood-framed partitions, and bricks spread across the street by the shattering of the toppled exterior walls. Yet the possibility of earthquake damage to what could have become the new headquarters was never a factor in her fight to block the relocation initiative. It had all been about prestige, stature, a corner office with a gorgeous view, and, now, luck. If not for that decision to thwart the planned move, driven by despotic aspirations, instead of cussing at a digital reader, she would have been contemplating piles of bricks where there used to be a front door.

Surrendering to the stubbornness of innate electronics, she abandoned her car in the no-parking zone of a deserted side-street, confident of her authority and determined that any fine and fees would be the responsibility of her employer—failing to recognize that parking restrictions would not be enforced given the circumstances. She then tried to enter the building through a number of controlled-access points, but, in spite of her vigorous and determined card-swiping attempts, all back, side, and front doors, denied her rights—treating her like an evicted tenant. By design, all electronic access mechanisms for this secured facility defaulted into locked position during power failures. There was a regular passageway to this otherwise keyless castle, an override to the system, but she had forgotten about its existence as soon as she had dropped its key in the kitchen drawer dedicated to collect all the useless, unlabeled items she was compelled to keep but didn't care about.

Given that the dumb, discourteous electronic system unbreakable from the outside had been deployed on all entryways, she resolved that, as director of the *Organisation*, she was empowered to smash one of the large glass panes of the lobby. Her immediate access was imperative, and her resoluteness absolute, but her ability to break tempered glass was deficient. The glass resisted all impacts from her shoes, purse, and briefcase, as well as small rocks found on the ground. The search for heavier projectiles led her to retrieve the crowbar from her trunk.

As she was about to test the effectiveness of this last tool, the building superintendent appeared in the glow of emergency lighting, gratified to have discovered the source of this insistent banging. Having duly assessed Lise's credentials by inspecting the photo-ID she assertively pressed on the glass door, he let her into the complex through a low-tech side door that could be mechanically unlocked from the inside.

He did not escort Lise to her office, as his immediate priority was to fix the power generator damaged by a toppled, unsecured heavy shelving. And the elevator was obviously out-of-service.

The prestigious executive office, 45 floors up, lost some of its glamor during the long, strenuous climb through the poorly lit staircase. Each step, each landing weighed like an insult to her status, the physical expression of her anger solely kept in check by the fatigue of hauling her heavy frame up hundreds of steps and dozens of landings, while her blood boiled. Fueled by the raw energy of rage, feeling at war with the universe, she reached the glass door of her palatial office only to be met by an electronic lock.

In a climax of fury, she hurled her 250 pounds through, smashing the door to the *Bureau Chef de l'Organisation de sécurité civile du Québec*, in a powerful release of her accumulated frustration.

Sprawling on the floor among the pebbles of shattered tempered glass, exhausted, she mentally searched the office, trying to guess where her staff could have strategically stowed the flash light mandatory to any self-respecting emergency preparedness office. Clueless, she instead resolved that pulling the blinds and waiting for dawn might be the simpler solution. As she completed that thought, the fluorescent lights came to life and a subdued bell noise from the hallway announced the opening of an elevator door. Had anybody been in that elevator, they would have been greeted by a howl of obscenities directed at those cynical gods who enjoy creating chaos as the purest form of sarcastic expression.

Following this thunder of cursing, physically and mentally exhausted, still lying on the floor, Lise attempted to collect her energy and gather her thoughts, slowly drowsing into an uncharacteristic calmness, when the fear of being discovered sleeping on the floor of the agency most urgently needed in this national emergency sparked her to "resurrect." The dread of such a photograph on the front cover of all newspapers and magazines—fancy the headlines—rekindled her resolve.

She pulled herself up and started to shuffle across the office, taking a moment to assess the situation. Through the blinds, the city remained in complete darkness, the nearest visible lights being on the south shore.

No doubt, there was an emergency, and, no doubt, there was an emergency response plan for that type of emergency. There had to be one, as it was the sole purpose of the existence of this office. It was just a matter of finding it, an operation that started rather calmly, but became more vigorous as the intensifying search failed to yield results, up to the point where Lise Letarte was slamming the doors of the file cabinets that lined the walls of her office.

The worn labels on those easy-to-find thick manilla folders that addressed ice storms, floods, terrorist attacks, and chemical spills, attested to the extensive developments, consultations, and revisions bestowed on plans for emergency response to future disasters that would be identical to those of the recent past. Conspicuously missing was the folder labeled "Earthquakes."

Then, amidst a classification system that defied logic, rearranged to suit the fancy of successive directors, and possibly compounded by the random shuffling of disinterested movers packing and unpacking boxes as fast as possible, the miracle discovery occurred. The thin earthquake response plan folder, free of wrinkles and with its pristine label, was found hidden at the back of a file cabinet drawer, curled and buried—presumably pushed down below eye level when adjacent fat folders had been force-fitted into the drawer.

Relieved, Lise retreated to her office with the precious document and sat in her plush executive chair to peruse this earthquake emergency response plan. Her first reaction upon opening the folder, before even going beyond the lead page, was one of great disappointment when reading that the plan had been authored by the former director of the agency. That man had publicly expressed his bitterness to have been replaced by a political appointee, told all that he was pleased to abandon the province to its "incompetent cronies," and moved to Deerfield Beach, Florida, under an unlisted number. Lise knew full well that even a "hailstorm of cow dung" splattering over the Province would not prompt this 50-year-old retiree to call his successor. Nothing would make him cancel his morning walk on the beach, or whatever other enjoyable pleasures of a life of leisure made possible by courtesy of an obscenely generous pre-retirement package, offered by the government in its zeal to get rid of "dead-wood" bureaucrats and reduce its deficit during the previous fiscal crisis. All the wisdom or advice she would ever get from him presumably had to be in this folder.

The executive summary of the document explained that the *Organization's* earthquake emergency response plan was modeled on one developed by a Long Island power company, for the purpose of public hearings, to demonstrate its ability to deploy an effective response in the case of an incident at the nuclear power plant it intended to construct. Lise recognized the long-held tradition of acknowledging an American document as the reference template upon which is molded a Canadian/Québécois document, as a sure way to give the latter a greater aura of credibility and fend off potential criticisms—a particularly useful strategy when the expertise of a panel, and its ability to develop a document from scratch, is debatable. The executive summary clarified that the Long Island plan was duly adapted to account for the differences between a nuclear incident and an earthquake disaster, and to recognize special conditions attributable to the distinctness of the Québec society—a vague and undefined term, but yet an essential and politically correct part of any statement needed to ensure endorsement of such a national plan.

A copy of the Long Island document had been acquired by her predecessor by serendipity during a conference of emergency responders in New York City, and in light of its convenient availability, it was deemed adequate by the *Organisation de sécurité civile du Québec* to serve as a basis to develop its earthquake response plan policy—in lieu of a master document developed from scratch and tailored specifically to address earthquake response. The elegant simplicity of the plan had impressed him most. For example, following the declaration of a nuclear incident, the Long Island plan heavily relied on school bus drivers to immediately pick up children from schools within a certain radius of the power plant, and drive them to pre-designated safe havens; a bastardized variation on this concept was thus embedded in the *Organisation's* plan. The absurdity of mashing a response plan to evacuate the population from a region with sound infrastructure but air fouled by a radiological incident, into a plan to evacuate a region with pure air but failed infrastructure, just got lost in the translation.

He had also filtered out from the master document, by necessity, the need to conduct regular drills to assess the effectiveness of the plan, because his agency's operating budget barely allowed for the conducting of such rehearsals for small-scale emergencies—simulations at the scale needed for earthquake disasters were deemed fiscally impossible. He justified his decision on the basis that the Long Island plan thoroughly documented that all drills conducted to show the effectiveness of the plan worked smoothly. Undocumented were the serious doubts expressed throughout the hearings as to whether the bus drivers paid to participate in the drills would as eagerly dash into the radioactively contaminated zone during a real emergency, or would even bother to show up at all.

Another key part of the plan, partly reflecting the military training of its author, contained a detailed operational chain of command and a list delegating responsibilities for a complex telephone chain, identifying who would phone each of the key players in the hierarchy of emergency responders. Upon close scrutiny of names on that list, Lise recognized at least a dozen individuals who had also benefitted from various early-retirement packages and who probably too lived as snow-birds where neither snow nor earthquakes were considerations. Not that it really mattered anyhow, since there was no way to make any phone calls out of Montréal until service was restored.

After a few chapters, Lise stopped reading. She found the plan of limited practical use, being lean in specifics and peppered with convoluted and vague statements concocted by the masterminds of civil service, such as, "Based on early information collected by assessment of on-site conditions throughout the affected area, response resources should be deployed to areas based on relative risk of increased casualties and severe injuries, unless other priorities require dispatch to other more critical and strategic targets."

She concluded that, even if she memorized the entire plan, it would be of no benefit for the current crisis.

She pulled out a yellow pad, a pencil, and stared at it, trying to figure out what to do next. The absolute silence in the room echoed that in her mind, as if there was no script, no template, no model to follow. Where common-sense data was in fact plentiful, nothing came to mind, as if a database laid dormant engraved on a hard-disk, waiting for its magnetic platters frozen by rust to start spinning again. Ideas just refused to get in gear.

And she wondered, "Where the hell is my staff when I need it?"

Montréal, 8:00 a.m.

They had agreed to avoid residential neighborhoods. James didn't want to interfere with people trying to put their lives back together—or be pestered by homeowners eager for free professional advice on the safety of their damaged dwelling. Richard didn't want to be seen profiting from people's misery—or be diverted from his higher-purpose agenda by inescapable human-interest stories instead of real news. Assuming that nobody would rush to the office in the aftermath of a disaster, grieving for the loss of a cubicle, it was judged safe to focus on industrial and business districts.

This strategy worked as the streets along their itinerary were devoid of people, except for a few souls who appeared to linger next to specific collapsed buildings, either searching for personal belongings or devoted to not abandoning trapped loved ones who had hopefully survived, not yet frozen to death. James had witnessed similar behavior in prior earthquakes, but was shocked that, in this instance, most of the persons they passed by were alone. No altruistic strangers had converged to offer them unsolicited assistance. He guessed that maybe it was easier to play hero in the California sunshine, where there is nothing else to do while awaiting help, than in a Siberian winter when there is an overwhelming need to find shelter from cold air that drills to the bone.

Richard stopped the snowmobile next to piles of bricks. Buildings had shed their masonry facades over the entire length of their top story, revealing their inside partitions and divisions, much like a full-scale version of the archetypical dollhouse. Exposed pipes froze and burst, nourishing long streaking icicles that glazed the remaining walls below and stretched to the ground—pilasters of ice creating the illusion of arctic Greek temples.

Outward failure of unreinforced brick masonry walls at the top stories of buildings were quite common for that type of construction, although their Nordic expression in sub-zero temperatures provided for some visually striking variations on a known theme. James snapped a few photographs for the sake of documenting this unusually artistic expression of what he considered to be an otherwise rather mundane failure, but beyond the few minutes this required, he was driven to push the expedition further, eager to collect the bounty of truly significant data sure to await discovery elsewhere. Yet, by the time he finished shooting his photos from various angles, apertures, and zoom distances, Richard had already set the satellite dish and was ready for another CHOK-AM report, "live from the disaster zone."

James was determined to avoid further exchanges devoid of technical merit, and warned Richard that this partnership was conditional on keeping the focus of the interviews on descriptive matters, without frenzied debates on who was to blame for the damage that had happened. This seemed like a viable proposition, and Richard somewhat reluctantly promised to stick to technical matters, however unsure whether he could honor such a commitment, being such a consummate, passionate shock-radio professional. After the usual station identification, introductory hype, and a vivid description of the damage, Richard lunged into another questioning session.

"Dr. Laroque, in your assessment, could pedestrians be killed by falling bricks or other types of falling debris?"

Another trap. Nightrock was determined to follow the proven journalistic tricks of the trade to capture the broadest possible audience, focusing on blood for the time being. James wondered if Nightrock would soon find a way to interject sex scandals and sports events into the interview, to further spruce up the ratings. There was no escaping the truth on this one, but opportunities existed to spin it into an educational piece.

"Indeed, Mr. Nightrock, falling debris of that size can be life-threatening. This is why one is best served to remain inside a building during an earthquake. In fact, because the risk of being injured by falling objects is also significant indoors, as one can easily visualize toppling bookcases and other bibelots becoming dangerous projectiles during an earthquake, it is highly recommended to duck under a table throughout the severe shaking, as a simple protective measure. It is only safe to proceed outdoors once the earthquake is over."

"Or the outdoors will come to you if your building decides to shed its skin, as the tenants of this particularly building painfully discovered," added Richard, in a lame attempt to be funny.

In the absence of a laugh track, and facing a stoic James, Richard remembered the forlorn look of those deluded individuals waiting in front of collapsed buildings for rescuers that would come too late. He shelved the tasteless humor attempts and pursued with a tenuously related thought.

"Would you recommend that people gather in churches seeking divine protection while waiting for this turmoil to abate?"

A most surprising comment considering the mostly atheistic Québécois society. This was certainly not a technical issue, and Richard was moving further astray from his promises, but another infomercial was in order here.

"Mr. Nightrock. That would be a most terrible mistake. Although all churches are stylistically different, most old churches are built of the same unreinforced masonry construction as the building in front of us, even though stone masonry may have been used instead of brick masonry. This type of construction is known to be the most vulnerable to earthquakes, and aftershocks could conceivably trigger the collapse of a structure previously weakened by the main shock."

Lecturing like a professor—his missed vocation—he continued.

"Furthermore, earthquakes are not acts of God to punish sinners, but rather 'equal opportunity' killers. In fact, this was convincingly proven during the 1755 Lisbon earthquake, which struck on All Saints' Day, when 250,000 faithful were in church in a city known in Europe to be a bastion of Catholic piety at the time. A first shock terrified the worshipers who rapidly exited all the churches and congregated outside into the narrow public squares to pray for almighty protection. Disregarding their pious callings, a second more powerful earthquake followed minutes later, during which the masonry facades of every church and building overturned and collapsed toward the squares, turning the cobblestone plazas into graveyards for all the devotees who had assembled there. The earthquake also knocked off candles from church altars, igniting a conflagration that lasted days. The final tally was 60,000 dead Christians.

"More significantly, the quake also killed the prevailing philosophy at the time that all laws of the universe were divinely ordered, as the Lisbon earthquake swept humanity away indiscriminately."

Richard, overwhelmed by this impromptu lecture, returned to familiar territory.

"So what is your estimate of casualties and deaths resulting from this earthquake, Dr. Laroque?"

"It would be extremely hazardous to risk an estimate at this time."

"Would a thousand deaths be possible?"

"No number is impossible. It depends on a number of factors, but earthquakes that occur at night have typically resulted in fewer deaths for obvious reasons: fewer cars on the roads, no kids in schools, no workers in the offices—all potential casualties when infrastructure fails during daytime."

"One tenth of a percent of Montréal's population would correspond to 3,000 people. Would 3,000 deaths be realistic?"

James felt all his attempts to steer the conversation back towards technical issues—even if only superficially—were futile, as Richard was not listening to his answers and not responding to his cues. So he walked away, leaving Richard enthralled in his leitmotif.

"Our leaders, by their sheer incompetence, could be accountable for the death of 3,000 law-abiding citizens, regular taxpayers, honest individuals who have made the mistake of entrusting their lives to the hands of shylocks and liars more interested in padding their cushioned bank accounts with fat compensation packages and obscene retirement benefits than in the welfare and safety of their constituency. Where are the responsible officials when hardworking common men are being chased by pianos in their living rooms, crushed against walls, and buried under debris?"

The technical content and educational value of the remaining broadcast vanished, another casualty of this disaster.

Montréal, 8:15 a.m.

Jean-Pierre and Audréanne felt like they had spent most of the past seven hours walking, waiting, and freezing, all while failing to fulfill their destiny—a destiny thrown upon them with the insidiousness of a spell, a curse under the guise of a blessing, but a destiny nonetheless, etched in their minds when a shaking bed had thrown them on the floor.

This intensity of their conviction was only matched by that of the peculiar and vivid call to duty at the root of the day: a frightening, jerky freefall, the deafening thunder of tons of crashing materials, a brutal, uneven landing leaving the floor settling at a substantial angle from horizontal, and an energetic bounce from the mattress onto the floor. The theatrical effects of a descent to hell in an out-of-control mechanical ride, with the power to crush.

Dazed by the rapid passage from serene dreams to a nightmarish reality, Jean-Pierre had first thought that the building had been bombed by a terrorist, and that they were going to die in its collapse—civilian martyrs of the modern crusades, collateral damage in a holy war. No terrorists in their right mind would waste precious explosives on a lowly student dorm when so many other high-impact prestigious or symbolic targets abound, but Jean-Pierre unabashedly fantasized that students in medicine should be considered as prime targets by fanatic Muslim fundamentalists in their attempt to destabilize western societies, a fear fueled by his inflated view of the value of medical doctors to society. In that perspective, while he was sorry that being alive impugned this egotistical belief, he nonetheless was pleased to have escaped death, especially if it had come as the only relief from excruciatingly painful debilitating injuries and the random tinkering of dispassionate doctors driven by imperfect science and financial rewards.

More pragmatic, Audréanne had first thought that a runaway truck had impacted the building at full speed, hence the large demolition noise and vibrations. But, after being thrown across the room by the raging bed, spread out on the leaning floor as a rag doll, left wondering whether this was all a dream or reality, and whether the never-ending residual vibrations she felt were physiological or really the building still vibrating from its violent outburst of fury, she had guessed that this was possibly the result of an earthquake. She had taken a freshman geology class as a technical elective, and had been stunned to learn that Québec was a seismically active region. At the time, only valuing cause-effect science that can lead to immediate observable outcomes, and because she had never felt an earthquake before, she was incredulous of theories which she attributed—for lack of better knowledge—to the wild imagination of unemployable scientists seeking attention. She never expected such a baptism by fire.

In the first peaceful moments following the wreckage, grateful to have suffered no worse than a few bruises, they had initially assessed that the best course of action was to stay put, in total darkness, taking refuge in their leaning yet apparently stable apartment until outside assistance materialized, like patients in a waiting room. However, without electricity, light or heat, as the air was becoming quite cold due to broken windows in other apartments, it dawned on them that, contrary to a limb, a stabilized building would not proceed to heal itself. Just like those poor souls in pain awaiting help that seemingly never arrives, piled up in the same cold room irrespective of the severity of their ailment, ignored by an indifferent triage nurse immersed in a crossword puzzle, Jean-Pierre and Audréanne's hope for prompt assistance was a desperate, futile one.

In the stillness of time, during their anxious wait for miracles, they slowly realized that if an earthquake really was at the root of this mayhem, then thousands of partially collapsed buildings filled with thousands of partially crushed occupants would compete for the attention and limited resources of emergency responders. This cold and leaning apartment would likely remain cold and leaning for months. Recognizing that they were responsible for their own survival, they resolved that exiting the building was the sensible option.

Navigating in darkness amidst the cluttered, spilled content of familiar rooms, as spelunkers grabbing solid edges to guide their venture, they had grabbed whatever familiar clothes they found, hoping for some color coordination. Beyond underwear and comfortable sportswear, the objective was to dress as warmly as possible. Ideally, the anticipation of a range of possible weather conditions would have dictated the strategic selection of shirts and pants that could be added or peeled off in layers as harsher or milder climate was to be encountered, but dressing up like a giant onion would have been impractical given the circumstances—carrying unnecessary layers would have been cumbersome as Jean-Pierre and Audréanne did not own a car, and finding clothes that could be overlaid comfortably to implement such a scheme was difficult in the dark. Instead, by blind touch in a random search through drawers and closets, they identified—to their relief—their warmest wool sweaters, winter coats, gloves, scarves and boots. Ready to confront the cold, they had also instinctively grabbed leather briefcases containing their tools of the trade, indispensable clothing of the medical intern.

The usually straightforward emergency route down to exit the building had become a somewhat circuitous, but still manageable, obstacle course bathed in the glow of a few functional battery-powered emergency lights. The door of their dorm room, jammed and broken off its hinges when the entire story shifted askew by a few inches, had also been bent outward enough to allow them to crawl through the small resulting opening.

They found themselves alone in the hallway, theirs being the only faint amber shadows stretched by the emergency lights. Amidst the muffled shouts that came from every direction, echoes emanating from the staircases confirmed that others were also attempting to escape the leaning building. The door of the emergency exit at the end of the corridor had remained serviceable as its more robust steel frame had stayed square, the surrounding weaker partition walls instead having crushed on it as the story distorted.

Echoing voices could still be heard, but, disappointingly, there was no one in sight in the staircase. Whether the other "escapees" were far ahead or behind them didn't matter. There was no stopping on their path in search of freedom.

The stairs were free of debris from the third to the second floor, but inexplicably stopped in a pile of debris at the second landing. Not stopping to seek a logical explanation for this discontinuity, Jean-Pierre and Audréanne had straddled the chunks of concrete and masonry blocks to exit on the second floor, determined to find another stair shaft free of such obstructions, but while proceeding down along the corridor, they noticed through a broken window adjacent to the staircase that the second floor was now at ground level. They escaped through that window.

Time had stopped at that moment. All the theoretical classes, all the rote learning from textbooks, all the rational metabolism structures and lymphatic systems, all abstractions from a dry curricula, ceased to exist, swept aside by the raw power of colliding emotions unleashed by an explosive cocktail of raw hormones. They felt exhilarated as kids who found a labyrinth's exit, freed from the oppressing fear of being trapped, but at the same time distressed by the loss of a comfortable and predictable life, perturbed by the pressures of immediate survival, stressed by the anxiety of an uncertain future. And horrified, standing in front of a dorm building clearly amputated of its first floor, in the brutal cold of the night, realizing that students living on the first floor experienced the earthquake in a dramatic way, possibly waking up just in time to see their ceiling crashing down. For those few who may have survived the crushing, the obvious prognosis was death, perishing from hypothermia while waiting for rescuers.

They were part of a small group of students transfixed by the sight and sounds: the screams of agony and calls of distress from the cavernous concrete maze; the flashlight beams randomly sweeping rooms; the eerie alarms and sirens wailing in the night; the pervasive surrounding darkness atop a layer of snow reflecting the moonlight. And the smell of death.

Speechless and shivering, it was then that they had started to grasp the potential magnitude of the disaster, that they had recognized the small wreck of a building to be merely the tip of the iceberg, that they had found themselves surrounded by wounded giants of steel and concrete, by shelters that failed to shelter their occupants. Only then, they understood the enormity of the situation. They felt all the broken bones and mangled flesh, all the hypovolemic shocks and cardiac arrests, all the punctured lungs and impaled bodies, awaiting the soothing balm of anesthesia, the expert compassionate hands that can heal, the benevolence of modern medicine. Imbued by the virtues of their higher calling, pride pulsing though their veins; empowered by the stature of their profession, they were compelled to help, to find a hospital where their supreme knowledge would save lives. Roaming the wreckage to comfort those trapped or mutilated and waiting to run out of blood, or to provide first aid to those bruised or battered, would have been an option, but they felt anyone could have done that; to tap their special skills to the fullest required the full infrastructure and support that only a hospital could provide.

Their long trek through the city had started from that point, driven by that urge to seek where their professional service would be unquestionably needed, where hordes of injured and maimed humanity would forever be grateful to receive treatments and care, even at the hands of lowly interns.

Indeed, this was the implicit ultimate incentive, the true opportunity. In the dire circumstances of such a disaster, they believed that whoever was lucky enough to make it to a hospital wouldn't mind receiving personalized care from the two interns having scored the lowest grades in the graduating class—grades just a hair above the minimum required to avoid being expelled from the school of medicine, thanks to a generous school-wide policy of grade inflation implemented to artificially pump the ego of its graduates, but most importantly to impress the non-medical schools on campus.

Ego fully bolstered in spite of dismal academic performance, Jean-Pierre always reasoned that, "No patient in pain has ever cared to know the grade point average behind the diploma of an M.D.! A diploma is a threshold, not a bell-curve or an Olympic podium." Consistently, he upheld the idea that those injured by the earthquake would care even less, readier than ever to suffer the miscellaneous ignominies of the healthcare system—even though he realized that senior patients often repressed in silence their disgust of being treated by immature, pompous, and disrespectful M.D.s whom they considered to be arrogant and ignorant "kids" in their early twenties freshly minted by a faculty of medicine that they loathed for admitting teenagers on the strength of 13 years of a feeble pre-university education, per the dictates of Québec's Ministry of Education.

Jean-Pierre and Audréanne were on a mission, a single-minded pursuit, on target like a missile. As such, along the way, they were blind to the injuries, the distress, and the agony, that surrounded them. They were undisturbed and unfazed by the desperate humanity gathered next to buildings just like the one they'd escaped and abandoned, and unresponsive to those who implored assistance. They only saw the bigger picture that mattered to them.

The hospital closest to the student dorms was affiliated with the medical school. As a logical point of convergence, Jean-Pierre and Audréanne had arrived there along with other interns who either shared the same luck of having been on floors that did not collapse—beneficiaries of a serendipitous assignment of dorm rooms—or lived in off-campus apartments constructed to more modern codes. All were eager to serve and saw it as their duty to put their newly learned skills to practice. Some, like Jean-Pierre, also rejoiced at this unique opportunity to execute an outstanding number of billable procedures in a very short time—the crass alternative way to express human compassion that originally attracted him to this great profession.

While the hospital staff had been grateful for this outpouring of altruistic and energetic interns eager to put their freshly acquired knowledge to practice, this sentiment did not extend to Audréanne and Jean-Pierre, whose lackluster academic career was well known—their ludicrous responses to some exam questions were legendary, "confidentially" disclosed to staff by professors for entertainment purposes. Even in the prevailing extreme emergency conditions, which stretched beyond the ability of the hospital's emergency rooms to cope with the influx of badly mingled bodies, no responsible physician dared entrust a soul to the hands of this enthusiastic yet dangerous duo of interns. The expectation for Jean-Pierre and Audréanne was that, after graduation, intelligent enough to recognize their limits, they would establish a small practice to deal with sore throats, strained muscles, immunizations, and other mundane ills, to generously prescribe pills, and to duly dispatch real patients to the appropriate specialists. Hard-core medicine would be off-limits, and that included serving in an emergency room providing MASH-like services. Given that no senior physician had time to tightly supervise them, they had been relegated to serve as glorified nurses.

Under strict orders, the triage nurse thus only dispatched minor injury cases to Jean-Pierre and Audréanne, individuals more scared than hurt, whose wounds and scratches were more emotional than physical. After seeing all the bloody cases bypass them for four hours, and having no opportunity to apply stronger medicine than Tylenol and Band-aids, Jean-Pierre and Audréanne's enthusiasm morphed into a sour dissatisfaction. How could a hospital stressed beyond surge capacity, and which turned-away tons of patients, have nothing better to offer them than insignificant, menial tasks? They realized that the system was askew, that management failed to value their talent, and they agreed to bail out, to investigate whether greater income-generating opportunities existed at other hospitals where the helping hands of even lowly interns would be welcomed. It was also a matter of respect, but only subordinate to the primary drive.

After a brisk 30-minute walk in the miserable cold, they reached the next hospital, one not affiliated with the university. They were pleased that their offer for assistance was immediately and warmly welcomed, and needed at once. However, many of the hospital wings had suffered crippling damage, both to the equipment and the building structure itself. The emergency power generators had failed to operate, lines for medical gases were punctured, and some windows were broken. This raised severe safety concerns and, barely half-an-hour after Jean-Pierre and Audréanne had arrived, the upper administration decided to close the hospital.

Hundreds of patients had to be relocated to other hospitals on the island—in spite of the gross overcrowding of these other healthcare facilities, it was inconceivable to move patients to regular emergency shelters where basic health services were unavailable. Jean-Pierre and Audréanne thus spent a few hours under the glow of emergency lights, helping the staff move heavy hospital beds down staircases, striving to keep patients and ancillary medical apparatus on the beds as much as possible, and pleased to have dropped far fewer patients than medical equipment. After a few staggering bad slips, they were reassigned to move patients from less intensive care units, down the same staircases but on stretchers instead, which they accomplished with a much lower drop rate.

Once assembled at ground level, patients were then moved into the automobiles of dedicated staff and volunteers—the sports utility vehicles and station wagons being reserved for those with the most debilitating injuries and unable to sit. As mandated by law, the hospital had a standing service contract that called for the prompt dispatch of ambulances if the hospital had to be evacuated, but unknown to the administrators, the same ambulance company had signed with all hospitals in the region to provide the same emergency service, on the assumption that such evacuations are rare and unlikely to be needed at two institutions simultaneously. In addition, irrespective of this gross overbooking, the ambulance service was not operational, as not a single crew member had yet reported to work, presumably to tend to the urgent needs of family members or to deal with other personal emergencies related to the earthquake.

Exhausted, as they watched cars leave the premises, shuffling staff and patients to other hospitals, a very few at a time, back and forth in the cold morning, they realized that the entire operation with the limited number of cars available would take the best part of the day, particularly considering the exceptional traffic snarls they had witnessed along the way. At the bottom of the hierarchy, they understood that they would not be given a chance to hop in one of the cars until the very end, and only if space was available then. Nobody would come back just to pick up interns. Staying longer would not provide opportunities to practice medicine, and they surmised that it was best to move on again to another hospital.

The closest hospital to which patients were dispatched was a good three hours' walk away, but given that the carloads of patients to that institution came back empty, at least it was known to be open and operational, which justified the trek. There was not much else to do in the circumstances and, after a brief pit stop to grab some stale pastries and other nonperishable tasteless food at the hospital cafeteria, Jean-Pierre and Audréanne embarked on their long walk in the cold, briefcases in hand, ideals and hope in heart, and dollar signs in mind.

Ottawa, 8:30 a.m.

The discovery of scattered pockets of earthquake damage in Ottawa, more than 100 miles from the epicenter, was surprising. From sunrise, desperate journalists had been roaming the town prospecting for news, and were delighted to have unearthed such easy-to-pick news nuggets, local stories always taking precedence over any other news in captivating the public's interest.

By contrast, Brendon Decker was upset. Arguably, he was of a somewhat permanently upset nature, but over the past few hours, as stories of local damage emerged, his level of agitation rose a few notches above normal. Every time he first learned from the media of instances of significant damage to a federally owned facility, instead of from informants within his own government agencies, he fumed, swearing to hunt down the fat bureaucrats serving as custodians of the national capital's infrastructure and reassign them to inconsequential, menial jobs at an Inuvik office or an outpost even closer to the North Pole if such existed. He'd prefer to fire them or, better yet, impale and roast them alive over charcoals, but the mighty Public Service Alliance of Canada protected all its unionized members against such abuses and ensured them a paycheck for life, even if it entailed no specific related work duties.

At sunrise, a reporter discovered large vertical cracks in the masonry piers supporting the large steel trusses of the Royal Alexandra Interprovincial Bridge connecting Ottawa to Gatineau. This revelation prompted the owner, Public Works and Government Services Canada, to immediately close the bridge to traffic, creating a most unintentional but symbolic disconnection of communications between Québec and Ontario—even though other undamaged bridges upriver and downstream preserved lifelines, like umbilical cords across the river, and ensured that the civil servants residing in Québec could still commute to Ottawa a few days per week, as necessary.

Another news crew reported damage to the new headquarters of the Department of National Defence, in the suburb of Orléans. Many large reinforced concrete columns exhibited wide diagonal cracks. The building had been evacuated during the night and declared unsafe pending an investigation of its structural integrity. Guards at the doors, a safe distance from the building, prevented all access to the facility—where access was once restricted, it was now prohibited altogether. Puzzling to all was why such a brand new building suffered so much damage where all surrounding buildings, of smaller size and older vintage, had survived the distant earthquake undamaged.

Brendon was furious that damage to such a vital arm of government, the Department of National Defence of all things, remained unknown for so long. Even though the top brass of the armed forces communicated from home using cell phones during most of the past night, Brendon was convinced that they had to know the situation at their own headquarters and were just too callous to admit any failures that could give an impression of diminished capabilities to serve in this time of emergency. Even if they had spent every second of the night building an improvised makeshift headquarters at the Petawawa base a hundred miles west of Ottawa, there were no excuses for keeping him in the dark.

At least, if it was of any consolation, when he had arrived at his office hours earlier, he did not need the media to notice the cracks in the sandstone masonry of the Parliament building and the miscellaneous fallen gargoyles splattered across the entrances—and in total darkness to boot.

Montréal, 8:50 a.m.

The "deal," recalled James, was that in exchange for hourly interviews, Richard would drive him to where he could do some work. However, in both previous cases, Richard steered toward collapsed structures that, while spectacular to the uninitiated, were simply the Canadian versions of collapses identical to what had been observed following numerous prior earthquakes in other countries sharing similar construction practices and design codes—therefore damage of little engineering or scientific interest.

Part of the problem stemmed from Richard's self-imposed target of hourly live broadcasts, each time from a different venue. Jim Sunshine manned the master studio, filling the time between his broadcasts with indiscriminate calls from birds of all feathers and the replaying of highlights rapidly becoming stale, so fresh live broadcasts were needed on the hour to keep the audience tuned in. Each of those broadcast lasted approximately 15 minutes, most of which consisted of the politically charged solo ranting of a disc jockey starved for fame, during which James could accomplish some work collecting data if the site was rich in new discoveries. At each stop, to those minutes of actual broadcasting were added 10 minutes to set up the transmitters and 5 minutes to dismantle and pack the transmission station. This left only 15 minutes of undisturbed on-site research work and 15 minutes of travel time in search of the next damaged infrastructure.

Such a pace was not conductive to research. To James, the new and truly valuable engineering lessons lied as undiscovered treasures waiting to be found by a discerning eye, having the time to recognize and analyze subtle external clues hinting of complex internal hidden problems, and 15 minutes zigzagging at a blazing speed on the back of a snowmobile rushing in the hunt for failures spectacular to the laymen would not allow it.

James had made it clear that he would select the next structure of interest, and he directed Richard to park in front of a staid looking office building apparently without damage, across the street from one with severely damaged concrete columns. It was perfect, as there was nobody around—in the middle of a business district unlikely to attract looting if a desperate population came to that sooner or later. Off the snowmobile, Richard proceeded to carry the transmission gear next to the concrete columns, when he noticed that James was about to disappear into the plain, undamaged building through a broken bay window.

"Hey, what are you doing? The busted concrete is here."

"The 'busted' concrete is of absolutely no interest."

"What are you talking about? There are huge four inches wide cracks crisscrossing in an X-shape, and all kinds of bent and twisted steel bars are exposed."

"It's just a regular shear-failure in a reinforced concrete column without adequate hoop reinforcements. I've got CD-ROMs full of identical pictures. Everybody knows what that is, everybody knows why it failed, and everybody knows how to fix it."

James stopped short of saying, "It's not an engineering problem, it's a political one," aware that it would take no less to ignite Richard's frenzy, but he knew it to be the truth. The deficient seismic resistance of older reinforced concrete buildings, designed and built at a time when seismic design requirements did not exist or were far less stringent than considered necessary today, was a problem well documented and widely recognized within the profession. James was fully aware of the existing engineering knowledge and techniques to retrofit such structures, but he also knew that there existed no public policy to force these buildings into compliance; since there were no "recalls" of dangerous buildings, they could forever remain "seismic deathtraps." Only if extensive architectural renovations were undertaken, beyond a certain cost-threshold, could full-blown compliance with the latest building code requirements be enforced—the "trigger" often taking owners by surprise.

Just like one couldn't be forced to add air bags to an old car only because safety standards and knowledge on how to build safer cars had evolved in the past decades, building owners couldn't be required to upgrade the structural integrity of their buildings. Some might have been willing to perform such upgrades for the public good, if provided with obscenely generous incentives—such as a government program that would have relieved them of any financial burden—given that the retrofit costs for deficient buildings were prohibitive and that demolition and reconstruction anew was often the only economical alternative. But, with limited exceptions, there was neither public outcry nor political will to enact legislation that would provide such monetary assistance. Hence, the thousands of old buildings having obsolete and hazardous details in their reinforced concrete framing remained in service, like ticking bombs, waiting to either someday "retire of old age," decommissioned to be naturally replaced by more modern facilities, or to face a sudden "early retirement" prompted by an earthquake, destroyed or damaged beyond repair.

"In your ivory tower, maybe everybody knows why it failed and how to fix it," argued Richard, "but the public does not know. The public has to know."

"Maybe, but the deal was that you would get to follow me, not the other way around."

"Follow you maybe, but follow you to where there is damage, not to the post-office. There is nothing to see in that other building."

"Actually, lots to see. For one thing, it is leaning by approximately one degree. Barring foundation failures, this could only happen if there is either substantial damage to the structural system, or important permanent residual inelastic deformations—the former a design failure, the latter in full compliance meeting the design intent, even though it may be an undesirable outcome if one wishes to reoccupy a fully operational building following the earthquake."

Richard squinted, trying to see such a subtle inclination of the building, wondering if a single degree of lean meant that this 100-foot tall building was a foot out-of-plumb. James was getting technical on him, but he did not have time to ask for clarification, as more justifications on the merit of studying this particular building followed.

"Second, the architectural style suggests mid-1990s construction, a time during which fairly decent seismic design and detailing requirements were in place in building codes. Third, the spacing of columns suggests steel construction, possibly relying on braced frames for lateral load resistance, since this type of structural system has been popular in Montréal for steel frame construction. So, I'm the expert and I'm telling you: this is the building from which new knowledge can be extracted; this is the building in which a careful study of damage can reveal deep insights on the seismic behavior of modern steel structures; this is the building that has possibly failed in a surprising way and that could serve as the benchmark case study that will change practice forever. And it's going to take a good hour to do a decent job here."

"An hour? We've got a broadcast to do in five minutes. What am I going to do?"

"Just do your usual improv about the incompetents that govern us."

"James, James, James," sighed Richard. "Give me 10 minutes of your time. Just describe the creepy concrete column failure, get the interview started with your technobabble, and then you can spend the next hour in your bland post office, or whatever it is. Help me here, buddy. We had a deal."

Richard extended his hand. James kept him waiting, feigning hesitation, before agreeing by a grunt—without shaking hands. James felt the message had gotten through, and that he might be able to finally get some work done, albeit after another dose of populist radio.

He briefly toured the steel building while Richard set up the equipment in front of the concrete one. Searching for large diagonal steel bracing members whose sole purpose was to resist and restrain the lateral sways produced by either wind or earthquakes, he found them surrounding the elevator core. Buckling of the braces had pushed the unreinforced concrete block finishes to collapse outward, revealing the entire structural system. The detailing indeed appeared to have been done in compliance with the latest codified requirements, but the steel gusset plates connecting the brace to the columns and beams had fractured after severe cycles of large deformations and buckling. That behavior had been observed in laboratories and after large earthquakes in Japan, and thus predicted to occur in future earthquakes, but not identified to have occurred in the field yet in North America. This building was typical North American construction of that era, which suggested that many more similar failures had likely occurred in other buildings throughout the city. The big question was to figure out why the building did not collapse given that its structural integrity had been severely impaired by these fractures. The steel diagonal braces—the only structural elements engineered to resist the lateral forces imparted to the building by the earthquake—had been killed, so something else yet unidentified kept the overall structure alive, standing.

"James! Ready to broadcast!" yelled Richard a few times until James heard from across the street.

James emerged from the leaning building with a broad smile suspended from both earlobes, and Richard understood that his expert had found his long-awaited engineering playground. James's exhilaration was such that he even seemed to enjoy Richard's usual excited introductory remarks. He was basking in the warmth of a radiating rainbow-colored aura, as if in a daydream, oblivious to Richard's nonsensical ratings-raising sermon castigating the political elite. A goading question broke the hazy spell.

"Dr. Laroque, please tell us what has happened to this severely wrecked building, visibly in imminent danger of collapse, right in front of us. Why are all its columns split open by large diagonal cracks that expose its guts of steel bars?"

James wondered how to describe a concrete column shear failure in such explicit detail that a radio auditor could mentally reconstruct the picture. He settled for a brief, boring engineering tutorial that would lead to the image depicted by Richard—anything, just to free himself and return to his study of the other building.

"Reinforced concrete is a material that consists of concrete, strong in compression but weak in tension, and reinforcing bars made of steel that provide excellent strength in tension. It is the structural engineer's job to add those bars in concrete members where tension is expected to develop. For example, imagine for a moment a concrete telephone pole sticking out of the ground. Think of it as pure concrete—no reinforcing steel bars in it. Imagine grabbing the top end of the pole and moving it to the right. When doing so, the concrete on the right side of the pole is compressed downward—that side of the pole is pushed down to become shorter. Concrete has enough strength to resist that compression, so it is not a problem. However, on the left side of the pole, the concrete is in tension—that side of the pole wants to elongate. Since concrete as a material is unable to stretch, the left side of the pole fractures under tension, and the resulting crack propagates across the width of the all-concrete pole, snapping it in two like a dry twig.

"However, if a vertical reinforcing bar is embedded in the concrete on the left side of the pole, when the concrete fractures, the bar takes over and acts like a stitch across the crack, resisting the tension forces that the concrete has failed to resist. To reverse the problem, if the tip of the pole is moved to the left instead, then a vertical reinforcing bar would be needed on the right side of the pole.

"This scheme of vertical bars works well and is sufficient for a slender pole. However, imagine that instead of having a slender pole, it is a very squat one, no taller than wide—more a stump than a pole actually. By grabbing its tip and moving it to the right, it does not really bend because it is not long enough, not flexible enough. The stump deforms more like a parallelogram, with its top part remaining flat as it displaces to the right. As a result of this movement, the distance between the top-left and the bottom-right corners of the stub becomes shorter and is accordingly compressed. Likewise, the distance from the top-right to bottom-left corners of the stub increases, and is in tension. Since the concrete stub can't stretch, it fractures into two big wedges, with one big crack spanning from the top-left to bottom-right corners where tension was the largest, and the two resulting concrete triangles separate. To prevent such a fracture, steel bars oriented perpendicular to the crack are needed to stitch the pieces together—or, more practically, horizontal bars can be added to create a regular mesh of bars, that can work in combination with the vertical bars already present to resist flexure of the squat stump. In other words, vertical bars alone are ineffective to prevent this fracture, being at the wrong location and in the wrong direction. The complementary horizontal bars are essential. Now, again, imagine reversing the direction of loading, and moving the top of the stub to the left instead; as a mirror image, this would result in a diagonal crack spreading from the top-right to bottom-left corners instead. The two diagonal cracks—one generated from loading in each direction—would crisscross, checking the concrete stump with an X created by the intersecting cracks."

Richard was yawning. He wondered if James was purposely trying to put the audience to sleep. But he didn't interrupt, as James was at least filling air time and was doing the best he could to answer his question.

"The columns in the building in front of us behave just the same. All the columns connecting two floors together flex and shear, like the tall and stubby poles in the previous example. As the earthquake made the floor above move left and right respective to the one below, concrete cracked everywhere tension developed in the columns, and the steel reinforcing bars crossing the cracks were engaged, trying to keep the pieces from separating. Because there were not enough horizontal bars to resist these severe earthquake-induced motions, the big X patterns of cracks developed, revealing all the 'guts' of the columns, as you described it."

Anticipating Richard's zeal to indict and condemn all those he deemed fit to be culprits, he further clarified: "Research in the 1960s generated the knowledge on how to duly detail reinforced concrete columns to prevent this type of failure. Buildings designed and constructed before building codes embodied these discoveries will inevitably suffer during earthquakes, lacking the benefits of this special reinforcement."

The dull mini-lecture left unfulfilled Richard's desire for front-page news.

"Dr. Laroque, we have literally seen hundreds of buildings afflicted with this type of fatal damage, and as far as we know there could be thousands similarly destroyed."

James did not flinch at Richard's lies and exaggerations. James's exhilaration worked like morphine. Richard didn't bother to rationalize why James's defenses were down. Whether James just wanted to get through the interview to get back to his data mining activities, or felt vindicated by his discovery and thirsty for the blood of elected officials for one reason or another, it didn't matter. A window of opportunity had opened, and Richard was jumping through it.

"Dr. Laroque, are buildings with such kind of damage at high risk of collapsing at any time?"

"Absolutely. A small aftershock could suffice to tear them down."

"So these buildings should not be used until they are properly repaired?"

"Correct."

"And would repairing them be expensive?"

"Very. In fact, it could be so expensive, that in some cases, it would be more economical to demolish them and rebuild anew."

"Seems to me that could be a lengthy process: months, probably years."

"Indeed."

The exchange was so smooth, and the end-goal so clearly in sight, that Richard understood that he was not manipulating James.

They were both dancing along a well-choreographed storyline, and approaching the climax.

"Dr. Laroque, in your experience, what would be the impact of such extensive damage?"

"All of this would translate into substantial direct and indirect economic losses."

"What is the difference?" asked Richard.

"Direct losses account for property damage, lost inventories, and other immediate losses. Indirect losses are consequential losses that occur often in the long term, such as loss of employment or business activity from closures or bankruptcies related to the earthquake. For example, the 1995 Kobe earthquake in Japan caused 50 billion U.S. dollars in direct losses, and probably four times more in indirect losses."

"Could you estimate those losses for Montréal?"

"Impossible to give a precise estimate. But for sure, based on what we've seen so far, this earthquake will most significantly disrupt the country's economy, certainly wreck the province's economy, and will likely bankrupt the city."

Richard got what he wanted. All wrapped in the glow of authority of an expert opinion, and delivered without the need to agitate. This last citation from James would be CHOK-AM's mantra for the rest of the day, replayed every 10 minutes for the benefit of all, until the entire province became glued to CHOK-AM.

Longueuil/Montréal, 9:35 a.m.

Léandre's voice crackled on the short waves: "Am I supposed to say '10-4' or something like that after each sentence?"

"You may treat this as if it was a telephone conversation, with the difference that the transmission is encrypted, and that other communications on this frequency are filtered out by the system software. It is a public frequency, but made secure."

The sophisticated technology presumed to work, and no secret jargon necessary, Léandre wondered why his repeated attempts at establishing communication remained unanswered, and how much had been robbed from the public purse to purchase expensive gadgets that proved useless when most needed.

"Headquarters of *Organisation de sécurité civile du Québec* here, responding to your call!"

Lise Letarte's cordial yet businesslike greeting sounded sincere—concealing well her anger and frustration at leading an "agency of absentees and deserters" at a critical time when a dedicated staff was sorely needed. Fortunately, one of her technicians had arrived to the headquarters just an instant after the C.B. radio started to beg for a response to the calls from Longueuil, saving his befuddled boss the embarrassment of admitting her technological ineptitude.

Before Léandre could utter his relief, a technician jumped on the line blasting a cryptic sequence of telecommunication protocols and configurations, asking for an acknowledgment in reciprocal terms. Words dutifully poured in Lise's ear by her sycophant were repeated verbatim, wrapped in the authoritative tone needed to feign competency. Satisfied that encryption tools and secure protocols to prevent eavesdropping were engaged, the technician nodded to all, certifying the qualifications of the invisible team on the island. An aura of confidence permeated the room, as this preliminary contact with professional emergency responders across the river provided hope that things there might not be as dysfunctional as feared.

Léandre's request for a preliminary ground-level assessment of damage on the island was answered by a solemn narrative of the obstacles Lise serendipitously encountered on her way to the office: the burning tanks, the dropped bridge spans, the highway closures, the debris in the street, the stubbornly inoperative electronic locks—a series of near-trivial anecdotes masquerading as a significant subset from complete and substantive data collected by crews already in the field, as random samples selected from reports already being assembled.

The summary of fallen infrastructure and broken gadgets was fine, but the consummate politician wanted to know how the population was coping. Caught in her own world on the way to the office, she had noticed the citizens roaming the streets but hadn't paid much attention to assess their actual activities, well-being, or morale. So she improvised, painting a rosy picture of optimism amidst resilience, an imaginary tableau of capable emergency responders diligently answering every call for assistance bolstered by an army of volunteers, on the canvas of a well-oiled coordinated operation.

While Léandre was impressed by the thoroughness of this briefing, Florent was unmoved. In his advisor role, it fell within his responsibility to know the true capabilities and leadership of the various provincial government agencies. He had not scrutinized the *Organisation de sécurité civile du Québec* as intensively as other agencies more relevant to promoting the separatist agenda, but recollected highlighting substantial leadership deficiencies in his prior assessments of that agency. Léandre's initial enthusiasm dampened a notch as he noticed Florent's concerned demeanor. A revealing squint by his longtime advisor underscored his skepticism. Florent slipped a note to his boss, two bullet items underlined.

Léandre inquired: "Is the landing pad serviceable?"

Lise, unable to fathom how a flat surface on a roof could possibly be damaged by an earthquake, ventured: "Sure, helicopter landings should not be a problem." Her technician frowned, as he knew the pad to be an elevated platform that would have to be quickly inspected following this conversation.

"I am told you have a state-of-the-art press room in the building. We would like to use it as our main briefing room, and would fly over selected journalists—"

"I'm afraid it is not serviceable," Lise snapped.

The technician was stunned by her assertiveness, as she had never seen the $500,000 facility recently built a few stories below. In fact, she had ignored or declined all invitations from her staff to visit the facility, always pretending to be too busy, or finding other convenient lame excuses to circumvent the fact that she steadfastly refused to acknowledge the existence of a half-a-million-dollar press room created by her predecessor. Not only did she boycott it because it was not her brainchild, but most importantly because this lavish investment was deemed frivolous by higher authorities and previously used as an argument to justify cutting her agency's budget, thus forestalling a later phase of her personal office renovation project and depriving her of a status-enhancing private bathroom with shower.

"Anything that could be quickly fixed?" insisted Léandre, inexorable, convinced that an on-site press conference would have a flamboyance that the insubstantial ones hastily slapped together to fulfill the imperatives of the news would definitely lack.

"We've had an earthquake here!"

Cold silence for a moment. All those gathered around the decrepit short-wave radio knew that Léandre did not like to be lectured. Florent suspected in this arrogance a possible deceit, but wondered how they could operate around her at this time. Léandre's response closed that option.

"We will fly over to your office tomorrow at 6:00 a.m. with reporters for a press briefing at 6:30 a.m. Get the landing lights working, get the briefing room ready. Then we will borrow one of your four-wheel drive vehicles to perform a local reconnaissance of damage within the vicinity of—"

"It may not be possible to get the vehicles out of the under-ground garage, we would have to check—"

Interrupting in turn, louder: "We will drop a limo and a chauffeur in front of your building, just in case."

Léandre stood up, threw the headphones on the table, and walked away. The staffers looked at each other, wondering whether a limousine was within the payload range of the available helicopters, but unequivocally certain that the request had better be met.

Lise concluded that the exchange "Did not go too bad," as she convincingly expressed to her technician. Accustomed to her delusions, he knew better than to argue, and proceeded instead to undertake the tasks needed to meet the Premier's request, while making his immediate boss look good.

Longueuil, 10:00 a.m.

A media room had been improvised by stacking all the Québec flags that could be gathered into a small conference room. Any evidence of the site ever having been a military facility for the Canadian government had been long erased, but extra efforts were nonetheless made to ensure no maple leaf, no beaver, no picture of moose or Mounties, no signs from Transport Canada, or any other federal symbols could be accidentally encountered.

Only a few journalists could make it to the impromptu press conference, dispatched in a rush from Sherbrooke, Trois-Riviere, and Québec City, and representing the top media groups of the province—those with the resources to react on such a short notice. The few large conglomerates that controlled all news and entertainment outlets in Québec were headquartered on the island, still cut off from the world, incapacitated by damaged broadcasting equipment and emergency generators, understaffed and deprived of their star reporters, themselves dealing with their own problems. However, there was enough depth and breadth of expertise scattered across the adjoining regions for each organization to compensate for the absence of their local star correspondents, commentators, or columnists.

The seasoned reporters present knew it was imperative to attend this press conference, to officially take the pulse of the government, yet recognized the futility of the exercise and expected to learn nothing useful so soon after the disaster. They suspected that the strategy of the provincial government was to show itself "in-command" and reassuring, first on the site and first on the "tube," to bolster the separatist claim that Québec did not have any need for the Federal government. On the basis of those expectations, the pro-separatist members of the press, a majority, as well as the federalists, mostly from the English media, had already decided how to report the event, before a word was even uttered.

The Premier entered the room with a coterie of his advisers, and rushed directly to the podium. He cast a furtive look at his watch to subliminally reinforce to members of the press the message that they should feel lucky to get some of his precious time during this crisis. Dispensing with any formal introduction achieved the same goal.

"You have all received a copy of our 7:15 a.m. communique, so I will not repeat this information. As you can gather from that earlier press release, in accordance with Québec's Civil Protection Act, our government has declared a state of emergency and assumed responsibility for the functions that normally fall within local and regional jurisdictions until those jurisdiction are able to administer those powers anew. We have been in contact with the *Organisation de sécurité civile du Québec*, and mechanisms are already underway for our government to appropriately respond to this disaster. It is premature at this time to provide any details with respect to the extent or nature of the damage, but we want to reassure all citizens that we are diligently and systematically doing everything in our power to restore all essential services as soon as possible and provide the necessary emergency services. I will now answer a few questions, recognizing that we only have a limited amount of information at this time."

In spite of such an explicit opening statement, a first journalist was compelled to ask the mandatory unoriginal question, so that the obvious answer could be "on the record."

"How long will it take to bring life back to normal in the city?"

Léandre knew that "normal" was a relative term. In the sense of "the same as before," he suspected that this would probably never happen, as the lives of many individuals and businesses would likely be shattered by the event.

"It is too soon to make such predictions. However, our fellow Québécois and Québécoises have overcome many challenges in the past, and I am confident that the resolve, solidarity, and resourcefulness of the people of this grand nation will triumph in making it possible for the citizens of Montréal to regain a strong foothold in the best possible time. However, our number-one priority is to first get a solid assessment of the situation on-site, to form the basis on which we can build our recovery."

"Sir, in that perspective, one radio station has been broadcasting detailed accounts of damage from downtown Montréal all morning, and your government has yet to provide an assessment of the situation."

Léandre restrained an urge to turn towards his staff, a distress gesture that would have signaled ignorance and lack of commandership. He was fuming that nobody had bothered informing him that the media already had teams on-site, but he never lost composure. He guessed that his colleagues had to share his surprise, as none would have hidden such valuable information, so he concluded that the content of such reports had to be slim in actual credible information, anecdotal at best.

"You must realize that isolated reports by non-experts possibly providing information with a sensationalist slant on cases of isolated damage, do not necessarily nor reliably depict the actual condition in downtown Montréal."

"Sir, these reports have been co-provided by an expert from the National Research Council of Canada conducting engineering assessment of buildings. This team, based on field observations, has estimated that direct losses could exceed 50 billion dollars, and produce extensive closures and bankruptcies. They have forecasted bankruptcy for the city, and possibly the province. What is your government's plan to prevent this from happening?"

He feared having made a wrong guess out on a limb, and was burning to make incompetent staffers pay for their stupidity and lack of meticulousness and thoroughness in collecting information on the crisis. A powerful image of staff members crucified naked on Québec's Parliament Hill, in sub-zero temperatures, using rusted nails, ran through Léandre's mind. Those staff members in the room were all simultaneously struck by the same chilling vision. Léandre did not flinch in spite of his sudden lust for a torture-fest. Solidly anchored by the decorum of the briefing room and with a commanding resolve to show his government in full control of the situation, he offered some banal platitudes in avoiding an answer to the question, either in words or body language.

"Our teams in the field will provide us with credible documented assessments and reports from which our government will construct a realistic assessment of the situation, and will formulate appropriate plans to ensure minimal disturbance to our citizens. Any alarmist commentaries pandering to sensationalism should not mislead the Québécois and Québécoises."

Léandre knew that the media representatives in the room, this early in the game, were not the "regulars," not the national intelligentsia of journalism, not those with the strongest political science bias. It was beyond them to check whether or not there was an official team on the site, and Léandre never doubted that he could get away with such a minor embellishment of reality (never to be called a lie). The politically loaded follow-through question was so predictable that Léandre was already busy formulating his response into the 10 second sound-bite mandatory to fit the evening news broadcast format when the reporter from Radio-Canada sought the following "clarification."

"Mr. Laliberté. Is your government openly disregarding any assessment of damage and losses provided by technical experts from the Canadian government?"

"Federal government employees had been mandated to spread lies and apocalyptic visions on the future of Québec before any earthquake struck. I am confident that our compatriots cannot be fooled anymore by the scare tactics of these hallucinating bureaucrats."

Léandre read in the gleeful eyes of those scribes that he'd scored a goal, and that he needed not say more.

"On this, ladies and gentlemen, you'll have to excuse us, we have important work to do!"

Longueuil, 11:00 a.m.

"We found one!" cheered the jubilant bureaucrat on the phone.

Réal Chaput-Vigneault's staffers in the capital had searched the web, called all the academic institutions, awakened citizens, raked through all the "Who's who," and rummaged through other similar vanity lists and databases, to find an earthquake specialist who also happened to be a member in good standing of the *Parti National.* The initial plan was to obtain a list of experts knowledgeable about earthquakes, from some learned society or professional association, and cross-reference it against the available one of party loyalists—looking for the overlapping intersection of two giant circles of a virtual Venn diagram. However, failing to find any organization regrouping such experts, the staffers soon discovered the lopsidedness of the Venn diagram, one of the two circles being a mere point compared to the other, and the process became instead a hunt for experts.

Sure enough, universities teemed with individuals boasting expertise about everything, but what was sought, beyond competence in geology, was a deep and solid understanding of how infrastructures perform during earthquakes. As the challenge burned the morning hours, it was deemed that a "deep understanding" would be as good as a "deep and solid understanding," and a few hours later, that a "good understanding," or even later a "credible understanding," would be just as acceptable. The exhausting hunt for that rare gem yielded someone with "some understanding" of how infrastructures behave during earthquakes, and with a definite deep and solid membership in the *Parti National.*

"So, who is the egghead?" enquired Réal.

"Louis Riopelle. He's a fairly senior professor at the *CEGEP de Limoilou.* He's only teaching a general science introduction course there, but he has a general B.S. in education with a minor in geology."

The credibility of a teacher from a *College d'Enseignement Général et Professionel (CEGEP*—as a College of General and Vocational Education) was a far cry from the prestigious authority that an emeritus university professor could have provided, but Réal kept silent.

Aware that these were insufficient qualifications against the expectations, the bureaucrat expanded: "He also has written an entire book chapter in which he describes the damage done to the built infrastructure by past earthquakes."

"What's the title of the book?"

"Actually, it is a chapter in his class notes. He emailed us a copy; it's actually nicely done, well illustrated."

Réal remembered, from his CEGEP days, the typewritten class notes, photocopied, spiral bound and sold by the student association. Decades later, the quality of the end product presumably had benefited from the emergence of desktop publishing, but class notes still carried the stigma of an unpublished work, even against the authors' claim that their manuscript had been rejected for lack of a market rather than lack of quality. Réal recalled that, in those days, only the courses on the required path for university admission were blessed by the support of a real publisher. Students enrolled in the mathematics and fundamental sciences classes, mandatory literature and philosophy courses, and a few wildly popular and entertaining electives, had to fork over extra dollars for the luxury of a bound book, the others having access to stacks of Xeroxed papers glued to cheap cardboard wrap-around covers.

Réal refrained from asking "Is he any good?" knowing that his sleep-deprived team had worked hard to unearth this expert on short notice—whatever they got would have to do for now.

"Good work! How fast can you get to him for a chat with Léandre?"

"He's already been picked up and on the way to *Complexe H*."

"OK, check him out a bit, give me an off-line assessment, and we'll have him talk to Léandre at 1 p.m., no matter what you find."

Réal was somewhat disappointed that they couldn't find a true academic. Universities are supposed to be full of separatists—couldn't there be one somewhere interested in earthquakes as a hobby and in politics as a religion, or vice versa? At the same time, he wasn't outright negative about CEGEP teachers, as he had fond memories of his two years there. Two formative years, trapped in one of these giant career-sorting facilities that gather all the youth with ambitions beyond the terminal Grade 11 of Québec's high schools, and let them float unsupervised adrift various career paths, either as part of a 2-year curriculum leading to the doors of a university, or a 3-year one leading to a technical-skills trade. Let loose in a tuition-free and parent-free jungle, he, like every other student, faced a smorgasbord of experiments and choices, from a track of intense and deep study, to the opportunity for swimming cross-current, or even to abandon all life ambitions and become a "professional student" supported by generous government need-based scholarships supplemented by interest-free loans. Not to forget the palette of available extra-curricular options that complement the all-encompassing life experience of CEGEP as a microcosm of the Québec society—but excluding the bluest of the blue collars and those who didn't graduate from high-school.

That's where Réal had discovered his passion for political science, brushed by the winds of Marxism, communism, utopianism, anarchism, socialism, reformed capitalism, and nationalism. That's where he'd gotten deeply involved in the national student association, staging student manifestations and strikes to protest anything and everything, from government cuts in the student financial aids program to the same government's occasional support for imperialist U.S. policies—always submitting reports of his agitatorial and rebellious activities as term papers under the wing of a supportive teacher with social-democrat inclinations. That's where he'd joined the militant youth wing of the *Parti National*, setting foot on the first rung of a long ladder.

CEGEP teachers were mostly hard-core separatists then, unabashed missionaries of their convictions to captive audiences—irrespective of relevance to the class taught—and Réal knew that polls confirmed this to still be the case, with allegiances recovering from a substantial drop in support to the *Cause* that lasted nearly a decade. Also, beyond statistics, as a name, Riopelle sounded *Québécois de souche* (with roots deep in the motherland), which boded well unless he turned out to be a ranting zealot.

In any event, any registered member of the Party with a professed scientific expertise on the topic would surface at some point, exposed by the media. Réal preferred to be the first to discover and screen any self-promoting, self-aggrandizing opportunist who fit the bill and who could be bewitched by the limelight. Riopelle might as well be heard in private. If a good match was established, he could serve a useful purpose.

Ottawa, 11:15 a.m.

From an authoritative stance, the 6:30 a.m. communique from the Canadian government painted an exceptional grasp of the tactical response to unfold, driven with a steadfast resolve. It referred to the mobilized Government Operations Centre to coordinate all activities under the jurisdiction of the federal agencies responding to the emergency. It volunteered satellite-based imagery to map and quantify the extent of damage. It hinted at the deployment of well-trained first responders, and even of the venerable Mounties, to the rescue. It teased with the prospect of a windfall of disaster financial assistance, and even tax relief. All the carrots were out.

It was, without a doubt, a great press release, flaunting the government aptitude and skillful readiness to respond. The staffers working for Kaylee, Graham, Wayne, and Shirley had masterfully briefed them on the theoretical federal emergency response capabilities. However, beyond theory, with respect to implementation, a number of glitches prevented a smooth unfolding of these capabilities.

First, the entire leadership team of the Government Operations Centre had been enjoying lunch at the World Emergency Preparedness and Response Conference in Taiwan when news of the disaster reached them. It would be another 30 hours before its return to Ottawa, on account of the awkward time difference and inconvenient flight schedules. Compounding the stress on the smaller and less experienced B-team left to operate the Centre, key technical staff members were enjoying the beaches of Florida. These staffers, like many Canadian public servants, had long in advance specifically scheduled a vacation for one of those weeks known to be coldest of the year in Ottawa, and, by the God-blessed right given to every union employee of the powerful Public Service Alliance of Canada, no boss could have prevented them from picking that week to "cash-in" some "accumulated sick-days," even if it coincided with the World Conference.

In spite of all these hurdles, unfaltering and of enduring resiliency, the Government Operation Centre was still functional and fired up—just propelled by a smaller engine. For sure, moving forward, but as if limping on three flat tires, yet determined to reach the next service station before the rims sliced the steel-belted radials to shreds.

Second, even accounting for the possibility of off-nadir viewing, the satellites needed to provide the images promised in the communique only orbited above Montréal at best once every three days. The next passage was scheduled to take place in 26 hours, by itself a reasonable delay, but if the weather forecast from Environment Canada were to hold true, the high-resolution pictures from outer-space would only capture, in its heavenly beauty, the thick, impenetrable cloud shield hovering a few thousand feet above the ground.

Third, the federal emergency responders had to remain on standby, hands tied until Québec officially requested help, something it seemed disinclined to do, or until the Federal government unilaterally declared its omnipotent jurisdiction to step in to assist provincial authorities presumably overwhelmed by the disaster. Brendon's politically concealed desire was that the extent of the disaster, of the destruction, of the pain and suffering, was such that the helpless Québec Premier would have no alternative other than to crawl and beg for help for his incapacitated province. However, realistically, he knew Léandre would either charge fists in the air, arrogantly requesting due return on the billions of dollars in income taxes funneled to the federal coffers, or make no request at all. The former scenario, in spite of the grandstanding, would be a debilitating political concession, an admission of weakness that no public relations spin could undo. The latter scenario, however, was not an acceptable position, and Brendon had long concluded on the necessity to act in his best interests, in spite of constitutional protocol. He was planning to invade.

Fearing Brendon's mistakes more than his anger, given that the public backlash from a calamitous blunder might abbreviate their political careers, Graham Murdoch and Kaylee Carling timidly cautioned him that some tact and sensitivity to historical precedents might be befitting. The nationalist intelligentsia in Québec always resented "October 1970," when the federal government, in response to a formal request by the Québec Prime Minister, declared the War Measures Act, suspended civil rights, deployed the Canadian army to take control of the province, and worked with the police to arrest overnight nearly 500 citizens deemed "suspect" on the basis of their support for separatism. In total confusion, journalists, union leaders, writers, artists, even musicians and poets, were treated worse than criminals, apprehended without warrants from the sanctity of their home, handcuffed in front of their family, and jailed for their support for the struggle for national independence, while the handful of terrorists that scared the provincial government out of its wit in the first place by kidnapping and killing the Minister of Labor and the British Trade Commissioner remained at large for two more months until they negotiated their safe exile to Cuba.

Brendon scolded his advisors for confusing deployment of the army with the suspension of habeas corpus, dismissing any suggestion that the Canadian army might not be welcome in Québec, even if to serve in a humanitarian function following a disaster. For the few hundred terrified sons who'd seen their father wrestled away without cause decades ago, there were hundreds of thousands of despondent citizens thrown into the freezing dead of winter by a destructive earthquake and who would embrace emergency responders even if outfitted with camouflage helmets. The province had to be freed from the thugs who not only kept its internal affairs at arm's length from the federal government, as if a sovereign nation, but who also always dictated how the rest of Canada should think, feel, and act, on all matter of national interest. To Brendon, this was a matter of national security, but first and foremost, the time to assert his vision of Canadian federalism, the time to quench his thirst for power, the time to unleash his unabashed ego, the time to forever engrave his name in history. It was the day before D-Day.

Brendon's lackeys were tasked to ready all agencies for the decisive charge. This should have been a smooth enterprise in light of the oft-proclaimed government aptitude and skillful readiness to respond, but the hodgepodge they encountered rather revealed total government inaptitude and ineptitude to respond. Compounding the aforementioned glitches, many agency leaders, department executives, and lower level senior managers were also missing, having joined the merry flock of Canadian snow-birds vacationing in Florida and the Caribbean, attracted like flies to the bright light of a sunny beach. In a more mundane way, many federal employees had elected to stay home, either to cocoon loved ones against obvious imminent dangers, out of concern for unreachable relatives in Montréal, or in fear of having received but not understood God's garbled message of perceptible displeasure.

All good intentions, sometimes bathing in an undertone of laziness in sub-zero temperatures.

Nonetheless, undeterred by this conspiracy of absenteeism that emptied the halls of power on and around Ottawa's iced Parliament Hill, the wheels of government were in motion. A slow but steady motion.

In addition to their oversight and information-gathering role, Wayne, Graham, Kaylee and Shirley participated in strategic meetings to plan a press briefing to be attended by a mob of national and international journalists. It would serve to announce Brendon's plans, and briefly outline some of the logistics of the process he triggered. But one major point was left to resolve: whether the country's Prime Minister would go on site. Whether the leader of the nation would inspect the disaster-stricken area, meet and comfort victims, sympathize with their pain, be a visible and compassionate commander-in-chief.

Here lied Brendon's existential crisis.

As shrewd a politician as he was, as much as he didn't mind lying his way to power, he resented shaking hands and kissing babies, pretending to care. Throughout his political career, his demeanor had been trained to cultivate those friendships in power and abandon the befallen ones. Flatter those who could serve his purpose, politely ignore those who couldn't anymore. Gravitate to those with ideas, leech vital information, gain prestige by association, reap the benefits, claim intellectual ownership and unequaled expertise, and move on to the next host. Strangely, while he excelled at socializing at the high level of power, he didn't care to charm the public, to peddle an image of conviviality with the common folk. He had found other effective ways to win a majority of votes without needing to reach down to ground level.

Brendon was fully aware that in this crisis, some symbolic tableaux would have to be staged to satiate a society focused on images, where one's worth was appraised by form rather than content, where foundations and structure were irrelevant provided the facade was appealing. He could not ignore how the public would react to his actions.

The compassionate option was to set foot amidst the debris, visit hospitals, hug victims and pretend to feel their grief and pain, the media in tow ready to beam the spectacle live across the world. The vision of a savior-in-chief, on the ground, leading his army to save the country, as a godsend to help Canadians recover from a vicious seismic attack, piped through airwaves, cable, or internet. Ideally.

The only risk for that option being that agitators could take advantage of the concentration of media to pelt him with detritus, sending worldwide the powerful message that the wrath of an earthquake was still better than appurtenance to the federation. Should such an unexpected situation arise, Brendon would have to display a stern resolve and sufficient arrogance to stand his ground, like a modern-day version of Pierre Elliot Trudeau, the former Canadian Premier, who, during the Québec national holiday parade, against the wishes of his security guards, refused to leave the grandstand when bombarded by rocks and bottles thrown by supporters of Québec's independence rioting to protest his symbolic attendance at the event. Although an unappealing possible worst-case scenario, there was solace that, in a Canadian context, where the possession of firearms was regulated, heads of state were not likely to be killed by lunatics, contrary to tradition in the land of opportunity south of the border.

The commander-in-chief option was to remain in Ottawa, as a master tactician, an army general, making key decisions from a central operation center. The vision of a strong reflective father, a reassuring wise elder who oversees and analyzes the continuous barrage of information with aplomb, able to masterfully distills order from an otherwise deplorable mess.

Ideally (again).

The only risk for that option being to appear aloof and isolated if the anticipated torrent of information turned out to be a trickle, choked by clogged communication pipes. Should such a situation arise, the decisions and announcements of his office would be overshadowed by the deluge of data streaming from the media's battery of cameras deployed in the field where all the action lied, and Brendon would have to change strategy and parachute himself to the field to catch up lost time—just like Microsoft's intense drive for web-browser supremacy which started a few years after its CEO called the internet a passing fad. Although an unappealing possible worst-case scenario, there was solace that, in a Canadian context, where Premiers are not held up as standards of moral rectitude, political leaders could be forgiven for changing their minds—even, at the extreme, for changing political party affiliation—contrary to tradition in countries whose rulers must please moralists or religious zealots.

Brendon's existential crisis was rooted in an obsession with his legacy, as a springboard for immortality. As such, his decision hinged on how he believed his actions would be remembered henceforth, engraved in the subjective annals of history. A sad fixation—an unfortunate staple of modern democracy—on which images would garnish history books and encyclopedias, which video clips would endure as stock footage for the documentaries screened in classrooms to shape pride in Canadian heritage or streamed online to mold public opinion. The same obsession with name recognition for posterity that drives some to become artists, preachers, serial killers, pornographers, or politicians.

Would future academics dissert on the vanity of futile and hypocritical leaders who trampled disaster scenes in search of positive press, or praise their humanity? Would history praise a cool-headed chief executive who launched effective policies and directed their implementation with a steady hand, or judge it a distant ruler, disconnected from both the electorate and the battle field, more a Nero than an Eisenhower, at odds with the public expectations of a glorified, chivalrous hero bathing in the deadly cross-fire of a bloody battlefield?

Sadly, all about image.

Did McKenzie King, when serving as 10th Prime Minister of Canada, think himself a visionary judge of character when he denied entry to Canada to Jewish refugees fleeing Nazi Germany, and wrote in his journal that Adolf Hitler was "a reasonable and caring man who might be thought of as one of the saviors of the world"? Did he expect history to reveal his occult interest and séances seeking advise from his dead mother, his dead dogs, and dead celebrities?

Did Richard Bedford Bennett, when serving as 11th Prime Minister of Canada, expect that his confidential communications, agreeing to fund the publishers of a fascist anti-Semitic newspaper in return for favorable propaganda to help win an election, would one day be unearthed by historians?

Did John George Diefenbaker, when serving as 13th Prime Minister of Canada, anticipate that he would be best remembered for having killed, in one fell-swoop policy decision, development and manufacturing of the all-Canadian Avro CF-105 Arrow—

arguably the world's most advanced supersonic fighter plane at the time—and ordered the systematic destruction of all Avro aircrafts, engines, facilities, and technical data, leading to the demise of the Canadian aerospace industry and the exile of its best engineers?

Sadly, all about image.

Sadly, all beyond one's control.

Unlike Sir John Alexander Macdonald, the 1st Prime Minister of Canada, who hadn't been concerned about his legacy when showing up drunk as a skunk for his parliamentary debates, Brendon worried, fearing that video clips showing him ducking a shower of tomatoes while feigning empathy inspecting an earthquake-ravaged city could be downloaded from the internet at a dizzying frequency.

Brendon decided to stay in command, in the Ottawa seat of power, at least for the time being. Aware of the missed golden opportunity to confound his detractors and exude some human warmth, cognizant of the road not taken whose destination will never be reached, at this juncture, Brendon settled for the beaten path rather than the unexplored one, for certainty over adventure. Brendon was certain that episodes of national compassion would continue to shine by their absence from history books, to the benefit of detailed analyses of forceful leadership and significant conflicts.

So images of forceful leadership it would be, packaged and released by his diligent public relations experts.

Brendon's entourage was convinced this was the wrong choice—they instinctively feared it would backfire within a few days at most, so they started to plan in parallel all the needed logistics for the "parachuting of Brendon" worst-case scenario.

As the case for all his decisions, Brendon was cocksure he had made the right choice this time again. True to himself, he did not listen to any advice, disregarded any benevolent caution, couldn't care less about other opinions, because he had an unwavering, absolute confidence in his superior intellect and leadership skills. Suggestions discordant with his views always rang like repulsive orders that he was loath to acknowledge, given his stature, experience, and seniority. His intelligence and political acumen, second only to God in his assessment, conferred on him an incontestable rightness. From that Olympus where he ruled, he could do and undo anything, just toying with his tightly woven political relationships. In Brendon's world, to move anything, achieve anything, it all boiled down to relationships, and he was the virtuoso of masterminding and playing relationships. And in the end, after all, being right or wrong was irrelevant. What mattered was forceful and convincing demagogy that could paint an unpleasant wrong into a desirable right, thinking enough moves ahead in the chess game to circumvent any possible logical escape, killing from the outset the possibility of alternative solutions. To Brendon, truth was a relative and illusive concept, a mirage to manipulate and reach personal goals. Brendon was a sophist working for the best interest of no one but himself.

Montréal, 12:00 p.m.

Richard was irritated. James had spent the past two hours fully invested in unspectacular damage, measuring and photographing bent steel plates, oddly distorted members, barely visible cracks, and other subtle damage that only a boring engineer could appreciate, moving from one slightly leaning building to another, as a bumble bee methodically collecting the pollen of succulent yet identical adjacent flowers.

To Richard, this "procrastination" was unproductive, even more so after he realized, while waiting outside for James, that the four-story building across the street was actually a five-story building whose top four stories had moved down one level, crushing whatever once existed at ground level. The concrete slab of the first floor now rested a few feet above ground, propped a few feet up by crushed furniture, file cabinets, and marble counters. A minivan parked in what once was a delivery bay had also been flattened into crumpled steel oozing oil and gas.

As Richard circled the building, stupefied by the sheer magnitude of this sobering discovery, trying to comprehend this surreal vision, he encountered a second building, previously hidden behind the injured kneeling building. Landscaping features between the two buildings, even though shrouded under a winter veil, evinced that they were bound as two parts of a complex, presumably of similar architecture and construction. This presumption could not be directly verified as the second building had completely collapsed—not only the first story, but all stories had failed. Five massive concrete slabs were stacked atop each other like pancakes, almost touching, kept a few feet apart by miscellaneous debris that could not be further compressed. All the amenities of what had once been livable office space now served as the mashed-up filling of a giant quintuple-decker sandwich. Pieces of cladding, broken glass, and torn adornments lying in the snow hinted at the rubble's prior fabric and character. A carefully crafted style and signature erased in an instant from the urban drawing board.

Perusing the awful, disjointed, nonsensical pile of debris, Richard recognized a familiar form, barely visible deep in the stack, pinned between large unidentifiable masses. Familiar but abnormally folded. A human body articulated in defiance of anatomy, in unfamiliar directions, where no articulation exists.

The reality of death shook Richard. The abstract fatalities that had populated his discourse, sprinkled in his broadcasts for effect, had just emerged from the bins conveniently stashed in the back of his mind, to invade and occupy his entire thoughts, commanding absolute attention and respect.

Stupefied, eyes closed, he saw himself floating inside the collapsed building, searching for survivors the instant after collapse, slithering amidst the clutter and the dust, seeking human souls amidst the paste of ground flesh and bones soaked in its own fluids. He saw his hands clutching slimy remains, still warm from the infinite pain, and reconstructing the lives that were destroyed.

Outraged, eyes open, he still saw the mound of destruction in the clutches of a grey cold winter, with its frozen content of death. Not a collapsed building, but the mass grave of innocent bystanders indiscriminately slaughtered without rhyme or reason.

In reality, in an era that empowered insomniac workaholics to connect to the office from the comfort of their home, the janitor was the only victim of the collapsed building. No one else was entombed there. Yet, it was just the same for Richard, as he imagined the scene around apartment buildings that had similarly collapsed. The mayhem in residential neighborhoods that they purposely avoided flashed into his mind: the crying mothers, the contorted broken bodies, the intrepid rescue efforts, the bloody debris, the squashed lives, the eviscerated communities, the amputated society. Richard's visceral anger was flared by his sudden grasp of the pain, death, and destruction, bolstering his crusade to crucify those responsible for this carnage.

Perfect weapons for the cause, Richard saw the slain buildings in front of him as deflated monuments to the ineptitude and shortsightedness of governments, to the inability of Québec to break away from its Third-World colonial mentality, and to the overall poor state of affairs in the "kingdom"—or, at least, the perfect pretense to proclaim so live, on the air, even though one would be hard-pressed to establish credible cause-effect linkages supporting his thesis. As such, it was unacceptable that the one all-important expert within his grasp and that he could manipulate to shore up his credibility was fully absorbed in measuring the length of near-invisible cracks along near-invisible welds keeping together two insipid steel plates whose existence and purpose was unknown but to a few engineers—those few nerds passionate about selecting the right steel plates the way some women can immerse in endless shopping to select the right shoes to match the clothes.

Richard felt he had respected his side of the deal and that the time for scientific pursuit had run its course. He found James outside one of the dull, uninspiring buildings.

"James, you must give me some air time on this one," pointing to the stack of concrete slabs across the street.

"It's not interesting. It just a boring, stupid, soft-story collapse mechanism."

"I don't care that you have boxes of photos of buildings trashed just like those—"

"More than you can imagine."

"Still, nobody knows what that means, except for a bunch of... specialists," stopping short of saying "geeks." "You have a responsibility to educate the public."

James stopped a moment and looked at Richard. A raised eyebrow and lashing look said it all. He was incensed that Richard could even lecture him on the "responsibility to educate," as if he were delinquent in his duties to provide substantive information, as if CHOK-AM ever had an educational and enlightenment mission, as if he had any reason to be satisfied and impressed by the promotional packaging that Richard wrapped around his previous remarks. By virtue of which pedagogical sleight did a piano slightly sliding across a room morph into a raging bull pursuing hapless citizens across an entire home, and, why not, across town. By which scholastic delusion of grandeur did a cautious and tentative economic loss assessment transform into an omen of national financial apocalypse. But none of those thoughts broke the heavy silence.

A still moment between two men, one now disinvested from the initial partnership, the other still trying to overspend the benefits of his investment, like a satiated leech unwilling to loosen its grip.

When James stopped his work and walked toward the microphone with an assertive pace, Richard almost hesitated to start the broadcast, fearing an explosion of impulsive, unrestrained statements that could include virulent personal attacks.

Only almost.

The enraged testimony of a presumed expert, irrespective of content, made too good radio to censor; unable to override his greed for fame and journalistic ambitions, Richard could not miss such an opportunity. He barely completed the station identification, when James ripped the microphone away.

"Mr. Nightrock, we are standing here in front of a five-story building. Imagine the top four stories as a rigid box, as a series of small offices divided by numerous rigid dividing walls and partitions, some added by the architect, some by the owner, some by the tenants. Imagine that rigid box supported on top of a completely open ground story. Imagine that open ground story to be taller, a welcoming yet inspiring height, suggesting the grand and solemn spaces of old banks or churches. Imagine that ground floor free of obstructions, a wide-open space broken only by a few unfortunate columns inconveniently inserted to support the above stories. This is a typical building, as our society likes them, as all societies like them, and as architects like to provide to clients who like them. Mr. Nightrock, we all love these buildings, and we would love them even more if only we could get rid of these pesky columns that obstruct the view, that violate the sense of freedom and spaciousness, and that reduce the number of square feet that can be leased.

"Now imagine this building swaying during an earthquake, imagine the entire rigid four-stories-tall box supported on its tiny first-story legs, moving left and right as the columns distort during an earthquake, like an enormous concrete block supported by the swaying legs of a cheap plastic kitchen table, struggling to hold this huge weight, moving sideways until the table legs give.

"Imagine yourself, inside this building—it looks just like the one in front of us. Maybe it's a bank and you're making a deposit. Maybe it's a doctor's office and you're getting a physical. Maybe it's a restaurant where you're sipping wine in good company. All the same, you're feeling the strange sway, the first small disturbance that keeps amplifying, wondering if it will stop or endlessly intensify, worrying whether your loved ones are safe.

"Imagine yourself, unable to decide whether running for the exits is safer than remaining inside, while everything is thrown on the floor and the bulbs from the violently swirling chandeliers break as they hit the ceiling.

"Imagine yourself, seeing the ceiling coming towards you, with no time to react, to move, or to even think who to blame.

"Imagine the columns busting, the ceiling touching the floor, and the clump of warm flesh that remains of yourself, squashed between two slabs of concrete.

"Imagine yourself, not splatted like a fly on a windshield, but only half-crushed, mangled from the waist down, still conscious, able to contemplate your mutilated body.

"Imagine yourself, tortured by the excruciating pain that tears your brain apart and burns your body, as if nails were driven through your skull while a meat slicer amputated your limbs a sliver at the time.

"Imagine yourself, deafened by the agonizing screams of your loved ones, and many others, all half-dead, scattered throughout the building, sharing your plight in a desperate chorus of the doomed.

"Imagine yourself, aware there will be no help, watching your life drain with the escaping blood, crying in hope for the unbearable pain to end soon, praying to find relief in death.

"Imagine yourself, desperately counting every second, devastated that the count doesn't stop and that you must live longer.

"Imagine yourself, swearing at the gods for annihilating you, possibly with cause, certainly without warning, definitely as cruelly as conceivable.

"Imagine yourself, desperate for the uneventful, peaceful, boring life you had before the ceiling illogically dropped to kiss the floor, before your cocoon imploded.

"That, Mr. Nightrock, when ceilings come to kiss their floors, in engineering terms, is what we call a soft-story collapse mechanism. A building that was originally designed as a five-story building, but did not behave like one because the top four stories were locked together by a multiplicity of rigid partitions inserted at one time or another by various parties, transforming the building into a massive rigid block supported by a single story, completely against the original design intent. Just like deactivating the airbags deployment mechanism in a car, or not replacing batteries in home fire alarms, or swimming during a thunderstorm, or driving home after drinking half-a-dozen beers. Now who is to blame, Mr. Nightrock? I'm sure you'll be able to tell me. Because had this earthquake occurred at 1 p.m. today instead of 1 a.m., this office building in front of us would have been fully occupied when it collapsed and you'd be wading in a blood-soaked slush, nauseated by the stench of death, and surrounded by hysteric survivors assaulting your microphone, instead of freezing your butt off on a pristine snow bank."

A pause.

Richard was awed. This was shock radio at its best. He could not have done better. James had dispensed his terrifying and gory portrayal of dark fate and irresponsibility under an aura of professional credibility that he could never aspire to attain. He also recognized that his unabashed delight disgusted James. There was nothing to add.

"Thank you Dr. Laroque, thank you, thank you, thank you for this description with chilling realism of the horrible damage we are witnessing in downtown Montréal, subsequent to today's terrible and deadly earthquake. I am confident our auditors appreciated your edifying remarks, and am hopeful our government officials also heard you and fully understood the dramatic implications of years of faulty policy and complacency for which they are fully responsible."

Richard and James understood that their circumstantial partnership ended here.

Longueuil, 1:00 p.m.

The leadership team was assembled around the speakerphone base, a relic of bygone technology whose annoying hiss was only randomly interrupted by loud clicks of unknown origin. The major concern however was not the obsoleteness of the equipment available, but rather the disappointing profile of Riopelle drawn by Réal's team, privately reported to him half an hour earlier. Their assessment of his capabilities and allegiances was devoid of the glowing praises originally anticipated. They had already downgraded their high hopes to find a superstar technical expert on earthquakes and resigned themselves to the pragmatic resolution that a CEGEP teacher masquerading as one would be acceptable provided he was unconditionally partisan of the sovereigntist cause. Unfortunately, their interrogations of Riopelle revealed that his allegiance to the party was at best tenuous: He was a hardliner frustrated that the government wasted time with sterile referendums rather than declaring independence outright. Yet it appeared that he kept his membership to the party because it provided him with an opportunity to vent his anger during the party's conventions and other public forums, and because there was no other viable party on the Québec political map that could satisfy his hard-core and extremist positions.

Concluding their private report, Réal's staff apologized for their inadequate and deficient judgment in inferring Riopelle's allegiance on the basis of his professional tenure, and for their failure in further checking his background before bringing him to attention. They suggested that this "loose cannon" shouldn't talk to Léandre after all, and indicated that they would at once resume their arduous search for a more suitable expert and scientific advisor. However, Réal insisted that Riopelle be heard now, on the grounds that it was better to hear his point of view firsthand than from the media at the least-expected moment. In the best-case scenario, he might even have some valuable information to share.

As such, huddled around the speakerphone on the small table, Léandre and his leadership team were ready to scan every word of this expert, hoping to harvest ammunition to shoot down the federal government in future showdowns.

"So in your scientific opinion, Mr. Riopelle," asked Léandre, suggesting a desirable answer, "would you qualify this disaster as a highly improbable and unforeseen geological event?"

"No."

Off to a bad start.

The upbeat and anticipating mood, already tainted by the profile report, dropped a few more notches. The hissing silence compounded the gloom. Riopelle's silent treatment was his eerie way of discomforting an audience and achieving full attention. He then started lecturing.

"A disaster is the result of a hazard event involving injury or loss of human life, damage or loss of property, or disruption of economic activity. For the case at hand, a hazard is a natural phenomenon—that may result in a disaster when occurring in a populated, commercial, or industrial area. Risk is the likelihood and probability of loss. A disaster risk is the chance of a hazard event occurring and resulting in disaster, while the hazard risk is the chance of a hazard event occurring."

Riopelle was already losing his audience, which Léandre saw as a reassuring attribute—a bumbling professor wading in semantic and theoretical abstractions would be harmless to his government, as the media abhor sheer, incomprehensible technobabble. Unfortunately, Riopelle quickly translated the high-level concepts into layman's terms.

"In that perspective, this *hazard* is not an unforeseen event, and given this geological event, this *disaster* is not highly improbable. Earthquakes are documented to have occurred in Québec going as far back as the 16th century. The disaster has occurred simply because there has not been any will to duly prepare to prevent such a disaster, no will to mitigate the risk. No interest from the population, and thus no political will."

All around the table kept silent but shared outrage at the deliberate upsetting and provocative choice of words. Riopelle's accusations killed all interest to discuss the relative merit of various political strategies in the pre-disaster context.

Attempting to find some redeeming value in a post-disaster situation, Léandre suggested, "On a positive spin, would it be reasonable to assume earthquakes are rare events and that it might be many centuries before another one of this intensity will happen?"

Riopelle reverted to his condescending and theatrical lecturing tone, but none interrupted, all craving a few nuggets of usable information from the heap of scientific mumbo-jumbo.

"The intensity of an earthquake is a measure of its impact, measured qualitatively in terms of damage observed for certain types of construction, or from some other natural observations of the earthquake effects. As such, a single earthquake has many different intensities, depending on how close one is situated with respect to the zone of most severe shaking, where the maximum intensity is assigned to a particular earthquake. The magnitude of an earthquake is a single scientific measure of the strength of the earthquake, as recorded by an instrument. There are many different types of magnitude scales, but they all share the common characteristic that they are values along a logarithmic scale, meaning that a Magnitude 7 earthquake is 10 times more powerful than a Magnitude 6 one, itself 10 times stronger than a 5."

All were confused as this failed to answer Léandre's question. Yet, Riopelle was pleased with his scientific rigor, having first laid out the fundamental concept of earthquake magnitude that is intertwined and inseparable from that of recurrence interval.

Sharing the roadmap of his thought process, Riopelle added, "The question of how frequently will earthquakes occur at a particular geographic location can only be answered in relation to their sizes, and the average number of years between events of a certain magnitude is defined as the return period for such earthquakes."

Had the teacher been able to see the puzzled face of his students, he might have instead volunteered this clarification at the outset of his long exposé.

"The return period of larger earthquakes is such that there will be on average a larger number of years between two Magnitude 7 events than between two Magnitude 6 events, but this is true only in a probabilistic sense. History has shown that return periods are poor predictors for policy planning purposes. For example, two earthquakes, of Magnitude 6 and 6.5, have occurred in Québec within 10 years of each other, in 1860 and 1870, in the Charlevoix region, even though the return period for such earthquakes averages approximately 70 years. In an extreme case, three Magnitude 8 earthquakes have occurred within a few weeks of each other in the New Madrid area of the Central United States along the Mississippi valley, even though the return period for such large earthquakes exceeds 500 years. Therefore, while it is tempting and arguably reasonable to wish to assume that a period of 'earthquake quietude' follows a major event and that a similar earthquake will only re-occur after a number of years equal to its return period, it is ill advised and not scientifically justifiable to plan on the basis of that expectation because this is only true in an average sense. Only one who does not respect earthquakes and does not care about their impact could take such a stance."

Léandre needed not hear more. He had an aversion for arrogant, pompous and long-winded, self-righteous 'experts' of Riopelle's caliber, who wore their bitterness on their sleeves. As a seasoned politician, he had learned early on to ignore such "clowns," denying them the pleasure of a debate that would aggrandize their credibility—like navigating a sailboat around shallow waters to avoid being stuck on a sandbar until high tide. However, as much as he wanted to dismiss this abject low-grade scholar, Léandre recognized that the conjuncture was ripe for Riopelle's deranged rants to escape the confines of his classroom, and that an earthquake expert with long-standing official affiliation to the *Parti National* was a possible political liability that could be tapped by the party's foes. Best to ensure Riopelle was invisible for a few days.

"Mr. Riopelle, we understand that you have thoroughly studied this topic over the years, and we would sincerely appreciate if you could, on the basis of your extensive knowledge and expertise, draft a detailed report that would provide us with some of your understanding of the subject matter, in layman's terms, particularly outlining what measures should have been taken to avoid this disaster, and which mechanisms we should be able to implement to prevent recurrence of such catastrophe."

Unaccustomed to a responsive audience, far less an appreciative one, Riopelle was speechless. Even though he forever longed for due professional recognition, he never foresaw it being ever granted by such happenstance. He was overwhelmingly surprised and flattered.

Léandre further buttered him up, stroking his ego and nationalistic pride.

"Allow me to stress that this is a unique opportunity to produce a landmark document that would make a historical contribution to the seismic safety of the nation. The 'Riopelle Report' will be referenced as one of the foundation stones of our seismically safe new country."

Léandre continued for a while, alluding to this legacy as a trigger to the intangible recognition showered on those that answer the imperatives of higher service. Yet, Riopelle didn't need to hear the rest. He succumbed to the charm of an eloquent orator who could sell bottled air, delighted to have been hooked and reeled in without much of a fight.

It was emphasized that, for agreeing to this assignment, Riopelle was bestowed the privilege of a dedicated office in the *Complexe H* (omitting the fact that it would be in a windowless, secluded part of the building), a powerful computer with word processing (without internet access), and a personal assistant (whose primary function was to ensure that he wouldn't leave the office unescorted). The conference call ended with Riopelle thrilled, convinced to be a VIP, unaware that he actually was a pariah.

With the thorny matter so dispensed, the leadership team returned its attention to the pressing matter of strategically planning the recovery to this disaster, first in physical, logistical terms to pick up the pieces and return society to normalcy, but also in political terms to prevent the federal government from using this event to torpedo the nationalistic aspirations of the Québec government.

While the leadership team conferred on strategic issues, brainstorming ideas in a rapid crossfire, a staffer whose primary duty so far had been to fuel the team with gallons of coffee felt compelled to interject with a well-intentioned suggestion—deluded by the belief that volunteering a bright, unsolicited idea was a sure way to climb the political echelons.

"It might be a good idea to call the army to help."

The intense chattering stopped abruptly. Cold stares converged on the staffer.

Like an angry mob ready to pummel the fool who accidentally pushed the needle off the turntable in a crowded disco because it generated a multi-thousand-watts scratching noise that pierced their eardrums and killed the dancing, Léandre's team was menacing. From the wrathful faces staring him down, the embarrassed staffer realized his hope for recognition and possible future promotion had just evaporated, but didn't understand why.

Léandre's friends and colleagues knew well the one word that should never be uttered in his presence, the one word that could at any moment instantly ignite his most passionate anger, the one word that would trigger his dithyrambic assault of the Canadian defense forces, a speech never delivered in public but oft forced on those who inadvertently dropped the dreaded word.

"The *army?*" shouted Léandre with fiery eyes.

A single word that triggered his distressed and resentful memories of October 1970, when a cowardly policeman, emboldened by the strength of an armed soldier and the War Measures Act, had broken into his home, without a warrant and without due cause, to arrest and incarcerate his older brother, a peaceful young man who happened to teach a political science course with a separatist bias, beating him into submission and dragging him into an army vehicle serving as a makeshift paddy wagon.

"What army? There are no military ground forces in Canada! There is only a *crisse de* bunch of pubescent boy scouts allowed to drive *des tabarnak de* 40-year-old trucks whose thick coat of green paint hides *des osties de* rust holes the size of your ass. What is this *sacrament de bâtard de* group of unemployable drop-outs and bureaucrats ever going to be able to do for Québec with their *viarge de* shovels and slingshots? With all their military might, they couldn't even defend *la Citadelle* for an *ostie d'*hour against an attack by a busload of Alzheimer's disease-afflicted geriatric pirates, unless it was rescued by its U.S. Big Brother. The Canadian Department of 'so-called' National Defence is an army all right: an army *de ciboire* of paper-pushing bureaucrats that is all brass and no *ostie de* soldiers. The 'forces' is so full of them, that the only bombs Canadian planes can drop are file cabinets full of reports that document the *calvaire de* various misconducts of its *crisse de* personnel, like the undisciplined outbreaks of sex-abuses and spurs of cruelty that excusably overtake those dispatched with blue UN helmets when they snap under stress and lose their *viarge de* tenuous grip on sanity when they discover, *baptême de* cruel reality of war, that they amount to nothing more than *des ti-culs de* target practice for the mercenary warlords and thugs of despotic regimes. You can hear the enemy scream in fear: 'Watch-out! Here comes the *osties de* Canadians! We're going to get squashed by these *osties de* file cabinets again!' *Saint-ciboire de crisse!* The last thing we need is *des sacrament d'*teenagers in khaki parading their *tabarnak d'*acne and Canadian flags in front of TV cameras, pretending to help the 'poor helpless Québécois who could not survive without the benevolence of the federal government.' No! As long as Québécois will have balls and deep convictions, their *crisse d'ostie de tabarnak de* convoys of rust-buckets will not sully our streets with their defiance. As long as there will remain one drop of warm blood in my veins, this bastard army *d'enfants de chiennes* will not trample our soil with its *crisse d'*arrogance."

There it was.

The terrorized staffer whose self-esteem was crushed to pulp didn't know how to react, but most in the room knew to just let it go, patiently waiting while the steam was released, listening anew to the harangue, memorized like a script, that Léandre loved to declaim. All members of Léandre's team wholeheartedly endorsed this philosophy, fully committed to it in spirit, but often expressing the same point of view using their own less polite words, and weren't alarmed by the outburst.

However, Julien felt the poor staffer had unknowingly raised a valid point in that the Québec government might have been, until now, too focused on mitigating the political damage. Twelve hours into the disaster, and Québec had yet to develop and implement an effective strategy to deal with response and recovery. Maintaining this course for too long would play into the hands of a federal government lurking for opportunities to claim ineptitude of the provincial government and justifiably send the army to deal with the situation.

Julien cleared his throat to break the tension, and volunteered: "I could not agree with you more, Léandre. However, this raises the issue that by this time tomorrow, all of the world's media will have converged to the island. Even with all the bridges down, they'll find their way in somehow. If our rescue and recovery operations are not in place and rolling by then, we will look like a banana republic. The feds will milk the negative news stories to their benefit, and further leverage this opportunity by feeding the international media all the lies and delusions it needs to quench its endless thirst for sensationalism. Forget the truth; they'll perpetuate the distorted and derisive portrayal of our inability to self-govern. They'll escalate the rhetoric and paint us like a bunch of drunk hillbillies completely disconnected from reality."

"Same old same old," said Léandre. "The *viarge de* suckers who jump in the arms of a *crisse de* sugar daddy will get what they deserve."

"If we rely on the federal government to bail us out, we are no better off, as our support for the referendum will go into free fall," added Réal. "It's the old 'Sovereignty-Association' story. People will never understand the difference between the two. We can explain till we are blue in the face that mutual aid between equal sovereign nations is normal and expected, it will go over people's head. This will be seen as dependency, promoted as such by the feds propagandists. We may never recover from it."

Réal's allusion to "equal sovereign nations" sparked a thought.

"That's an idea! What would Canada do if they needed to be bailed out after a disaster?" asked Julien, scanning the room to see if anybody could anticipate the punch line.

"Big Brother!" he said, hitting the table with his fist with uncharacteristic exuberance, proudly answering his own rhetorical question. "They would call south... just like a sovereign Québécois government would."

The overwhelming enthusiasm Julien expected was not forthcoming, but intense frowning and contorted facial expressions suggested that the idea was being dissected by the brain trust. Like a piece on a Rubik cube, it was studied from all sides and angles, spun and displaced around, successively juxtaposed along other ideas in search of a perfect alignment for which all pieces of the puzzle would match to produce the ideal solution.

"We don't have a direct line to the president. The U.S. embassy does not even maintain formal ties with us, at the bequest of the Canadian government," posed Léandre.

"We could call FEMA," suggested Julien.

Seeing some clueless gazes amid the group, he clarified, "That's the Federal Emergency Management Agency, the arm of the U.S. government tasked with disaster mitigation, preparedness, response and recovery planning. A logical argument could be made that FEMA has experience responding to earthquake disasters, an expertise the Canadian government clearly does not have."

"Having U.S. marines on our soil won't help us any more than having Canadian troops," replied Réal.

"No, no, we don't ask for troops," clarified Julien. "Let's argue for now that our police forces can handle emergency response on the field. After all, they're called *Sûreté du Québec*, and report to the *Ministère de la Sécurité Publique*, so their name embodies their mandate to take care of security. They'll feel important and will appreciate our vote of confidence in their capabilities. Considering our substantial investments in the salaries and equipment of the police force, at times possibly more than the feds invest in their armed forces, they are likely to super-achieve—if only to justify those investments and be in a position of strength when entering negotiations for the next collective agreement. Incidentally, before then, in the forthcoming referendum, our show of trust and goodwill today could translate into solid votes through a valuable endorsement by their union."

"So, we have the security forces and first responders," asked Réal. "What do we need?"

"What we really want from the U.S. at this time, though, is humanitarian assistance, things that do not threaten our sovereignty, but that show we can easily do without Canada in such crises."

"Seems to me it's only poor despondent countries that seek and receive international aid following earthquakes," questioned Réal.

"Not true. I remember sending a check to the Red Cross to help Japan after their earthquake in the 1990s—mostly because I didn't want to contribute to the special fund put in place by the Canadian government. TV coverage was intensive and I recall that Japan received help from all over the world back then. That certainly did not threaten their identity as a nation," added Julien.

"They may have received containers full of emergency supplies, but I remember one of the big stories then was that emergency responders had a hard time getting into the country as the Japanese felt they did not need anybody's help to conduct their recovery activities," questioned Léandre. "They even quarantined the search dogs of international search and rescue teams, effectively rendering the teams useless."

"Sorry, my long-term memory isn't that sharp. But most people don't know this, or won't bother with such subtle differences anyhow. The fact that Japan got the supplies is all that matters," countered Julien. "The rest, if it's true, was Japan's own decision. It's easy to spin our way."

"So what do we request from FEMA?" asked Réal.

"Everybody will find some ways to keep warm for a while, running car heaters, fireplaces, basement wood stoves—whatever works," answered Léandre. "Until they run out of gas or wood supply. When that happens, people will go to shelters, waiting for power to return. These are the school gymnasiums and other large public spaces where back-up generators are operating, right? So they have space, but no facility to host all of these people for an extended period. We need cots, blankets, dry food, that kind of stuff. Would a million units be a reasonable estimate?"

Montréal, 1:30 p.m.

Except for a few weeks during which the entire office had been jolted by the whirlwind of his destructive outrage to be forced into retirement, Lise Letarte's predecessor had been a calm, unassuming bureaucrat for the length of his tenure. His leadership philosophy in guarding the outpost—for lack of a work ethic—had rested on three fundamental axioms: limiting disruption to the order of established systems; delegating all and everything to subordinates who presumably knew what to do and how to do it; and continuously praising the staff for its support, essentially performing his work. This management strategy afforded him plenty of time to read and reflect on organizational structures, inter-agency relationships, and mission agency mandates, and to use that knowledge for "networking" to establish professional relationships. He so intensely enjoyed and practiced the latter activity, that his staff had come to freely associate "my boss is networking" with "my boss is not working."

Given the inescapable compromise that to enjoy life one must waste part of it earning a living, there was no better outcome than this relaxed and delightful position. It was the agony of losing it that had fueled his stormy anger for the better part of a week during which he spilled his bitterness to the media, publicly discrediting a successor whose qualifications he did not know but alleged to be incompetent, in hopes of sparking a controversy and getting his job back. After a government's spokesperson dismissed these harsh words as unfounded misogynist accusations, the whole affair fizzled out at once. Facing this failure, and the irremediable fatality of his impending forced retirement, he had returned to his more composed nature, and reflected on his legacy. All those days invested in developing policies, white papers, recommendations, implementation briefs, could not come to naught. In spite of the abominable closure on this chapter of his life, and of his successor being a "despicable political appointee," he concluded that to preserve his body of work for posterity—and for the betterment of the nation—Lise was entitled to inherit the benefit of his wisdom.

As such, on his last day before retirement, while still feigning anger in public to save face, he carefully selected a number of documents that outlined the duties and responsibilities of the organization, as well as its place within the government hierarchy, and left them in a neat pile on his desk, diligently sorted so that the documents could be logically read from first to last, and also in relation to their significance. He penned a short welcoming note, taped it to the top of the pile, switched off the light, and left, as satisfied as a librarian would be that all was left properly organized and stacked, and pretending to be thrilled that he would never, ever have to be stuck twice a day in rush hour for the punishing privilege of having no harder labor than shuffling paper and pretending to work to receive a paycheck. And on he went, disappearing forever in Florida, at peace with his civil servant legacy, yet determined that his allegiance to the province could never be resurrected.

Upon first entering her office after being appointed as head of the *Organisation de sécurité civile du Québec*, Lise had sat in the executive chair, leaned back, put her feet on the desk, and reveled in the empowering rush. She surveyed the room, its walls, its paintings, its carpet, its furniture, and the neat stack of reports next to her feet. Without reading a line of it, Lise diligently moved and stored that pile of document into a file cabinet for future reference, and embarked on her first self-appointed mission: restructuring the office—an extensive reorganization, although not one concerned with the reassignment of personnel duties and the moving of names on an organization chart, but rather one focused on the remodeling of her executive office.

She invested her efforts in the selection of expensive furniture and wall coverings, but quickly realized that the existing floor layout and architectural constraints would not allow the construction of a private bathroom and shower directly connected to her office—not a practical necessity, given the clean public restrooms conveniently located adjacent to the elevators, but certainly one of stature. She thus undertook a bureaucratic battle to secure the funding to justify an expansion by acquisition of additional floor space on the above story to which her personal office would be moved and redesigned to provide the prestige and amenities she assessed herself to rightfully deserve.

She won a partial victory by getting the extra floor space, and lavish office, but the private amenities were vetoed by an anonymous accountant charged to disallow frivolous expenses that could catch the eye of the auditor general and end up embarrassing the current administration. She huffed and screamed, threatened the

---

"despicable" accountant, machinated ways to have him fired, and waged unremitting psychological terrorism to reverse the accountant's ruling, but to no avail.

She resigned herself to the compromise of new floor space without the ceramic throne and accessories, crabby, but nonetheless confident that a new request submitted in a subsequent fiscal year could be successful given that governmental agencies have no institutional memory. Failing that, she anticipated that some amounts could be carved yearly from her operating budget and saved in special accounts, hidden below the radar range of stuffy accountants, and used to advance her construction projects in small, incremental steps.

In the meantime, the expansion project (amputated of amenities) briskly moved forward and consumed her entire energies for the first few months of her tenure, until the day she finally took possession of her new palatial office. In an inaugural mood, with a great sense of accomplishment, she sat in the plush, deluxe leather ergonomic executive chair, leaned back, put her feet on the mahogany desk, and savored the sumptuous decor at last commensurate with her new dominion. While she surveyed the room, its marble and glass panel walls, its glamorous art, its hardwood flooring, and its signature furniture, unencumbered of reports or paperwork, she watched the information technology specialist hook her new top-of-the-line computer into the internet. IP addresses, DNS, subnet masks, WINS server, and other cryptic communication protocols shook hands, magically christening her cyberidentity.

From that moment onward, the fulfilling backlog of email and requests drove her daily routine, the message-carrying streaming bytes giving a purpose to the job, with the constant flow of new information drowning that contained in file cabinets and unpacked boxes of documents stacked in a closet after the move from her old office one floor below. Whatever she needed to know about the chain of command and inter-agency relationships, she was confident that it could be eventually inferred from the email trail, mapping the virtual links forged by the recipients on the "To," "From," and "Cc" headers. Besides, most requests to her office pertained to paperwork duties that could reliably be dispatched to staffers whose tenure in the office had outlasted multiple changes of furniture, and familiar with the quirks of miscellaneous cryptic forms, obscure procedures, and arcane regulations. This arm's length approach to operations provided her with ample time to represent the organization at various venues, the highest priority given to conferences on disaster-response management held in exotic locations, where she would read slides prepared by staffers and provide evasive answers to questions, or declining to answer, claiming duty to honor the inviolable veil of secrecy drawn on matters of national security as a convenient shield to hide her ignorance.

Those were the good days.

Now, Lise, pen in hand, was staring at her yellow legal pad, still blank, awaiting the bullets enunciating the strategic steps of her action plan, a plan that had to be ready before the Prime Minister and his cohorts landed on her roof. Something better than the meaningless and useless disaster-response plan from the manilla folder found in the file cabinets a few hours earlier.

She was exasperated and frustrated that, more than half a day into the emergency response phase, no other staff had reported to work other than the lone technician. She was incensed by such a blatant lack of professionalism, unaware that her entire staff, paid barely above minimum wage, could only afford housing for their young families on the south shore of the St-Lawrence river, a long commute away from the now-inaccessible island.

The cyber-world was of no help either. Her internet browser shouted "HTTP/1.1 500 Server Error" in bold large font, depriving her of the ability to locate any of the documents she felt she could confidently "google" under normal circumstances.

Only then, racking her brain for clues on where else the precious information could be stored, in a bedazzling flash of serendipity sparking like a short-circuit across parallel universes, did she remember the mountain of paper that welcomed her in her old substandard office on the first day of her reign. Maybe the precious information she needed was available, logically organized in that neat stack of documents stashed in one of the boxes hidden in her closet.

Latching onto the hope that one of those documents had to be relevant, she spent hours unpacking boxes. Although immune to stress as a result of her obliviousness to the pain of others and her brash cockiness, she spilled the contents of every box on her office's floor, intensely sifting through for the golden nugget that would duly empower her to drive all agencies into a highly coordinated and effective response under her stewardship—not for the satisfaction of exerting power over other various agencies, but rather for the enormous possible political benefits that would ensue from the considerable media exposure she anticipated from such an activity.

The hand-written note from her predecessor slipped from a stack of documents crashing on the floor. She could not quite determine which of the documents were part of the original pile, but she randomly perused a few of them.

A first document provided a list of major disasters that struck the Province of Québec in the late 20th century. Lise remembered all these events, like eerie milestones that strangely connect one's life to tragedies covered by the news, but only as a spectator to parallel, disturbed universes—at best mirages of remote events marking time as the world collectively navigates through its journey.

She read the list like a familiar history book, already knowing the end of each chapter, the outcome of each event:

The 1984 shooting at the National Assembly in Québec City, when a deranged corporal from the Canadian armed forces, dressed in combat fatigues, entered the parliament building intent on killing the Prime Minister and other members of his separatist party, but, arriving hours before the parliamentary committee had convened, resorted instead to randomly killing a few simple employees—Lise always considered military types to be nuts by definition;

A small, magnitude 5.9 earthquake that struck in the middle of a national park close to Chicoutimi, alarming the wildlife there but also damaging a number of weak masonry structures up to hundreds of miles away—Lise believed owners of shabbily constructed buildings get what they deserve;

A fire in a warehouse storing PCB's in Saint-Basile-Le-Grand, resulting in the evacuation of angry citizens living along the path of the toxic cloud—Lise thought only fools would live next to ticking environmental time bombs;

A toxic spill following a train derailment in Saint-Léonard d'Aston—another type of environmental time bomb to Lise;

The massacre of 14 women engineering students at the *École Polytechnique* in Montréal at the hands of an anti-feminist psychotic gunman—Lise dreamt of hanging all male chauvinists by their balls until death;

Millions of tires burning for days in St. Amble, transforming a mountain of rubber into a cloud of dangerous pollutants—Lise thought living next to a dump was just as stupid as living in one;

A First nations crisis in Oka and Châteauguay that pitted Mohawks in a standoff against the Canadian forces for more than two months—Lise harbored racist sentiments toward the natives and had no sympathy for their claims;

A small tornado, of intensity F3 on the Fujita scale, destroying 90 homes in 27 seconds of terror in Maskinongé—Lise was skeptical, suspecting that exaggerated damage was reported as a scheme to fleece insurance companies;

Some forest fires—Lise wondered why these were considered disasters since wood is made to burn after all;

The Saguenay flash floods of 1996 that overtopped levees and leveled an entire neighborhood—Lise considered living downstream of a levee to be sheer insanity—and;

A massive ice storm hitting Montréal in 1998 that disabled the entire power grid, an unlucky few being left without electricity for over a month—Lise, then without power for an entire week, deemed this critical infrastructure failure totally unacceptable.

The report noted that the latter two events respectively affected 16,000 people, and 1,300,000 people, although to quite variable degrees.

It was puzzling to Lise that this list lumped a colossal ice storm that required 450 shelters together with more pedestrian disasters such as a madman taking hostage members of the National Assembly. Given its inclusion of so many mundane events, she wondered why the list did not also include the concrete beam that unexpectedly fell by itself from the Olympic stadium structure, or the bridges everywhere that suddenly collapsed just under regular traffic conditions—wondering whether crashes due to the wear and tear of shoddy construction weren't considered disasters for political reasons. Following that thought, she deduced that if the city's infrastructure was so decrepit that it crumbled on its own from disrepair alone, then the damage induced by the recent earthquake had to be quite substantial, far more than she could notice on her way to the office.

Reading a different report, Lise discovered that the last two disasters—the flood and the ice storm—led to a reform of the civil protection system in Québec, through the Civil Protection Act. She learned that the act formalized the hierarchy and distribution of responsibilities between citizens, municipalities and the government of Québec. She made a bullet list summarizing key points from the legalese-heavy treatise. In the act:

The citizen was defined as being the first person responsible for his or her own safety—as if legislation was required to state the obvious, sighed Lise;

The municipality was tasked to provide additional support in a disaster situation, and it could in turn rely on the support of government resources, as needed—likely to happen all the time if dollars are involved, she thought;

Each municipality was required to formulate a plan to be approved by the government—which likely resulted in the kind of well-intentioned but useless paperwork and phone lists that she'd unearthed from her files earlier in the day.

She also noted that, according to the act, local authorities had the power to declare a state of emergency, and the role of the provincial government was limited to setting policies to reduce risks or mitigate the consequences of a potential disaster, or to provide effective disaster response and recovery operations. However, if local authorities were unable or failed to declare a state of emergency in a major disaster situation, the government could assume that responsibility, and order implementation of the emergency response or recovery measures provided for in Québec's National Civil Protection Plan.

She circled with a highlighter the stated goals and scope of the law, that the plan was intended to provide support to local groups or government departments and government bodies when a major disaster exceeds their capacity for action in the areas under their jurisdiction, with respect to either risk mitigation, response or recovery. The plan also provided for financial assistance programs, the government having the option to set eligibility requirements, as well as scales and terms and conditions of payments on a case-by-case basis.

As such, in disaster conditions, the plan gave the government the opportunity to provide compensation for the extra housing, food and clothing costs incurred by victims during the event or the recovery period (which could be achieved by providing shelters), and compensation for the extra costs incurred by local authorities in carrying out emergency response or recovery operations. It also provided the government with the option to dole out financial assistance with great largesse for the repair of damage caused to: any principal residence or essential belongings of its occupants; any property essential to a business or essential to the livelihood of a person or that person's family; any facilities of a nonprofit organization that were useful to the community and readily accessible to the public (except facilities used exclusively for recreational purposes); any property essential to a local or regional authority, an intermunicipal board or a civil protection authority; and any vital installations, such as transport, telecommunications, power generation and distribution, water supply systems, and systems used by the police, firemen, civil protection services, and government services responsible for public security and human health and welfare. Lise envisioned the length of that grocery bill and laughed—as if a government would wittingly bankrupt itself to fulfill silly promises.

A call-out box highlighted a passage of legislation stating that the role of the *Organisation de sécurité civile du Québec* was to plan civil protection measures for the entire province and, when a major disaster occurred, to coordinate the operations to be carried out by each mission director specified in the Québec's National Civil Protection Plan—Lise assumed that, for the case of earthquake, the plan might have amounted to no more than the contact list in the damn manilla folder.

Reviewing the information on the legal framework of disaster response proved useful in helping Lise identify a few avenues to deflect blame in many possible directions. Foremost, by law, prime responsibility for preparedness and mitigation fell on the shoulders of local authorities, and lack of preparedness and mitigation was certainly at the root of the current disaster. Given that most municipalities struggled to reduce accumulated deficits—some tethering on the brink of insolvency—without further increasing municipal taxes, the pressures to meet the daily maintenance and operation needs in times of insufficient financial resources pretty much ensured that fixing potholes and conducting tasks with immediate benefits and high visibility would be allocated the highest priority, sucking their budget dry before any attention could be devoted to the development of protection plans, guaranteeing that mitigation would never occur. At the very best, in wealthy cities and townships, some funds could be allocated for preparedness activities to generate thick stacks of paper and hold a few drills choreographed under ideal conditions. In addition to faulting the local authorities, Lise appreciated that blame could also be deflected upward, since the *Organisation* fell under the *Ministère de la Sécurité Publique*, an agency essentially focused on law enforcement. The broad portfolio it had to manage, including police and private security, fire, detention and rehabilitation, police ethics, gambling equipment certification, and many other departments, effectively ensured that civil protection matters pertaining to natural disasters got little attention when competing for resources. Lise envisioned that, in light of all these mandates competing for limited resources, when the ministry's decision-makers argued on how to cut the financial pie, those favoring investment into policing work above all other interests needed only rhetorically ask how much more crime would citizens tolerate to achieve a slight increase in protection against natural disasters—given the professional inclination of those at the table, civil protection was sure to be left with crumbs. However, Lise recognized that deflecting blame upward could be unwise, since she had been directly appointed in her position by the Minister of Public Security.

While Lise was pondering her miscellaneous options on how to escape accountability, her technician diligently responded to Léandre's executive order by prepping the state-of-the-art press room, climbing to the roof to realign the satellite dish and inspecting the integrity of the helicopter landing pad to the best of his limited ability, essentially ensuring that none of the steel members supporting the platform were bent or fractured. He randomly checked if bolts were tight (thinking that a fractured bolt might be easy to dislodge by hand) and that none were missing (assuming a hole without its bolt would be conspicuous). Realignment of the dish was more challenging, as axles and sliders in the mechanism supporting its steel post had been distorted by the severe shaking experience at the top of the building during the earthquake. Even though the high-rise itself showed no signs of structural damage, seismic waves propagating from the ground up the building had evidently, like a whiplash, brutally jerked the rooftop equipment.

Using a combination of crowbar, blowtorch, hammer, and duct tape, he managed to force it to a position that provided an acceptable signal level.

He was still working on the roof and thus unable to respond when a call from one of Léandre's staffers came on the C.B. radio. Lise, upset that her sole available technician had apparently failed in his duty to man the emergency control room, perused the switches and labels on the radio front panel and correctly guessed the rudimentary principles to operate the device.

She answered by identifying herself as head of the agency, as if her title should inspire respect from the caller.

Unimpressed, the staffer pressed on with his requests.

"We have a list of the key journalists that have confirmed they will attend Léandre's briefing tomorrow morning, as well as a protocol agenda for the event. We also would like to confirm that the media room and landing pad will be operational."

"I told you earlier that we have been very severely affected by the earthquake here. We will tell you when we are ready to entertain such a request," responded Lise.

Léandre's staffer had been briefed on Lise's belligerent attitude, and snapped back as instructed, "Let me be clear. This is a non-negotiable position. In addition, Léandre also requests that you provide to all media a list of available shelters in time for the 6 p.m. news."

Unintimidated, to assert her authority while faking respect for the chain of command, she dryly retorted, "We are operating in emergency conditions here, with no support staff and the full responsibility to coordinate the response of all agencies in accordance to the National Civil Protection Plan. You have to set the priorities here, as to whether the list of shelters or the media briefing is more important at this time."

The staffer recognized this ploy to force answering with a choice, to acknowledge that failure to meet one of the two goals was acceptable right from the onset. He didn't take the bait.

"They both have to be done. Léandre expects no less. He intends to name the chair of a National Task Force for Disaster Recovery during tomorrow's briefing, and he wants the *Organisation de sécurité civile du Québec* to issue key needed emergency response information today to ensure that the press will not attempt to highjack the briefing agenda. Having the room ready to broadcast is essential, just as is the list of shelters."

Strangely, some of those words just didn't register, forever vanishing, while other words excited to a frenzy a select group of neurons in Lise's brain; the compounded cerebral mix triggering odd behaviors. As a result, Lise remained firm and uncooperative, somehow felt vindicated in her strategy, and yet entertained the delusion that Léandre was planning to name her chair of the Task Force on Disaster Recovery. The electrical charges that wildly pulse through synapses can work in mysterious ways, and no conceptual scientific model could rationalize the semi-logical process that had just brewed out of this impenetrable neural network.

Washington, 1:45 p.m.

Bill Treegherapy's eyes did not loosen their grip from the computer monitor. Nor did they need to, as his secretary's shy coughing and limp door-knocking were his calling card, distinguishing features he bore like an annoying trademark. Bill's disdain for his effeminate assistant was so intense that he never bothered to remember his name—in his mind, it was just "Basketcase Wuss." More a clerk than a secretary, more a paper-shuffler than a private secretary, always a pen pusher, never an executive secretary—and, worse, one with no military training whatsoever.

Bill's office was cluttered with reports never read in boxes never opened, stacked on shelves that hid all walls, sparing one window with a view on the National Mall where only peaceful battles were ever waged—wimpy wars of words, without guns, thus devoid of interest to Bill. To him, the vast rectangular expanse of grass was a boring and meaningless garden, the wet dream of a disgraced temperamental 18th-century foreign urban designer rescued from obscurity in the 20th century by senators, nobles, and bureaucrats eager to beautify an uncharacteristically drab national capital. To him, it was aptly named, as he found it no more inspiring than a shopping mall. Square and neat, it was the appropriate metaphor for a city busy writing unread policy reports that collected dust on library shelves. Bill, once a man of action, now lived a life chained to a computer screen, adding to the mountain of paper generated by the federal government.

Unanswered the first time, the shy coughing and limp door-knocking resumed.

"What now?" asked Bill, still a captive of his computer monitor.

Answering the invitation, Basketcase looped around the ajar door, avoiding contact like a limbo dancer squeezing under a stick, as if it would minimize the disturbance from his intrusion.

"Sir, we have received a special request for assistance from Quebec, sir."

"Kwebek?"

"The Canadian province, sir."

Treegherapy freed himself from his monitor, swiveled his chair around, and frowned while looking at Wuss straight in the eyes, knowing it would intimidate him.

"Why would the Canadian government request assistance from the Federal Emergency Management Agency?" asked Bill with the authority of a congressional inquiry.

"It's not the Canadian government, sir, it's the Quebec government who's making a request, sir."

Treegherapy looked at the large map of the United States pinned on the back of his door and perused the beige nondescript territories clustered along its northern border, searching for any edifying annotations qualifying what lied above the colorful states of immediate national interest. In vain.

"What do they want anyhow?"

"They specifically requested bunk beds, and blankets, sir. As many as possible, sir. Apparently possibly as much as a million, sir."

"A million?"

"Apparently on loan only, sir."

"Jesus Christ! What the..."

Treegherapy shuffled paper on his desk looking for an official release or morning memo reporting a possible national emergency in Canada. No luck. He banged a few keystrokes on his computer searching for an equivalent email notification.

"Sir, the Department of Homeland Security's Office of Cyberinfrastructure Protection has suspended internet external links and email communications beyond the intranet today, sir, awaiting a resolution to the 'I-8-US' worm attack threat."

Treegherapy had accepted the curse of upper administration in exchange for better remuneration to please his wife, but ever since, deeply resented that sellout. He hated the futile pressure of producing thick boring reports, for audiences that barely read them. He hated spending days editing the impractical proposals of dumb public policy wonks who never went on field missions. He hated the job that turned him into an office peg and effectively isolated him from all the "action" at ground level.

Sensing his boss in dire need of a briefing, Basketcase volunteered some information in a carefully structured sentence not threatening to reveal Bill's ignorance.

"As you know, sir, we do not have accurate information on the extent of this morning's earthquake in Canada, other than it was located near Montreal, and probably of Magnitude 7."

Treegherapy glanced again at the map, if only to remind himself of its uselessness beyond the confines of national boundaries.

"No reliable communications have been received to date from our consulate in Canada, sir."

"How close to Montreal is Toronto?"

"Uh, sir, Toronto is roughly 400 miles from Montreal, sir. Your concern for this central nerve of the Canadian economy is most appropriate, sir, but it is fair to assume that at such a distance from the epicenter, they probably suffered little from this earthquake. On the other hand, our consulate in the National Capital of Canada could have suffered, sir, since Ottawa is only roughly 250 miles from Montreal, sir."

Basketcase's veiled geography lessons did not please Treegherapy. "Decision-making skills are promoted, not encyclopedic mastery of trivial information on neighboring countries," thought Treegherapy. His innate urge to make impulsive decisions and give orders took over.

"Call the jokers at NSA, CIA, FBI and State Department, and tell them that I want their experts on Kwebek on the line at 16:00 hours. Tell them to scrounge around their basements for the best they can find. Tell them I don't care about commerce statistics or tourism information. Also stress that I don't give a damn about how many Muslim teenagers are reading bomb recipes on the internet in hopes of blowing themselves up for the paradisiacal reward of 72 virgins—'cause that's all that seems to matter to agencies nowadays, and they'll send me busloads of those experts. Tell them I want someone that can provide historical and political substance. In the meantime, I'll warn the FEMA director to check with the White House on the availability of the President. The 'big guy' might need to get involved in answering such an international request for assistance."

Longueuil, 2:00 p.m.

Still awaiting any useful information out of the *Organisation de sécurité civile du Québec*, and given that all accesses to the island were impracticable, Léandre and his staff decided it would be prudent leadership to declare Montréal a "closed city." The official communique dispatched to broadcasting agencies across the country's "open cities" would only emphasize to everyone that they should avoid unnecessary and futile attempts to reach the island, and declared the airspace above the city a no-fly zone, to preclude interfering with emergency response and recovery operations.

The rest was implicit. Bridges closed. Airports closed. Subway closed. Grocery stores closed. Pharmacies closed. Garages, gas stations and repair shops closed. Plumber and electrician services closed. Dentist and chiropractor offices closed. Stores and businesses closed. Grade schools, high schools, CEGEPs, universities closed. Government offices closed. Warmth and cozy homes closed. Happiness closed.

More than a mere statement of facts, it was a proclamation on the world stage that one of the peaceful and highly organized civilizations, a member of the high society of prosperous nations, had incurred a disaster that would possibly result in hardship significantly exceeding the level of suffering customary deemed acceptable by those few nations that basked in the luxuries of this technological age. It was a signal that this earthquake had not buried 100 million despondent peasants in their collapsed mud homes, but had rather clipped one node from the global network of critical interconnections—a small tear in the modern economic fabric that could rip through in unknown and uncontrollable ways and possibly destabilize the precarious financial equilibrium at the foundation of many institutions. It was a warning that some key links of the planet's interdependent supply chains were broken, and that, like toppling dominos, the shockwaves of these failures would ripple across the world.

Deadlines would be grossly missed, suppliers would not deliver. No computer generated animations for Hollywood; no video game releases for Silicon Valley; no subway cars for New York; no electronic components for Texas; no luxury furniture for Chicago; no car components for Detroit; no turboprops for Brazil. Unanticipated sudden interruptions in the flow of goods, cascading worldwide, slowing or stopping operations, generating losses and economical damage thousands of miles away from the epicenter.

This dire announcement was intended to put Québec on the front page of every newspaper of the industrialized world, on the scrolling news ticker of every television channel, and at the top of millions of web pages. The ultimate goal was not to provide propagandist visibility for the nation, but rather officially acknowledge and underscore the gravity of the situation to elicit the solidarity of co-citizens of the modern connected world. A subtle mea culpa to remind other advanced nations that shared similar exposure to potentially devastating hazards and similar lack of preparedness, that the next large-scale disaster could be in their own backyard. A symbolic expression of a painful reality to prime the sympathies of allies toward possible subsequent necessary targeted calls for assistance.

Québec City, 2:45 p.m.

He couldn't care less.

Assaulting him as he paid for his cigarettes, piled on the counter next to the cash register, the special edition of the *Journal de Québec* blasted "Montréal in Ruins" in tall red letters fit to its tabloid format, to fill the space in absence of pictures or substance. Clearly a revised cover shoddily slapped atop the earlier morning edition in a rushed effort to sell more papers, proposing to fill an information void with speculative opinions devoid of usefulness.

"So what?" he thought.

He woke up late, hung over from an evening of web surfing, one pathetic drink after another, hopping from one social networking website to another in search of cyber-relationships, possibly cyber-sex, definitely not cyber-romance. He wore his unkempt appearance—wrinkled shirttail partly hanging out of torn jeans, mismatched socks, disheveled hair, a three-day beard, and a cigarette parked atop his ear—as a revolt against his privileged background, higher education, and cushy, nondescript job as a civil servant not serving any specific purpose; as a living tease to dare challenge the rights conferred by the powerful union of government employees.

"They apparently got hit real hard," said the cashier, trying to capitalize on his glance at the headlines.

He took his change back, and grunted out some unintelligible words in a gruff voice. He couldn't care less, and wasn't about to buy a copy of a newspaper he deeply despised. So what if Montréal was burning, sinking, flooding, crumbling, dying, or whatever else. He'd never liked Montréal anyhow. He had his own problems.

One life—his—was plenty to manage. Nobody cared when he smashed his toe on the corner of the bed to start the day on a good note. Nobody cared that it took him an hour to find a parking space. Nobody cared that his grocery bag ripped open and spilled.

Certainly, nobody cared about his cum laude diploma in sexology, nor about his contemptible job unrelated to that expertise. Nobody cared that he blew up taxpayers' money, sitting in a corner, pretending to reflect on some complex and deep problems, sometimes falling asleep in the process.

That's life. "Just suck it up and shut up" was his universally applicable motto.

Montréal in ruins was not his problem. He hated the pompous metropolis, its cold, morose, decrepit infrastructure of concrete abuses, its infinite boasts of hockey supremacy clinging to distant irrelevant glories, its arrogant pretension to be the navel of the world, its snub for Québec City and contempt for the rest of a province it considered medieval, its determination to first address customers in English, its encroaching hordes of immigrants who subtly disdained Québec's French roots and culture, and its increasing willingness to trample hard-acquired freedoms to accommodate an ever-expanding list of multicultural sensitivities.

A disaster in Montréal had no impact whatsoever on him, just like it had no bearing on those around him, all busy running errands as slaves answering to the always-urgent demands from a multiplicity of insatiable masters. Too busy to care.

Except for those with relatives or loved ones potentially victimized by the disaster, it was only a distant crisis. A distant crisis to distant neighbors. In the absence of an emotional bond, no cries of distress mattered. The greater the distance, the greater the detachment—be it a distance in miles, from Québec City, to Toronto, to Vancouver, to New York, to Los Angeles, to Paris, to Tokyo, or Johannesburg, or a distance in humanity, from the senses to the brain, to the heart, or to the soul.

He, for one, lived far, far away. He would not feel pain if they all died. He recognized it as a fact of life, and righteously held this blunt truth as the only sincere emotion one could avow. The rest was contemptible hypocrisy: the sympathetic wailing of social covenants to feign grief and compassion toward strangers for a few days; the purporting altruistic generous donations conveniently over-assessed for tax-credit purposes; the elusive timespan during which an obsessive and perverse curiosity towards the misfortune of others was mistaken for solicitude. All soon forgotten as the routine of daily life retook control, recapturing all attention and emotions for selfish purposes and sensible endeavors—shoveling snow from the driveway, grocery shopping, washing dishes, doing the laundry, repairing the car, paying the bills, epilating legs and clipping nails.

This was his perspective on the nature of humanity, proven true countless times by virtue of actual human behavior. The pain felt by unpierced and unscathed skin, like the loss felt by an uncommitted heart, was a superficial and imaginary construct that could only engender tears destined to evaporate like a morning dew of unjustified sorrows. Against a millennium of literature praising the higher virtues of humanity, a millennium of natural and human-made catastrophes underscored an absolute disconnectedness and inhumanity, an inability of mankind to reach beyond its immediate narrow connections, an all-encompassing focus on intimate relationships comfortable in complete ignorance of anything significant in a global perspective.

Acknowledging the political incorrectness of what he considered to be inalienable truths, this philosophy was condemned to remain unstated. Notwithstanding, he was determined to live abiding to his honest beliefs and feelings, not "caving in to the bullshit" of misplaced emotionality.

Besides, today was his day off. An entire day to relax and clear his mind from the frustration of being a sexologist forcefitted into a meaningless bureaucrat job. An entire day to the pursuit of entertainment and the miscellaneous pleasures of life, and it was not to be wasted by the misfortunes of strangers. Only after a fulfilling good day of rest and leisure would he report to duty at the Québec City district office of the *Organisation de sécurité civile du Québec.*

Montréal, 3:00 p.m.

While her technician was busy completing work to ensure that the press-room and helicopter pad would be ready for the morning visitors, Lise focused on setting up the list of emergency disaster shelters. A well-structured list culled from a database and formatted using the latest word processor was surely engraved into a magnetic medium as a string of bits set to zero or one, somewhere in the local computer server of the *Organisation de sécurité civile du Québec*, along with all the other precious critical data that needed to be protected and available following a disaster. In accordance with the standards of care for every respectable emergency response agency, that server was secured against toppling, sliding, or other damaging effects. It was elevated from the ground, to protect it from accidental kicks, and the *Organization* staff had located it in a special metal enclosure to protect it from other damaging impacts, with vents at the top to prevent it from overheating.

The *Organisation*'s technology experts recognized that, in a pernicious way, life is fraught with hazards that can attack the physical and cyber infrastructure in multiple ways, and that the strategies to defend against these onslaughts may conflict with one another. In this multi-hazard arena, strategies and devices implemented to protect against one hazard may create conditions that clash against the needs dictated to protect against another hazard, and vice versa. Some of these specially trained experts even knew that elevating the first floor of a building, to reduce its risk of being flooded, made it more susceptible to overturning or collapse during an earthquake, and that replacing heavy masonry facades and partitions by lighter ones to reduce undesirable seismically-generated inertia forces made the building cladding more vulnerable to debris impact during hurricanes. However, this knowledge was of little benefit as they rarely were afforded the opportunity to review design concepts for new physical infrastructure—the agency always rented space in existing buildings. At best, they conducted audits of premises, seeking to identify all the potential problems and to reach the best possible compromises, aware that unless all hazards and their potential consequences were holistically addressed from the onset, competing priorities aligned to reflect the biases of their constituency when facing conflicting demands that couldn't be simultaneously satisfied. Given that the hazards having the highest perceived probability of occurrence always received preferential consideration over the more esoteric hazards that few expected to see within their lifetime, their task was to buck this human tendency, think beyond the obvious, and impose physical changes as necessary to make the infrastructure more resilient to a wide range of hazards.

Prior to moving into their new headquarters offices, the *Organization*'s information technology experts requested that the sprinkler system in the designated server room be de-activated, and the building owner confirmed that he was pleased to oblige. This reassurance, however, was an empty promise to alleviate the fears of the new tenant. The owner had no intention of putting his property at risk by partly disabling the fire protection system and possibly being fined or sued for a building code violation. The deceit could have remained unrevealed forever without the earthquake. During the severe shaking, tiles from the suspended ceiling system that swayed violently impacted and broke the sprinkler head just above the server. This triggered a shower that not only flooded the computer room and part of the surrounding offices on that lower floor, but also filled the server's nice metallic enclosure to the rim with water oozing through the vents of its top cover, drowning the badly needed zeros and ones beyond recovery.

Lise's technician was convinced he could figure out a way to extract the inestimably valuable stream of data from the dead hard-drive, but at a considerable investment of time and effort. Lise was more pragmatic. Contemplating her options, she envisioned two possible short-term solutions. First, she was convinced that a printed version of the list of disaster shelters probably existed in one of the boxes stacked in her office, but an archeological expedition into a mountain of manilla folders was most unappealing. It was also risky, as the search could be futile, failing to provide results by the stated deadline. The second and more expeditious approach was to regenerate the list from scratch.

"After all," she thought, "how hard can it be to construct a dumb list of public facilities that have lots of space and the ability to serve cafeteria-style meals?"

She pulled the phone book from the shelf, and started to make a list of high schools and hospitals. A list was a list.

As she was handwriting the list, Lise provided her own assessment of the institutions she reviewed, on the basis of her past experience and biases growing up in the city. Empowered like a critique on assignment for a travel guide and dispensing the precious stars that reward or destroy reputations, scheming to reward or deprive friends and foes of government assistance dollars per her subjective evaluation scheme, she excluded from the list all private schools catering to snob kids that had once antagonized her, and those hospitals where she'd received bad service in the past. The institutions where her few close acquaintances—in absence of friends—worked rose to the top of the list. This careful screening of all entries in the yellow pages required careful deliberations that slowed down the process, but she was confident the greater quality of the resulting product justified her meticulous approach.

Ottawa, 3:15 p.m.

Graham Murdoch was worried by the hard-line stance of his Premier. Brendon Decker could commit political suicide if he so wished, and Graham wouldn't shed a tear watching the self-destruction, but if the money that kept the party flush were to dry up, it would hamper his own climb up the power ladder. All those years at Queens learning how to schmooze the aristocrats and influentials of the establishment, all those years in the lower rungs of the party building a network of strategic connections, all those years buttering up to powerful deputy ministers to earn his entry in the select club of invited running candidates, all those years campaigning, crisscrossing his district to propagandize the party's program and profess genuine compassion and commitment for his constituency; all those blood, sweat and tears invested in the party would go to waste if the party contributors that he had himself harvested, upset with the actions of the government, were to discontinue their generous financial support of the party. The blame for this flight of allegiance and capital under his responsibility would fall on his shoulders, severely diminishing his influence and curtailing his ambitions.

Graham thus undertook to spend a few hours taking the pulse of key donors across the country—old money and new money alike.

The ancestors of Buckminster Winston Axworthy, III, set foot in Canada on opening day of the Gassy Jack Deighton saloon—the first dive on the land that would eventually become Vancouver. They made a small fortune exploiting the Chinese indentured labor that survived malnutrition, diseases, or other mistreatment on the packed vessels that shipped them to slave on the construction of the Canadian Pacific Railway. Nineteen years later, they made a bigger fortune rebuilding the city from its ashes after the conflagration that spared only a handful of buildings. Buckminster wore his arrogant humor as a proud symbol of British heritage and loved dispensing his views as absolute truths. To religious groups that solicited his support, he responded that, "churches and temples are nothing but the sad refuge of gutless cowards afraid of women." To charitable organizations that approached him to contribute to international poverty relief efforts, he blurted that he would "never give a penny to blokes that suck bleeding hearts and fuck the Third World under the same satin sheets."

It greatly impressed many power brokers in the Democratic Canadian Rightist Alliance Party that Graham miraculously and continuously extorted rich donations from Axworthy, III, and Graham never revealed the secrets of how he achieved this feat. One needed not befriend Buckminster to be showered by his unsolicited, alleged gems of wisdom, but these were mostly shocking hyperboles dispensed to flaunt his immunity against political incorrectness as one of the perks conferred by accumulated wealth. Whereas few truths could be distilled from the ludicrous rhetoric of the public persona, Graham believed he could take the pulse of a whole segment of British Columbia by dissecting the more private, candid views of his sponsor—something possible on the strength of his privileged relationship.

Direct as always and true to his style—even when speaking from the heart—Buckminster summarized his thoughts in a series of adages.

"Leave the goddamn frogs alone. No one is married to an old prostitute. Canada can live with one kidney. As for the immediate hemorrhage, it's their bloody mess, it's their bloody band-aids. Nobody cares because it would never happen here."

Chéng-gong Shing, in compliance with Canada's fast-track immigration policy, invested $400,000 in Canada in exchange for his immigration visa, and soon thereafter, his Canadian citizenship. He was one of the 110,000 who had moved from Hong Kong to Vancouver in the decade leading to July 1, 1997, when the sovereignty of his motherland was returned to China. To Chéng-gong and his compatriots, Vancouver was a politically stable and relatively close member of the British Commonwealth that proved convenient and welcoming, and shared the familiar sight of high-rise towers at the foot of mountains. They were well aware that, under the fear of being assaulted by endless horses of Asians, the city and its institutions became less welcoming—cynical residents referring to the city as "Hong Kouver" and others seeking to legislate against the disturbances and excesses of unbridled foreign capital investments on community life—but it remained a privileged and favorite adopted base of operations for the expatriates.

Except for an occasional trip to Niagara Falls, and vacations in Europe, Chéng-gong's frequent flyer points all accrued for trans-Pacific travel. He spent most of his time tending to his business in Hong Kong, his Canadian Passport serving as an insurance policy against the fickleness of the Chinese communist government, while his family enjoyed the open space, lush nature, and comparatively cheap cost of living of British Columbia. Graham believed Chéng-gong's opinions reflected the views of the new money in British Columbia, and possibly of a large segment of the 30% of Vancouver residents and 5% of Canadians who were of Chinese decent.

Matter-of-factly, Chéng-gong supported all political parties, out of tradition, as a way to ensure smooth business operations. As long as Canadian politics did not impact the value of his condominium investments along English Bay, False Creek, and Burrard Inlet, Chéng-gong was willing to grease the political wheels for the privilege of periodically sharing his thoughts with Graham on what should be the government's priorities.

Diplomatically, consistent to his distrust of central governments, he told Graham, "Give them humanitarian assistance if they ask for it, don't if they don't. Bottom line, economic prosperity on the west coast will not be affected, so nobody really cares. By the way, something like that would likely not happen here, nor in Hong Kong for that matter, because of superior construction quality and code enforcement there."

Rowland Tosch's first Canadian ancestors, German European Catholics, initially settled in Saskatchewan, but soon thereafter moved to Alberta in the 1920s to escape the intimidation of the Ku Klux Klan who were busy burning crosses to capitalize on the fears of rural communities, promising to protect them against the encroaching dangers of Roman Catholics, the French language, and immigrants from Eastern Europe. Although a few years later, Alberta became the only province to have officially allowed the Klan to register as an incorporated registered society, Rowland's ancestors felt safe in Fort McMurray, a northern village in the middle of nowhere focused on oil exploration rather than agrarian concerns. Not much happened there for generations, but Rowland always upheld that living and building operations atop the Athabasca oil sands was like incubating gold. His Fort McMurray business would have long been bankrupt if not bolstered by decades of federal government subsidies to the oil sand industries, but after years of hardship, the egg finally hatched.

When the world price for crude went through the roof, massive production of oil sands turned wildly profitable, Alberta envisioned becoming the new Saudi Arabia, and Rowland's business at last thrived. The new redneck sheiks of the North were busy milking the world's second largest known oil reserves, and Rowland's share of the cake amounted to crumbs. Yet, with crumbs commensurate to the size of the feast, he was inebriated by the insane profits and overwhelming demand for his subcontractor services.

Rowland's allegiance to the party predated his good fortune, but he had been pleased to supplement his moral support with generous financial donations from his new-found wealth—if only to underline that he was from the same province as the Premier and for the opportunity to provide a grassroots perspective from Alberta.

"Graham, given that Alberta might itself secede if Canada doesn't scrap its traditional transfer payment program which robs Alberta for the sake of providing welfare to the others, I don't think you'll find much sympathy here for anything you do in Quebec. Besides, that kind of disaster would never happen here as people are much more self-reliant."

Wellesley Bowell, descendant of sir MacKenzie Bowell, fifth Prime Minister of Canada and once Grandmaster of the Orange Order of British North America, shared much of his ancestor's conservatism, disdain, and occasionally hate, for all human beings not protestant and Anglo-Saxon. One of his forefathers paid to have the infamous sign "No Dogs or Jews Allowed" built and posted on Toronto's beaches in the 1930s, and Wellesley's philosophy of life hadn't evolved much above those basic precepts. Heir to his family fortune, pampered in his Rosedale residence of luxury, entertained by all of the world's high-tech gadgets, consuming like a forest fire, and wasting life without passion, his only interest was to distribute money to seek influence, for self-aggrandizing purposes. Graham only called him to prevent the aggravation that would ensue should Wellesley learn that the opinion of other large contributors to the party had been solicited, but not his.

Wellesley's long diatribe against the debilitating powers that lied outside of Toronto and the ill-advised willingness to pander to Québec's endless demands was summarized by his closing remarks: "Let them rot in their own feces. If such an earthquake was to happen in Toronto, with all the capital, all the brainpower, and all the manpower in place, we'd be back to fully operational within a week."

The Canadian forefather of Stephen Alexis settled in Digby, Nova Scotia, in 1783. He had been among the thousands of slaves emancipated for having fought with the British troops during the American Revolutionary War and attracted to settle in Canada by the promise of 100 acres of land. As Stephen established through genealogical searches to trace his roots, the white Loyalists were indeed granted the promised acres, but through some convoluted and deliberate twist of logic to serve the British sensibilities of the era, the government reneged on its promise, and the black Loyalist received a one-acre parcel of non-fertile rocky land on which to settle—a destituteness only matched by that of Acadians returning to this motherland years after their deportation. Many blacks died of starvation or froze to death after selling all their belongings in exchange for food; others indentured their family or sold themselves as slaves; a large group embarked on a trip to another promised land, on the hope that Sierra Leone would be their home of freedom and equality.

Stephen's ancestor remained in Canada, providing generations of cheap labor, managing to avoid channelling their anger in any of the sporadic riots that failed and proved fatal for their proponents, and luckily escaping the bouts of violence by former soldiers rampaging through black settlements in attempts to eliminate a competing labor force that toiled at depressed wages or for free. Lo and behold, they survived through the abominable conditions of an unacknowledged Canadian apartheid until all reference to race and separate education facilities were erased from the Nova Scotia laws in the 1960s. Treading through emerging education opportunities as escape hatches from the hegemony of the Maritimes, and breaking their chains by tapping the progressively expanding equal opportunity business propositions created by successive governments seeking redemption from a shameful past of institutionalized and socialized racism, Alexis's family's outlook brightened.

Stephen, as the greatest beneficiary of the province's Black Business Initiative, understood the value of lubricating the political parties in power on the federal and provincial stages, however repugnant they might be. Graham only knew Stephen through the generosity of his support, his public convivial facade, and his relentless enthusiasm to preach a vision of government programs and financial investments designed to elevate the ideal of pan-Canadian diversity and to promote the beauty and uniqueness of the Canadian mosaic. Graham ignored the fact that Stephen's sympathies to the misery of others had been atrophied by centuries of self-dependence on the urge to survive, and that his true interest in a mosaic focused on those few identical tiles he could inlay in it.

"Graham my man, there ain't one bit we can do for them folks. For the almighty pride that flows in them veins, it's their duty to pick themselves up by the bootstraps, and get out of that awful mess they're in. You know you wouldn't catch us folks here beggin' for that kinda stuff. Hell, in Scotia we wouldn't end up in that kinda mess in the first place!"

Clyde Falkland had settled in Newfoundland during construction of the Hibernia oil platform 200 miles offshore, as a site project operations manager for one of the oil giants that owned and operated the integrated drilling and processing facility. He left the comfort and lifetime security of a federal government job in Ottawa for the rich rewards of a private sector executive position. He had recognized that to climb to the upper echelon of federal government agencies, one needed to be bilingual, a concept he inherently loathed. As a middle manager while in Ottawa, as part of a federal government training program, he'd been dispatched to a west coast government-language institute, all expenses paid, with full salary, for an entire year, to learn French. He had a good time living in a resort-like setting on the Pacific coast, but upon return, his command of a second language remained sketchy, to the extent that he would steadfastly respond in English to all those who addressed him in French.

His unwillingness to play the "despicable bilingualism game" for the sake of advancement, and the strong financial incentives intrinsic to the "oil oligarchy," were Clyde's sole motives to relocate to a cold, remote, and sparsely populated island-province that he previously only knew for the distinction of having joined Canada in 1949 as a result of a referendum on the political fate of the island won by a slim of margin of 2%. In spite of Clyde's shallow roots in Newfoundland, he felt at home. He didn't mind the rabid monarchists imposing the display of gigantic portraits of the Queen of England in public institutions, nor the fact that

Newfoundland reneged on its word and prevented passage of a constitutional amendment that would have allowed Québec to join the Canadian Constitution patriated in the early 1980s. He didn't care about the province's history, its Viking settlements, its challenged fisheries, its years of financial hardships and welfare dependency. All he cared for was the prosperity brought about by the black gold flowing up from the sea bottom.

Clyde didn't even know that an earthquake had happened in Montréal when Graham called. That was a world apart, 2,000 miles away.

"Graham, I don't care. That's not even on my radar screen. I'm sure they'll be fine on their own. We'd be fine too, although I have to admit that this kind of stuff wouldn't happen here, you know."

Graham didn't need to make more calls. All was in order. If anything, instead of a softening of the party's usual hard line, which he had expected maybe as a compassionate response to the human tragedy unfolding in Montréal, he found his constituency to be ruthlessly entrenched and dogmatic in waving the party's rightist flag. If anything, he sensed a barely concealed glee—maybe they saw poetic justice in seeing the province that wanted to break Canada being itself broken up, struck a fatal blow at its heart.

Graham recognized that his brief survey was not conducted on a representative sample group and knew that a large segment of the country's population was far more liberal and would not share the views of those he'd called. But the financial pillars of the Democratic Canadian Rightist Alliance Party did, and that was all that mattered.

Washington, 4:00 p.m.

Within a few hours, a conference call was the best that could be arranged. Even if a meeting room had been conveniently available, given that the key divisions of the National Security Agency, Central Intelligence Agency, Federal Bureau of Investigation, and Department of State were scattered all over town, their representatives wouldn't have been able to come to the FEMA offices of the Department of Homeland Security in due time. Besides, participation to the call was an inter-agency courtesy more than an obligation—expecting them to commit the extra time for a face-to-face meeting would have been unrealistic, unless a genuine shared interest existed at the outset. Whether such an interest existed, and on whose turf it would fall, remained to be established.

Treegherapy described to all participants the circumstances that had led to the conference call, summarizing the situation from talking points prepared by Basketcase Wuss, carefully emphasizing that the request for assistance came to FEMA from a Canadian provincial jurisdiction, therefore bypassing the expected and official lines of communication, that is, the Canadian federal government.

"Gentlemen, I would sincerely appreciate if you could enlighten us on what is going on here, so that we can map an appropriate course of action. Please, intervene in any particular order, as you feel appropriate."

Treegherapy believed that asking individuals to randomly volunteer information was a horrible strategy to manage a conference call. In this case though, he wanted to determine if the participants to the call were truly experts on Canadian matters, or rather mid-level staffers filling in to serve as rapporteurs, instructed to notify their respective bosses if the discussion took a turn that warranted them to jump into the fray. The long silence betrayed the discomfort of the polite placeholders. Treegherapy, with no great gift for gab himself, allowed the tension to hang a few more moments, assuming that those on the line were eggheads without much interpersonal skills to start with—the nerds he'd loved to abuse as a high school jock.

In reality, most on the conference call were just eager to continue answering their emails, shielded by the invisibility granted by telephony, confident that they could convincingly feign interest and improvise meaningful comments at a moment's notice if called upon or if awakened by a relevant thread of conversation. None of the other agencies were affected by the DHS's self-imposed temporary isolation from the internet and all waited for someone to break the sustained muteness that disrupted their business.

Dr. Dick Brausmard, the assigned representative from the State Department, emboldened by the hesitation from the call participants, jumped at the opportunity. Once a young exuberant graduate from the Canadian Studies Program of Saint-Chretistic Technological University, dulled by frustrating years of service during which his expertise laid untapped in a country more concerned about the turmoil and crises in the Middle East and Asia than the phlegmatic posturing of Canadian peons, reduced to depressively counting the days before cashing in the barely deserved rewards of a golden federal employees retirement program he'd studied in its most arcane intricacies, Dr. Brausmard was delighted by this unique opportunity to showcase his expertise.

"The State Department has amassed considerable knowledge on the tense relationship between the governments of Quebec and Canada," opened Brausmard, mostly referring to his expertise on this topic.

With great relief, now that one lamb had self-sacrificed, all in attendance returned to reading their emails, except for Treegherapy, bound to listen to the experts he had convened. None of the names on the hastily assembled list of participants and titles were familiar to him, and he could only presume that a Ph.D. from the State Department would be knowledgeable. Yet, on the breadth of a single sentence, Treegherapy was already irritated by Brausmard's shrill voice and preaching tone. He hated suffering the futile ramblings of eggheads let loose, but elected to patiently remain silent as long as possible, because he badly needed snippets of key strategic information to instruct his decisions. He controlled his breathing to cool his innate temper and restrain his urge to tell Brausmard to shut up, giving him instead some space to elaborate.

Brausmard continued, "One could say that the political problems of Canada effectively go back to the early colonization times. A sizeable French contingent had colonized the land known nowadays as Quebec when the British, at war with France, took possession of it in 1763. As a result of the British's primary interest in developing business and commerce to 'milk' the colony, and to prevent unrest, the more populous French-speaking 'habitants' were allowed to keep the right to exercise their religion, to teach in French in their own schools, to enforce French civil laws for private transactions, and, to various degrees at different times, to maintain some level of autonomous government. The ruling cast assumed that, over time, the habitants would inevitably assimilate into the English culture as they would come to recognize the presumed benefits of the British empire—the better education, the better culture, the better jobs, the better society, and the privileges of integration into the ruling class—all above the cesspool of inequity and misery of a marginalized underclass. Of course, this presumptuous and contemptuous British attitude was faulty, and assimilation never occurred. The French culture thrived over the years, with periodic attempts by various groups to assert their strength beyond the legal political arena and recapture full autonomy from the British dominance."

Still irritated from the earlier Canadian geography primer, Treegherapy could not bear a long Canadian history lesson. He started to regret his specific instructions to Basketcase to find experts who could provide historical and political substance.

"Dr. Brausmard, with all due respect, our time is fairly limited. Could you please focus on information relevant to the case at hand?"

"Sure, sure. It's all very relevant, as it is this same British-French cultural clash that led to near political chaos during the second half of the 20th century. See, over the years, the British kept thinking of Canada as an English colony, namely the Dominion of Canada, and of themselves as British citizens. In fact, many never bothered to acquire a Canadian passport, but rather revered and carried a British passport. The French inhabitants though, isolated from their European motherland, became 'French Canadians,' outright citizens of what they believed to be a country, much like we did in the U.S., with the exception that severance of their ties with the former homeland was imposed, not revolutionary."

At that very instant in the middle of Brausmard's extensive commentary, DHS's servers reconnected to the internet. Treegherapy's computer screen flooded with hundreds of new emails, including a few high-priority ones that monopolized his attention for a few minutes, leaving Brausmard free to ramble unchecked. Treegherapy had suffered so many meetings during which all attendees, in blatant violation of office etiquette, in everyone's faces, sitting around a conference table, pretended to write notes on their laptop while actually checking emails or working on over-due reports, that he didn't feel any guilt in letting the conference call drift into irrelevance for a moment while he tended to impor-tant business.

Brausmard continued, speaking a bit faster, hoping to squeeze as much important factual background information as possible before being interrupted anew, unable to fathom that a rational and judicious political decision could be made without a minimum of historical perspective.

"Co-existence of two parallel societies having unequal rights and powers, and vastly different ambitions and purposes, has been a constant source of tensions. In the decades following the British conquest, the English colonists continuously pressured for a rever-sal of the cultural concessions made to the French. They were bitterly discontent to live under French civil laws and unfamiliar institutions and eager to structure government and constitution per the British model. Their numbers swelled by the surge of loyalists displaced North by the United States' drive to independence, but still representing only 10% of the population, unable to abrogate those laws and concessions, the English colonists settled in 1791 for a constitutional separation of what was then the broader Prov-ince of Quebec territory into a Lower Canada (today's Quebec) and an Upper Canada (today's Ontario), allowing each group to pursue its aspirations under laws and governments that reflected their own character, under the stewardship of a Governor General serving the interests of the British Crown."

At this juncture, Brausmard could have skipped a few para-graphs from his notes, but as nobody complained, he assumed that his captive audience was spellbound. The history buff was elated by this opportunity to expand on riveting details that he believed to be of immense interest and value in setting the stage for under-standing the issues at stake.

"This split opened up the relatively sparsely populated land of Upper Canada for business, but left unpleased the British set-tlers in Lower Canada. As the total number of English settlers grew over the subsequent decades, approaching that of the French Canadians, they strategized and conspired to unite the two Canadas into a single British colony under a single language and common laws, without distinct status and accommodations provided to the French Canadians. The assembly of Lower Canada, in substantial majority French Canadians, responded by demanding responsible government and political sovereignty. That self-affirmation attempt did not go well. Violence erupted and escalated into the 1837-38 populist rebellion. Martial law was declared and the British army brutally squashed the outnumbered rebels. Twelve prisoners were hanged to set an example, dozens others were deported, and a large number were freed on the strength of a controversial amnesty.

"Lord Durham, a renowned liberal and radical thinker from London charged to assess the situation and recommend a solution, concluded that the French Canadians were a backward people without history or culture, and that it was in their best interest and betterment to be assimilated into the more progressive British culture. Given that by the time of his report, the merging of Upper and Lower Canada would have given the English population an absolute majority, Durham's recommendation for a federal central government to which the two provinces would be subordinate was enacted by the 1840 Union Act. The act banished the use of French in official government activities and suspended specific French Canadian education and legal institutions—although, within a decade, Quebec politicians, working within the system, succeeded in having the clauses related to language and culture repealed. The act also unfairly consolidated the debts of both provinces, transferring much of the fiscal burden of Upper Canada onto the more financially responsible Lower Canada, and apportioned the same number of seats in federal legislative assembly to both provinces, even though Lower Canada was 50% more populated. Two decades later, as further immigration made the English population a dominant majority, the Union was expanded into a Confederation with representation by population, by the addition of two more provinces in 1867, and six more thereafter."

Treegherapy, between two emails, seeing the clock, snapped back into the mission at hand, and realized that Brausmard was lost in his own lucubration on historical injustices and double standards.

"Dr. Brausmard, could you please come to the point?"

"Yes, exactly!"

Stressed that he might not be able to reach the key points of his presentation, Brausmard truncated a century of history from his rehearsed exposé to focus on relatively more recent events.

"As time went by, the French Canadians felt alienated in the federation. They were deprived of access to the best jobs in the Canadian Government, and were generally discriminated against everywhere but in the province of Quebec. For example, unable to control their destiny through the political process, they suffered at the beginning of the 20th century as the government of the province of Ontario declared French schools and the teaching of French illegal. Everywhere, French culture was threatened, except in Quebec where government and the clergy successfully cooperated to protect the French culture, to some degree. However, in the 1960s, a cultural revolution took place in the province of Quebec, relying on disfranchisement from the clergy and a newly established nearly free system of upper education. This resulted in a more politicized and educated population that undertook to use political means to take over progressively more control of their destiny as a nation."

"Dr. Brausmard, please cut to the chase! This is all very interesting, but could you stick to the bottom line please. Why did we receive this request of assistance from the Kwebek government, not the Canadian government?"

Brausmard truly hated these military-type zealots, oblivious to history, disrespectful of cultural traditions, anxious to bark orders, ready to kill, in complete ignorance of the consequence of their actions. Frustrated, he shuffled his papers, searching for nuggets of information that could quench Treegherapy's impatience.

"Sorry. Here are the facts. The government of Quebec, although it is legally a provincial government that is related to the Canadian government as part of a federation, thinks of itself as a National government. Its legislative body is called the 'National Assembly', and Quebec City is called the 'National Capital.' It has not succeeded in seceding from Canada through political means, or even through radical non-democratic means."

Treegherapy's secretary, head poked through the ajar door, waved at him, caught his attention, and conveyed, like a clumsy mime, the message that his boss was on the other line. Treegherapy left to take the call in the adjacent room confident that Brausmard would just continue unchecked, but turned up the volume of the speaker phone to monitor the noise and be able to return without revealing his temporary absence in case Brausmard reached a full stop.

"As a result of popular dissatisfaction with the ruling party's handling of the economy, work conflicts, and laws to protect French language, a separatist Quebec government was elected in 1976."

Brausmard hesitated a few seconds, concerned that Treegherapy would rush him again if he was to dwell on this particular point, providing a bit more depth than necessary. The silence on the line encouraged him to try, always pleased to display his erudition. He read from some of the notes he had prepared for the meeting.

"This led to a referendum in 1980, in which the population was asked: *The Government of Quebec has made public its proposal to negotiate a new agreement with the rest of Canada, based on the equality of nations; this agreement would enable Quebec to acquire the exclusive power to make its laws, levy its taxes and establish relations abroad—in other words, sovereignty—and at the same time to maintain with Canada an economic association including a common currency; any change in political status resulting from these negotiations will only be implemented with popular approval through another referendum; on these terms, do you give the Government of Quebec the mandate to negotiate the proposed agreement between Quebec and Canada?'* Early polls suggested that 55% of the population supported this proposed mandate, but following a number of political gaffes, an inability to provide substantiated evidence to counter doomsday scenarios of economic and political collapses painted by their opponents, and unrestrained spending by the federal government campaigning to defeat the motion, the proposal to negotiate sovereignty association was defeated by a 59.6% to 40.4% margin."

Amazed that Treegherapy had not interrupted him on these small details, he continued.

"Pretending to interpret the referendum results as an implicit mandate for change, the federal government unilaterally undertook to write a new Constitution and Bill of Rights in replacement of the British one. It was endorsed in 1982 by nine of the ten provinces after lengthy negotiations. Only the province of Quebec refused to sign, as it felt that the new proposed constitutional accord reduced its power and eliminated its veto power on constitutional matters.

"Almost a decade later, after a change of government in Quebec and Canada, the Meech Lake Accord was reached, hailed as a landmark agreement between all the provincial and federal governments to modify the Constitution in a way acceptable to Quebec, with five meager symbolic amendment requests. It collapsed when the provinces of Newfoundland and Manitoba failed to ratify the agreement within their own legislatures. Within two years, a highly heterogeneous set of amendments slapped together to please an even broader constituency, called the Charlottetown Accord, failed miserably, rejected in a Canada-wide referendum by 54% of Canadians, and by Quebec. Offended by the brutal collapse of both of these amendment attempts, Quebec has withdrawn ever since from further constitutional negotiations."

Brausmard shuffled his cue-cards looking for an exact citation.

"Re-election of the separatist party to power in Quebec, in 1995, led to a second attempt to separate from Canada, with a referendum question asking: *Do you agree that Québec should become sovereign after having made a formal offer to Canada for a new economic and political partnership within the scope of the bill respecting the future of Québec and of the agreement signed on June 12, 1995?*—that was an agreement on sovereignty signed by all three of the major political parties having seats at the National Assembly. At the start of the campaign, polls predicted a defeat by 67% to 33%, but the sovereignist proposal garnered an impressive momentum up to a few days before the vote, with polls forecasting a 55%-45% victory. Inundated by a flurry of last minute mega-events and poignant promises, the population voted to stay in Canada by a margin of 50.6% to 49.4%, with 94% of the eligible voters casting a ballot.

"Exhausted by nearly two decades of political turmoil and little effective results, all further attempts to change the political power-sharing formula or to amend the Constitution were put on ice. In spite of not having signed the Constitution, and by default still technically being a part of Canada, Quebec has instead continued to use its jurisdiction on a vast body of powers to ensure its future and to differentiate itself from the rest of Canada. This tactic, predating all these constitutional battles, has been successful before. For example, in the late 1970s, the Quebec government had declared that commercial advertising in the province had to be done in French, and has since enacted many other similar laws to protect its culture and right to work, live, and be educated in French.

"However, in recent years, the country has seen the election of a polarized right-wing and uncompromising federal government, and in response, a resurgence of separatism in the more socialist-leaning Quebec population. After a few years of new federal initiatives clashing with the culture and identity of Quebeckers, the long-simmering aspirations to nationhood are boiling anew. Indeed, the current Quebec government had scheduled a referendum on sovereignty to be held a week from now, and the latest polls indicated that the vote would support separation by a 55-45 margin."

Brausmard stopped, certain that this was more information than Treegherapy could absorb in one serving, and that questions were inevitable. The few seconds of silence being more than he expected, he dared wonder whether he had impressed his audience to the point of speechlessness.

At that very moment, done with his other call, Treegherapy quietly slipped back into the room. In spite of his best intentions and the boosted speakerphone volume, he had failed to partition his mind to monitor the on-going conference call, and worried at the absence of noise. The expensive cyberspace void had to be promptly filled to dispel suspicions that the conference call was adrift.

"Um. Are there any concerns that this Kwebek government could harbor any terrorists?" asked Treegherapy, as if coming back from a deep reflection.

Brausmard was abashed. This didn't make a whit of sense to him. But before he could even take a breath to respond, let alone figure out how to determine which part (if any) of his erudite exposé had been actually understood, the NAS, CIA and FBI representatives, awakened from their email-induced drowsiness by the mere mention of "terrorists," were tripping onto each other, storming into the call, to describe the extent of their activities to foil the plans of multiple terrorist groups harbored in Canada. Extravagant claims, as irrelevant as incredible, were made about groups of all stripes, from congregations of middle-aged, creedless spiritualists awaiting redemption in mass-extraterrestrial abductions, to clubs of disparate misfits and social outcasts channeling their countercultural angst through aggressive anti-imperialist slogans and nihilist heavy metal lyrics—groups that saw death as means to different ends, but without the means or desperate convictions to implement these consoling leitmotifs to their deadly ends.

Even though they were passionately and emotionally entangled in the same intense hunt for "bad guys" with ill intent, the NAS, CIA, and FBI representatives never danced like a well-tuned corps. Rather, they all blitzed to the stage and hogged the spotlight as long as possible, as narcissistic soloists, trumpeting their disparate opinions as gospel. Yet, some rhythm to this incongruous rampage of egos was found in the cyclic succession of repeated political dogmas: each representative monopolized the line for a long enough time to loudly proclaim an elaborate series of absolutely non-negotiable beliefs, before returning his full attention to preoccupying urgent emails, totally disinterested in the points of views or assertions of others, only leaving his keyboard to reiterate his beliefs as soon as the line was free anew. An endless recitation of discordant mantras, growing louder each cycle, in a room of deaf pontificators.

Brausmard knew that Québec's request for emergency assistance bore no relationship to homeland security issues. He understood the entire discussion on the plausible existence of terrorist cells in Québec and the highly speculative assessments on the risk of providing assistance to a terrorist-harboring state, to be simply by-products of the hallucinations of "security" experts who saw terrorists everywhere. He recognized that it was futile and unwise for anyone to argue otherwise. He instead acknowledged with the occasional "uh uh" all assertions of potential—yet unproven—threats to national security, aware that the momentary blip of insanity would recede in due course, after all the experts finish reciting their agency propaganda wrapped in the latest buzzwords.

However, before this recession of insanity happened, to make things worse, in one last climactic round of passionate preaching, the proselytizers were forced to further raise the volume of their rhetoric when one of them, working on his computer while awaiting his turn on the soapbox, oblivious to conference-call etiquette, carelessly launched his printer, a vintage decibel-belching box located next to his speakerphone. The sophisticated intelligence analyses and eloquent hyperboles empty of substance were drowned in a cacophony of squeaks, clangs, pops, clicks and whooshes as every sheet of paper screamed in panic, dragged against its will by rubber rollers on rusty unlubricated hinges through an unnatural tortuous course, rubbing on skewed steel edges, flipping against sharp plastic rims, pressed against gluey rotating drums, unsuccessfully attempting to jam the device to escape an uncertain and horrifying fate, courtesy of a bureaucrat who didn't know, didn't care, or didn't care to know the purpose of the mute button on his phone.

Treegherapy put an end to the chaos, thanking the speakers for their thorough coverage of the issues, and barking orders to the unidentified noisemaker to stop the racket at once—which he did, after recognizing himself as the culprit, by briskly unplugging his printer from the wall, ignorant of how else to proceed to kill the disturbing noise, embarrassed but grateful for the anonymity of telephone communications.

Treegherapy was satisfied that the mandatory security issues had been covered by the conference call participants, and that no one could be accused in some unforeseen future of not having duly assessed the potential risk of a terrorist attack related to this situation. He could then return to the search for a proper response to the request from the Québec government, seeking to summarize the situation in a few simple words to conclude the call and proceed to action.

"So, Dr. Brausmard, in your own opinion, why do you think the Quebec government contacted us directly?"

Brausmard decided to sum it all up by jumping to his "summary and conclusions" cue cards.

"As I indicated earlier, the Quebec government is in the middle of a secessionist referendum campaign. According to the latest polls, they have a significant lead, with voting intentions in support of separation by a 55-45 margin. Clearly, the vote will have to be postponed because of this earthquake. Until then, however, any sign of dependency on the central federal government would erode their position and jeopardize their chances of winning this referendum. Note that the Quebeckers perceive the United States to be a greater friend than the Canadian government, if only for our common ancient history of sour relationships with the British. They certainly have no allegiance to the British monarchy, which they perceive as nothing but a trite symbol by one linguistic group to subjugate all the others. Throughout history, and now more than ever, the Quebec government has aligned closely to U.S. policies, as the province's economy is more tied to the U.S. than to the rest of Canada. Quebec has expressed the strongest support for the North American Free Trade Agreement with the U.S., before and after its signature, and exports more to the U.S. than to the rest of Canada—not to forget that it sells a substantial part of its hydro-electricity production to the northeastern states. Hence, their call to FEMA is simply a way to assert their national aspirations. A positive response from the United States to their appeal, without prior approval from the Canadian government through the traditional diplomatic channels, would be tantamount to a recognition of Quebec's sovereignty by the U.S., prior to the outcome of the referendum, thus a priori sealing the fate of that popular ballot."

"That's exactly what I thought," snapped back Treegherapy, in a clumsy attempt to steal the spotlight. He didn't understand the geopolitical issues at stake, but the word "secessionist" resonated. He remembered stories about his ancestors who fought for the Union during the Civil War, the detailed recounting of the blood shed and sacrifices made to keep the nation whole. He had been born to a family of proud military heritage, tracing his lineage to a soldier rowing across the ice-clogged Delaware alongside General Washington's canoe on course to change history. Proud and decorated, with medals and trinkets pinned on the bark of a family tree blemished by amputated limbs, amputated lives, amputated pride, and decimated wealth—the severe tolls for the privilege of a free country and the unalienable rights of life, liberty, and the pursuit of happiness; concepts drilled down his memory as absolute and inescapable truths.

"Thank you very much gentlemen, for your contributions. This has been most helpful. As a result of our discussions, I firmly believe and have concluded that this should be handled at the highest political level. Our President will be briefed at once and advised to get in touch with the President of Canada to discuss this matter," affirmed Treegherapy in a self-important way, as if he were the President's golf buddy and would bring him up to speed himself, while sharing a Scotch whisky and slapping him on the back at the punchline of saucy jokes.

The fact that Canada does not have a president but rather a prime minister did not matter to Treegherapy, undeterred in his resolve. According to the schedule obtained from the White House by Wuss, the President was not to be disturbed between "15:00 and 17:00 hours," official time of the presidential nap.

Like baseball players who religiously follow the same ritual before every game, the presidential nap had become an important tradition respected as the mark of successful presidents. In fact, the length of the nap had increased with each successive presidency after some researchers documented a definite strong positive correlation between the length of naps taken by presidents and the positive popular remembrance of their impact on history. This observation enticed successive superstitious presidents to progressively nap longer to secure a better place in the historical collective memory, even though no one questioned that this trend could lead, by extrapolation, if followed to its logical conclusion, to permanently napping but extremely popular presidents in a not-so-distant future.

Since this Canadian skirmish was far from a matter of U.S. national interest, awakening the President was out of the question. However, this would give Treegherapy sufficient time to prepare material for a presidential briefing by the head of FEMA.

As he hung up, Brausmard pondered whether there would ever be another Canadian crisis someday that could rescue him from his otherwise useless job. If only the referendum would pass, maybe...

Ottawa, 4:15 p.m.

Wayne Greenbriar, Graham Murdoch, Kaylee Carling, and Shirley Coulthard were meeting with Brendon to review the communique to be released at 5 p.m. Most of it consisted of bland generalities promoting the federal government agencies and tools to be deployed to deal with the disaster. The write-up was purposely vague to suggest that most were already deployed. Propaganda from a distance, per the party line. A few potentially controversial points remained to be resolved to be able to complete the final draft and release the communique—small items in a long document, but that better be cleared knowing Brendon's compulsive obsession with details.

Graham was struggling with the political implications of the various return periods provided to him by experts at his Department of Natural Resources. As he understood it, the latest Canadian codes required that buildings be designed to protect the life of their occupants, even during some of the most severe earthquakes—specifically, the large ones that were deemed likely to reoccur on average only once every 2,500 years. The buildings designed in compliance to code for such rare events could end up being so damaged that they would become total write-offs, but they were not expected to collapse or get damaged in a way that would endanger the life of occupants—although occupants could get injured if hit by falling objects or harmed by unsecured items for which they were themselves responsible. This was called the "life-safety design level." A few decades ago, life-safety design was accomplished for earthquakes with a recurrence period of only 500 years; a few more decades earlier, only a 100 years recurrence period was considered in design; before then, building codes simply ignored the earthquake threat. As large earthquakes occur less frequently than small ones, logically, the smaller return periods considered by the older codes only provided protection against correspondingly smaller earthquakes.

Yet, in all cases, even as codes became more sophisticated and complex, there remained no absolute way to ensure that no death would ever occur. This remained only a probabilistic expectation. Compliance with the codified provisions was only deemed to meet the life-safety objective, without any ironclad guarantees against loss of life.

Graham was comfortable with the absence of certainty, which in his mind was no different than most things in life; after all, the global economy operates without explicit guaranties against financial panic and stock market crashes, peace is a fragile equilibrium at the mercy of unpredictable political conflicts, the medical profession is most prosperous without ever promising any success, and lawyers are statistically certain to fail half the time.

What bothered him was the juggling of various return periods in the mind of the public. One could profess that the latest Canadian codes were safe and right in promoting the use of a 2,500 year return period, because, as explained to him, considering that a building is built to have a life of at least 50 years on average—some being demolished and replaced by more modern ones before then, and others outlasting that multiple times over—using that kind of return period left only a 2% chance that an earthquake greater than considered by the design code could occur in a span of 50 years.

At first, all things being relative, this seemed to be an acceptably small probability.

However, depending on how one looked at the numbers, it seemed riskier than desirable. Graham felt he wouldn't cross a street blindfolded if he was told there was a 2% chance of being hit by a bus. Likewise, he felt people would buy bagfuls of lottery tickets if they were promised a 2% chance of winning a multi-million dollar jackpot in their lifetime—a substantial improvement over the near statistically anomalous odds of winning nowadays.

At the same time, jacking up the return period to consider in the design of any standard building seemed inconceivable—he was told that only nuclear power plants and offshore oil platforms were designed to resist rarer earthquakes having a 10,000 year return period. If anything, Graham felt that one could already accuse the Canadian codes of being wasteful to design infrastructure for events that have a one-in-2,500 chance of happening every year. No matter how one sliced it, 25 centuries was a very long time. After all, the entire written history of civilization spanned approximately 5,000 years, the first three millenniums sketchy at best. In the last 2,500 years, entire civilizations, empires, and dynasties had come and gone, large religions had emerged, and thousands of wars had killed millions. Over that period, Europe went through dark ages, medieval times, the renaissance, and conquered and lost possession of America, whereas maybe one earthquake as large as those considered by the Canadian building code had occurred in Montréal.

Graham could not come up with a single satisfactory way to present this information. When does "very safe" become incomprehensible to the public? Ideally, it would be an unstated figure, an annoying and inconvenient number swept under the rug, but he knew that the question would eventually be asked and was unavoidable.

Graham decided instead to defuse the issue by stating the facts, and by emphasizing that the Canadian design standards, in this regard, followed the practice south of the border. He understood this to be philosophically correct, except that the Canadian codified values were somewhat higher on account of some subtle technical differences that had been explained to him but that he failed to understand—and that he thus considered unlikely to be challenged. In context of the Canadian psyche, where great pride is found in doing more than the Americans when it came to safety nets and quality of life, nobody could be faulted for being at least as safe as the Americans.

However, considering Brendon's aversion to all things American, Graham needed to test the proposed paragraph on him. As expected, Brendon wasn't pleased, but he nonetheless accepted the proposed approach when briefed on the problems caused by the alternatives.

Wayne Greenbriar's list of communique items to review was short and mostly uncontroversial, but were aired to allow support or dissent before final release—and fulfill his obsession with "covering his ass." These items were dispatched expeditiously. All agreed with the proposed statements emphasizing that graduates of the federal government's Canadian Emergency Management College had been most effective in response to prior Canadian disasters. All endorsed the brief description of the Canadian Forces' ready-to-deploy Reverse Osmosis Water Purification Units, each capable of providing 50,000 liters of safe-to-drink purified water per day, assuming these units would be operated inside heated trucks given the current sub-zero temperatures. All endorsed the statements on Canada's international network of friends ready to help should the need arise; even though only a few ambassadors were able to confirm that such assistance had been offered, nobody in the room doubted that Canada could tap external aid from the unlimited reserve of goodwill it had built by spreading peacekeeping efforts and generous donations worldwide. Tactfully and tactically, this was presented as friends helping each other, as it was clear that Canada would not accept aid, especially U.S. aid, in the context of the national political sovereignty crisis.

Kaylee Carling, confident in all the aspects she contributed to the communique, did not bring any issues for discussion.

The last item to debate was whether to include a statement on economic impact from the disaster. Shirley had contacted the ministers in charge of economic development and industry, seeking data to assess the anticipated negative impact of the disaster on the economy, and from there speculate on measures that could be enacted by the Canadian government to save the day. At first, she was disappointed that nobody was willing to volunteer such numbers, even coarse estimates, without the benefit of computer simulations to substantiate any data provided. Then, counter to expectations, she ran into an expert who claimed that the economical impact from the disaster could actually be positive, instead of negative, but who was also unwilling to commit to actual numbers without running computational models. Although totally lacking any data, Shirley wondered whether it would be valuable to build on the optimistic prediction of that last expert, if only to provide encouragements to the population, and brought this matter to the floor.

Her proposed contribution to the communique read: "While this earthquake will be a disaster with dire consequences for many Canadians, Canada's economy remains robust and resilient, and is expected to recover rapidly as the positive demands in some business sectors overcome the losses from other negatively impacted sectors."

The statement, drafted by her expert, was purposely left vague.

"Why would there be benefits?" asked Kaylee, upset that this had been done without first consulting with her department of finance, and puzzled by such counter-intuitive claims that appeared disconnected from reality and askew with the mainstream thinking.

Shirley replied, "In essence, the argument is that the able-bodied population recovering from the disaster will be eager and highly active to repair all damage and see life return to normal. As a result, all sectors tied to the construction sector will be booming. There will be high demand on building materials and supplies as well as labor to repair the damaged infrastructure, with indirect positive impacts on the service industries that support these activities. In addition, the region will be the point of convergence for all kind of special teams, many from the U.S. and from the rest of the world, including emergency repair crews, media crews, and many more. These groups, usually sustained by generous per-diem allocations for meals, hotels, and incidentals, will pour truckloads of dollars into the local economy, like a sudden convention camping in town indeterminately—not to forget the sustained flow of curious 'disaster tourists' coming to gawk at the extent of damage. There will also be other inordinate surges of economic activities in various sectors, such as in the news media, moving companies, insurance industry, sales of specific goods (such as camping equipment, emergency supplies, warm clothing)."

Brendon remained silent for a moment, pondering the merit of such unusual statements from a political perspective. Then, with an icy tone more glacial than ever, told his Cabinet member, "Shirley. This makes no goddamn sense whatsoever. If this were really the case, then the best way to recover from a recession would be to just destroy a city. So why don't we just drop a fucking nuclear bomb on Vancouver, or bulldoze Toronto to the ground, to create new jobs and pump up the economy while we're at it?"

Those statements wouldn't go in the communique.

Toronto, 4:35 p.m.

The drab offices overlooking the Canadian Broadcasting Corporation newsroom were abuzz with activity. All day, the baritone exhilaration of the Director of Information had reverberated, echoing through the monotonic rung of metal trinkets and crystals within reach.

"Manna! This is manna!" he had been shouting all day, moving from office to office, dispatching assignments like an adrenalin-pumped coach trying to protect a one-goal lead in the last seconds of Game 7 of the Stanley Cup finals.

To him, it was always a joyous day in Canada when the media did not have to rely on the news feed from U.S. broadcasters to keep the audience tuned in. Market necessities unfortunately did not facilitate this process. He often repeated to his staff, as if a dictum, "Failing to pay attention to any twitch of the giant next door is fraught with danger—just as hazardous as sharing a bed with an elephant who has a tendency to toss and turn in its sleep."

With an audience from a country captive to the luxury of exporting more than 80% of its goods to the U.S., he felt—like all of his colleagues—that Canadian newscasters were compelled to report any social, financial, economical, or political event than may have cross-border ripple effects on the bottom line of many family budgets. With an audience addicted to the escapism provided by products and productions from U.S. entertainment giants able to penetrate Canadian homes in ever-expanding ingenious ways, bypassing feeble Canadian legislation intended to protect local creative arts against the U.S. cultural onslaught, Canadian infotainment had to mix stories from both sides of the border in a seamless whole, yet patriotically over-emphasizing the achievements of local heroes. As an odd juxtaposition of curse and blessing, he recognized that it would have been suicidal for any media conglomerate to ignore the public's fascination with the empire next door, yet he was delighted that the southern neighbor had enough population and shortcomings to statistically ensure a full supply of wackos, and enough social problems and corrupt ambitions to generate crises faster than solutions.

On an almost daily basis, some frenzied, gun-toting lunatic, preferably unleashed at the friendly neighborhood school, post office, or fast-food joint, went on a rampage ending in a gross bloodbath in time to feed the dinner-hour news. On an almost daily basis, the political machine of the most powerful country on earth acted out in some newsworthy way, disparaging, alienating, freedom-frying, threatening, bullying, tariffing, invading a dissenting or hostile nation, or disparaging, threatening, bullying, tariffing its allies—intentionally or not—castrating part of the Canadian economy in the process. On an almost daily basis, findings from some presumably scientific survey on the mores of this perpetually self-examining society were released in a way that could be massaged to make Canadians look better—for example, wallowing in the pleasure of learning that 99% of Americans were dangerously obese whereas only 80% of Canadians were grossly overweight.

With that predicament, any day self-sufficient in national content was a delight for the Canadian news media. A prestigious victory in national self-affirmation.

Yet, this was already a time without any shortage of Canadian news. With the country completely wrapped in the referendum hysteria of the past weeks, the President of the United States himself, in a spurious moment of dementia, could have taken hostage a group of weight-watchers visiting the White House and shot all those that admitted to having previously binged on Canadian bacon, and this juicy newsworthy saga would not have been allocated a single minute of air time north of the border.

Canadian content more than filled the available airwaves, cyberspace, and print space. The Anglophone media proclaimed "Unconstitutional Referendum Non-Binding Says Premier," "Quebeckers to be Denied Canadian Pension if Separate," "No Common Money Says Finance Minister," "Emperor Léandre Laliberté's Republic Dreams to be Foiled," "*Parti National* Proposes a Racist Hegemony." The Francophone media countered with their own propagandist accusations.

Never a dull moment in the enthralling would-be secession's war of words. All the available bandwidth, the available ink, and the available air-time was saturated with Canadian content. No need to resort to stories on the "plight of the Maritimes fishermen," documentaries on "Inuit stone-carving," and the other usual fillers, to meet the legislated Canadian content minimums.

Now, an earthquake topped it all.

Normal operations were configured to cope with a volume of newsworthy material that tended to fluctuate, as a succession of drought and floods. However, already deluged with stories on the

Canadian political crisis, the events of the day now had the potential to over-saturate the Canadian media.

"Manna!"

Undoubtedly, eventually.

Some of that "manna" had even started to pour in by late afternoon. But the day started bleakly, with inane press releases from the Canadian and Québec governments, and no live feed from Montréal. News has to be manufactured, and frustration built as it was found that no broadcast trucks could be dispatched to the island as all road access was cut. Worse, because of the no-fly-zone order, no slick news anchor with blow-dried hair and feigned compassion could be flown in to report live standing on top of debris or holding the hand of children crying in pain—although plans were underway to circumvent this restriction.

Early in the day, the only documents circulating throughout the newsroom were emails volunteered by homegrown diviners, prophets, and other mentally deranged souls. In normal circumstances, these would be useless, but given the current drought of solid information, the Director of Information ordered his staff to run these emails through the teleprompters, as if legitimate news, and forced the anchormen to read them non-stop. This was done off the air and off-line, not for public consumption but rather just to embarrass the journalists and pressure them to dig out the real news.

As such, from the newsroom desk, impeccably dressed and staid news crews solemnly cycled through the available information for the benefit of the closed-circuit television audience.

"The CBC has learned from reliable sources that 'Mohamed Delta' was contacted by God yesterday and forewarned of this morning's earthquake. Mr. Delta, informing us via electronic communication, has stated: 'Allah is Great! Allah, through the voice of Mohamed Delta, has warned the Prime Minister of Canada for the past two years that he should convert to Islam and recognize the supreme truth of the Koran at once, or risk the wrath of Allah and imperil his population. I have warned Mr. Decker of Allah's impeding wrath, and he disrespectfully disregarded my emails, refused to answer my calls, and avoided me. In doing so, this infidel has rejected Allah! Today's earthquake is only the first pounding of Allah's fist on this land of infidels. Allah will destroy all of Canada, unless Mr. Decker leads his nation to faithfully serve Allah at once! Allah is great!' Mr. Decker has yet to indicate whether he will convert at once to abate the risk of further disasters. The CBC will be investigating this matter further and would welcome any further information on the designs of Allah for Canada's future. In the meantime, we enjoin Mr. Delta to warn all Canadians of the next impending calamity, if possible beforehand this time."

As a mean and merciless, violent tag team on steroids, the co-anchors took turns reading from the teleprompter, haranguing the inept, embarrassed reporters scattered at desks and computer terminals around the studio floor.

"Ms. Stanfield, from Rosedale in Toronto has informed the CBC that her poodle, Fluffy, has demonstrated the ability to predict earthquakes. Fluffy has been reported to uncharacteristically relieve itself on the living room carpet, a behavior unequivocally attributed to the recent earthquake felt just seconds later. Ms. Stanfield has volunteered the services of her canine 'seismologic urinometer' to Earthquakes Canada, which has yet to officially respond to this generous offer.

"In Squamish, British Columbia, a man arrested this morning and accused of the murder of his wife, claims that shaking from the earthquake waves traveling nearly 2,500 miles across the country have loosened a loaded hunting riffle from a basement wall, which accidentally fired as it hit the ground. The suspect alleges that the circuitous path followed by the bullet from the basement to the second floor bedroom is attributable to a seismic-related electromagnetic field that unfortunately traveled through the house at the exact time of the accident, resulting in the reported casualty. The accused man's lawyer plans to bring expert testimony from seismologists to establish his client's innocence on the basis of scientific evidence, including in-depth forensic analysis of large cracks on the basement walls attributed to the earthquake.

"According to a woman in St. Johns, this earthquake had been predicted all along by Pink Floyd. Mrs. Moon is a self-described lyrics-analyst who considers rock music to be a channel through which the spirit of Nostradamus lives as a distributed consciousness. According to Mrs. Moon, Pink Floyd's lyrics stating 'One of these days, I'm going to cut you into little pieces,' from the album *Meddle*, together with 'And deep beneath the ground the early morning sounds' from *Pillow of Winds*, and 'Did you ever wonder why we had to run for shelter when the promise of a brave new world unfurled beneath a clear blue sky' from the album *The Wall*, combine to send a clear message of an early-morning destructive earthquake shattering the infrastructure of a new world city on the edge of a social revolution, most evidently Montréal, where political independence is promised as a new freedom under the blue banner of the *Parti National* of Léandre Laliberté. Unfortunately, CBC reporters forgot to ask Mrs. Moon how she interprets the lyrics 'The lunatic is on the grass' from *Dark Side of the Moon*.

"Mr. Kross from Fanny Bay, British Columbia, has developed an earthquake prediction machine that promises to forecast any earthquake 24 hours ahead of time, with a 97% accuracy. Mr. Kross's machine continuously analyzes cloud patterns, electromagnetic atmospheric fluctuations, ground temperatures, and a number of other important environmental parameters that are recognized as potential earthquake precursors. Through a patented complex mathematical algorithm, the machine will trigger an alarm if a probable earthquake is predicted, and provide an estimate of Richter magnitude and time before event. Mr. Kross is confident that many lives would have been saved had his machine been implemented in Eastern Canada. In solidarity for the victims of this disaster, Mr. Kross has offered to donate one free machine to local municipalities for each machine purchased by the Canadian government.

"An ounce of prevention always worth a pound of cure: an inventor from Hope, British Columbia, is promoting his innovative 'Float-KR-free' design concept for 100% guaranteed earthquake-resistant construction. The inventor, Mr. Ikasama, has designed a residential home system that has a water-tight foundation wall and literally floats in a recessed bathtub-like enclosure. Given that seismic waves cannot transmit across fluids, the Float-KR-free home, like a boat in its very own small harbor, is completely isolated from the earthquake by the little inch-wide moat that surrounds it. Mr. Ikasama imagined this isolation system subsequently to prior unsuccessful attempts to design buildings with large hemispherical bases that would gently rock during earthquakes. The alleged advantage of the Float-KR-free system over that other rocking concept is that the entire house is expected to stay put—floors remaining horizontal at all times—instead of rocking and spilling its contents as it rolls back and forth."

So went the quality of the information reaching the newsroom during the first half of the day. To counter this drought of meaningful news, the Director of Information dispatched a first "home" team to the streets to interview anybody with an opinion or anecdotal story to share. Rapidly, the airwaves filled with recollections of broken bottles in Etobicoke, swinging chandeliers in Scarborough, howling dogs in Mississauga, and other "Made in Canada" insipid stories.

A second team was tasked to call every University of Toronto professor and seek their expert opinion on a myriad of entertaining trivia: Should the country expect a baby boom in nine months as a result of this catastrophe? How to ensure pets are treated humanely during such disasters? Will the intense reconstruction following this disaster translate into a massive boom for the economy? Should instances of cannibalism be expected as people freeze to death? Will this disaster have a negative or positive impact on tourism next summer? Can fat people survive without food and water longer than slim ones?

The strategy was to generate a sustained flow of filler infotainment material that would give enough time for the Ottawa news bureau—the still-operating affiliate closest to the epicenter—to provide various reports on the impact of the earthquake there. Anything was fair game: minor injuries from miscellaneous falling objects; heart attacks of people scared witless; minute cracks in roadways or bridges; reports by curious onlookers; traffic jams; anything that could be speculatively attributed to the earthquake.

Combined, the Toronto and Ottawa stories would add up to a sufficient pile of pseudo-news to keep Canadians watching the tube until the teams dispatched to the real disaster could report. Unfortunately, as winter darkness fell, none of those CBC teams had been able to cross onto the island. And nothing but bleak silence from the reporters who lived on the island—although there was hope that, professional ethics above all, overcoming extreme hardship in conducting investigative work, they would eventually find ways to communicate with the outside world.

As headquarters faced the unenviable prospect of further stretching the inconsequential news further, the CBC crews close to Montréal caught the CHOK-AM feed, apparently the only radio station broadcasting tangible damage reports live from Montréal. The crews undertook to transcribe the juiciest parts and pieces, and fed this secondhand, repackaged information from CHOK-AM to the venerable and wealthy CBC, always careful to identify the source of their information to avoid lawsuits against the deep-pocket national institution on charges of plagiarism and copyright violations.

To complement this scant information, a briefing from the Québec Premier live from the old St-Hubert airport was scheduled for 5 p.m., and the CBC, like every other news agency equally frustrated by the island's inaccessibility, had microphones, cameras, and reporters awaiting the event that would keep Canadians glued to their television, for a little while longer.

"Manna! Manna!" Sort of.

Longueuil, 5:00 p.m.

Released almost simultaneously, the federal and provincial communiques rehashed the same platitudes issued earlier in the day. Tenuous claims on the capabilities of various government agencies, coupled with assertions on the effectiveness and relevance of their programs, wrapped into generous propagandist embellishments fully disconnected from ground-truth data, amounted to nothing more than chest-thumping by entrenched foes.

The provincial government attempted to take the upper hand in the courtship of public opinion by staging a press conference immediately after the release of the document. Léandre provided an upbeat summary of the high points of his government's communique and opened the floor for questions, fully aware that the few reporters in the room, beyond their usual egocentric drive to be seen as asking the tough questions, were starved for news and would be far from satiated by the meager official communique alone.

One question cut through the roar of reporters jockeying for attention: "Is your government planning to request assistance from the Canadian army?"

The media noise abated slightly, as the few savvy reporters who privately knew of Léandre's passionate opinion on this topic awaited to see whether he would dare publicly deliver his famous dithyrambic assault of the Canadian defense forces. Léandre paused a moment, and slowly translated his private tempestuous tirade into diplomatic and strategically suitable language.

"The army?" asked Léandre with surprised eyes. "There are no military ground forces in Canada with adequate training and experience on how to respond to this disaster unique in history."

Léandre expanded, with a calm authority.

"Furthermore, the relatively young and inexperienced Canadian troops are ill-equipped to provide the reliable field assistance needed by the affected population. All the equipment and resources required to respond to this disaster are already in place in Québec, and the small additional manpower and management assistance that can be provided by the Canadian Department of Defence is unnecessary.

"While we recognize that, in recent history, the mission of the Canadian army has not been to maintain offensive or defensive power, but rather to be of assistance in peacekeeping activities, and that as such it may have had some successes in providing limited logistical support after smaller disasters like floods or ice storms, the particular expertise that the Canadian army could provide at this time is not required and, if anything, could interfere with our own response and recovery activities. The extensive overhead required to integrate them into a complex operation to which they are ill-equipped to contribute would distract from the key actions undertaken by our own coordinated response and recovery activities.

"At this time, our government feels it is in our collective best interest to refuse any assistance from the Canadian military, with the proviso that we will advise if the situation were to change in the near future."

Léandre smiled to the press, confident that those few who knew him intimately recognized the uncompromised virulence of his position, under a diplomatic disguise. Indeed, Réal Chaput-Vigneault decoded this response to be a verbatim, politically correct version of Léandre's explosive rant of four hours earlier.

The rest of the press conference was uneventful, proceeding within the bounds of a standard pattern, with reporters asking for clarifications on points highlighted in the communique, and Léandre restating those points in ways that gave a new guise to the same information to fulfill each reporter's impetus and vainglorious drive to pry out guarded, valuable information.

This pointless massaging of information lasted for a period after which one reporter, cued by Réal, asked a planted question.

"When will you set foot on the island to assess firsthand the state of damage and the needs of the population?"

Léandre responded, "Before sunrise, my cabinet and I will fly, by helicopter, to the *Organisation de sécurité civile du Québec* headquarters in Montréal, together with a small contingent of invited journalists. Only a small group will be ferried along with us to the inaccessible island so as to minimize disruption to the response and recovery operations. From there, at 6:30 a.m. tomorrow, the director of the *Organization* and I will provide a brief summary report of the conditions on the island where I intend to spend considerable time over the next few days."

He hated long question periods and tried to never stretch them beyond a single high point, in an attempt to control the headlines. Pleased to leave on a teaser, he concluded, "Thanks for your time. Looking forward to reporting to you live from Montréal tomorrow morning."

With that, Léandre briskly walked off the podium, ending the press conference and leaving the audience wondering who among them would be invited to partake in that field trip. Very few. The lucky guests would be a select group of influential journalists, aficionados partial to the *Parti National* agenda.

Montréal, 5:30 p.m.

By 10:30 a.m., after miles of snow, slush, and ice—and hours of cold, frost, and wind chill—Jean-Pierre and Audréanne had reached another hospital. A seemingly operational hospital where health services were dispensed by a staff stretched thin, at the limit of its capabilities.

They had spent their first hour in the waiting room, thawing in silence, frustrated and scarred, exhausted by their trek through the frozen and demoralizing urban landscape of damaged infrastructure and helpless, wandering population. As blood started to flow again to their extremities, they had devoted much time to refocus, soul-searching to rediscover their deepest inner motivation and energy, and to rekindle the passion needed to care for the well-being of perfect strangers—or bolster their cupidity for other incentives that could lead to a similar outcome. Once reconnected with their selves, they had invested another hour searching for the head of operations, from whom they secured permission to dispense health services under the direction of a more experienced professional.

Unfortunately, they only had had time to apply a few balms and band-aids before management announced immediate closure of the hospital. Lack of justification for this decision generated a sizeable consternation, as all systems seemed operational and the few small cracks in the walls were far from intimidating. The announcement had thus been treated as a misguided and ill-informed management decision, probably by some distant bureaucrats on the basis of flawed data and a fair dose of conservatism, and the dispensing of care continued undeterred, assuming that a subsequent announcement would rectify the error.

However, a second announcement, counter to anticipations, had included a detailed technical brief by the chief physician. Water damage had been found propagating downward from the top stories. The cause of this flooding was traced back to ruptured pipe connections at the water reservoirs on the top story of the building, damage that likely occurred during the earthquake. The water infiltration was already extensive by the time of the announcement, and even if the sizeable leak could have been plugged, the flow of the accumulated water spill would have eventually reached the lower stories. From a medical perspective, this water was contaminated and created a substantial health hazard.

It was assessed that health services should not, could not, and would not be provided under a slow shower of dripping, contaminated water.

So again, Jean-Pierre and Audréanne spent hours assisting with the makeshift evacuation of patients to the nearest hospital. However, wise of their earlier negative experience, they had planned this time to hitch a ride on one of the last sport utility vehicles substituting for ambulances. Not being left stranded anew was the ultimate objective, so while helping to load stretchers and wheel chairs, they assiduously monitored the flow of patients and the remaining number of staff. They were determined that their just place would not be denied.

Yet, in spite of their best assessment, endless quantities of additional medical personnel kept appearing from the confines of the hospital. Panicked at the thought of being again left behind, they elected to violate protocol; twice they sneaked onto the back of the improvised ambulances, as clandestine passengers hoping to reach a welcoming harbor in uncomfortable but warm transit, and twice they were discovered by the hospital personnel and "evicted" before the vehicle even departed. Staff with union seniority and full employment at the hospital, and who had relied on public transportation to commute to their job, were not about to let two kids, volunteers at that, deny them their due.

As they had feared, to their greatest chagrin, the last surrogate ambulance left the two interns on the sidewalk, dousing them in a thick white smoke of tailpipe condensation as it took off, a brutal reminder of the Siberian cold and the miles of snow, slush, and ice—and hours of cold, frost, and wind chill—necessary to reach the next hospital.

They could have found some solace from the fact that the degrading experience was shared by a large group of lower-grade employees similarly abandoned at the deserted facility, but the disheartening prospect of another long trek to reach the next nearest hospital was overwhelming. Their energy had been sapped by a dark, negative force.

Consumed by doubts and pounded by the crashing waves of repeated failures, estranged from the pampered environment in which they had been groomed, they contemplated the abyss of depression. One side of their brain urged them to relinquish their idealistic pursuit of service, to abdicate their conceited perception of indispensability, and focus instead of the immediate need to survive. Yet, another side of their brain, still driven by the pursuit of recognition, adulation, and riches, couldn't surrender to the despair, couldn't tolerate the indelible taint of failure. The pride, the vanity, the irrational desire to force admiration, to be a hero, just wouldn't let the flame die. That driving force overtook all other emotions, mustered all the strength and adrenaline it could find, and pushed them through another dreadful sub-zero expedition.

A few hours later, they sat in the corner of another waiting room, in another hospital, starting the thawing process anew. The place was abuzz, and resources were stretched to the seams, which presaged well for employment of extra talent to cope with the surge of emergencies. A sign posted by management and indicating that thorough inspection of the entire building revealed no damage also augured well against closure of the hospital due to leaks or other unforeseen surprises.

Jean-Pierre and Audréanne, immobile while waiting for sensitivity to return to their frozen limbs, were entertained by staff gossips. Indiscreetly, nurses were spewing their disgruntlement in the open, with complete disregard to the impact this could have on the patients, buttressed against any possible consequences by the absolute protection provided by the union.

Much of the resentment centered on the unfair distribution of labor. Some expressed outrage at being abused, as no clause in the collective agreement required them to work excessive overtime, even in emergency situations. The problem was compounded by the fact that some staff had apparently snuck out without notice, and that others had never shown up for their shifts. Possible attenuating circumstances due to hardships related to family or personal losses were promptly dismissed by the staff on duty, who were unequivocal in condemning the absent parties as unabashed slackers with a track record of playing the system—even in the absence of emergencies. Some of the nurses voiced a resolve to also leave within a short time, if not at once, irrespective of the number of bloody patients clogging the waiting rooms, on the grounds of fairness and equity.

Jean-Pierre and Audréanne rooted for the slackers, hoping that the perspective of a severely depleted staff and a growing influx of patients would incite the management to be more receptive to two interns offering their services. In such circumstances, two lowly interns should be worth something—if not gold, at least respect and some financial recognition. A reasonable assumption, to be sure.

More disturbing, though, the professional complainers then directed their acrimony toward the paramedics and ambulance drivers, without whom the most severely injured patients were denied safe access to hospitals. The nurses bemoaned their utter unprofessional disappearance at the time they were most needed, accusing them of being rotten, unworthy scum that would not flinch at the thought of taking a union break in front a dying patient.

Jean-Pierre and Audréanne suspected that some paramedics and ambulance drivers never missed a chance to shirk their responsibilities and blame others for their failures. It was known throughout the health care community that some ambulance drivers with extreme union activist tendencies had not hesitated to let persons in distress die in their homes waiting for paramedics for hours—homes sometimes within striking distance of a hospital—simply to make a point during tense periods of negotiations for renewal of collective agreements. However, they had never anticipated that their potential employment, one day, would have hinged on the simultaneous conditions of having enough slackers not report to work at a hospital, and having enough patients show up on their own in spite of the failure to perform by other slackers.

Washington, 6:30 p.m.

President Butler hated complex, comprehensive briefs, and never read them. Neither did he read text that stretched beyond one 8.5-by-11-inch page. To survive, those around him had learned to prepare concise, factual bullet lists on which presidential actions, simple and decisive, could be made. They had mastered the skill of drafting briefs in ways that contrasted all points against the good old-fashioned values held by the proud people of Butler's native God-fearing Tennessee, which Butler upheld, with his full heart and soul, as a beacon of America's roots, traditions, and constitutional truths. All issues were thus either compatible or discordant with these beliefs. The world's geopolitics, the global economy, environmental policies, the social fabric of the nation, and the spectrum of political beliefs, were sifted through Butler's sieve, separating all matters into good or evil, black or white. Never half-good, never grey. A hand on the bible as assurance to impose self-righteous decisions, Butler never doubted or questioned his decisions, never changed his mind.

Treegherapy had prepared a 5-page executive summary outlining his perception of the geopolitical forces at play, tainting the narrative by his personal beliefs, leading to the recommendation that the director of FEMA should meet with the President, who would ultimately decide on what should be the official position of the United States in response to this direct request for humanitarian assistance.

After having perused Treegherapy's document and met with him to further pick his brain, the FEMA director summarized the information in a few succinct paragraphs, which stated:

"It is the consensus opinion of the CIA, FBI, NSA, and FEMA experts on Canadian relations that Quebec is committing a grievous offense against protocol by contacting FEMA directly in search of humanitarian assistance to sustain its recovery effort following a large-magnitude earthquake that has struck Montreal early morning today. Half of the province's population and industrial base is located in Montreal, as well as the headquarters of many international agencies. Although the extent of damage to the infrastructure is unknown at this time, massive direct and indirect losses, as well as human casualties, are expected following an event of this magnitude.

"Canada is a long-time ally and trade partner who has generally, but not consistently, supported U.S. national and international policies. It has encountered challenges in its attempts to meet tight homeland security objectives, due to its lax law enforcement capabilities and excessively distorted protection of civil liberties. Canada's demographics and economic system resemble those of the U.S., except that the Canadian government has woven a tight social net, with extensive 'cradle to grave' benefits for its population in exchange for an aggressive taxation basis.

"The country is currently under a constitutional crisis due to the rise of secessionist pressures in the province of Quebec, where an impending referendum will consult the population on its desire to leave the federation. It is unknown how Canada would respond to a declaration of independence; the possibility of escalation to civil war seems remote in a country highly regarded for its peacemaking tradition, but there are no precedents in Canadian history.

"The immediate matter of concern is the Quebec government's request for humanitarian assistance from FEMA, specifically a million bunk beds and blankets presumably to be used in emergency shelters for the population displaced by the disaster. There is a possibility that this request, since routed through nonconventional communication channels in breach of protocol, has not been vetted by the Canadian government, and a direct response to the Quebec (provincial) government without prior consultation with the Canadian (federal) government could create a diplomatic incident."

The President's Chief of Staff read this convoluted FEMA brief and, familiar to the desires and aptitudes of his boss, rearranged the information into a bullet list that sorted statements into a number of black or white outcomes, adding clarifications of his own when appropriate.

"Positive points:
- "Canada is a reliable trade-partner, with a population predominantly of Christian denominations;
- "Canada is a friendly nation with an insignificant army;
- "Quebec is a Canadian province (like a state);
- "Quebec turned towards the U.S. for assistance after a damaging earthquake has hit at the heart of its economic hub (Montreal) today;

"Negative Points:

- "Canada is not effective (by U.S. security standards) in tracking, arresting, and prosecuting suspected terrorists;
- "Quebec is led by a secessionist government, with socialist/communist tendencies, that wants to separate from Canada;
- "Quebec has directly requested assistance from FEMA, bypassing the official channels of communication with Canada;
- "It is not known if Canada is aware of Quebec's request;

"To decide: Official response and course of action."

The President hated complex briefs from which obvious decisions couldn't be inferred. The balance of positive and negative points left him perplexed. He loved campaigning, talking to his people, shaking their hands, kissing their babies, dispensing affectionate slaps in the back—the human side of representing the nation. He abhorred geopolitics.

Through the oval office's windows, he could only see trees and a patch of lawn unfolding from the West Wing, permanently deserted except for the occasional mad streaker dashing through before being tasered, tackled, trampled, and pummeled by Secret Service forces. He wished he could have an unobstructed view on the National Mall, the fascinating rectangular expanse of grass where so many peaceful battles were waged on the strength of clear unambiguous mandates, the symbolic and inspiring garden of the National Capital City, seat of the government, where thousands of skillful policies were crafted and implemented to better one nation under God. He had visions of General Washington strolling along the mall, pondering what bright future laid ahead for the land of the free, visions of President Lincoln lecturing the elite of the young nation gathered along the mall in celebration of national pride, and other similarly exalting anachronistic visions, all factually incorrect recollections of American history lessons poorly learned and distorted by the fuzziness of time.

He turned and looked at the director of FEMA patiently awaiting the presidential decision.

"As a courtesy, I should call the President of Canada to better inform my decision on this complex matter."

He turned to his Chief of Staff who understood, no words exchanged, that it was his task to arrange this.

Montréal, 7:15 p.m.

Lise had invested her afternoon drafting a thorough list of emergency shelters that reflected her own biases and prejudices, trampling upon all standards of political correctness. She edited and re-edited the list, deleting and undeleting entries, reordering it, until she deemed it to be duly massaged and presentable. Unwilling to entrust the raw outcome of her deliberations to a lowly staff who could betray her intents, given the sensitive personal annotations peppered over the pages, and also because the document was plainly illegible, she devoted another hour to word-process the document on a laptop computer which was loaded with all the necessary software and could operate independent of the dead central server.

The six o'clock deadline had long come and gone, as Lise was aware. Just prior to that deadline, the product had been nearly ready. The list of all venues she deemed acceptable to serve as possible shelters was complete, with addresses and phone numbers for each institution (in case phone service was to resume), but it was an unpolished product. Its main sins were that the information was lumped in paragraphs, that the list of institutions was not alphabetized, and that a number of typographical errors had to be fixed. Lise was determined that such an important document had to be perfected to a level commensurate with its status. No deadline was to ever have supremacy over her own job satisfaction. Better to not release anything than release a half-baked product. Therefore, she spent an extra hour in formatting tasks, building a nice multicolumn table into which she cut and pasted all the information, sorting the data to display all entries A-to-Z, and, most time consuming, double checking all the phone numbers she had painstakingly transcribed from the yellow pages.

The final product was ready to distribute at 7 p.m. As a result, the early evening news was deprived of this vital information.

Contemplating the aesthetically pleasing yet informative pages, fulfilled with the satisfaction of a job well done, it finally dawned on her that there were significant challenges in communicating this information. The pernicious effect of anchoring emergency response central operations into a high-technology platform only became obvious to her then, for the first time, when faced by the insurmountable challenge of using this technology to share with the world the few pages she had created. Lavish investments in advanced multimedia electronic tools were fashionable and convenient to justify the need for an ever-increasing agency budget, but the resulting addiction and total dependency on that technology translated into the inability to transmit a simple letter, in either its digital or analog version, once the gadgets were broken. No server implied no email. No phones implied no faxes.

She surmised that getting a copy of the communique to Radio Canada would be sufficient, on the basic assumption that all media essentially plagiarize each other. She thus devised a two-pronged plan to deliver this data to the national broadcaster.

First, she would arm her technician with copies of the document, and dispatch him to the headquarters of the national television agency. The expedition was a good two miles' walk in the crisp cold of the evening, which she saw as positive, providing much-needed exercise for her geeky aide who, by her assessment, spent too much time crouched over keyboards staring at computer monitors. The expectation was that, even in a highly dysfunctional Radio Canada office, enough of the young blood would have reported to work, seeking an opportunity to shine and eager to dislodge some of the senior staff from the best-paid media jobs in Montréal. Putting the document in the hands of these hungry wolves nested within the most resourceful media organization in Canada ensured that it would somehow reach the masses.

Second, as a back up, Lise radioed the list to the government staff temporary headquartered in Longueuil, laboriously spelling each word to ensure that this perfect, useless list suffered the least possible degradation in quality as it filtered through the communication link.

Now, those in dire need of food and shelter, assuming they could somehow receive this governmental roadmap, would be provided with a unique opportunity to roam door-to-door, from one useless address to another, frustrated to find only locked doors and dark buildings—like trick-or-treaters spending Halloween night in a gated community restricted to "mature living"—until reaching, out of luck or by sheer perseverance, one of the institutions on Lise's list that would coincidentally happen to have taken the initiative to open its doors to serve as a shelter.

Montréal, 7:30 p.m.

Collecting his random thoughts and impulses into a coherent whole had always been challenging—an exercise better deferred till absolutely required, either by danger or the need to survive.

"What a day! What a day! What a day!" repeated Clément Légaré incessantly to himself, as a mantra recited to ignite the mysterious, uncontrollable process by which he sometimes could probe into his mind, hoping that a retrospective approach, slowly replaying the day's series of incomprehensible events, might help, maybe even lead to the right decision.

It had all started so suddenly.

Was it a thief, or mischievous teenagers? Or some evil god?

Somebody, whoever it was, had shaken his bench in the middle of the night. The culprit had been quick to run and hide because no one was around the bench when he opened his eyes, which had occurred as he was falling off, the instant before hitting the ground.

A lame joke on a destitute, harmless soul minding his own business, not asking anything of anyone.

"At least it wasn't a beating," he thought, a late-night activity enjoyed by young thugs which he felt had been happening with increasing frequency; or maybe the collapse of time between rancid memories was just a psychosomatic byproduct from the digestion of gallons of Listerine?

"Damn cold, damn cold, too damn cold," he had whispered as his mantra then, trying to refocus on the problem.

"And all that noise, and noise, and noise!" he had yelled, for the sirens in the night made it impossible to regain sleep in spite of the unusual total darkness. Lampposts, buildings, traffic lights, and neon signs had strangely died, with only the headlights of traffic assaulting him.

And the sirens. So many of them.

He had lied back on his bench, puzzled, eyes wide open, pulling tight on layers of newspapers he could not read, wrapped in the political rants of professional analysts weighing the possible economical dangers of a secession from the glorious Canadian nation, a 96-point headline deploring a 4-3 overtime loss by the Montréal Canadiens, and colorful pages proclaiming unbeatable low prices for Canadian Grade A beef and Florida oranges. Had grocery chains ever contemplated the possibility that their multifold inserts displaying weekly bargains could serve to wrap and preserve human meat in an outdoor fridge?

And light had come, as it always does, without asking if he wanted another day. But the routine was askew.

He had remained lying on the bench, wondering why this day was different, why the almighty enforcers of the city's authority had not yet poked him in the ribs and ordered him to move. Granted this reprieve from the need to wander aimlessly away from the public eye, he had rested on his bench, cocooned in his torn garbs against the sub-zero temperature, wondering how long he could enjoy this vacation.

From this prime location, in a park encircled by rows of turn-of-the-century renovated townhouses stacked together in blocks like the roots of pastel rainbows, displaying their faint colors as tributes to the wealth and poor tastes of their young urban professional owners, Clément had observed the unfolding of this strange day.

He had paid a particular attention to the events at the pink house that he could barely see between a few big trees at the edge of the park. Uncharacteristically, its windows were broken—oddly enough, the only house around the park with such damage. But what had attracted Clément's attention to that particular house was the burst of activity there... and all the swearing.

Over the years, many charitable souls, presumably driven by divine guidance, had tried to save Clément by praising the virtues of work and the redeeming qualities of a steady job, but he never fulfilled the expectations of those generous overtures. The intense swearing that accompanied the man's labor at the pink house had vindicated Clément's aversion—if work was indeed so enjoyable, that working man should have been singing hymns instead of being a foul-mouthed wretch.

Yet, it was the nature of the specific activity itself that had captivated him, for hours. The man was boarding windows! He had nailed large plywood sheets on the first window frames, consistently with the rules of the art to convert an occupied dwelling into a condemned slum. But strangely, after a few windows, the man changed strategy and proceeded to cover the other windows with single boards and planks, and again, finally, as the intense hammering mutated into the screeching of unrolling tape, with cardboard and polystyrene.

How could one of those infinitely wealthy owners rooted around the park be too lazy to purchase the proper supplies to do the job right, using instead whatever makeshift material could be found, as if his stash of suitable supplies had dwindled to extinction and pragmatic solutions prevailed over effective ones?

Final surprise, once all the gaps had been filled one way or another, the man had driven away, abandoning the house.

There lied the torture.

A boarded-up house.

The attraction was innate, the signal unambiguous. An abandoned house as an inviting shelter. Yet, the disconnectedness of the surrounding neighborhood, the cleanliness of the finishes, the orderliness of the landscaping in its winter skeleton.

Clément's random thoughts could not converge. How could such a dump appear overnight? Weren't slums the slow by-product of urban decay as neighborhoods were overtaken by criminals and economic outcasts? Did a single boarded-up house make a ghetto? Could the expanse of a ghetto be reduced to a single house, and if so, how it could mushroom in such a well-groomed community, and how it could be pink?

As night fell, as the air grew colder, as the man never returned, the coherent whole his brain had tried to assembled never materialized. The torture, however, had to cease. So Clément left his bench for the abandoned sanctuary. All he had to do to trespass into the house was to punch through one of the flimsily boarded-up windows; he sacrificed a cardboard window for the reward of a roof.

He had never so easily entered into a vacant property before, but he knew that care was still required. A rotten floor failing under weight, co-habitation with rats, and hostile squatters were part of the occupational hazard. Memories had for the most part been washed from his brain cells by the cleansing effect of alcohol, but knowledge engendered by pain is forever tattooed into the grey matter. So entering new, uncharted territory, he remembered to take time to assess the lay of the land.

His first steps into the dark new shelter had suggested an unstable, mushy ground. He had kneeled and removed his shredded gloves to feel the floor. It felt like wool, in a tightly packed coating on top of a solid floor. He had sprawled on the floor, squashing his nose on it. The sweet citrus smell cajoled him, soothing his ache, melting his fear, warming his spirit.

"What a day! What a day! What a day!" he incessantly repeated.

After replaying the entire day in his mind, at great effort, like a collage of disparate patches, it still made no sense. So Clément stopped trying to make sense of it, like he had stopped trying to make sense of anything a long time ago. Most of life to him was senseless, pointless. Begging wasn't rewarded in a county proud of its social net built on the strength of merciless taxes, but he knew as a visceral truth that, as few realize, no matter how strong it can be, a net essentially consists of holes woven together. Sure as the arthritis eating his bones told him, homelessness was harsh in a country abandoned by most living forms, vegetable or animal, for six months of the year. Pity and charity were scarce resources not randomly wasted on the stupid fools that refused to latch onto the largesse of government programs for their survival and that instead preferred to be autonomous individuals left to succumb to the failings of their defective brain, inadequate judgment, minimal education, excessive pride, and whatever else led through the holes of the net.

"What a day! But a good one!" Clément thought, never one to complain, in making his final assessment.

He had found a better place to sleep.

Warm—if only relatively so.

Sleep was still the best part of the day, a complete evasion from his heavy burden, the respite from the insanity of it all, second only to death as the great healer of all pains. Clément was convinced of that—dying wouldn't be bad. When falling asleep, Clément often hoped not to wake up, because killing himself didn't come naturally. He reasoned, as he could, that life had already given him all that he was entitled to receive and that it had been a good life overall; staying any longer was pointless, being like the guest that never leaves. Nobody would notice the absence of a single star in a sky of billions of lights, and to Clément, here lied the significance of insignificance. He was ready to burn off, unnoticed, as he knew that he was insignificant, even to himself.

But the abandoned house was too warm and comfortable to die in.

Not there.

Instead, as his unstructured thoughts wandered aimlessly, he fell asleep on the soft carpet.

Ottawa, 8:00 p.m.

Per protocol, the ringing started punctually. The Premier picked up the phone, and strained to greet the President's call with an upbeat, yet diplomatic, "Brendon Decker speaking."

"Premier Decker? President Butler will be with you in a moment."

Brendon fumed at the "I'm so important that you need to first talk to the secretary that set up my call" routine from his American counterpart. This was particularly offensive coming from Butler, whom Brendon considered to be a lazy bum addicted to talk shows, video games, junk food, soft porn, fart jokes, and other mindless cultural pursuits in vogue south of the border.

"Brendon! Ron here. It's been a while!" a voice said—the President refraining from adding, "I still remember your horrible golf swing, and that tee-off drive into the clubhouse."

"Ronald. It's always a pleasure to talk to you," he replied, thinking, "as long as you keep your ass in your fucking country."

"I hear you have some problems up there?" the other said, dying to editorialize with "What else is new in a country run by inbred frozen morons?"

The virulent feelings of mutual disrespect between the two statesmen were so intense that even though protocol forced them to keep their true feelings to parenthetical thoughts they could not openly express, they were both aptly able, like mind-readers, to translate casual statements wrapped into a disingenuous aura of friendship into their real meaning.

"Well, they're not really problems (you pompous arrogant Yankee). I think we have it all under control, and will be able to bring back normalcy within a few days, except for a rogue provincial government who is trying to make political capital out of the whole deal (although so many fucking words in a single sentence will likely logjam your minuscule brain)."

"We certainly can relate to such political problems (but the morons in our House and Senate are amateurs compared to the fuck-masters that run your poor excuse of a country). I am confident that you will successfully manage any crisis that comes your way (by pumping more hot air per minute than anybody I know). Besides, you can always trust in our long friendship with Canada to be of assistance in times of difficulties (but we would force you to publicly kiss our ass and acknowledge that Canada is just a goddamn despondent banana republic before sending a single dollar your way)."

"The most sincere and long-standing friendship of the United States is truly appreciated (we just love being fucked from behind by a 300-pound gorilla)."

"It's always a pleasure to be of assistance to our most respected neighbors (and rape Canada all we can)."

"In that perspective, there is a small issue for which we would appreciate your collaboration (and hope that we won't have to trade our sovereignty over the arctic passage waterways for it, you greedy bastards). And I trust our diplomatic corps have already exchanged on that topic, and likely briefed you on that matter (they might even have played the tapes while you napped since I hear that's how you get educated)."

"Sure. It's this thing about Kwebek, right? (and I've started the meter... this will cost you)."

"Exactly (even though you can't pronounce any foreign word right, like most of your illiterate compatriots). That province is led by a secessionist government (that's a word you should understand and fear), and for political reasons, we understand that they have requested assistance from FEMA (where did they get the idea that the U.S. gave a shit about anybody)."

"Yes, that's our understanding, too (dumb ass, we're the ones that told your stupid overpaid and asleep-at-the-switch bureaucrats)."

"This was a serious lack of judgment on their part, and we would prefer to deal with this problem internally. Any intervention from the U.S. in Canadian politics could be negatively construed by the world's political and economical communities as an objurgation of our sovereignty (go screw up third world countries, foreign dictatorships, and the Middle East until the entire world wishes to blow you up to smithereens and we'll pretend to morally support you publicly, but don't fuck with us)."

"That should not be a problem (as if we cared for a 51st state filled with a bunch of igloos and a few million assholes that can't be assimilated). We have never intervened in Canadian internal affairs and politics (if you are so stupid to believe this), and certainly don't intend to change our policy in light of the recent events (we never give away freebies; let the secessionists go to the bank). However, we would like to take this matter into deliberation for an hour or so (just to piss you off and show you who's in charge here)."

"Certainly, that is not a problem (we know you need to ask your advisors to decide because you don't have the brains to do so by yourself, just as you need their help to wipe your ass or to bang your wife). We trust you will come to the right conclusions ('cause your advisors actually have real diplomas and are highly paid to jackhammer some common sense into your hollow head)."

"So that's it, Brendon. It certainly was nice to talk to you. I hope we will have some chance to play golf in Canada again some time in the near future (it was a riot to see you drive divots the size of Rhode Island, and I will always keep reminding you over and over of your shot into the clubhouse)."

"Likewise, Ronald. Looking forward to same (I dream every-day of using my sand wedge to carve out the arrogant smirk from your ugly face, and my wood driver to whack your balls back to the alligator-infested swamp where you grew up)."

The President hung up first, as always. He cherished the thought of hanging up on world leaders, especially those endowed with an inflated view of their importance, and, in his opinion, Brendon "Dick-less" ranked very high on that list of irrelevant leaders

Brendon, annoyed as always to hear the sustained tone signaling that the other party had hung up first, shut the speakerphone and turned to his advisers. In his usual monotone manner, he summarized.

"I think we're fine. The goddamn lazy bastard will never commit a dollar for something he can't find on a map."

Montréal, 8:45 p.m.

All television stations, radio stations, and newspapers assigned teams of interns to diligently copy and replicate the list of shelters from the ticker scrolling at the bottom of the Radio Canada screen. Nobody knew how the national broadcasting agency managed such an exclusive, but all wondered how it could be so low as to scoop them on such key information of vital public interest.

The document hand-delivered to the Radio Canada headquarters had landed in the hands of a couple of aggressive and resourceful budding reporters who found a way to dispatch it to affiliate stations before the official list from the government was issued—hungry young wolves evidently transcribing faster than civil servants more mindful of the dangers of high blood pressure. Armed with laptops in various states of partially discharged batteries, they drove towards the eastern tip of the island, stopping to check phone booths every mile or so, until a working one could be found. A decrepit payphone east of Highway 25, like a beat-up soldier on guard, offered a weak but steady dial tone, to which they hooked the acoustic coupler of an archaic dial-up modem to email the transcribed list. The triumphant satisfaction of their mission accomplished was absolute; the fact that they ended up stranded out of gas a few miles later—by lack of foresight in their youthful eagerness—without an open service station on the island, couldn't dampen their spirits and the certitude that the self-sacrifice was worthwhile and likely to pay rewarding professional dividends in the long run.

The list prepared by Lise Letarte included a number of civil buildings that could be of potential use during the disaster, but did not group them in categories differentiating their specific use. With a blatant disregard for new immigrants or even tourists, Lise assumed that the citizens of Montréal worth helping had lived there long enough to understand how specific institutions would operate in a crisis. As a result, the names, addresses and phone numbers of civic halls, hospitals, grade schools, high schools, *polyvalentes*, CEGEPs, morgues, churches, bingo halls, shopping malls, and museums were lumped together as one long string of institutions contributing to the emergency effort.

By the evening, all Québécois outside of Montréal knew where to find a shelter on the island, although some iterations would be necessary to sort through those that accepted cold or warm bodies. The challenge was to convey this information to those who needed it. Those residents of Montréal without power but with phone service could be reached by concerned family members. Those immersed in absolute power and communications blackout had to resort to portable radios, stretching battery life through parsimonious usage, in some instances trading off flashlight and radio needs on shared batteries, hoping to catch the weaker signals from distant Sherbrooke or Trois-Rivières for a broader perspective. The one radio station broadcasting from Montréal remained long uninformed of the existence of the list, unable to serve its community until callers brought the information forward. Those without batteries, isolated from the outside world, would wait for the information to slowly filter down, by word of mouth.

In the meantime, Lise had undertaken an archeological dig of significant proportions, opening countless boxes in search of additional reports documenting how the earthquake emergency response plan had been created and validated, or any additional information that she could use to start coordinating the emergency response activities and assert the important role of her office.

Numerous policy documents outlined the key role of her office in providing training and assistance to municipalities that were bound by law to implement effective emergency preparedness measures. Twice as many related memos and briefs systematically emphasized that a gentle, cooperative approach was recommended to entice and encourage the local emergency responders to participate in those training and assistance programs, as coaxing was deemed more effective to preserve the respectful and collegial climate needed to achieve better preparedness than the threat of rigorously enforcing the law and enacting sanctions against the noncompliant parties. A high level of "collaborative communications" was sought as the primary objective of the government's agenda, rather than massive, expensive investments. Within a large cadre of activities that could be conducted to meet the mandated level of emergency preparedness, programs that funded abundant discussions and studies on what should be done to enhance emergency response capabilities were given top priority, a convenient, unstated strategy to indefinitely postpone major financial investments and commitments from both the municipal and provincial jurisdictions. The municipalities quickly mastered the game, recognizing that the time invested to pursue an ongoing dialogue between levels of government on possible future actions that could be undertaken, was being credited—no differently than actual actions—as preparedness activities in fulfillment of their mandate. The teeth in the legislation displayed to reassure the public were actually dentures, removed to soften the bite when it came to enforcement.

Emergency response plans for all kind of contingencies were available, in 4- to 6-inch-thick binders, providing in excruciating detail the responsibilities for awarding financial assistance and the respective role of each level of government in that process, the paperwork and documentation that would have to be assembled to justify each said request, the forms that would have to be filled in, the eligible and noneligible expenses, the role of each agency during the response process and their interdependency through a distributed chain of command, the desirable frequency of training exercises (pending available funding), and other minute details well-intended to ensure the smoothest possible response and recovery. A plan for flood, another one for chemical spills, plans for each kind of natural or technological disasters, and plans for any flavor of terrorist attack. Great plans assembled by policy and planning wonks, never exercised outside the confines of a file cabinet. All because the task of generating the plans, while itself convenient in fulfilling a significant part of the mandate, was achieved at costs that were manageable compared to the exorbitant expenses required for implementation and effective preparedness.

Lise guessed that the development of a plan over 2,000 slow hours by one bureaucrat, factoring in salary, a myriad of benefits, sick leave days taken when not sick, generous vacations, training days, long breaks and lunches that over-spilled negotiated boundaries, and even wasted time—such as taking breakfast after punching the clock using a toaster conveniently hidden in one's desk bottom drawer—was still less expensive than a full-blown, all-agencies field exercise that would have required planning and coordination efforts by hundreds of bureaucrats over many months. Furthermore, generating reams of plans likely not only exploited a skill in which administrations excelled, but also provided the mountains of paper by which one could document accomplishments to justify raises and career advancement.

Yet, to wrap plans in an aura of credibility and anchor them into real-life data ready for implementation, each plan duly ended with the obligatory chain of phone numbers to be dialed in the most effective way to mobilize the entire emergency response team as promptly as possible, built on the assumption that all links of the chain would be alive and eager to report to duty following a catastrophic event, a wishful but inane assumption, as Lise had discovered earlier in the day. To further compound the futility of the contact list, Lise noticed that most lists had not been updated in years, a substantial oversight given the immense rotation in leadership throughout agencies, where up to 50% of decision-makers had been promoted to other positions in the past two-year period, or had retired and not been replaced in many cases due to budget constrictions.

Lise fell asleep among the pile of reports, a juicy financial monograph on the municipal subsidy needed for new fire trucks serving as a pillow, and other surrounding binders keeping her warm—the fruits of the labor of an army of bureaucrats at last finding a purpose.

Montréal, 9:00 p.m.

In spite of periodic exercises to generate body heat, to compensate for the relative quasi-immobility inherent to making notes and taking pictures, the cold of the night had permeated through the layers of Gore-tex, nylon, wool, and other diverse natural and synthetic fabrics, and proceeded to bite the skin of his hands and feet. Furthermore, determination and passion could not overcome the challenges of darkness, which had reduced the flow of data collection to a trickle over the past five hours. Seeking an appropriate shelter for the night seemed the wise course of action.

James had considered a number of options. Seeking shelter from a charitable homeowner or tenant was not one of them. First, the absence of smoking chimneys within sight underscored the scarcity of operating fireplaces in the vicinity, a sure indication that most families had either abandoned their homes in the search for a state-provided temporary shelter, or set camp in their basements, cuddled together, cocooned in layers of blankets or quasi-hermetically zipped into sleeping bags. Second, James believed an engineer would be unwelcome in the current circumstances. Engineers had been the targets of public hostility in the aftermath of past destructive earthquakes, specifically when failed and collapsed infrastructures (known to be designed by engineers) were directly responsible for much of the public's suffering in the weeks following the main shock. As a result, in those instances, easily identifiable members of the profession—as convenient scapegoats—had been victimized by resentful and unforgiving violent mobs, being severely brutalized, even sometimes lynched. To date, such spontaneous mob frenzy and executions had been confined to undeveloped countries with lax or corrupt building officials, or to countries where building codes consisted of a simple clause stating that contractors and engineers shall be killed if their building fails and kills one or more occupants—a statement usually surrounded by text praising God for the enlightenment to formulate such a fair and effective building code provision. Further, this barbaric behavior had typically occurred following damaging earthquakes in warm climates where loss of shelters exposed excitable souls to the burning sun. Yet, James did not feel any urge to investigate if subzero temperatures in a modern civilization wrecked by an earthquake could tempt the frozen locals to adopt the customs and rituals of the world's uneducated masses.

At the same time, while James wasn't eager to disclose his professional qualifications to a homeowner in seeking refuge for the night, no amount of denial could overcome the fact that his white hard-hat, measuring tapes, fluorescent orange jacket overlay, and other miscellaneous gadgets, convincingly screamed "Look at me! I'm am engineer!" to anyone who might harbor a primal desire to hang "one of them bastards" from a telephone pole. If this were a real concern, stuffing the engineer gear in his backpack would only require removing his gloves for a few minutes, possibly hiding from the wind in a bus shelter to partly abate the duress of the -40°F air. In reality, the more worrisome and probable risk was to be mistaken for a looter, and the engineer paraphernalia provided some appearance of officialdom guarding against that danger, the outfit alone justifying his right to roam abandoned buildings without scrutiny of his credentials—leaving observers to assume that his efforts were contributing to implementing the eagerly awaited restoration of normalcy.

The real reason he was loath to seek shelter in a private dwelling was that he was completely exhausted, and resented the idea of having to spend an evening conversing with his hosts as a courtesy, to avoid being rude. Furthermore, once such connections were established, they unavoidably led to some sort of linked destiny, and the impossibility of escaping without paying back the hospitality by sharing in some task or chore—an infinite number of which would urgently need to be accomplished in any home of survivors in these harsh and trying times. He was not a social type by nature, even less so at work. He'd left the warmth of his Ottawa home to undertake a scientific earthquake reconnaissance mission, and any situation that would tie him down and distract from this objective was not worth this self-imposed suffering.

Sleeping in an office building deprived of power, and thus heating, offered the promise of some possible residual warm air still held captive by building insulation (assuming unbroken windows) and protection from the wind, but remained unappealing. It could have been the last resort in any other northern city, but he had long ago identified a far better solution.

As he'd expected, the windows of the metro station entrance were already broken. This could have been attributed to the earthquake by an untrained eye, but the radiating cracks on the remaining glass converged toward a point of impact that could have only been induced by human activity. Circumventing the locked doors of the station through this impromptu entrance, James navigated the station with his flashlight, following the signs to the metro ramps.

Down the steps of the first immobile escalator, penetrating deeper into the earth's insulating mantle, he could feel the receding coldness, and even hints of warmth, surely in a relative way. He stored all his engineering gear in his backpack. By the time he reached the platform along the metro tracks, already densely populated by others who had deducted from the same logic that the dark shelter could provide a suitable environment to weather the crisis, the temperature was bearable even without a winter coat.

He first settled on an isolated spot at the end of the platform, about 20 feet from the next closest refugee, but soon pondered whether it was preferable to proceed into the metro tunnel, not because the air seemed still warmer there, but rather to more safely secure his possessions by increasing the safe distance to possible scavengers. His enormous backpack was substantially more voluminous that those he could see when he had proceeded down the platform, and he suspected that some of the desperate and hungry citizens resting on the hard concrete floor probably inferred that this bulkiness was attributable to a sizeable food reserve and other sorely needed goods—unless they were momentarily blinded by his flashlight.

Sleeping on the narrow concrete ledge adjacent to the metro tracks inside the tunnel could have been hazardous if power resumed and trains started to circulate anew, but he gambled that this was unlikely given the state of the infrastructure he'd observed during the day, and entered the tunnel.

Washington, 9:30 p.m.

Moe, Larry and Curly filled the void, crushing the opportunity for a propitious silence. As dictator, field marshal, and minister of propaganda of Moronica, they complotted to foil a female spy's attempt to commit mayhem, with the usual violent abuse and chaotic racket of their black-and-white vaudeville slapstick. Even in high definition on a swank plasma screen, The Three Stooges' absurdities clashed with the solemn decor. The president, adrift in his thoughts, occasionally glimpsed at the screen when strident screaming or an outbreak of pandemonium summoned his attention. He otherwise stared out the window at the grass on which nobody walked and the trees that blocked the view.

Both a curse and blessing, he was a living, breathing cliché caught in the trappings of his own ambition. He embodied the shallow one-dimensional profile that perfectly matched the ultimate optimal stereotype that polls, focus groups, image consultants, public relations specialists, and other charisma professionals established to be the persona most electable in the grand republic. The genetic expression, educational background, and moral beliefs that coincidentally met the dosage of all ingredients contained in the secret recipe that defined the ideal president. The one bland person in conformance to the nation's archetypal desires of leadership, for a given demographic profile in time, and able to recite the pre-scripted formulas of platitudes needed to gather the right percentage of voters in the right states having the right number of Electoral College delegates to win.

So there stood the winner, bolstered by his slim education and moral beliefs, propped by the briefs of experts and the interested support of countless advisors, alone to formulate his final decision on a minor point of international policy of little national interest.

About Canada, of all things! A country he loathed and perceived to be nothing more than a wasteland of consanguineous turpitude endlessly moralizing with a despicable and annoying smug self-righteousness. A banana republic of parasites living on the fat proceeds of its unbounded natural resources, culturally and financially leeching from the USA for its survival. An arctic Saudi Arabia lazily sucking oil from its frozen sands to fund its decrepit socialist agenda by showering dollars on an unaccomplished citizenry only united in its hate of the southern giant. An arrogant weakling deserving of a good beating, unable to defend its borders, yet allowed to exist by the sheer democratic magnanimity of its allies and the unattractiveness of invading a burdensome population of ingrates, loyalists, secessionists, natives, and terrorists that could never be assimilated. An unprincipled and rudderless bureaucratic atheist state, without moral rigor and self-respect, encouraging a free-for-all of creeds and superstitions to trample its venerable institutions and traditions, in the ridiculous belief that its superior intellect could accommodate the endless demands of all sectarian rituals and dogmatic fairy tales.

"A nation without the balls of a nation!" thought the President.

A rumbling noise distracted the President from his aimlessly wandering bigoted thoughts. In the new short playing, one of the earthquakes that happened every five minutes in the tropical country of Valeska, simulated with all the clumsiness of the golden age of cinema, destroyed an adobe wall of the prison that kept the Stooges captive.

A decision had to be made. He gratefully welcomed and praised the timely divine intervention that inserted Valeska as a metaphor in his reflection to solve the problem at hand. Valeska just seemed like another incompetent country that got what it deserved. It all became clear.

So clear that he didn't need to read the thick report that had been dropped on his desk, describing the geopolitical stakes, the risk of earthquakes on the West Coast of the United States or in the Mississippi Valley, and all the other relevant and irrelevant details. Nor did he need to read the executive summary, or anything for that matter. The electorate had spoken and it did not choose an intellectual who would pretend to anchor all its decisions in cold, objective scholarly facts documented in thick, spiral-bound theses.

All clear that earthquakes were divine punishments dispensed to sinful unrepentant societies, that no matter what scientists predicted, the seismic lashing of California was the result of its continued open embrace of gays, just like the flooding of New Orleans by Hurricane Katrina was just retribution to a wicked sin city addicted to hedonism, laziness, and voodoo.

All clear that the God-fearing people of the Bible Belt could dismiss all forecasted scenarios of cataclysmic earthquakes, recognizing those predictions to be nothing more than misguided scientific fallacies extrapolated from historical religious transgressions no longer applicable.

All clear that reliance on building codes to prevent disasters and government support to recover from disasters were equally misguided approaches at odds with the core American values of faith and self-responsibility, and that one could gauge an individual's compliance with those almighty values by the financial wealth and rewards dispensed from above.

The president genuinely believed that quarterbacks owed their mega-salaries to saluting the sky after each touchdown, not surprisingly earning more than the agnostic liberals and free thinkers who had overtaken the country's academic institutions and polluted youths' minds with their heretic propaganda. He believed that poverty and destitution were a plague dispensed with Calvinist rigor upon those addicted to government handouts, as much after disasters as in normal times—those too lazy or too dumb to embrace the land of opportunity bestowed upon the young nation by a God whose citizenship was never in doubt, in a land where education was optional on the path to riches.

From there, it was a simple matter for the president to coalesce his random thoughts and prejudices into a final decision. Canada's earthquake was not a coincidence. He didn't need to know for which part of its liberal agenda of secular humanism the country had been stricken—castigated for its acceptance of gay marriage or chastised for its socialist policies—but it was clear that he had to deny Québec's request for humanitarian assistance. One should never interfere with celestial designs, and certainly not rub balm after a holy spanking.

He left it to FEMA to translate this denial into diplomatically correct language and forward an official communication in answer to the original request.

Exhausted by this exercise of executive power, he retired to his living quarters, hoping that his staff had found a plumber to fix the overflowing toilet and an electrician to replace the batteries in the fire alarm that beeped all morning, as "someone ought to know how to fix those."

Ottawa, 10:30 p.m.

Two hours late, Republic Airlines flight 0401 landed at the Ottawa International airport. Although the flight crew conveniently blamed the late arrival on the turmoil created by the recent earthquake, and while some of the delay could legitimately be attributed to it, frequent flyers knew that Republic could not get an on-time arrival even if the itinerary only required them to taxi the plane from Terminal 1 to Terminal 2 at the same airport. On par with most other North American airline carriers, responsive scheduling was just not part of Republic's corporate culture—nor was courtesy to customers, for that matter.

The flight attendants, based in California, knew near-empty planes to be the norm following earthquakes. Weary travelers bound to destinations within a large radius of the epicenter typically canceled prior reservations, out of precaution, unable to assess the attenuating effects of distance on the severity of shaking. Remaining passengers included residents from the earthquake-stricken region unhappy to be rerouted to the nearest open airport, a few business travelers whose financial interests and deadlines were imperturbable by world events or mother nature's caprices—direct descendants of the Pony Express riders—and, finally, those who specifically booked their tickets after the earthquake, in fact because of it.

From that last category, among the few disembarking from the old Boeing 737, stood Yago Krapo (also known as *shit-head* by his detractors) of Saint-Chretistic Technological University, the prestigious research-intensive institution known for its controversial scholarly pursuits and unorthodox views on academic excellence.

Professor Krapo carried the Saint-Chretistic Technological University label as a badge of honor, a calling card warning his interlocutors that his words were wisdom, his statements truths, his expertise beyond challenge. In Krapo's view of academic gamesmanship, it was the sum of knowledge held by its esteemed faculty that lent credibility and prestige to an academic institution, and by inference to all of its members equally—even to those less distinguished professors whose futile academic pursuits had no redeeming intellectual value or whose scholarly contributions were of a quality many standard deviations below the national average. Through the distorting glasses of this skewed elitist perspective, the same dead wood that befouled a pond, choking it by overbearing encumbrance, was seen to embellish a sandy beach, providing romantic ornament to an otherwise dull shoreline.

For Krapo, this strategy worked well with outsiders, those who relied on status and perception to establish credentials. However, experts and insiders who weighted accomplishments over image recognized dead wood for what it was, and all knew that without the crutch provided by Saint-Chretistic Technological University's reputation, *shit-head* would not have survived, dragged down the abyss of professional irrelevance by the weight of his bombastic and egocentric persona.

Professor Krapo's professional credibility was tainted beyond redemption among his peers, a sour embarrassment to his faculty colleagues who never recovered from the terrible momentary lapse of judgment when they'd offered him a position with full tenure. To many in academia, that privileged academic status of permanent and irrevocable lifetime employment, usually granted after a probationary period upon critical scrutiny of a scholarly portfolio, was the golden threshold of academic life. A life-lasting armored refuge from criticism and dissatisfaction, bestowed upon budding professors on the assumption that the promising early accomplishments of developing faculty members could be extrapolated beyond the bounds of certainty, and on the wishful hope that absolute job security would not entice one to slacken the pace, to answer to distractions ahead of duties, to dissociate from responsibilities, to disengage from intellectual pursuits to let the brain rot unattended, and to progressively turn into dead wood—effectively retiring on the job until death or mandatory retirement. To them, the granting of tenure was that absolute defining moment when, after having seen the high jumper launch as high as possible to impress—unaware of where the bar to clear is exactly located—a jury of peers must decide if the candidate is bound for the stars or at the apex of a career, on a downfall to a brutal crash after brushing the wobbly bar, never to soar above that personal best achieved under intense pressure. An uncertain decision at best, clouded by biases and human foibles, as underneath Krapo's execrable vanity lied a shameless sycophant and master manipulator who systematically invested himself only in those tasks and assignments that generated political capital to be redeemed against favors in due time. To Krapo, the tenure-granting process had only been a matter of forging the right allegiances.

Yet, Yago Krapo was charming and eloquent, absolute sugar to the media flies who interpreted his off-the-cuff, unsubstantiated remarks as gospel from the gods of Saint-Chretistic Technological University. Abusing the implicit leverage afforded to him by Nobel Prize winners and other giants of the venerable institution, presuming to stand on their shoulders, Krapo's outrageous statements ignited controversies, bringing the university into headlines with recurring regularity. Although unwelcome on the shoulders of the institution's giants, who treated Krapo as the academic equivalent of dandruff, the university brass loved the media coverage and promoted him for it. The formula was simple and Krapo knew when and how to milk that political capital.

Determined to be the first U.S. "expert" on site, providing his infinite wisdom as a resource to assist "our friendly neighbors to the north," and fully aware that he would never receive an invitation to serve on an official U.S. earthquake reconnaissance team, Krapo had secured special emergency travel funds from the discretionary account of the university president on the promise of favorable reputation-building international press and front-page headlines. He intended to deliver.

Saint-Chretistic Technological University was endowed with wealthy and generous alumni, and its president's discretionary account was almost bottomless, allowing Yago to conduct a reconnaissance visit in style. Therefore, before even collecting his bags, he undertook to roam the entire airport in search of a helicopter charter service. To his surprise, in less than a single minute, he had crossed the entire airport, leading him to sneeringly conclude that the "international" qualifier in the name of the airport was probably more a matter of national pride than reality, notwithstanding the occasional U.S.-bound flight. Without finding any evidence of a helicopter service, Yago surmised that a better approach might be to consult the phone book at a pay phone.

As he waited through the rings and the messages of the automated answering systems that he reached, Krapo watched the evening news broadcast on the flat-screen monitors above the baggage carousel. While the volume was turned off, the scrolling banner and closed captions, respectively displayed at the bottom and top of the screen, although small characters to read from the phone booth, allowed Krapo to capture the essence of the issues being discussed.

The featured story, closed captions and silent images from Repentigny, east of the Montréal island, showed emergency responders forcing citizens to evacuate homes in the path of a toxic cloud allegedly generated by burning petrochemical plants and tank farms in Pointe-Aux-Trembles. Footage of the fire itself was conspicuously absent. Dramatic testimonials from displaced and distressed citizens were followed by expert estimates suggesting that the dangerous fires could burn unrestrained for up to a week, maps showing the probable eastward spread of the noxious cloud over populated regions, and concerns that snow showers expected to start during the night could drag some of the hazardous contaminants to the ground, with the risk of infiltration into the aquifer, streams, and rivers, and severe ecological and public health consequences throughout the province.

A brief weather report inlaid into a left computer-generated column on the television screen, flashed a winter storm warning for southern Ontario and Québec, predicting warmer temperatures but intense snow falls with accumulation of up to half an inch per hour. Also forecasted were high gusty winds which, when combined with the falling snow, could create near blizzard conditions. Travel conditions were predicted to deteriorate rapidly within 12 hours, becoming impossible at times due to the heavy snow and increasing winds. Travel of any kind was strongly discouraged through the storm, and those who couldn't avoid it were warned to prepare for severe winter driving conditions and reminded to pack extra clothing, blankets, and emergency supplies in their car—essential survival gears should they become trapped for hours.

At the same time, the bottom-scrolling banner displayed a series of institutions on the island presumably enlisted to serve as emergency shelters, with a disclaimer in red on a second ticker line warning that, "Some of these emergency shelters may not be operational at this time—the validity of the information received has not been confirmed and the CBC assumes no responsibility for errors in the list provided," an advisory prompted by staffers from the broadcasting agency familiar with Montréal who became suspicious after noting that the official list included some institutions that had become insolvent and closed operations during the year, and who doubted that abandoned buildings could be resurrected to serve as emergency shelters within a few hours.

All the while, Krapo's suitcase circled endlessly in the shiny metal cemetery of unclaimed luggage, eroding to shreds by the rubbing edges of the baggage carousel.

Krapo finally reached a company open for business, staffed by live operators slaving in a call center in India rather than artificial voices fed by bits of ones and zeros. He made arrangements with the National Capital Helicopter Charter service for a 5 a.m. departure next morning in front of Hangar #2 on the west side of the main terminal.

A short cab ride later, he checked into a suite at the Château Laurier and proceeded to empty the fully stocked mini-bar, just because he could.

Eastern Canada, 11:45 p.m.

In the skyward war where cold and hot fronts fight, exerting pressures and invading each other's vast territories, bands of clouds clash and shed their blood, trillions of droplets at a time. Mortal spectators of these celestial battles await their showering outcomes and, sometimes, blessings. However, blessings are few, and irony plentiful, when the accompanying prospect of warmer weather implies an escape from the lashing hell of -40°F into a crisp comfort zone barely under the freezing point. Snowstorms can be the currency of that trade-off, a rite of passage, an avalanche in slow motion from which the buried have a fighting chance. In the end, it's all about burial rate and duration, and in this case, it started at a quarter to midnight, to be sustained for the next couple of days. In a normal winter, this can be a challenge.

January 26th

It's Only Snow Business

Ottawa, 3:15 a.m.

Krapo grabbed the ringing phone off the hook, and brought the headset to his ear, more by reflex than by desire to listen to a lousy pre-recorded wake-up call message.

"Dr. Krapo?"

"Uh?" answered Yago, wondering what kind of fancy personalized wake-up call message tradition could possibly exist in up-scale Canadian hotels.

"Dr. Krapo... It's Graham from NCHC."

"Haynee cee Atchee?"

Yago opened an eye, scanning the unfamiliar room for a clock. In the middle of the night, every hotel room is just a dark, foreign cavern. The big red digital numbers next to the phone confirmed that the wake-up call was only due 15 minutes later.

"National Capital Helicopter Charter, you know. You called yesterday, for a reservation."

"Em, ya. Vat iz de prôblem?"

"Well it's the snowstorm, eh. Things are getting worse than predicted. You know, low ceiling. Maybe we can fly tomorrow. Got to cancel for today though. Just thought we would let you know so you don't come to the airport for nothing, eh."

"Gud. OK, OK. I vill kall you layter," he said as he hung up.

Looking at the empty mini-bottles on the floor, Yago called reception to reschedule his wake-up call for 7 a.m., and dropped back into a slumber. Decisions could wait a few more hours.

Québec City, 4:00 a.m.

Riopelle had worked all night, invigorated by the belief that, for once, his work would have an impact. A redeeming impact. Thirty years of teaching science to late-teenagers had dulled his early post-graduation enthusiasm. As he became convinced over time that the few who cared about science would learn in spite of him, and that those who didn't simply wouldn't, his lecture morphed into boring narratives of material regurgitated from the standard mandatory textbook sanctified by the Ministry of Education. Progressively deteriorating student evaluations of his teaching accelerated this degeneration in the quality of his lectures, which further deteriorated the class evaluations, in a vicious spiral of demotivation that left in its middle a mumbling fool ignored by most, inaudible to all. And if the students didn't care, as long as they were anointed with the minimum passing grade without effort, the CEGEP administration was not about to pick a fight with the union either. This amounted to a mutually agreed-upon pact to endorse and embrace incompetence across the board, in all its forms and expressions.

Riopelle's report was still an early draft, but given the current crisis, he judged it appropriate to distribute it at once, after one last proofreading.

The first few paragraphs captured almost verbatim his earlier comments in answer to the Premier's questions. Since the differences between hazards, disasters, and risk, and the issues related to return period, seemed to be at the fore of the Premier's mind, a brief review and clarification of these significant concepts provided an adequate entry into the topic. It also afforded a most appropriate segue into answering what appeared to be the next most important question: "Where does responsibility lie for this disaster?"

The document's second section began by declaring, "Responsibility for this disaster most clearly lies with the government."

Riopelle was fully aware that the gods had never granted him the gifts of effective prose and structure, so shooting for maximum impact had been his approach. To a tired mind in the middle of the night, it might even have appeared to be a brilliant strategy. Miscellaneous points followed each other in a disorderly fashion, emphasizing how things could evolve to such an unpleasant outcome.

"Fundamentally, governments are in power to execute the will of the population, while simultaneously fulfilling their own personal agenda. At a fundamental level, the public wants 'bread and games,' expressed in its insatiable pursuit of enhanced quality of life, of immediate satisfaction to endless desires, and of entertainment and pleasures. Given that an endless number of burdensome responsibilities must be managed to make possible the pursuit of such miscellaneous pleasures and consumption, a few important fundamental needs will receive full attention of the masses, and all others will be delegated. In short, the public can only deeply care about matters that have a direct impact on their 'bread and games;' for example reducing taxes is a priority, as the extra dollar at hand has the most immediate impact on one's ability to enhance its personal quality of life. Deciding which activity of the government must be curtailed or postponed as a result of the reduced taxes is a delegated responsibility."

Riopelle was proud of his forays into philosophy and sociology. As misguided as they might be, they made him feel like a renaissance man, worthy of excommunication like the best of them.

"Those entrusted with the responsibility to make the millions of other important societal decisions must therefore gauge the public opinion and set priorities in accordance with this perception. Given unbounded and frequently unrealistic societal expectations, needs significantly exceed all available resources. In that context, and because governments must demonstrate tangible accomplishments to get re-elected every few years, policies that favor short-term rewards will be given priority over those policies that may contribute to public welfare over the long term. Policy makers must also cope with the consequences of unrealistic public expectations, and make adjustments within the constraints of the existing framework.

"For example, while the public may believe that a reduction in income tax will force the government to critically review its workforce and fire non-producing employees, the powerful Canadian labor unions virtually ensure that losses in government income will translate either to greater deficits, to new fees charged directly for specific services, or to the curtailment of some government services. At the extreme, in difficult fiscal times, as a result of budget cuts, some government departments end up staffed with a full contingent of union employees with inalienable job security but without government projects or expenses to manage, thus re-orienting their attention to busywork that only consumes relatively cheap office supplies, such as the development of white papers for policies that can't be implemented for lack of funding, in a vicious circle of futility."

Living in the national capital, Riopelle had many friends working for the provincial government whom he had had the opportunity to quiz over the years on his favorite topic, never expecting that these casual conversations could one day become vital statistics in a strategic government document that he would author.

"For example, the Ministry of Transportation submits each year its list of project priorities and attached budgets to the Minister of Transportation—in this instance, for the current government, Mr. Réal Chaput-Vigneault. Repairing and replacing rusted steel bridges, deteriorated concrete bridges, roads with holes the size of lunar craters, and other deficient civil infrastructure are at the top of the list, implicitly to be done after the more mundane maintenance items like snow removal from the roads. Enhancing the ability of this infrastructure to resist earthquakes, while recognized as a worthwhile thing to do, is a task close to the bottom of the list. The Minister of Transportation's budget allocation for any fiscal year allows it to address, at best, the top few priorities, by removing as many eyesores as possible, making the changes that are visible and can be claimed as progressive investments in subsequent political campaigns."

The document proceeded to provide other examples, without concern for accuracy as Riopelle's memory suffered from the ignominy of a lack of academic rigor he attributed to the task of teaching the exact same material for 30 years. All these examples led to the inescapable conclusion of his brief, to the crowning finding of his thesis.

"Governments don't care about earthquakes because people don't give a damn about earthquakes. People care about matters that affect their personal financial well-being (increasing their net income, reducing taxes, black market work), material things (cars, boats, homes, and other toys), leisure and hobbies (shows, vacations, collecting trinkets, pornography on the internet), and the latest hockey scores. When it comes to responsibilities to protect their well-being, they care about health insurance because they expect to be sick, and they care about unemployment insurance because they fear that unfair employers and disingenuous national and international enterprises could move their offices and operations offshore in search of cheaper labor. Some will care about liability insurance, because they believe the law is an institution that provides wealth redistribution in an incoherent and unpredictable way. Some will care about property insurance because they constantly hear about criminals, car crashes and fires on the news. Some will care about life insurance, because they know they'll die and wish to avoid creating a financial hardship to their beloved who will remain. A rare few will care about floods if they live in flood plains, maybe hurricanes if they live in coastal regions. But, generally, nobody gives a shit about earthquakes!"

Riopelle didn't think "shit" should be in the final draft, but at 2 a.m., when he wrote that sentence, he couldn't find a sufficiently powerful substitute that packed enough shock value without being too wordy. He jotted a red note in the margin, showing to the eventual reader his awareness that proper language should be inserted there, while awaiting inspiration.

"As evinced worldwide, after any earthquake, the public does express shock and outrage that its government has failed to ensure the safety of public infrastructure against all possible disasters, particularly when it is revealed after the fact that the earthquake in question was known 'likely to occur'—and has evidently happened. And therein lies the unsolvable dilemma: How can a government establish public policies in expectation of new public priorities that will only emerge after a disaster, for a disaster that has a very low likelihood of occurrence during one's term in office? How to answer the irrational public behavior toward the risk of disasters?"

This was the crux of the matter in Riopelle's mind. Given the thesis that nobody cared, why should the government care, and if it did, what reasonable actions should it undertake to provide an adequate level of national safety? To him, answering these questions exposed one's expectations and belief in the role of government in society. Given Riopelle's strong belief that the government was ultimately responsible, cradle to grave, for the well-being of its citizens, and his conviction that this government had strong socialist desires, he felt confident of reaching a receptive audience by proclaiming unabashedly: "Responsibility for this disaster most clearly lies with the government." However, this deserved some further clarifications—hoping that his awkward prose could actually enlighten anyone.

"Society has adjusted well to 'progressive continuous losses' distributed uniformly across the country, such as road accidents, heart attacks, and other fatal technological failures and diseases. Even though these small incidents are collectively an enormous societal and economical problem—and of devastating impact for the affected individuals, families, or small businesses—society and the economy are accustomed to this continued flow of small incidents and have developed an ability to systematically absorb its impact. Each person is a unique individual valued by a close circle of colleagues, friends and family, but in a societal, economical, political, or organizational perspective, no one is irreplaceable, and everyone is indeed eventually successfully replaced—aren't cemeteries full of individuals who had bragged of being indispensable?

"For most employers, death is just one of the many causes of staff turn-over. Death is part of the circle of life, and for some it is even just a business activity ensured by a continuous and quite stable flow of clients—an enterprise mostly insensitive to fluctuations of the economy, for that matter.

"Given the frequent occurrence of those incidents that fall into the category of 'progressive continuous losses,' any measure by a government to alleviate (or give the perception of alleviating) the risk for any of those unfortunate events is perceived most positively. Arguably, personal responsibility can contribute significantly more than the government to mitigating the risk of road accidents or heart attacks, but governments can reap the short-term political benefit of laws that enforce harsh penalties for drunk drivers, of programs to eliminate junk food from school cafeterias, or of public health information campaigns to encourage exercise—all low-cost measures that are popular and for which quantitative and reliable results (or any results for that matter) from implementation are not needed to have a positive psychological impact by the time of the next election. It is capitalizing on the fear of death."

In a first draft, Riopelle had expanded on the inescapable human balancing act between an unhealthy and unrealistic fear of death requiring one to ignore it just to be able to function, and a morbid obsession with death leading one to conclude that life was meaningless—the poles of devastation, from denying death to denying life. While he truly loved that passage, upon proofreading, he realized it to be grossly out of context and distracting, and exercised self-restraint by editing it out. Returning to the main argument, after expanding on normal death, he now turned to mass casualties.

"Society, however, is far less adapted to cope with extensive casualties or losses concentrated at one single point in time, due to one single event. No business can cope when 70% of its employees or customers die, or fail to show up because their personal lives have been devastated by the impact of a disaster and their entire attention and energies must be redirected to recovering. Such a massive diversion of resources bluntly swipes all chance of business continuity. The good business citizens adapted to operate in normal conditions as pillars of the community are thus starved, day by day edging closer to bankruptcy, awaiting a return to normalcy that may never come.

"For community survival, recovery is imperative. Yet, the ability to recover (and the cost of this recovery) depends on how many contractors and businesses have been sufficiently lucky to remain mostly undisturbed in their ability to operate, and how many with similar capabilities and fair-trade intents can be temporarily transplanted from remote areas. However, alongside those with noble goals, invading the market with vile profiteering business practices will be the buzzards of the disaster-recovery business. Contrary to businesses that provide honorable services as contributors to the normal economy, even including funeral enterprises that respectfully live and thrive from death, those that deviously profit from the ad-hoc business of disaster recovery often capitalize on the scarcity of available services to greedily gouge those in greatest need.

"Communities are not inherently able to adapt to these societal shocks: disappeared customers and employees, shifted market needs, and rampant opportunistic inflation. Some survive, some are doomed.

"The only way to prevent falling into such unplanned despondency is preparedness and mitigation. Yet, what incentive is there for the government to enact measures to prevent against a disaster that has a rather low probability of occurring before the next electoral campaign?

"To further overwhelm decision-makers, the entire spectrum of possible disasters must be considered. Beyond earthquakes, one should consider landslides, volcanic eruptions, hurricanes, tornados, floods, droughts, blizzards, ice storms, extreme cold or heat waves, desertification, forest fires, pest invasions, pandemics, not to forget the human-made disasters of civil war, conventional war, nuclear war, genocide, physical terrorism, biological terrorism, chemical terrorism, nuclear terrorism, psychological terrorism, agricultural terrorism, totalitarian regime, dictatorship, famine, global warming, climate change, sea-level rise, coastal erosion, stock market collapse, and the endless list of technological disasters, such as transportation system failures (train derailment, plane crash, ship sinking), accidental contamination (oil or chemical spill, nuclear release, industrial/radioactive waste), unsustainable development (overgrazing, overfishing, deforestation, genetically modified or displaced species), etc.

"Strategies must be developed to decide how to set priorities in allocating scarce resources to address these pressing problems while addressing other competing priorities. A first way to sort through this list is to respond ad-hoc to various interest groups, the most powerful lobbies getting the most attention. Banks and financial institutions want to prevent stock market collapses, and will ensure that measures will be enacted to protect their portfolios to the extent possible should such a disaster occur, or that the government will bail them out of foolish investment schemes. Second in line are those small disasters that are easy to cope with, such as plane crashes or train derailments. Third are those that have the highest visibility due to their frequent occurrence, such as forest fires or small chemical spills.

"In some pernicious ways, the ability to deal with small events gives the population some measure of confidence that a similar ability to cope with rare larger-scale events may exist. However, this is not the case. Given limited resources, limited public interest, and low probability of occurrence within one political term in office, large and rare natural disasters rarely get the attention they deserve."

Riopelle recognized that his argumentation could be seen by some as suffering from repetitions, but he reasoned that presenting the same conclusion from a few different perspectives was pedagogically sound and that there was merit to continuing to hammer the same nail.

"It is convenient to governments that disasters occur mostly due to failure of the infrastructure. For example, an earthquake is in essence shaking of the ground. Except for the consequential occurrence of tsunamis and landslides that are sometimes triggered by an earthquake, there are no negative natural consequences to an earthquake. Ecosystems are not disturbed by this shaking. Rather, it is the very infrastructure that is constructed to shelter society against nature that fails in an earthquake and kills its occupants or users. It is convenient to government, because infrastructure is constructed by engineers who write design codes and standards presumed to provide safety against such catastrophes, allowing the politicians to partly deflect the blame when a disaster occurs (but not completely, because government is the regulatory body for many civil works of significance). The fallacy of this argument, of course, is that engineers are people too, and represent the interest of various constituencies. Many thus reflect the general skepticism of their employers towards risk-mitigating measures, and advance financial, political, or societal arguments to argue against the adoption of design requirements intended to protect against disasters.

"The challenge in dealing with rare events lies exactly in their infrequent occurrence. Competing with all other more urgent priorities, few are willing to invest in the prevention of a disaster with a low probability of occurrence in any given year. The hidden message of this discourse is that it is simpler to take a chance: await the disaster and cope with it. Yet, few are openly willing to co-endorse responsibility for (say) 50,000 deaths and $100 billion in losses in any natural disaster, and prefer to claim ignorance of the problem than recognize their implicit decision to just take a chance and see if a disaster will really happen in their lifetime. This is problematic, in that what is often perceived as a reasonable assumption of risk and cost-saving measure prior to an event, is unavoidably treated as a lack to responsible duty in lawsuits after the fact."

Riopelle hesitated on whether or not to introduce here a discussion on the general population's inability to understand risk and act consequently. On one hand, he felt that it was important to put in perspective irrational behaviors with regards to risk, but on the other hand felt that this was a complex question that would warrant an entire exposé by itself. He couldn't think of a simple way to explain in a few lines how an individual could drink 10 beers just before driving home one day, fully aware that a third of fatalities in crashes involved an alcohol-impaired driver, and the next day, join a class-action suit against a landlord who refuses to spend millions of dollars in abatement measures to remove traces of asbestos in his office buildings, even though documented air-quality measurements showed a concentration of asbestos fibers orders of magnitude below the level that could theoretically lead to cancer in one out of 10 million individuals—and only if they would continuously breathe air containing that concentration of asbestos fibers over an entire lifetime. Would it be sufficient to state that most people have zero tolerance to unwelcome risks imposed on them by others, no matter how minute the risk, and yet are willing participants in the most risky self-imposed endeavors when they believe to have some level of control and responsibility over the outcome, even if that perception is flawed? Would it needlessly confuse the reader, or enrich the report, to explain the effect of positive or negative outcomes on the tolerance and appeals of risks? How to explain that the same individual buying lottery tickets faced with odds of one in 14 million to win the jackpot (an outcome with positive appeal), avoids a medical exam that could detect prostate or breast cancer (an outcome with negative appeal) that is almost a million times more probable? How to explain that the same individual who smokes, avoids exercise at all cost, and suffers from obesity, can militate passionately against nuclear energy?

Riopelle couldn't find a way, in light of the tight deadline, to elegantly weave such a narrative into the text, and elected to altogether omit such considerations. He assessed that the key conclusions of his thesis didn't suffer from this voluntary omission and that focusing on issues contrasting responsibility within a legal framework was preferable at this stage of the document.

"The problem is often compounded by the fact that there now exists voluminous accumulated engineering knowledge on how to mitigate risk against such disasters; this makes reliance on the 'act of God' theory indefensible in a court of law.

"Therefore, in this context, any legal entity (e.g. an agency, a state, or an owner) would be ill-advised to affirm that it has willingly elected to ignore the earthquake risk and openly acknowledge that it was willing to deal with the aftermath of a disaster rather than invest in planning and preparedness. The government has nonetheless taken this approach, and has not duly considered the full range of actions it could have taken to mitigate the risk of a major disaster due to an earthquake."

In re-reading this last sentence, Riopelle felt that it might be a bit harsh. All along, he wrote candidly under the impression that this government was truly interested in his erudite professional opinion, and was ready to assume responsibility and own up to the population. However, as a card-carrying member of the *Parti National*, he felt compelled to soften the message to shelter the current government from unfair criticism by the media, mostly from what he considered to be unethical English Canadian journalists.

He accordingly rewrote the last sentence to inject it with some personal political commentary.

"All past Canadian (Federal and Provincial) governments have nonetheless taken this approach in the past, and have not duly considered the full range of actions they could have taken to mitigate the risk of a major disaster due to an earthquake. This failure of imagination is systemic across the entire country, and even (with some exceptions) across the United States, where some governments are in full denial of the seismic risk, as well as the risk of other disasters, and are not taking any action to mitigate the risks, gambling instead with the lives of millions—essentially betting that their natural deaths will precede death by disaster. Fortuitously for those governments, although they could be the first blamed and targeted by lawsuits, more commonly, they fail in subsequent elections."

Riopelle liked ending his lectures with a dramatic climax, but it usually fell on the deaf ears of his disinterested, sleeping students. This time, dealing with an interested reader, he was anxious to see whether the punch of the closing paragraphs summarizing the above ideas into sharp, constructive criticisms would energize the reader into action. The lead sentence of those closing remarks started with: "Denial is the root cause of the disaster we are facing today." This set the stage for a few final examples and an inspiring call to action. It would only take him a few minutes to draft those closing remarks.

Then, all that was left to do was to wake up his temporary assistant and see that he found a way to forward to the Premier this most eagerly awaited document.

Ottawa, 4:15 a.m.

A few logs on the glowing embers revived the flames. The flaring blades of light dancing in the stone fireplace of 24 Sussex Drive painted vibrant gold and crimson hues on the walls, like the random soothing caresses of a massage. The spasms of relative brightness bathed the room, as a fickle protection against the invading darkness. The trembling shadows wrapping the two men cast a medieval aura to the meeting.

Brendon's friend and confident never refused an opportunity for a double scotch and an opportunity to chat with the most powerful man in the country. To the Evangelical Protestant priest, this friendship had the means to serve his agenda. To Brendon, it provided the moral bracing he sometimes needed to empower his deep political convictions. It was one of those friendships that had morphed over the years, from a respectful shared interest and concern for each other, into a like-minded relationship of convenience, corrupted by the decades of calculations that had come with power and influence.

The priest's long-term prophetic vision was to establish a government ruled by the Scriptures, in their most rigorous, pure fundamentalist reading without the liberal interpretations of free-thinkers and new-age gurus. He recognized that, undeniably, this was an ambitious goal given Canada's support for religious pluralism and demographics. Nonetheless, it was one he pursued with great urgency, alarmed that the number of Catholics and Protestants was in slight decline—even when counting the baptized "non-practicing" ones—while, in the past decade alone, the number of declared atheists, agnostics, and humanists grew 20%, and the number of Muslims, Buddhists, Hindus and Sikhs doubled. If religion was the opiate of the people, his mission was to create addiction to his brand of narcotics. In the eternal crusade for the supremacy of ideals, in which victory couldn't be claimed until dissenting opinions were obliterated or drowned to inconsequence in a sea of converts, tolerance was a suicidal virtue. The Canadian mosaic concept, praised by the national underdogs of organized religion, was anathema to the dogmatic leaders.

The two friends basked in the pleasure of very different powers: one anointed by the borrowed blessings of a capricious and temperamental democracy, the other usurped by alleged divine rights shrouded in the spiritual canons of a metaphysical war. Two masters of the deceptions required by the unstoppable machine of power. Two powers that have too often shared a bed for the convenient persecution and desecration of humanity, justified by an inane belief of supremacy, to protect them from an inconvenient difference.

The two didn't have to say much. The double scotch set the pace.

They shared news of friends and families, exchanged fond stories of childhood in the prairies, praised the militant activities of committed moral leaders across the modest Canadian Bible Belt, and shared their different perspectives on the pulse of the nation, as they usually did at any other time. But in the wee hours of the morning, the unwritten agenda included some business matters.

"What do you think about sending in the army?" asked Brendon, knowing that his friend had an ear tuned into the daily concerns of regular folks, and could be relied upon as an honest poll of opinion.

A couple of sips later, the priest responded, with the assurance and authority conferred by his divine connections, "It's just unavoidable. Unquestionable. Better to do it sooner than later."

They thought alike and needed not expand. With the unquestioned rigor that drove Orangists to parade across unfriendly Irish communities to flaunt the symbols of Orange domination, with the same blind fervor that led Papal Zouaves to march to their death, with the same conniving determination to persecute gay "deviants" that openly married while hiding pedophile priests under the protective wing of the church, they knew what was right.

There was only one Canada. Only one that made sense to them. One in which the sanctity of the RCMP uniform could not be violated to allow Sikhs to wear their turbans as an alternative. One in which a single brand of religious symbols could be displayed in public places and government buildings. One where nonsensical accommodations had no place.

One where a lot of past mistakes had to be undone.

Longueuil, 5:00 a.m.

"Denial is the root cause of the disaster we are facing today" said Réal monotonously.

"*L'ostie de câlice d'enfant de chienne!*" shouted Léandre, a feeling shared by all members of the emergency cabinet.

Réal was nearly done reading aloud the draft Riopelle had forwarded him earlier. He never expected the "old fart" to so rapidly produce a first draft. As far as he knew, he had not been given speech recognition software, and there were no word processors capable of reading thoughts straight from the mind and translating them directly into coherent and grammatically correct sentences. Had he known the bugger to be a 100-word-per-minute touch-typist, he would have saddled him with an old Remington typewriter with sticky keys and a faded ribbon—or just a yellow pad and a leaky pen.

When Réal had received a fax of the draft document, he guessed that, given the quick turn-around time, it had to be a bullet-list of headers, or at best a poor, incoherent sequence of ill-conceived ideas, and that a quick phone call, encouraging him to polish the crude bits into a full-fledged document, would suffice to return Riopelle to his virtual dungeon. However, his "diagonal read" of the document turned into a slower browse, and eventually an attentive perusal. The multiple pages of curled fax paper already added up to a compendium of mad rubbish and there was no point in commissioning more of the same.

Without grounds to simply dismiss the document, he promised Riopelle that he would share his document with the Premier and give him feedback within two hours.

Réal had almost flunked French in high school, and had never been a good reader. Yet, his atonal rendering of the text was effective, as the words themselves needed no Shakespearean execution to ignite the room. The quantity and intensity of cursing by all had crescendoed throughout the reading, up to a frantic level.

"The denial by all, in the face of well-known and undeniable scientific evidence, that a large earthquake could happen in the province of Québec, and consequent inaction by the government and other key civic authorities, is the only reason for the terrible disaster we are facing today."

"*Le tabarnak!*" added the Premier.

"Should I continue reading?" asked Réal.

"Yeah yeah, go through it all. I want to know all the damage that this *sacrament de chien sale de* egghead could do," answered Léandre.

Réal nodded, and resumed, with the prescience that the message and the messenger would not be confused when the audience would cringe.

"History repeats itself endlessly as all leaders live in denial. Preventable catastrophes are not prevented because governments conscientiously refuse to consider them as credible threats, thereby allowing them to invest public monies into other projects having desirable short-term political dividends. Simply said, disaster prevention is not free, and serves no purpose toward getting one re-elected.

"For example, in denial of the severe insalubrious conditions in London, the British government refused to invest in an upgrade of the city's sewer facilities until the smell from the Thames became so putrid one summer day in 1858 that it forced the legislative assembly out of Westminster Hall (located next to the river). For example, in-spite of intelligence reports to the contrary, all Western European governments lived in denial that Hitler was preparing an all-out invasion of Europe, thus avoiding expensive investments in defensive military capabilities until it was too late. For example, following the crash of the high-jacked 767 in Lockerbee, England, clear recommendations were made to reinforce the cockpit doors of commercial aircrafts, but airline executives and governments lived in denial, convincing themselves that such terrorist activities would not happen in their country, especially not in the United States, until it did happen on September 11, 2001. For example, the Québec government, aware that the province's infrastructure had for the most part never been designed to resist earthquakes, and risked suffering severe damage or collapse should a major earthquake occur, denied the evidence and convinced itself that it lived in a technologically advanced society where such disasters miraculously do not happen.

"And so preventable disasters are not prevented, as short-sighted politicians fail us, leading to unnecessary casualties and losses. Where leadership and far-reaching vision is needed, the blind lead the blind and the near-sighted focus their energies on mundane problems, answering to the narrow perspectives of voters unaware of (and often unable to understand) the comprehensive scientific and engineering knowledge on how to economically prepare against natural disasters."

Intuiting that the red faces around him couldn't stomach much more of this nonsense, Réal announced, "Last paragraph."

"Therefore, human nature, which underlies the socio-political mode of operation of a democracy, dictates that no money should be spent in preparing against a particular type of disaster, unless death and suffering at home attributable to that specific type of disaster still linger in the collective memory. This social behavior translates into an absolute lack of investment and total disinterest in preparedness for years or even decades. Then, when a disaster actually happens, in some amazing fulfillment of flawed logic, huge amounts of money suddenly become available to prepare the community where the disaster occurred against recurrence of the same event, which now has a most significantly lower probability of reoccurring so soon after the first one. This outpour of money and diligent work to enhance community disaster resilience against future disasters of the type that just occurred will span a few years, while the losses are still fresh in mind and painfully felt in the community, but will slow down and stop over time as people progressively forget and move on to address other concerns."

As if Riopelle, in an afterthought, worried that some sugar-coating might be necessary to make his candid and blunt thesis more palatable, he finished on a naively upbeat note: "Fortunately, the current government has the strong socialist convictions necessary to embrace such a responsibility and use these lessons to build a better Québec."

The collective silent rage, by some sort of negative aura, had noticeably increased the temperature in the room. Nobody asked whether Réal had reached the end of Riopelle's expose, just relieved that he had stopped.

Léandre abruptly broke the silence.

"You tell that *ostie de trou-de-cul* that he has to expand his report, that I want more explanations, more whatever. Make something up. Then, lock him up in that room with his *crisse de* word processor, and let him rot there. Make sure he does not get anywhere near the media. End of story!"

"I don't know how long we can really keep him out of the spotlight. We can trick him to stay there, but we can't forcefully keep him forever. Eventually, he'll get out and preach this crap to whoever wants to hear it."

"Maybe, but two days from now, the media will be inundated with good human interest stories to report. Heroes, grand rescues, amazing tales of survival, near frozen kids and grannies pulled from debris, updates on where to go for assistance, what to do to recover, and so on, and won't have much time to listen to crackpots like him. But now, all they have is a dark city and nothing to report. They are choked, dying for stories, and will air anything that says earthquake or looks like a witch hunt."

Léandre paused for a second, to emphasize that there was nothing else to discuss. His decision was final.

"Keep the *crisse de bâtard* locked up!

Montréal, 5:30 a.m.

Nested in a service recess in the concrete wall of the metro tunnel, James opened an eye. Noise was coming from the station platform a few hundred feet away. No light could be seen. Shouts and profanity hinted to theft as a possible cause for the commotion. He pulled on the straps wrapped around him and reached out to feel his backpack and other belongings, checking that they were free from tampering.

Half-asleep, James felt like a caveman. As if civilization had collapsed as a consequence of the failure of the modern infrastructure—as if those failures had single-handedly driven populations back to the Stone Age. Engineering megalomania at its best, convinced that humanity—irremediably enslaved into its web of interdependent technologies—would die once the gadgets that had emerged from the past two centuries stopped working. As if the Enlightenment had been a consequence of electricity and the combustion engine rather than an empowerment of science and engineering. To James though, at that very moment, sore from having slept on hard concrete, it was painfully undeniable that the downfall of those engineered infrastructures that moved the world out of caves would mark a return to prehistoric darkness, as evinced by the invisible savages screaming in the distance.

The glow-in-the-dark watch confirmed a 7-hour rest. Prudence suggested a return to the surface before the awakening of too many of the other cave dwellers—human or otherwise.

After feasting on a "breakfast" of dried food, and waiting until some time elapsed after the last noise was heard from the tunnel, James proceeded to discreetly escape the metro station, keeping a hand in front of his flashlight to muffle its light and weaving his way unnoticed toward the exit. As he crossed the broken window, he set foot into four inches of fresh snow. Although he couldn't say by how much, he definitely felt the outside air to be less forbiddingly cold as it had been the previous night. However, the powdery snow, propelled by strong winds, lashed without mercy all that stood in its way.

"This is going to be another brutal day on the job."

James was expecting that, after a few steps in the fresh air, the reawakened excitement and realization of the once-in-a-lifetime opportunities at hand alone would drive him to shake off the intense fatigue—as it normally had in similar past circumstances.

This time, however, it did not. Each limb was heavy, almost unresponsive. He felt drained of his vital energy by the harsh conditions. This was a bad omen at the outset of a long day. These were by far the harshest working conditions he had ever encountered in the 20 visits to earthquake-stricken areas he had conducted in his career. Compared to this, visits to the San Francisco Bay Area affected by the 1989 Loma Prieta earthquake had been a vacation. Even though a dramatic Canadian Broadcasting Corporation news anchor had then declared—live on prime time—the Californian city to be in ruins, this exaggeration was for Canadian consumption and ratings. Even though damage had been widespread and some major bridges had suffered debilitating damages, most of the infrastructure had been unaffected, power and water services hadn't been disrupted significantly, and many hotels had remained open. And it was warm by Canadian standards. The same held true for the 1994 Northridge earthquake in Los Angeles, except that even balmier weather prevailed. Even the catastrophic Hyogo-ken Nanbu earthquake that devastated Kobe in 1995, decommissioning hundreds of bridge spans and making transportation most difficult along this coastal region, had been more manageable in James's opinion, if only again for the more cooperating climate.

Exhausted, but unable to resign himself to terminate his mission at once, he decided, as a reasonable compromise, that this was to be the last day of his reconnaissance trip. The overwhelming extent of damage surrounding him ensured that there would be plenty left to see in multiple subsequent visits, to be conducted under more compliant and comfortable weather conditions.

For now, for one last day, it was showtime.

Montréal, 6:30 a.m.

Lise hadn't slept well—she had collapsed from exhaustion on reports never intended to serve as a comfortable mattress. She had tossed and turned on a blanket of spiral-bound documents for a few hours, tormented by a nightmare in which she endlessly rehearsed and fine-tuned in her mind the acceptance speech she planned to deliver following her official appointment as Chair of the National Task Force for Disaster Recovery. She was convinced her promotion and essential empowerment at this critical juncture was to be announced during the press briefing. Why else would the Premier bother to fly an entire crew of reporters to the headquarters of the *Organisation de sécurité civile du Québec*?

Airlifting a limo turned out to be unnecessary, as a couple of official town cars were parked in the underground garage. Not glamorous overstretched limousines, but one nonetheless dignified and relatively spacious oversized black luxury sedan that could squeeze six passengers in the back, and another one, nearly identical but slightly longer and more comfortable, that could be dressed to have the decorum of an official limo. Léandre's staffers were grateful for this fortunate discovery, as they had no clue whether helicopters able to transport this kind of payload could be found on such a short notice. They nonetheless spent hours searching for limo drivers and ended up flying two from Québec a few hours before the press conference.

The select group of six journalists partial to the government was also flown by helicopter, two at a time. Live broadcasting would not be possible from the room, but footage would be recorded for post-production—in addition to the usual scribbling of the printed press journalists. It was understood that, after the brief press conference, the real attraction was that they would be escorted across the city as a group in one of the town cars before being ferried back to Longueuil. The larger luxury sedan was reserved for the exclusive use of Léandre and his team. The team of reporters would tour alone for a couple of hours, returning by mid-morning to a few photogenic spots selected for their suitability to capture history, with Léandre heroically braving the elements to meet and comfort fellow Québécois and assess first hand, at ground level, the extend of damage to the nation's metropolis.

A brief meeting was scheduled between Léandre and Lise, to usefully fill the time while waiting for the reporters to arrive and set up. At first, Lise wasn't eager to meet the Premier face-to-face, as she resented the preposterous notion that she was subordinate and accountable to anyone, but in light of the impending nomination, she realized that the meeting was an opportunity that shouldn't be missed.

Léandre, briefed during the short flight to the headquarters, just couldn't believe that his staffers had to resort to the subterfuge of a possible chairmanship appointment to a prestigious task force to obtain any collaboration from Lise. He couldn't fathom why any professional—far less the leader of a key emergency response agency—short of being wheedled by such mirages of prestige, would do everything in her power to torpedo the government's attempts at holding a press conference. He wondered if the portrait depicted by his staffers was an unduly acerbic criticism, a by-product of their lack of sleep.

They met in Lise's plush office, she in the tall leather executive chair, directing him as he entered to sit across the desk on the smaller wing chair, like a busy CEO would greet a secretary, in command, without standing up. Léandre purposely reached across the desk, extending a vigorous handshake that pulled her up her seat a few inches.

After the usual exchange of empty and insincere courtesies, Léandre cut to his agenda, by outlining his expectations.

"Ms. Letarte, here's what the leading members of the press invited today will want to hear from you. First, your assessment of damage across the city; second, the status of your response and recovery operations; third, the plans to restore main services and the timetable per sector; fourth..."

Lise was reading Léandre's lips, filtering out and discarding all words that didn't align with her expectations, that didn't broach the anticipated topic, that didn't fulfil her longing. Her mind could only focus on the lustful ambition of fame and fortune.

After five minutes of unanswered monologue, not getting much reaction from her glazed stare, Léandre wondered if any of his instructions had registered. He paused, awaiting an acknowledgment, a sign of discerning intellect.

Lise, frustrated to be kept hanging, bored by excruciating details of mundane logistics instead of being promoted at once, broke her silence.

"Mr. Laliberté, I believe the matter of a salary increase is in order."

Léandre, stunned by the bizarre malapropos remark, convinced that he may have misunderstood, after a brief silence, slowly asked, emphasizing every one of his words, "Can you repeat that?"

Unabashed, she stressed, "These are extraordinary circumstances demanding extraordinary measures and an extraordinary level of commitment. Not only does it require the immediate implementation of a task force of agency leaders to coordinate the response and recovery efforts, but it requires capable chairmanship to ensure success of those operations. The pressures and excessive time demands to provide such a dedicated leadership is beyond the call of duty."

Impatient, Lise was acting as if her nomination was incontrovertible. In her mind, all discussions justifiably and expeditiously needed to proceed to the next stage of negotiations. She trusted Léandre would understand that time was of the essence.

Léandre was fuming. He stood up, pushing the chair back violently.

"*Sacrament!* What is an emergency response agency for if not to respond to *des tabarnak d'*emergencies? That, and only that, *ciboire,* is your call of duty! Nothing else!"

Lise, unimpressed by the outburst, retorted, "I know how to do my job! Don't lecture me about emergency response! Resources do not perfectly deploy, and recovery doesn't magically happen without massive prior investments of time and efforts by capable and qualified devoted experts—"

"No, no, no. That's it!" interrupted Léandre.

He wasn't about to argue or even negotiate with her. He regretted having dignified her outrageous demands by a response. He turned around and walked to the door.

He was amazed by her arrogance and insanity. Not only did she genuinely buy into the bogus task force story, but she was already living it; in a surreal reversal of roles, she was even giving him orders. Léandre was determined to remove this nutcase from her appointment at once.

Before he could exit the office, or even pursue these thoughts further, Réal rushed into the office and pulled him into the press conference.

A seasoned politician, keenly aware of the importance of public relations, Léandre regained his composure in the seconds it took to reach the rows of Québec flags lined along the wall leading to a centrally located podium. However, only as he reached the podium did he realize that Lise had followed him and planted herself on his right. Taken aback, Léandre couldn't just push her off the stage. As unwelcome as she had become, Léandre still wanted to preserve the image of a functional agency in front of the press. He, however, was to do all the talking.

"Good morning and thanks to you all for volunteering to come and serve as the eyes of the nation today," started Léandre, as if elevating to the status of "volunteers ready to serve" the handful of invited party disciples could extinguish criticisms and conceal the fact that they had all been carefully handpicked.

"We are pleased to welcome you here in downtown Montréal, at the Headquarters of the *Organisation de sécurité civile du Québec*, the state-of-the-art emergency operations center from where all response and recovery operations are coordinated," said Léandre, implying that the *Organisation* was open, functional, and operational.

Before Léandre could continue, one of his journalist friends asked point-blank, "Léandre. Who's that next to you?"

Léandre wasn't pleased by the troublesome interruption, but before he could even think of a smooth diplomatic response to deflect attention to other matters, Lise rushed to the microphone.

"I am Lise Letarte, director of the *Organisation de sécurité civile du Québec*. I would like to take advantage of this opportunity to inform the population that the measures outlined in effective and detailed response and recovery plans, designed and validated by experts having years of field experience, are being deployed as we speak. The population's well-being is in the safe and capable hands of the *Organisation*. However, I must also inform you that, as a result of a rift between the *Organisation* and the government, mostly due to the desire of politicians to micro-manage the emergency response operations and meddle with the *Organisation's* core values, I now officially present Premier Laliberté with my resignation from the directorship of the *Organisation de sécurité civile du Québec*."

In a solemn demeanor, she moved back from the microphone, turned on her heels, ignoring Léandre, and briskly walked out of the room towards her office. A smirk betrayed her bluff. Convinced of being irreplaceable in the current circumstances, she waited in her office for an envoy that would beg her to reconsider. Naively, and insanely, she was convinced that this coup would force Léandre to abandon his hard-line stance and bend to her requests, even though no politician could ever do that and save face at the same time.

However, this was a moot concern. Léandre silently laughed at her political ignorance. The friendship between Léandre and the six journalists in the room spanned decades, going back to early childhood in some cases, and Léandre had an ironclad certainty in their allegiance. Nothing would be written or said that would embarrass the government subsequent to this theatrical incident.

Thinking quickly, Léandre calmly announced, without even having to wink, "You'll forgive Ms. Letarte for her agitation and volatile temper, but I had just informed her before the press conference that she was to be dismissed of her functions because we were most dissatisfied with the slow speed of implementation of the response and recovery plan. Note that Mr. Réal Chaput-Vigneault had previously agreed to serve as interim director of the *Organisation*, on top of his regular duties as Minister of Transportation, until we appoint a new permanent director."

Leaning on the doorframe at the side of room, used to rolling with the flow and playing into Léandre's improvisations, Réal waived to the press, as if he'd known all along that this was to be announced.

The explanations were accepted at face value by the sympathetic crowd, ready to report them as incontestable facts.

"When do you expect to put in place the new permanent director?" asked a friend.

"We already have approached many good candidates," answered Réal. "Expect an announcement surprisingly soon."

Montréal, 7:00 a.m.

James first dismissed it as being impossible. He knew that critical exhaustion and hunger could lead a tortured brain to wild visions and imagined mirages, and thus believed the ghostly apparition in front of him to be unreal, not recorded by his eyes but rather a construct of his mind attributable to physical hardships impairing his judgement. It could have been a diabolic gremlin—a supernatural evil spirit given embodiment by the powerful fears that lurk inside each man. Some sort of archetypal nightmare lurking in a parallel universe, crossing the boundaries that imprison one's insanity, whose temporary visibility provides a faint testimonial of overwhelming spiritual powers.

However, James was also convinced that supernatural sighting must instill fear, something that few disc jockeys riding snowmobiles have had the distinction of achieving.

Under normal circumstances, the reappearance of Richard Nightrock would have been a horrible and unfortunate meeting that James might have been able to escape by feigning preoccupation with another matter. However, given that Nightrock swerved his machine, aiming directly toward Larocque right after the dark visor of his helmet locked in his direction, James understood that this was probably not a coincidence.

As the snowmobile braked past James, sliding on the fresh snow, he threw on the ground a bag full of cold, slightly stale Montréal-style bagels. The smirk on Nightrock's face as he pulled off his helmet confirmed that he'd snatched them from an abandoned commerce. James understood the price for this fortuitous encounter, but the availability of transportation at the day's start was too convenient. James thought that theirs was a repugnant, incompatible partnership of objectionable value, as far as their antipodal personalities went, but that it might be, after all, a strange symbiotic relationship in which each might find some redeeming benefits—just like the hippopotamus and the tickbird feeding off the ticks on its back, or the crocodile and the plover bird cleaning its teeth by picking up scraps of leftover food. For a moment, he wondered which of the two roles he played in this mutually beneficial interdependency, but concluded that it didn't matter.

He stuffed the bagels in his backpack and hopped on the snowmobile. At that signal, Nightrock pushed the engine to full throttle, the studded tracks simulating a burnout—free of the burned tire smell—propelling tons of soft snow backward while the stationary vehicle started to slowly accelerate, on the way to some carefully selected damaged building that Nightrock had staked out.

Without exchanging any words, it was mutually understood that there would be only one additional interview. For the time being at least.

Ottawa, 7:30 a.m.

Yago Krapo was flipping through the pages of the Ottawa Citizen, while chewing on the cold toasts delivered by Room Service. Accustomed to the thick daily of a large metropolitan area, rich in substance and international perspectives, the local paper of the national capital seemed parochial. The biases in the prose and editorial views left him with the distinct impression that reporters in Ottawa owed their longevity to having successfully pitched the federalist vision, with the closed doors of elected officials likely awaiting those who dared explore alternative perspectives. In his assessment, the prevailing local journalistic commentary seemed to spring from a distorted vision of all news being peripheral to the federation's navel and only significant in their relevance to it. All done democratically, without *force majeure* or dictatorial edicts. While this could be at best an unsustainable tenuous proposition for many news agency in other parts of the world, Krapo sensed that it provided the federal capital's journalists opportunities to spew vitriolic criticisms on all provincial differences, including Québec as a preferred target on account of its aspirations at a distinctiveness directly clashing with the federalist vision. He wouldn't have been surprised if someone had told him that this latter angle was made singularly more appealing by the prospect of being decorated by one of a slew of journalistic prizes and awards rewarding penmanship that scorned Québec in ever more creative and imaginative ways.

The *Ottawa Citizen*'s first section was entirely devoted to the events of the previous day. True to form, the cover page pitted Québec against Ottawa, with an unmistakable bias for the home team. The indelicate headline in red letters shouted, "Quebec: Crushed!" as if heralding a Stanley Cup victory. Pages 2 to 5 diligently reported the concerned statements of various caring politicians spinning the party line, while the spread on pages 6 and 7 provided some technical information on the earthquake itself, mostly abstracted from the information prepared by Earthquakes Canada. Pages 11 and 12 described some of the known damage in the vicinity of Montréal, after pages 8 to 10 focused on the limited damage inventoried in the National Capital Region.

These three pages reporting on local damage caught Krapo's attention, particularly the description of the new Headquarters of the Department of National Defence in Orleans, a recently constructed 2-million-square-foot complex of reinforced concrete buildings—allegedly closed while awaiting an in-depth engineering inspection to assess the extent and severity of damage inflicted by the earthquake and to determine its overall structural safety. The few grainy pictures in the paper showed spalled concrete revealing the reinforcing bars at the base of columns, two-inch-wide diagonal cracks in concrete walls, and other evidence of structural impairments, intended to impress the general public.

To the professionally trained eye of an experienced earthquake engineer, the information presented in the photos would have almost been sufficient to explain the type of failures experienced by various structural components. Unfortunately, Professor Krapo, by training, was an expert on the numerical modeling of visco-elastic thermo-dependent solids and the development of optimal three-dimensional shapes subjected to static load conditions; challenging engineering mechanics problems for which applications remained to be discovered, but at the same time not even remotely connected to earthquake engineering. Yet, in spite of his expertise in abstract theoretical constructs devoid of practical relevance, Krapo felt in authority to forcefully express an expert opinion on the seismic behavior of any type of structure, including reinforced concrete buildings, a competency he deemed to be granted by his tenure as a faculty member of the prestigious structural engineering department of Saint-Chretistic Technological University, and maybe by natural osmosis from being close to real experts in the field.

In light of time and climatic restrictions preventing his planned travel to Montréal for the foreseeable future, Yago decided that he could grace the locals with his wisdom by first concentrating his efforts on that most interesting building complex of the National Defence, presumably a short taxi ride away.

Leaning over the breakfast tray, he dialed the concierge to get the phone numbers of the top national news broadcasting companies.

Montréal, 8:00 a.m.

Léandre and his team were brainstorming on how to both regain control of the city, and prevent a potential erosion in public opinion. In most fights, be it in sports or in life, public sympathy goes with the underdog. His government should have been able to capitalize on this basic human idiosyncrasy, portraying itself as the epitomical victim of a natural disaster of unforeseen magnitude. Even heartless dictators have been embraced by public support when appearing genuinely hurt by the suffering of their people after tragic natural calamities. Hence, even federalists in the province might rally behind a separatist government truly fighting to help its citizens recover from a disaster that indiscriminately struck Québécois of all political creeds.

But that was "yesterday," before the aloofness of Lise Letarte had been discovered. Although she was kicked out of her office, dispossessed of her keys and credentials, and literally thrown on the sidewalk with her empty attaché case, and even though her weird antics during the press conference were easily dismissed by the partisan witnesses, Léandre was concerned that the mad lunatic might seek vindication publicly, booking interviews on every radio and television station she could find, providing insane sound bytes beyond the media's wildest dreams. Little clips of madness that would be played and replayed, infinitely looped during newscasts, revealing to the press that, for the most critical 30 hours after the disaster, a fool was in charge of coordinating all emergency response activities. This would then serve as the leitmotif of all subsequent news reports, to show how a poorly managed disaster could rapidly become a major catastrophe almost beyond recovery. Even stripped of her title and disgraced by her ruthless firing, the public display of sheer incompetence, arrogance, and utter imbecility would seriously damage the credibility of Léandre's government, and possibly melt any sympathetic support it could have enjoyed in the face of adversity.

Worse yet, short on substantive news to report, Léandre feared that the press might launch a hunt for other grossly unqualified political appointees whose irrelevant skills or dubious intelligence could be blamed for the current mess, and possibly succeed in establishing enough necessary linkages to uncover a full-blown political scandal. Finding incompetents at the helm of government agencies was not particularly difficult in a world of cronyism and patronage appointments, but of no journalistic value unless it could be tied to a major crisis to serve the higher purpose of derailing the government's greedy ambitions, or, as a consolation prize, to force a dishonorable deputy to assume the blame and resign. The national press always enjoyed flexing its muscles and instilling fear, for lack of respect as an alternative; it wouldn't miss a chance to dig out more gold by capitalizing on a credible lead, conducting a few rigorous investigations while simultaneously launching a number of other, unrelated witch hunts in the process.

This sort of intensive, inquisitive journalistic pressure had to be killed in the egg. The sore point of the morning's press conference was the government's lack of credible expertise. The strategy to counteract such damning criticisms was to bring aboard Léandre's team a recognized expert on all matters related to earthquakes. Yet, while the solution was simple, the challenge remained: All earlier attempts to find such an expert had been frustratingly unsuccessful. It would take Lise a while to escape the island and make her imbecilic views heard, which gave Léandre's government a small breather, but the "home team" couldn't go much longer without a credible voice.

"Where are the *ciboire d'*eggheads when we need them?" wondered an exasperated Léandre.

Julien, the usual pessimist, suggested, "Maybe the country plainly chased them away and never bothered to keep track of their whereabouts, because nobody cared"—as if Riopelle was right. "After all," he argued, "this is a uniquely Canadian trait."

All were perplexed.

Julien, with an almost condescending pleasure to flaunt his international academic experience, lectured his colleagues like an arrogant, erudite professor.

"When citizens of Europe or Asia become distinguished experts and leaders in North America, their motherland's intelligentsia find it worthy to bestow countless honors upon them: Many *Chevaliers de la Légion d'honneur* while in post riding Québec's hinterland were decorated by France for their achievements enlightening the local barbarians; China and India proudly award prizes and titles to sons and daughters that struck gold in the great American wonderland, glorifying entrepreneurs as role models and icons against which to benchmark aspirations for wealth and greatness at home. In Canada, by contrast, those that participate in the great exodus for better opportunities abroad are conveniently forgotten, politely ignored, and silently and collectively resented for the 'brain-drain' problem they have created. Exceptionally, when Canadians in exile win an Oscar or other prestigious prizes abroad, the motherland is proud to highlight the Canadian heritage of the recipient as a way to claim shared credit for the accomplishment, but overall, the tracks Canadians leave in the snow as they cross the southern border are rapidly erased by the winds of indifference, and they remain known only to colleagues and friends, until the last of them has also departed. This time, with respect to experts on disaster response and preparedness, the last one out did not forget to turn off the lights, and the network of cognoscenti will be difficult to reconstruct."

Julien's negativism didn't alter the fact that credible experts were badly needed. Léandre's brain trust was unanimous in this belief. If none could be found in Québec, then they would have to scour the earth for them. Experts that could be temporarily repatriated and put on the government's payroll just enough time to convince the population that if they were going to live through hell for a few months, it was the best that anybody else anywhere in the entire modern world could do in a similar circumstances, and that this would not be due to a lack of competence. Yet, in spite of the urgency, these experts had to willingly be an empathetic part of the team, so careful profiling was necessary to avoid another Riopelle.

Réal Chaput-Vigneault barged into the room, his cheap portable radio blasting excessive distortion.

"I think we found one!"

He had their undivided attention, curious to understand what was going on. Through the distortion of an anemic radio painfully screaming its inability to faithfully deliver more decibels, they latched on mid-sentence to what simply seemed to be another chapter of trash radio.

"...and this is again a failure of our government to take its responsibilities and enforce the very laws that exist to protect us. A government that really cared about the welfare of its citizens, instead of pretending to care about it, would simply not tolerate such shoddy construction and archaic practices that fail to provide the necessary level of protection against the natural hazards likely to periodically hit our developed urban centers and the infrastructure on which our entire economy depends."

Léandre raised an eyebrow, and looked at Réal, questioning the relevance of his "discovery." Réal waived him off, signing him to shut up and be patient.

"Mr. Nightrock, I believe you are misinterpreting my explanations. Allow me to clarify my earlier comments. What I said, to be more precise, is that this building has been designed and constructed per standards that reflected the state of practice and knowledge at the time, and that today, after much evolution on how civil works are conceived, we have standards and practices that are significantly more elaborate and effective in reducing seismic vulnerability. As such, like for much of the existing infrastructure, including key infrastructure lifelines that are the blood of our economy, this building was designed per a standard that is today archaic, meaning that it is not used anymore. Just like a Ford Model-T was the state of the art at one point in time, and today our safety standards and features in cars are significantly higher."

Léandre pouted in surprise. James sounded assertive and experienced, a person of conviction who knew that the "Nightrock" in question was entrenched in a visceral desire for sensationalism, who recognized that it was futile to attempt to convert him to responsible journalism, but who nonetheless did not tolerate that his message be distorted in his presence, as this would have amounted to a silent endorsement of Nightrock's lies.

"Yes sir, you said it well, our civil infrastructure is like a giant Model-T, the butt of ridicule, some rust bucket waiting to crumble. And crumble it did! The city hall that used to stand in front of us has been decimated by the revealing truth of yesterday's earthquake."

They all jumped. The city hall was only a few blocks away. Léandre nodded, answering the questions they all did not need to ask, as a signal to the start of a race. Réal and Julien dashed out of the room, with a clear mission.

"Mr. Nightrock, I cannot comment on the political commentaries and extrapolations you are freely dispensing, but I will again clarify that this building collapsed simply because it was constructed of unreinforced masonry, a construction material that has been used for centuries, and that continues to be used today in regions that are believed to be exposed to a lower seismic risk—meaning regions where the largest earthquakes that are reasonably expected to occur during the service life of a building remain of relatively modest size and less stressful to constructions. Masonry construction must otherwise be reinforced to provide some minimum structural integrity during earthquakes, and to prevent the complete and progressive collapses that risk developing as a result of the subsequent brittle failures of individual masonry components."

James then proceeded with elaborate explications of how reinforced masonry structures are constructed, describing the minutiae of this craft: the large reinforcement bars running vertically through the holes of staggered hollow cinder blocks then filled with mortar; the numerous smaller reinforcing bars tied into small trusses embedded flat into the horizontal mortar joints; the way walls lacking this reinforcement could be retrofitted using wide fiberglass strips glued on their faces to tie together the brittle masonry units. In spite of James's painstaking attempts to paint the process using verbal imagery that could be understood within the limitations of a radio broadcast, Léandre didn't understand a word of this technical mumbo-jumbo, but he was delighted that James expanded at great length on the topic, thus providing more time for Réal and Julien to reach them. He also appreciated that James thwarted all attempts by Nightrock to interrupt his technical exposé, showing strength of character and poise in dealing with the press.

Fifteen minutes later, after a long and comprehensive overview of techniques for the seismic design of new masonry structures and the retrofit of older ones, James concluded.

"In any event, Mr. Nightrock, it has been a pleasure to again provide you with some professional insights into the causes of some spectacular failures, but at this point, I must return to the pursuit of my research activities. Thanks to you and your audience for your interest in this work."

Léandre feared they might lose him, until he heard, faintly in the background, as Nightrock was signing off the air, his two out-of-breath colleagues calling out to James. The transmission ended before he could determine whether or not the mission was successful.

Time then decided to slow down.

Each second carefully pondered when to strike its beat, wavering in its usual determination to precipitate aging, a carefully orchestrated and familiar torture to the politician accustomed to periodically entrust his destiny to the hands of the electorate. The elasticity of time, crawling when it is an inconvenience that must be waited out, rushing away in punishment when life is enjoyable. As only time kept Léandre away from knowing if the eagerly sought expert had been found at last, the hollow tick of each second reverberated almost endlessly, filling the emptiness of the room before vanishing out of existence and moving to a different universe, making room for the next second marching along the frozen parade of eternity. This temporal stall turned into a skid when Réal and Julien returned, not only with their catch, but with Nightrock in tow.

"Mr. Premier. The population of Québec is dying to hear, straight from its leader, why you have not acted to prevent this disaster from happening in the first place, by conscientiously and decisively investing in repairs to the decrepit infrastructure necessary to sustain the economic engines upon which depend our entire societal fabric?"

"What the hell is this..." stopping short of saying "*crisse de joke, tabarnak?*" unsure if the fanatic reporter had a live microphone on him. At first glance, he didn't seem to be wired.

"He followed us, and there are no security guards in place in this building."

Regaining his composure, Léandre considered the options. His impulsive desire was to gang up on Nightrock and beat him to pulp. However, such a slugfest could have negatively impressed James—and it is usually poor politics to abuse those who operate some of the most important tools to chisel public opinion. To ignore him would require politely escorting him out of the building, a problematic task in the absence of security personnel whose imposing physical stature is usually needed to facilitate such an operation.

Léandre considered fanatic reporters with partisan agendas to be the unpleasant thorns that never get invited to parties. Part of the problem is also that they never leave, or never shut up once given an opportunity to start.

"Mr. Nightrock, members of my government and of my personal staff have been listening very attentively to all your broad-

casts since yesterday. We are most impressed by your dedication
to inform the population, and particularly by your excellent idea to
provide them with the sound situational and technical assessment
of an expert in this field. Unfortunately, as you know well, we are
in the middle of a crisis that requires our continued and urgent
attention, and we have therefore limited our interaction with the
media to a very few times during the day. It is most unfortunate
that you have missed this morning's press conference, but I sincerely wish we will be able to see you at the latter opportunities
tonight and over the next few days."

"Mr. Premier, Québec is in pain, and the blame for this pain
points at your government. You cannot continue to hide and
refuse to answer the burning questions that preoccupy the public."

Eager to rid himself of the jerk, Léandre gambled that the
young, annoying reporter would abide by the journalistic code of
honor to respect the terms of an agreement struck with a potential
interviewee.

"Mr. Nightrock, I'll go outside with you and answer two of
your questions. You'll have to be satisfied with that offer because
it is a 'take it or leave it' deal. Beyond that, if you persist with your
harassing questions, I'll have you arrested for obstruction of key
emergency response operations."

"Mr. Premier. There are no security forces here."

"We'll call some and patiently wait, and the longer we will
have to wait, the more severe the obstruction charges will be."

In normal circumstances, Nightrock would have relished the
badge of honor of having been arrested in the conduct of his
journalistic duties, akin to a graduation ceremony, an anointment
into the big leagues. However, having seen for the past two days
the state of the city's infrastructure, the thought of spending the
week in an unheated, unlit, and mostly unattended cell, possibly
without food, tarnished the badge. The deal was one-sided after
all but it was worth accepting.

On the way down, alone in the elevator with the Premier and
one of his right-hand men, Nightrock couldn't believe his amazing
luck. Within the space of a few hours, he had grown from an
obscure middle-of-the-night disc jockey to the only news reporter
on-site, likely listened to by more households than Radio Canada,
even counting the whole government and the Premier as key listeners. And now, he had secured the unique opportunity to ask

two questions to the Premier of Québec, in an exclusive interview, in the middle of the largest disaster ever to hit the country. The immensity of it all started to weigh on him. He suddenly started to feel like a debutante, developing a serious case of the jitters. What does one ask when limited to only two questions in this opportunity to make history? What would be the two most important questions to be aired repeatedly over the next decades in recollecting the turning moments in this disaster? He surmised that bombastic attacks would diminish his stature in the process of setting up a quote for posterity, and that he had to formulate some poised and grand question that would highlight his piercing acumen and substantial judgment, two of his most undeveloped strengths.

Outside the building, after Nightrock had quickly set his equipment and started the broadcast, as the early morning snow started to build up on their shoulders, Léandre was growing impatient, awaiting the first question, and hoping that the warmth of the building and Réal's gab would not fail to keep James captive. As this restlessness started to show, Nightrock further froze, worried that Léandre was about to call the deal off, and walk away, leaving him limp and sweating, having failed his biggest opportunity. He blurted out the first question that finally flashed across his mind after a long drought of intelligent thoughts.

"Mr. Premier. How much of the blame for this disaster are you willing to shoulder?"

Obviously, the drought did not end with a deluge. Léandre would breeze through this one, repeating old ideas.

"Mr. Nightrock, a natural event that occurs so suddenly as an earthquake, and with so devastating consequences, is a true tragedy. In my earlier comments to the media, I have clearly illustrated the shortcomings of the federal government in duly informing us of the risk to which we were exposed, and in their many other failings. Yet, no single person can be blamed for this disaster, as the terrible situation that afflicts many of our Québécois compatriots is not unlike the terrible hardship that has been suffered by our southern neighbors in recent disasters."

Léandre believed that benchmarking against the United States always worked, for whatever purpose. In his view, Canadians either envied the Americans for their exuberant sense of identify and creativity, or hated them for the same reason, faced with the enduring challenge of defining a unique Canadian culture. Québécois, confident of their distinct cultural identity, either envied their southern giant for having affirmed its sovereignty and rejected outright the colonial yoke of England, and hated them for the same reason, faced with the struggle of establishing their own. In either case, Léandre was confident that, while both groups were elated when beating the mighty neighbor in selected niches of business, arts, or sports, they felt exonerated from all blame if unable to avoid a failure that would also befall the more resourceful giant.

Nightrock was furious at himself for wasting half of this golden opportunity with a futile banality that was so easy to circumvent. It was down to one question.

Words twirled in his brain besieged by thousands of questions from the mundane to the outrageous: Will he apologize to the population, resign, fire his staff, kill his engineers, dance the Lambada, fully compensate all those who lost property, close the city forever, declare bankruptcy, jump off a bridge, recognize his incompetence, discontinue the pursuit of national sovereignty, raise taxes, play the violin as the city burns, nationalize private property, declare war, lie to the public, dunk his head in the sand, enact an emergency building code, create a new agency, appoint unqualified friends to lead it, issue emergency government contracts, swim in conflicts of interest, launch a special lottery, subsidize charity organizations, instigate mandatory national service, legislate against earthquakes, freeze all bank assets, defraud other nations, imprison incompetent bureaucrats, sniff cocaine, establish a parliamentary commission, find political redemption, cheat on his wife, ask forgiveness, lose sleep, go insane?

"Mr. Nightrock, I'm sorry but if you do not have another question at this time, I must return to—"

"Did anybody you love die because of this earthquake?" blurted Nightrock, without knowing how this particular thought emerged from the insane cocktail of cross-purpose references brewing in his mind.

Léandre remained silent. The easy, straightforward response was to profess that he loved all Québécois and Québécoises, like brothers and sisters, and knit empty niceties around that concept, but the surprise question somehow touched him. His immediate family was in Québec City, and unharmed. However, immersed in the whirlwind of activities generated by this great turmoil, he hadn't had time to take stock. His brother lived in Montréal, as well as many cousins, uncles, aunts, nephews, and nieces. His wife had admirably managed the network of communications with all the extended families, and was the one tasked with gathering and sharing news, and setting up the social agenda. She spared him the details about birthdays, graduations, weddings, births, and handled all with due protocol. In that perspective, no news had always meant good news. He had wrongly assumed that his wife, as her traditional role befitted, would have been able to diligently gather information on the health of the family tribe's members, and that absence of information again implied a positive outcome, but he suddenly realized that she must not have been able to reach anyone in Montréal.

In the recording that would be replayed over the world for years to come, one could hear a sober Prime Minister sigh, after a long silence, and say, "I'm sorry to say, I don't know. I really don't."

As Léandre returned into the building, a limousine hugged the curb and forced Nightrock to move away from the edge of the sidewalk. It had been clumsily decorated with numerous small Québec cardboard flags, in an attempt to informally grace it with an aura of legitimacy and disguise it as an official government vehicle. If cars had hearts, this one would be pumping with pride for having been enlisted to serve a higher calling under the flag for a day for the betterment of society, rather than play its usual "whorehouse on wheels" role for the benefit of kinky elite bureaucrats with access to the keys. As the limo idled in front of the building's entrance, following instructions and waiting as long as necessary for its customers, Nightrock carefully packed his equipment and rode his snowmobile away, fading into the blizzard, in search of other audio clips to sell to syndicated radio networks.

As Léandre rode up the elevator, he shook off the numbing sensation of his emotional lapse. To function as an effective leader, and fulfill his political goals, he had to devote his full attention to the glorious cause. One key step to advance the national agenda was to enroll James as the national expert earthquake advisor to the government. Léandre recognized that dangling the opportunity to tour the damaged city in a limo as a perk might be effective as an unstated incentive, but to put James in confidence, particularly in light of his recent trying partnership with Nightrock, the offer of such a comfortable study tour would have to be free of reporters or official photographers to remain appealing. This was a significant departure from his earlier plans, but Léandre assessed that he needed James more than the others as this time. Reporters were never hard to find and would soon start to track his every step every minute of every day over the recovery process—at least as soon as they could get their act together. Furthermore, as far as documenting his presence in the field to assist fellow Québécois, the small digital cameras in the pockets of his aides might better serve the purpose, being less conspicuous in capturing history in the making. These smaller cameras also yielded less professional, more grainy pictures, appropriately conveying a sense of emergency field action amidst a national crisis.

First task at hand, partly to tame James, was to request him to brief his cabinet on the basic principles of earthquake engineering. This would also serve to profile him and avoid a repeat of the Riopelle fiasco.

Ottawa, 8:45 a.m.

Waiting for Brendon, the reporters in the press room conjured wild theories to explain the overwhelming increase in prominently displayed and brightly lighted trifoliate symbols. One suggested that the two lone Canadian flags of the previous day had enjoyed an intense, steamy breeding session, as evinced by their abundant progeny draping the podium and the room in white and red. When another feigned disappointment that nobody had thought of using planters with full-size, mature maple trees, he was reminded by a reporter from British Columbia that the national symbol is a "bastard" generic stylized composite leaf that represents no specific maple species, that the look-alike sugar maple was non-indigenous to his province, that no native maple tree grew in the Northern Territories for that matter, and that a hockey stick would be a more appropriate symbol of national unity—particularly now that they all expected a good hockey fight to start the day. It seemed like the two favorite national pastimes, politics and hockey fights, were just about to collide in the same arena. The home team was on the ice, ready for the game, determined to crush an opponent invisible to the cameras but vividly real to all in the room. Excitement was high in anticipation.

Brendon stormed to the podium, nodded to the press, and, trying to look passionate and forceful, read his communique in his usual monotone way. Yet the press delighted in every word, sifting newsworthy gems out of the expressionless mumbling of the national leader.

"My government has a national responsibility toward the people of Quebec and their needs in this period of severe hardship."

As reporters scribbled, they subconsciously transmuted Brendon's droning into the frenzied voice of a sports announcer screaming the play-by-play of a Stanley Cup final: "He stole the puck right from the face-off."

Brendon continued, "It is most unfortunate that, for political reasons, prior to this earthquake, the Quebec government failed to take advantage of our free knowledge and programs on how to mitigate the potential dangers created by earthquakes, offered by our Earthquakes Canada and National Research Council of Canada, as many of these could have helped attenuate the severity of this disaster."

All heard, "Sharp stick-handling through the neutral zone, high-speed crossing the blue line, feigns a pass to the winger and beats the defense, almost breaking away..."

"However, at this time, after this devastating earthquake, we cannot dwell on the past. We must act."

"First shot on goal. Easy blocker save, deflected to the corner."

"Therefore, even though the Quebec government has not yet responded positively to our numerous offers of assistance, we cannot let our fellow Canadians from that province, from young children to senior citizens, suffer in the harshest of conditions as a consequence of the lack of leadership of their provincial government."

"Mucking it up in the corner, takes possession, rims it around the boards to the blue line. Stays in the zone. Keeps the pressure on."

"Therefore, my government has unilaterally decided, effective immediately, to dispatch the Canadian armed forces to Montreal."

"Lots of traffic in the crease. Centering Pass. Slapshot hits the cross bar! Saved by the goalie's best friend. He never saw it coming."

"The forces will report to Public Safety Canada, who will endeavor to provide logistic coordination with its provincial counterpart, the *Organisation de sécurité civile du Québec*."

"Takes the rebound, skates around the net, tries to sneak it in. Puck deflects off a player's skate away from the net."

"Our peacekeeping troops have been instructed to provide services to agencies and citizens in response to needs identified on site."

"Lose puck. Shoots on goal. Pad save."

"We expect the first contingent of military personnel to reach Montreal by 2 p.m. today."

"Back hand shot. Top shelf. *Scooooooooooores*! Great pressure. Amazing goal. Never had a chance. Complete domination. Bring on the Zamboni, this game is over."

Caught in their mental transmogrification, it took them a moment to read Brendon's body language and realize that the end of the dry speech meant the start of the question period.

Brendon first picked a few friends among the mob jockeying for questions. He pointed to the reporter from the *Toronto Star*.

"How do you think the Quebec government will react to your initiative?"

Brendon's immediate thought was,"The fucking bastards are screwed." Untranslatable into politically correct terms, he volunteered instead a harsh yet restrained critique.

"So far, the Quebec government has not displayed evidence that it has the ability and resources necessary to properly manage this crisis. With the cold temperatures and now inclement weather, there is an urgency to act. The safety and lives of thousands of Canadians are at stake."

"How much time do you expect it will take for the Canadian forces to bring the situation to some normalcy?" asked another friend from the *Ottawa Citizen*.

"Our forces are highly trained, and should bring back normalcy in less than a few weeks, provided the local authorities cooperate to ensure an effective deployment of resources and coordination of activities," responded Brendon, planting a disclaimer that would make it possible to later blame all failures on the Québec government.

The reporter from *Le Soleil de Québec* shouted above the noise, "How many troops will be available on each street corner of Montréal, and what is their special expertise in post-earthquake response?"

Brendon was tempted to dismiss the question, but noticed that the room quieted as journalistic professionalism took over partisanship. The pens, tape recorders, and cameras awaited the answer. As the reporter had likely established beforehand, simple mathematics would demonstrate that there were more street corners in Montréal than soldiers in the entire Canadian army, but facts did not matter as much as symbolic gestures and posturing in answering this challenge to the might of the armed forces. Brendon had to rebut the veiled accusation that Canadian soldiers would be no more effective than overpaid baby sitters in managing this crisis.

"Our soldiers have served worldwide, performing active peace-keeping duties in war-torn countries. Do you presume that an earthquake in our peaceful home country generates more disturbance than armed hostilities in Third-World nations abroad? Do you believe that a few snowflakes will be traumatic to hardened professionals used to performing their duties and saving lives surrounded by swishing bullets? Do you suppose that distributing supplies and lending a hand to Canadian friends and families in need is more challenging than preventing genocides by rogue governments or hostile para-militia?"

The press nodded, except for the reporter from *Le Soleil*, who remained skeptical. It was not lost on those present that serving abroad as sitting ducks in buffer zones between enemies in cease-fire situations was a more modest mandate than reconstructing a modern, highly developed infrastructure within weeks while coping with -30°F temperatures or hostile weather, but the journalists felt that Brendon had provided a decently effective and newsworthy political answer.

As in any good spectator sport, especially the national one, interest also stemmed from seeing how the other team would react to pressure. The puck had been dumped into their territory, from where they would regroup and mount an attack. The armchair coaches would have to return to the comfort of their offices to criticize the subsequent plays.

Québec City, 9:00 a.m.

In jagged letters shaped to convey a sense of crisis, the glistering words "Earthquake Catastrophe" were wrapped around the twirling colorful and sparkling three-dimensional program identification logo—a masterpiece of computer-generated animation designed to establish a bold image of journalistic dominance and confident professionalism. A baritone voice-over introduced, "CBC Newsworld, temporarily broadcasting from Québec City," leading to the news anchor's greetings.

"With us in studio is Mr. Louis Riopelle, an earth scientist, recently appointed advisor to the Québec government on earthquake-related matters."

A stern Riopelle, strangled by an ugly tie intended to ornament a wrinkled, mismatched jacket, strained to project the image of a blasé professional, hiding his gleeful delight at finally getting his day in the limelight. He saw this interview—his Warhol's 15 minutes of fame—as a long-awaited opportunity to have an impact, to redeem decades of intellect wasted in the meaningless tutoring of indolent teenagers, and more importantly to shape a small but important part of the future sovereign nation.

He relished being the center of attention and reveled in being formally acknowledged as a recognized expert, even, of all things, an advisor to the government. Admittedly a stretch. In reality, as a consequence of his escape from *Complexe H* a few hours earlier, he was more likely persona non grata with the *Parti National* by now.

Over the phone, Réal had personally thanked him for his valuable draft brief, called him a true patriot—an *enfant de la Patrie* to be sure—and had requested that he greatly expand the document, asking for a more in-depth treatment of each main idea, to be complemented by numerous factual examples. Réal had also enjoined him to sustain his narrative by extensive references from the available scholarly literature. He had insisted that the task be undertaken at once, as a confidential initiative, conducted from within the government complex, benefiting from the skillful supervision of a dedicated personal assistant.

Riopelle didn't believe that forever dwelling on the same ideas would strengthen the case, that expanding his document on the failures of the government into a treatise was in his best interest. Even though he recognized that his prose could benefit from some flourish, he was confident that his contributions were sound. He had been outright surprised by Réal's excessive enthusiasm and insincere flattery. At best, he had expected that the government's intelligentsia would have been startled by his provocative conclusions and eager to engage in a constructive discussion on various aspects of the document. As a result, he suspected that the earnest desire to enslave him, chained to a word-processor in the lower basements of the government complex, was a cunning measure to cloister him away from the media.

Yet, he knew that arguing against these impositions would have been futile, particularly when under the close guard of a "personal assistant" who suspiciously resembled a jailor. Instead, inspired by his lackadaisical students, he knew that the easiest course of action was to agree with over-enthusiasm to all assignments and simply not deliver.

In his mind, Riopelle glamorized his escape from *Complexe H* as an enterprise reminiscent of a spy-like thriller. In reality, it had been a rather mundane operation. First, he stashed a printed copy of his short report in a pant leg, held in place by his sock. Then, after an hour of docile compliance to execute the government's wishes, he took advantage of an unaccompanied toilet break to escape. As he ran through the confusing maze of endless corridors that spread like the dysfunctional signature of a bygone architectural era, following the signs toward emergency exits, he heard in his mind the nervous soundtrack of his favorite action movie when the hero flees hordes of ruthless bloodthirsty thugs in pursuit.

Bursting through a utilitarian exit into the icy morning wind, shoes into two feet of slippery snow, he had struggled to avoid slipping on the thick, buried ice layer that covered the sidewalk. Having had to abandon his winter clothes inside to avoid raising suspicions, dressed in nothing more than worn jeans and a long-sleeve shirt, he threaded his way through the snow up the *Grande Allée* to the nearest hotel where waiting taxis could be found. Jumping into a *calèche*—Québec's open-air buggies famous with tourists—although he crossed a few on his way, was not a viable option, for it was unfit to the image of a spy's escapade, but more importantly because he needed the comfort of a warm automobile to reach home where warmer clothes awaited.

From there, he had contacted the media, whom he believed would be keenly interested in his story. As much as he would have loved to gloat about how he cleverly evaded the attention of the government's watchdog and to recount the story of his successful escape, this fantasy was subordinate to (and would have discredited) his higher purpose as an expert who had a unique opportunity to directly influence the government's post-disaster policy.

To secure the interest of the venerable state-owned CBC, he had taken liberty to aggrandize his status, from bit contributor to educate the government on his views of seismic politics, to that of an "officially appointed advisor to the Québec government on earthquake-related matters."

Eager to gain leadership after a slow start on coverage of this disaster, and buckling to the pressures of unrealistic deadlines, there was no time to verify the credibility of sources. Given the political agenda of the Canadian Broadcast Corporation, it couldn't care less if Mr. Riopelle conveniently inflated his credentials. Any title he wished, from secret agent to personal manicurist or secret gay lover, would have been aired at face value. Besides, the venerable establishment could not risk being scooped again by the amateurish adult-contemporary soft-rock CHOK-AM, re-christened "CRAP-AM" by the enraged CBC top brass.

"Mr. Riopelle, please tell us, was the Québec government prepared for this disaster? Are you surprised by what you are seeing today?"

"Not at all!" snapped Louis.

His interviewer worked hard to keep the poker-faced expression required of television anchors, and to repress the exhilaration reporters instinctively wish to radiate when they succeed in igniting the type of controversy that pushes ratings skyward. Although he wanted to jump on the desk and pump his fist yelling "He shoots, he *scooooores!*" he calmly asked, with a sly gleam in his eyes, "Why is that the case?"

"Denial is the root cause of the disaster we are facing today," answered Louis professorially. He then launched into a well-rehearsed lecture.

"The denial by all, in the face of well-known and undeniable scientific evidence, that a large earthquake could happen in the province of Québec, and consequent inaction by the government and other key civic authorities—"

"So in your opinion, the government is entirely responsible for this disaster?"

Unaccustomed to be interrupted mid-sentence by unruly students, Riopelle was speechless for a short moment. In years, his CEGEP students, either disinterested, asleep, drunk, stoned, spineless, or mostly absent, had never interrupted him to ask, of all things, questions.

"Well... yes and no. It is more like—"

"Professor, it can't be both! Responsibility is like being pregnant—it is not a part-time job. You're in charge, or you're not!"

Flustered by the intellectual indiscipline of this obstacle to the public exposé of his enlightened theory of denial, Riopelle tried to resume his composure and directly address the national classroom.

Looking straight at the one camera crowned by a glowing red light, he restarted.

"The denial by all, in the face of well-known and undeniable scientific evidence, that a large earthquake could happen in the province of Québec, and consequent inaction by the government and other key civic authorities—"

"So you point the finger to the incompetence of our governments, and consequently of our political leaders, to prepare for this event. Now, in your accusations, do you hold that this incompetence, which has led to the suffering of many Québécois, is the result of political corruption?"

"Corruption? No, wait a minute! I'm talking about denial in a very broad sense here," corrected Riopelle, trying to prevent a small word taken out of context from his exacting essay from becoming a snowball triggering an avalanche.

"Broader? So do you allege that the unions are involved? Is there a broad collusion of the construction trades to explicitly violate building code requirements? Who are the key corrupt government officials who have been bribed to orchestrate these most severe transgressions to public safety, at a social cost that is becoming all too apparent today? Has this network of corruption infiltrated all the way up to the top? These are very important allegations, Mr. Riopelle. How conclusive is the evidence that you have accumulated to date? Can you share it with us?"

"I don't have anything of the sort to share!" responded Louis indignantly.

"So your sources are confidential. This is most understandable given that government employees who have become whistleblowers have received absolutely no protection in the past against the wrath of the powerful government and corporations whose unethical and criminal behavior they sought to expose."

Riopelle, untrained in the fine art of media control, felt helpless and overpowered by an anchorman with an axe to grind. He was navigating in deep fog, some of which was condensing on his forehead.

Shaking and suffocating, he attempted one last time to expose to the masses his theory of human nature and resource allocation from the perspective of rare disasters. Grabbing his essay and reading straight from the wet papers, Riopelle hoped that the venerable Canadian Broadcasting Company would respect the academic rigor of his arguments. A strained, uncertain voice delivered the thesis, almost from where it previously stopped.

"History repeats itself endlessly as all leaders live in denial. Preventable catastrophes are not prevented because governments conscientiously refuse to consider them as credible threats, thereby allowing them to invest public monies into other projects having desirable short-term political dividends. Simply said, disaster prevention is not free, and serves no purpose toward getting one re-elected—"

The news anchor's earpiece buzzed with instructions, indicating that all the needed juice had been squeezed from this lemon.

"We are out of time, but we clearly hear your eloquent argument, Professor Riopelle. Public monies have been diverted to serve the personal and political agenda of those in power, and those responsible will have to be held accountable," concluded the interviewer. "Stay tuned for a complete update on damage from this disaster, and ongoing emergency response activities."

From there, Riopelle's terse babble would be converted into sellable sound bites frequently replayed around the clock while awaiting fresher controversial material from other sources. More noise added to the cacophony of radio waves emanating from the globe and propagating through space, someday reaching infinitely distant civilizations unequipped with the keys to decode and discern the condescending elitism from the disdainful populism of distinct broadcasters, unable to sieve the relative absurdity of a self-centered species from the collective stupidity merged into a common stream of electromagnetic waves where all nonsense stood on equal footing.

Where it could be heard, ratings for this edition of the CBC National News soared, an unusual feat for a Canadian public television network that had previously upheld a strict journalistic code of conduct and refused to lower itself to the tabloid-quality level of the competition.

Among the listeners who contributed to these unusual ratings were the staff of two Premiers already developing very different strategies on how to cope with the unavoidable media frenzy that was likely to follow.

Montréal, 9:15 a.m.

Réal's staffers at the *Complexe H* in Québec City, in spite of much debate through the morning, hadn't resolved whether to inform him of their failure to seclude Riopelle. They agreed that they had been embarrassingly unvigilant, fooled by his feigned enthusiasm for the bogus mission to expand his report forever. Yet they had hoped that, after his escape, the uninspiring professor would have forever hidden in a damp basement away from the public eye, humiliated by the deception. However, when they heard the lunatic lecturing on the CBC, and the interview's most juicy sound bites repeated every quarter of an hour, they had no choice.

With the perennial admonition to not shoot the messenger, technicians brought the special broadcast to the attention of the executive team gathered in the conference room of the *Organisation de sécurité civile du Québec* headquarters in Montréal, by setting the shortwave radio microphone in Québec City in front of a television replaying the Newsworld broadcast in a loop, and by transmitting the bad news on a secure band. That was faster than waiting for a radio station version, particularly given the poor reception of the distant CBC affiliates in the bad weather.

Léandre and his team were glued to the shortwave radio, awaiting replays of Riopelle's interview. This provided a welcome break to James, who had spent the best of the past hour educating his hosts on various arcane issues germane to damaging earthquakes. In spite of his aversion to politicians, the reward of spending a few hours in a heated building with functional toilets in exchange for sharing his expertise and answering a bunch of simple questions seemed a fair trade of services. However, his earthquake engineering crash-course would have been faster had Léandre and his team not constantly interrupted him by their obsession with political gamesmanship.

"Who is responsible for writing the building codes?" "How has earthquake preparedness been dealt with in other countries?" "What governmental programs exist there to convey the seismic risk knowledge to various jurisdictions and agencies?" "What is the relationship between the States and the U.S. Federal government, in terms of post-disaster response, recovery, training, and resource allocations, for example, and is the model from our southern neighbor applicable to Canada?"—all questions that could have been translated as, "What can be blamed on the Canadian federal government?"

Composing himself to deal with his audience was not easy. He had to accept their genuine disinterest toward the technical and tactical challenges that had to be addressed if normalcy was to be promptly restored to the city, at least until their fixation on policy matters could be resolved. James was eager to "part with the clowns" and let them run their three-ring circus, but simultaneously worried that the absence of credible technical support to this hapless team of "political monkeys" would result in reckless decision-making and thus lead to unnecessary suffering for thousands of citizens as they blindly followed ill advice from their clueless leaders.

After a few minutes of general-interest stories, the awaited short interview was replayed. All words clearly cut through the transmission noise.

Léandre was not pleased by Riopelle's comments, but they didn't worry him. Some spinning would be required to disassociate the government from this fool "misrepresenting himself as an appointed advisor to the Québec government," but that would be the easy part as the government's position couldn't be disproved.

However, of great concern to Léandre were the stern accusations and attacks by the CBC reporter, most uncharacteristic of the moderate stance of the state agency that usually endeavored to instill a modicum of sanity on the airwaves. The media wolves were starting to howl and hunt for fresh meat, and the pack was getting tighter. Liberals were joining the radicals; weaklings were marching with the fanatics. That was serious.

On the positive side, after an hour of listening to James's lucid and eloquent lectures, Léandre knew he had found a credible technical voice that he could add to his team, and dangle to the media to assuage their voracious appetite for relevant data and irrelevant trivia. One who could bury them in endless technical lingo, but who could also massage and vulgarize the jargon to make it accessible for the masses, giving the appearance of a government fully in charge and with a solid understanding of the issues and solutions ahead. Better yet, an employee of the National Research Council of Canada who could testify that the Canadian earthquake engineering academic and expert community had been blown to smithereens by ruthless and insensitive policies dismantling the programs in that field across all government departments, including his own agency, and by re-focusing the research funding of the Natural Sciences and Engineering Research Council on nanotechnology, biotechnology, bioinformatics, and other disciplines promising riches and economic growth. One eager to testify with great acrimony that experts devoted to infrastructure protection, starved of research funding, had to expatriate to U.S., Europe or Asia. One who would subliminally highlight how the Québec government could work with federal assistance and experts, while the decision and steerage of this assistance was best left in the hands of the provincial jurisdiction.

On the negative side, giving a prominent public platform to a federalist was risky, a *beau risque*, particularly given that responsibility for the success or failure of the response and recovery operations would reflect on his government. What if venerable journalists from *The Gazette* skillfully manipulated him into promoting the agenda of the Anglo-Canadian establishment? A few maladroit remarks by James criticizing the Québec government, intentionally or inadvertently, and Léandre's constituency could turn against him, igniting a nearly unmanageable crisis within the *Parti*. James's allegiances deserved further scrutiny.

To everyone's surprise, to make things worse, following Riopelle's interview, CBC Newsworld had baited another expert, offering him the opportunity to shine and share his infinite wisdom, while reloading the venom-filled gun of political commentary. All ears were again glued to the blaring from the shortwave radio, this time broadcasting from the National Capital Studio in Ottawa.

"We are now joined on cell phone by Dr. Krapo, a world-renowned earthquake engineering expert from Saint-Chretistic Technological University, currently standing in front of the severely damaged headquarters of the Department of National Defence, in Orleans near Ottawa."

James was shocked. "Shithead" had once again managed to end up in the news, spewing errors and inaccuracies to the unfortunate, undiscerning public. "That's what happens when a University President rewards faculty for media coverage rather than academic accomplishments," sighed James silently.

"Dr. Krapo, these buildings were just recently constructed, and yet the report in today's *Ottawa Citizen* shows extensive structural damage. How do you explain such a state of ruin in buildings that presumably should have been built in compliance to the latest building codes?"

Pretending to speak as a sanctioned delegate, Krapo declared, "Ferst, Î vould lîke to tayke advântayge of dis platfôrm to exbpress de mozt deebply velt zympaty of de Yoonîted Ztaytes gôvernament and zitizens tôvardz our Kanadianz naybôrz fazin dis mozt tchallengin ertkuake aftërmat. Rrest assoore dat ve foolly undeirstan yoour tribulatiôns and stan reaydy to azsist our lon-tîme frayenz on deir rôad to rekôvery. Dis Kanadian-Amerikan parrtnerrzship iz ay môdel to de vorld, ay beekon of hôpe in dis trôuble—"

"Would you say that gross violations of the building code are to blame for the unusual failures you have observed in your inspection of the DND buildings?" said the CBC anchorman, annoyed by this meaningless grandstanding, and trying to refocus the interview.

Insulted by the impertinent interruption, Krapo tossed out all grand feelings of international compassion. Regaining his composure and confident of the authority conferred by his prestigious title, he did not hesitate to put both countries back in their respective places on the world stage.

"Ay bildin dezîgned to de laytest Amerikan kôdes vould not sufferr dis kînd of damayge. Î am not ayvare of de ztayte-of-de-art in Kanadian bildin kôdes, and vould derefôre hesitayte to difinitivily assîgn rezponsibility in dis mâtter, but one expekts beitter dezîgns from ayn advânce socîety."

"Bullshit!" exclaimed James. "The seismic provisions of the National Building Code of Canada are nearly identical to the U.S. ones."

Léandre and his colleagues were intrigued by this sudden outburst. Léandre was offended by Krapo's gratuitous claims of cross-border harmony, particularly in light of FEMA's rejection of their request for humanitarian assistance, but he didn't quite understand why a derision of Canadian codes would inflame James more than the faked sympathy.

"I know this guy. He's a fraud."

Conscious that such unqualified, harsh criticism leveled at an eminent professor from Saint-Chretistic Technological University might lack credibility, James clarified, "I'm sure the closest he has come to the DND buildings is from the back seat of a cab."

The CBC anchorman pursued further.

"How bad is the damage? In your opinion, can it be repaired?"

Squinting to better see the damage to the distant DND buildings through the 1000mm lens of his camera, Krapo wondered whether anything could ever be damaged beyond repair. Short of complete collapse, it surely might be possible to repair anything, but he wondered how such things could be done. In particular, how many broken pieces would have to be glued back together before a repair became so extensive that it was deemed equivalent to a complete reconstruction—essentially using old pieces as building materials, instead of new ones? Such academic semantics always captivated Krapo because broader nomenclature and classification issues were somewhat related, if only peripherally, to his sterile research pursuits on the topology of structural systems. Yet, he made an effort to answer the question.

"Shoore reepayrin iz alvays pôsible, at ay kost, but izn't de reeal qwestion vy it ad to be dâmage in de first place? Sôme of my reecent reesearch on de noomerikal modelin of bildins yoozin vizkô-elastik thermô-deependant materials shôz dat it iz pôsible to dezign and konstrukt bildins dat are virrtooally indestruktible by ertkuaykes."

The CBC anchorman in Ottawa was somewhat baffled by this answer. James in Montréal was shaking his head in disbelief at the inept response and empty claims. He hoped that all listeners across the country, erudite on the topic or not, would see the fraud and be shocked that such an arrogant clown had found his way onto the airwaves. Yet, on the contrary, many found him credible and wondered why Canadian engineers were unaware of these more advanced analysis methods, convinced the nation was plagued by an ingrained intellectual inferiority and predestined to forever lag behind the technological leadership of Uncle Sam.

"And so why was it damaged in the first place, Dr. Krapo? What do your analyses reveal?" he asked, pretending for a moment that this abstract research thesis had any relevance on the case at hand.

Delighted to describe his research rather than the building at hand, Krapo volunteered, "Sôme mikrôcellular fôams hav ay vizkô-elastik cell strukture vith anizôtrôpik and tîme-deependant thermô-depeendant prôperties. De organik tôpôlôgy of dese materrials kan be map yoozin brôadban spektrôscopy and krôskôrrelated to its frrangibility. Dis has many advantayges over sekond-ôrder statistiks of de vavelet transfôrm of non-statiônayry randôm prôcesses vich—"

The CBC anchorman cut short this gobbledygook by imposing another question on top of the technocratic exposé, stretching the preamble until Krapo stopped talking.

"It has been speculated that poor workmanship and poor quality inspection has been responsible for the damage to these buildings. More specifically, some confidential sources have alleged that concrete weaker than specified in the construction documents has been used. In your expert opinion, do you believe that this hypothesis has merit? Could such a construction error be responsible for the damage you are seeing?"

Krapo had no expertise on this topic, but familiar with some of the lingo from a colleague's research on concrete technology, he ventured an explanation.

"De qwality of de konkreete yoozed iz kee in enshoorin satizfaktôry seîzmik behayvior. Reesearch kondukted at Saint-Khreetistik Tekhnôlôgikal Yooniversity reevealed dat if ay 20 ksî konkreete iz yoozed instayd of 40 ksî one, ay signifikantly inadeqwayte seîzmik perfôrmance iz obtain," he said, failing to define what was meant by "inadequate," or even bothering to explain that "20 ksi" was a specified minimum strength for the concrete corresponding to its ability to resist a compressive load of 20,000 pounds per square inch of contact area under the load.

Sensing an opportunity to generate political controversy, the anchorman pursued, "So in your judgment, the wrong kind of concrete was used."

"Yoozed, ôr spaycified," emphasized Krapo, oblivious to the implications of his unprofessional, delusional speculations.

The news crew high-fived each other and gave the thumbs-up to the anchorman. A goal had been scored for the home team: An expert from one of the most reputable universities in North America, on record, indirectly accusing the contractor of gross negligence.

"We sincerely thank you, Dr. Krapo, for these perceptive, candid, and enlightening comments on the likely causes of this startling damage to this landmark building in the Ottawa region. We sincerely hope that the responsible authorities will avail themselves of your highly specialized expertise to promptly resolve the current crisis in the aftermath of this disaster, and raise the Canadian standards to a level on par with the other technologically advanced countries with which we attempt to compare and compete."

"It trooly vas ay playzoore. Î'm alvays lookin fôrvard to bee of serrvice to internaytiônal aygencies and gôvernaments in tîmes of dîre needz."

Imbued of self-satisfaction and a sense of a mission well accomplished, Krapo closed his cell phone, leaned forward, and instructed the taxi driver to return to Château Laurier. The crisp Canadian air was so deadly cold to him. Digital photos snapped aplenty from the warmth of that backseat, hundreds of yards away from the nearest cracked concrete, would suffice to pepper with visuals his self-published, self-promoting earthquake reconnaissance report—an expert report to be mailed to hundreds of libraries, government agencies, and, of course, media outlets, like bulky business cards looking for consulting opportunities.

To Léandre, the interview confirmed that the CBC had joined the fray: Canadian media were on the loose, and the theme was national technical incompetence and governmental irresponsibility. He had the wherewithal to easily rebut the latter accusations, but needed an ally to brace his vulnerability on the first front. He looked at James, still shaking his head in disbelief.

"I gather you disagree with the assessment of this expert," asked Léandre, pointing at the radio.

James was careful in responding. He had remained silent after his earlier outburst, somewhat ashamed of having lost his temper, afraid that his comments might be construed as mere professional jealousy. While it might have been of great therapeutic value to scream, "Krapo is a ridiculous imbecile!" while jumping on table, he wished his further comments to focus solely on technical issues without violating rules of professional ethics.

"Yes, in more ways than you can imagine. For example, even in the most simplistic terms, the seismic strength of reinforced concrete buildings does not significantly depend on the compressive strength of the concrete used in its structural members, but rather on the layout and strength of the steel reinforcing bars in these members. In fact, two building columns with identical concrete strength but different reinforcement layout could have dramatically different behavior during an earthquake, one completely failing and losing its ability to resist loads, the other sustaining only cosmetic damage when shedding the small concrete layer that covers the reinforcing bars, without loss of strength. At best, concrete strength plays a marginal role considering all the other things that require utmost attention. As qualified as this professor may be in other sub-disciplines of expertise, it is crystal clear that he is way over his head on this topic."

"In your opinion then, how can only a few buildings in Ottawa be so damaged compared to others?"

"Listen. Serious forensic engineering requires serious engineering data collection. One doesn't answer a question like that just looking at a building from the sidewalk. Experience may allow good engineers to identify the type of structural damage by observation alone, but to explain why two buildings next to each other performed differently, one needs to do some serious work. It could be a combination of many things. For example, I know that the DND buildings are the only ones of that size and type constructed where I live, in Orleans, on top of hundreds of feet of soft clay. Such soils are known to substantially amplify the severity of the ground motions felt on rock hundreds of feet under the surface.

"To make an analogy, imagine an earthquake shaking a table made of rock, but on which lies a gigantic bowl of Jell-O; an item sitting on top of the Jell-O would be more violently shaken than one resting directly on the table. Similarly, buildings constructed on top of a deep clay soil deposit (like the Jell-O) would shake more than those constructed on rock (the table).

"In addition, to continue with the analogy, it is possible to observe that irrespective of how randomly the table is jolted, the Jell-O more or less jiggles with the same rhythm—it has a well-defined vibration frequency, predominantly bouncing back and forth the same number of times every second. If one lays a small rigid block on top of the Jell-O, the block will just be transported along with the movements at the surface of the Jell-O, but if instead one adds another identical layer of Jell-O on top, the second one will deform even more as both layers vibrate in tune. In fact, any flexible second item added on top that will have the natural propensity to vibrate at the same frequency will be similarly excited, irrespective of what material it is made.

"This is what happened in Mexico City in 1985, a megapolis partly built on an ancient lake bed consisting of a very thick layer of soft soil. Waves from an earthquake of magnitude 8.1 on the Richter scale, epicentered 200 miles away from Mexico City, rolled across the country without damaging any structure, but when they reached the city, the ancient lake bed responded like a giant bowl of Jell-O, shaking with a period of vibration of two seconds—meaning one full cycle of back-and-forth motion every two seconds. The buildings most severely damaged were those that had the same period of vibration on their own, as they responded in resonance, further amplifying the motions at the top of the soil. Buildings that were more flexible or rigid than that, generally taller or shorter, suffered less damage."

James took a breath to confirm that Léandre was following, afraid to have become too technical. He reminded himself that talking about boring, endless technical matters was a sure way to end up alone at a party, and summarized his thoughts.

"All buildings are different, so there is a large number of factors at play here, an infinite number of possible reasons why some buildings survive an earthquake when others don't. In fact, since the DND buildings are new, it is even possible to speculate that they could have been conceived using a new kind of technology whose implementation failed to perform to the intended design level, shifting the responsibility to resist seismic vibrations after it failed to other structural elements not detailed to resist such severe demands. For all those reasons, there will be no shortage of self-proclaimed experts sharing their infinite wisdom over the next weeks, publicly depicting their speculations as credible scenarios for the observed failures."

Léandre partly understood James's desire to exert caution on all technical matters, but believed that a warm-hearted approach, rather than a hardcore, technocratic one, was required to console a fearful and anguished population.

"Surely, you understand that the population is terrified, and looking for answers that the media are trying to provide."

"The population is most certainly in great pain. Compassion is important and necessary, but not a surrogate for good science or good engineering. Outright lies or fallacious mental constructs are sure to deceive in the long run, which is counter to a genuinely compassionate approach. Better voodoo rituals, which might actually work in mysterious ways, than deceit in overdose. If you had a toothache, would you prefer a dentist eager for action who starts to drill solely on a vague description of where the pain seems to originate from, or would you prefer to suffer a few more minutes to undergo X-rays and have a true diagnosis of the source of the problem?"

Léandre appreciated the combination of rigorous approach and ability to put things in perspective. Yet political allegiance remained to be determined.

"The problem with your toothache analogy is that, here, the public wants to pin the blame on somebody. Heads will have to fall."

James paused for a moment.

The blame.

The eternal witch-hunt for that elusive, accountable public official, the one on whose desk the buck stops. For decades, he too had pinned the blame, mostly on spineless politicians, those ominous demagnetized compasses driven by capricious public opinions, those rudderless leaders responsible for countless budget cuts, chronic under-funding, and fatal strangulation of unpopular research activities. Although he had later recognized that his anger was misdirected, that holders of public office were just puppets of higher powers, interchangeable scapegoats cheaply rewarded with celebrity for posterity, he'd never had any compelling reason to admire or even trust politicians. Yet, Léandre's interest seemed genuine. Could it be that Léandre was sincerely looking for a solution to this morass?

"I have been... concerned..." hesitated James, not disclosing that it was a frustration more than a concern, "over the years by the widespread, rampant lack of disaster preparedness across all government levels, and to add insult to injury, the shifting of research funding in Canada to favor other fields deemed to be more cutting-edge and having an aura of long-term profitability for some high-tech industries. Professionals across all disciplines have made valiant efforts to operate under difficult constraints, attempting to sustain what they perceived to be essential activities to ensure the future disaster resilience of the nation, but there comes a point when parameters combine in unfavorable ways that can only lead to the demise of entire disciplines.

"So, when the media, in hindsight after a disaster, ask who's to blame for the mess, in fairness, one can only conclude that everybody's to blame. Buckling under economic pressures to perform at an ever-optimized level of productivity, no short-term return on investment is to be gained by planning for uncertain and highly improbable events, even if dire consequences are anticipated should they occur. Individuals crushed by the daily burden of life, running from one crisis to another, seeking evasion with whatever time they can scrounge from the week, stealing from sleep hours or family time, won't plan for emergencies unless an alarm is sounded by the media or the authorities. As such, if earthquakes aren't immediate concerns of industry or individuals, whose concern is it? Who can righteously point an accusing finger when disaster preparedness plays to an apathetic audience just too busy with everything else? Too few really cared, unable to do much with infinitely small resources."

Léandre, unconvinced, thinking that this was just a slick way to avoid facing the real issue, countered, "Isn't that easy rhetoric? Government agencies are entrusted all the time with responsibility to ensure safety of the public, for example, for safe air travel, or for safe drinking water. The public does not explicitly clamor for these everyday, but they certainly expect such protection, and will bring culprits to the hanging post when something goes wrong."

James, aware that he was playing devil's advocate to an extreme, wasn't surprised by such a counter-argument, expecting no less from someone making a living with public policies.

"I fully agree. The public is willing to pay for clean water and planes that don't crash, and has expressed outrage when these expectations were not met in the past, because these services are needed every day. There is an implicit social contract that these will be reliably available in perpetuity, as an integral part of our modern infrastructure. The corresponding expectation for buildings and bridges is that they will not unexpectedly collapse under their own weight, that they will always be designed to carry their full load of occupants or traffic, that they will not fly away in the first windstorm. However, public expectations and willingness to pay are harder to gauge when it comes to unusual circumstances likely to occur maybe once per lifetime."

"So what? That doesn't absolve anyone," interjected Léandre, thinking this just sounded like a poor excuse, especially from the perspective of a politician. "Everybody has to deal with the inability to anticipate what the public wants. That's just a fact of life in a democracy."

"Correct. And to deal with it, one must make some reasonable assumptions and guesses as to what would be acceptable. For example, the implicit philosophy underlying the seismic design requirements in all modern building codes is that earthquakes are accidents, just like car accidents for the sake of comparison. Both earthquakes and car crashes are rare events and the expectation is that, in both cases, the occupants will be able to leave the scene of the accident alive. Likewise, after a severe collision, an automobile may be totaled, but its specially designed body will have taken the brunt of the impact and protected the passengers from fatal injuries. After a severe earthquake, a building may be a write-off, damaged beyond repair and tethering at the brink of collapse, but its specially designed structure will have sustained the brunt of the violent shaking, affording the occupants a chance to escape alive. They may need to tread through much debris just to reach the exit, but they won't be trapped or crushed to death in a collapsed structure. Given the extraordinary strength of earthquakes, and their rare occurrence, this design philosophy is accepted world-wide."

Skeptical, Léandre questioned, "Very nice analogy, but it doesn't work. The intent is maybe laudable, for whatever reason, but what's the wisdom of a philosophy that gets us in this mess? There are hundreds, maybe thousands of damaged buildings out there. This is not one car accident. It is an infinitely long pile-up. It's miles of highways full of twisted metal and wrecked cars, and no tow truck in sight."

"So how much is the public willing to pay then?" asked James.

Léandre wondered if the argument had gone full circle.

James continued, "Everybody could own a Sherman tank and drive oblivious to the perils of the road, but these oversized Sport Utility Vehicles are inconvenient to park at the grocery store, lack cup-holders and sun roof options, and are a tad more expensive than your average sedan."

"That's extreme. There has to be some middle ground between a tank and a station wagon."

"Yes, indeed, but there still is an incremental cost to reach that middle ground. That shouldn't be a big barrier, but somehow it is. After all, why pay for something you may never need? In fact, it's often only a small premium to purchase an optional home insurance coverage to protect against the potential losses resulting from earthquake hazards. Yet, how many Canadians even bother to include that optional rider into their current policy? It seems that most people are just subdued and fatalistic with regards to earthquakes. And possibly complacent in the case of Canadians, as damaging earthquakes in the past century have mostly occurred in other countries."

Léandre nodded in agreement, unsure of exactly what coverage his home insurance provided.

Seeing that Léandre remained silent, James attempted to be more optimistic, stretching to find some redeeming benefit to the catastrophe.

"On the positive side, if there is such a thing in this case, this disaster may help change Canadians' perception of the risk, and hopefully encourage them to take actions towards enhancing their preparedness against such future disasters."

That didn't lift the spirits much.

Recalling Léandre's original comments, James added, "In the meantime, to come back to your original concern, maybe heads will fall, as you say, but I have no interest or patience for a witch-hunt to burn at the stake the presumed culprits."

James hoped this was a politically correct way of stating that, as far as he was concerned, the two levels of government could continue their childish attacks and power struggles, but he did not want to be played as part of those games. He was unaware that this indirectly laid out his conditions for helping the Québec government.

Léandre was delighted. James was technically competent, able to address controversial issues in relatively impartial terms, and disinterested in the blame-game. He could be integrated into the home team without having to worry about opening the door to a federalist Trojan horse.

Attempting to charm, he ventured, "You are correct that the population has probably not prepared itself, as attentively as it should, to the threat of a possible devastating earthquake. But the past is the past. Now, our government has a responsibility to respond in the most effective possible way to this crisis."

Léandre was deliberately inclusive, extending an arm beyond his jurisdictional reach. He added, "Our team could benefit from your technical expertise."

James, always leery of smooth-talking politicians, was concerned by this overture. Still exhausted from the hardships of his first day of field work and drained by his strenuous relationship with the leech from CHOK-AM, he wasn't eager to engage in another partnership given the risk that it might again only serve to advance the ambitious agenda of a selfish manipulator.

Seeing James's poorly concealed grimace, Léandre appealed to his altruism.

"We do not believe that anybody in the world has even had to endure the aftermath of a large destructive earthquake in such inclement cold weather. Time will tell and history will judge, but this might be the catastrophe of the millennium. We're in the middle of it; we can't escape it. Now is the crux of the recovery process. We have a task of inordinate proportion and we are alone in writing the rules and procedures of how to best raise our society back into normalcy. Toward that goal, we will need every experienced talent and technical skill we can muster. As such, you are most sincerely welcome to voluntarily participate in this endeavor, even if only for a small moment, for a few hours, or for a small expedition to assess the state of some select parts of our infrastructure."

While James was gratified that his highly relevant expertise was sought, flattery alone wouldn't suffice to buy his services. The incentive had to be potent.

Léandre added, "Our first expedition, departing in a few minutes, will attempt to reach the Olympic Stadium to assess the extent of its partial collapse."

A destroyed landmark was the ultimate incentive.

James promptly responded, "I certainly can tag along for a while, if you believe that my technical assistance can serve some useful purpose—maybe even having a positive influence on decision-making that could hopefully accelerate relief to the population."

This meant curtailing his earlier plans and somewhat extending his scientific expedition, but James felt justified in that the task at hand would provide exceptional access to exceptional damage. He also rationalized that it provided an opportunity to leverage his skills for the good of the public, something possibly more worthy than concentrating on the data-collection task he had originally set forth to undertake 35 hours ago.

His mind wandered. Who knows? The valuable knowledge he would gain in the process might even lead to a book deal—a substantial step up from his usual papers in scientific refereed journals.

The limo driver, asleep on the front seat since 6:30 a.m., was buzzed and ordered to get the engine revving and the car warm, as its passengers were on the way. He pulled a flask from his coat, gulped down a couple of shots of rum, and got out to wipe the snow off the car. Paid at triple overtime rate, he wished earthquakes happened more often.

Ottawa and Québec City, 10:30 a.m.

The Québec City's Jean Lesage International Airport and Ottawa Macdonald-Cartier International Airport had never been so jammed. Private jets from all over the world had been landing all morning and parking space for all these crafts was becoming scarce. Like invading armies, troops of journalists were ready to march on Montréal from their eastern and western positions, broadcast equipment and staff in tow; except that contrary to multi-national military campaigns benefiting from intense coordination by an international coalition, this was a haphazard assault by mobs of disparate teams competing for scoops. The foreseeable outcome was that the same chunks of debris and snippets of drama would be captured umpteen times, only with different talking heads in the foreground, yet offering to share resources was forbidden, for fear of losing an exclusive.

In each airport, through the morning, teams scurried in search of transportation to the epicenter, unsuccessfully fighting to rent the same helicopters and trucks—with pilots and drivers—settling at best for a minivan, at worst for a couple of sedans, and some road maps. Driving in a snowstorm for half a day would get them to the edge of the island, from where they would have to improvise, expecting to snatch a Good Samaritan on a snowmobile for a ride across the river and through city streets, like others before them.

The swarm of insensitive mercenaries had spent half of the previous day on standby, awaiting the green light from network executives who needed solid evidence of extensive material damage and financial losses in the earthquake-impacted areas before loosening the purse strings. They were unleashed by mid-afternoon, a decision triggered by Québec's official announcement that Montréal was to be considered a "closed city." Each network had spent the rest of the previous day planning its expedition, assembling teams, all the technical gears, and survival supplies for extended stays.

Like seasoned paparazzi in search of live adversity and human misery, but aware that dramatization could sell just as well, they also packed props to stage obligatory scenes: a realistic mannequin hand-painted with a light blue varnish to mimic a frozen hand reaching out from the debris of a collapsed building, in case the real hands found on-site were inconveniently located and in poor

lighting conditions; fake blood to sprinkle as necessary to accentu-
ate the harsh field conditions experienced during reporting; pre-
recorded rumble noises and survivor interviews to use if they
encountered delays accessing the site; and more. They worked for
big media empires built on the tenet that nobody reads anymore,
and that undertook to supply both visual news and fiction, often
at the same time, saving the population from the drudgery of the
printed word. Real or fake blood didn't matter in order to tell life
as a series of mini reality shows.

Given the organizational and meteorological obstacles that
stood in their way, none of the international teams dispatched to
prey on the province would make it to the edge of the treasure
island cut from civilization before darkness. By the next morning,
though, with more clement weather in sight, they expected to all
have figured out how to invade the precious isle.

Montréal, 12:45 p.m.

Again, light came, without asking if he'd wanted another day. Again, the "clubbing of the ribs" ritual was broken.

So he slept, as never before. Or at least for as long as a mind ravaged by the brutal erosion of alcohol allowed him to remember. As he slowly emerged from the temporary freedom of night, the cold reality did not feel as cold as usual. The sub-zero temperature had strangely lost its wind-chill whipping force. By reflex, his hands sought the gazettes and their imaginary warmth, but grabbed only air.

The puzzling failure of that search prompted the prying open of one eye. The colorful assault of blue popped both eyes open.

His face squashed on a powder-blue carpet, surrounded by blue walls and miscellaneous blue furnishings randomly planted in a tastelessly decorated room, he tried to reconstruct the past into a coherent whole. He wondered whether he was floating in some afterlife sky, or if this was just another dream soon to vanish disappointingly. Rolling over, he felt the biting cold of snow piled on the floor next to the breached window, and recognized reality.

"Damn cold, damn cold, too damn cold," he whispered.

He surveyed the room, searching for his bench. Broken windows, boarded-up from the outside, unequivocal features, yet, no rats, no squatters, no graffiti, no stench of urine. An abandoned building, fully furnished, ugly paintings on the wall, kitschy curtains waiving slowly, and, "goddamn it, praise the Lord," a fully equipped bar. Clément felt deeply blessed, convinced he had discovered the only 5-star abandoned dump in the world, and delighted that nobody else yet knew about its existence.

Leaving the wooly comfort of the floor, answering the call of the Bacardi bats and other longtime friends, Clément did not need a glass to let the redeeming liquids warm his soul and ignite his "central heating system," as he liked to call it. The first bottle of fuel rapidly emptied, Clément sat for better enjoyment of the second, cradling it lovingly between sips, in fulfillment of the dreams for which he'd abandoned a life long forgotten.

The numbing pleasure filled him with satisfaction as nothing else could. The alcohol cajoled him with the sweet caresses of a warm southern comfort. It never judged him, never faulted him, never nagged him, never crushed him with the myriad reproaches of being unlovable. It was peaceful in its essence of not being alive. It was the only negative, dark, and feminine yin running amuck with his yang, determined to influence his destiny. It didn't praise any more than it criticized, but he preferred this peaceful, neutral void to the pain of not being loved.

Liquor successfully made him forget, indiscriminately killing the offensive brain cells scarred by pain. Forget the wounds, the lacerations, the deep, deadly sadness of having dispensed an unreturned love, the pointless, fleeting beauty of a romance that never was, the despair of a desired, unachievable intimacy. The trauma of discovering life as a gargantuan lie, of disrobing truths to reveal a web of illusions and deceit, of being crushed and buried as the rotten foundations of trust fractured and collapsed under the weight of cynical fabrications. All those suicidal memories, once believed indelible, now scraped away by the continuous grind of hydroxylic organic compounds, dying one burned cell at the time. A pure liberation from the calvary of an accidental life worth trading for a brutal life of homelessness.

Slumped on the sofa, sweet bottle in hand, savoring the fruits of fermentation, Clément lived his eternal bliss. No questions, no distractions, no thoughts, no worries, no anxieties, no burden, no ego.

Halfway through his second bottle, keys rattled in a lock, the front door opened wide, and large plywood sheets entered the room, framed top and bottom by rows of fingers. Clément, already bathing in a blissful drowsiness, was impressed by the good manners of the plywood sheets wiping their boots on a corny welcome mat outside the door, and, always ready to uphold the streetwise creed of the drunk, wondered whether there would be enough bottles to share a friendly drink with a stack of lumber.

"*Crisse!*" yelled a stunned man as his eyes emerged above the lowering sheets.

The dropped plywood scratched a mahogany table and toppled a ceramic lamp before crushing a few exotic plants.

"Get out of here, *mon tabarnak!*" he snapped, mad that some "homeless trash" dared to violate his sanctuary.

"Hey chill man, there's enough booze for two here," volunteered Clément, with genuine intent to share his newfound paradise. He hopelessly tried to stand up as the hostile man dashed for the sofa.

"Move your ass out of my house, *ostie de* scumbag," answered the man, grabbing Clément by his oily shredded coat and propelling him toward the door.

Back were the questions, the distractions, the thoughts, the worries, the anxieties, the burden, the ego. The gripping nightmare. Blurry apocalyptic visions of doom, unleashed existential fears, demented burning excitations, and irrational paranoiac stimuli, all spasmodically collided and mixed within his damaged brain. Clément was drowning in the cerebral onslaught of a biochemical hormonal cocktail, panicking as if his out-of-control reactor was on the verge of a meltdown. All while being jolted and beaten by a furious maniac he had never met before.

Scared to death, he vigorously tried to wiggle out of the man's grip and run away. He frantically screamed and tightened in violent convulsions.

Thinking that Clément was undergoing an epileptic seizure and risked dying on his carpet, the madman freed him, with a violent push toward the door. Staggering after such a beating and because of a near-poisonous blood alcohol level, he rammed into the door frame in his escape, opening a gash on his forehead.

Freaked out, he blindly ran across the snow-packed driveway, tripping and stumbling, as far away as possible from the house, towards the park across the street, into the snowstorm, oblivious to the trappings of reality.

Montréal, 1:00 p.m.

Gusts of wind erased the world, drenching it in a hazy whiteout, like vandals throwing talc on a painting. One second a peaceful winter scene saturated with snowflakes falling on a city cloaked in a rare purity, another a violent swirl of ash dissolving all familiar references and fusing sky and earth into a senseless emptiness.

The limo plodded along, hugging the road as best as it could between spasms of blindness, carrying Léandre, Florent, Julien, Réal and James back towards the *Organisation de sécurité civile du Québec* headquarters. It could have looked like a normal winter storm. Except for the occasional audacious or desperate urban trekker threading across the desolate streets on snowshoes, the blizzard had cleared off those remaining few who had the temerity to endure the cold until then, forcing them to temporarily surrender the hope of lessening their losses, alleviating their pain, or promptly rebuilding their lives. The snow slowly enshrouded the debris and the squalls suppressed the other evidence.

At least the first hours of their tour, in the absence of any wind, had been productive, with the occasional stop at various places on their way to the Olympic Stadium, for some to record technical details of structural damage and collapse mechanisms, for others to stage photos and short videos of the nation's custodian appraising first-hand the severity of the crisis, knee-deep in the wounds of the motherland. Réal relished his role as official videographer and stage director, loading the memory card of his digital camera with striking images of history, counting on Julien's and James's digital cameras to serve as a back-ups should the splurge of videos ever fill his gigabytes of storage capacity.

From the ground up, at human scale rather than bird's-eye view, the Olympic Stadium's injuries were gigantic, more impressive and distressful to Léandre than what he remembered from the previous day. Beyond the awe of destruction, the architectural monument that had expressed national pride, broadcasted worldwide over two weeks in a distant summer, now laid in ruins. Yet, in a subliminal, perverse manner, it allowed photographs of unprecedented symbolism, documenting a pregnant moment in history, showing a nation's builder facing shattered ties to the past, a white canvas in hand to assume his obligations to the future.

James also snapped hundreds of photos, focusing his zoom lens on every visible fresh rupture point of engineering significance, but he was frustrated by the limited resolution and the mostly obstructed views from outside the giant structure. Broken windows at ground level in the general ticketing area provided partial access to the interior, but his burning desire to climb the tower for close inspection of the fractured post-tensioned cables and crushed concrete was thwarted by locked steel doors that effectively sealed the ticket area from the rest of the building. He could not reach the overturned, collapsed tower, see the mess of cables and fabric dome scattered over the field, or take pictures of the cantilevered ribs that failed inward into the stadium bowl.

Being deprived of this access prevented him from initiating the vital first steps of what would likely become the century's most fascinating forensic engineering study, leaving him deeply unsatisfied. Not even the luxury of conducting an earthquake reconnaissance visit from the comfort of a living room on wheels, traveling in style with a mini-bar and chauffeur, could compensate for this lost opportunity. As the limo headed back to headquarters, he was pondering the options for gaining subsequent access to this gold mine of knowledge, wondering how much longer he would benefit from the current royal treatment, absently gazing at the incessant snowfall through the tinted window of the limo.

At the relentless rate of precipitation over the past hours, the unplowed streets had become tracks—7-inch-deep grooves embracing the tires and steering the cars with an overpowering determination. The zigzag path laid hours ago circumvented hidden debris. Stepping outside those white tracks was inviting trouble. Now, worse, severe wind gusts traced thick white streaks across the windshield, severely impairing visibility—or outright obliterating it.

Speed limits rendered irrelevant by weather, driving conditions being equally horrible on all roads, the chauffeur veered the limo off the main artery to a side street running parallel to the park, seeking a shorter route given that driven miles directly determined travel time in those circumstances.

"Where are you going? You should stick to the main roads, we can't see *de l'ostie d'marde* here!" complained Léandre, jerked by the slippery turn.

"It's only a small shortcut, sir. Almost there," apologized the driver, briefly flashing a sincere smile and presumably reassuring expression to his V.I.P. passengers in the limo's back seats.

Before his eyes could reconnect with the road, a loud thump shook the limo. The driver slammed on the brakes; the repeated pumping of the Automatic Braking System eventually immobilized the car after it drifted some distance on the snow. Still shaken, he turned the flashers on.

"*Crisse*, what the hell was that?"

"I'll check immediately, sir," quipped the driver as he jumped out to inspect the situation.

He was most worried, fearful for his job. The position required an impeccable driving history. Any blemish on the car, any scratch, any dent from the impacted object would tarnish his record.

He first checked the front of the car. No damage. While bent to look for objects stuck under the frame, invisible from his passengers, he threw away as far as he could his flask of rum. He then hurried to the back of the car and beyond, following the tracks in the snow, desperately praying that he'd only run over a stray garbage can.

He discovered his worst fear lying beside the road 50 feet behind the limousine. Clément, drunk and unconscious, half buried in a snow bank, had gone from absolute fear and agitation to near-absolute peace and serenity. In his frenzy, he'd madly run across the street, at just the wrong time.

Inspecting the half of Clément protruding from the snow, the driver immediately noted the shabby clothes and conspicuous smell of homelessness. This presented some options. He glanced at the limo far behind, wrapped in thick, snow-laden whirlwinds, barely distinguishable, wondering what they could see, what they saw. The thickness of the blizzard hid the surrounding houses, making other witnesses highly improbable.

His conscience swirled, a moment. Residual pressures of a distant Catholic upbringing incited him to uphold higher moral principles, but burning memories of abuse at the hands of deeply immoral Catholic priests undermined such noble roots. As those impulses cancelled each other out, the decision was simple. Good jobs were hard to find and nobody would miss what appeared to be stray human debris. He proceeded to push more snow over the body to complete the burial.

All that time, in the car, James was appalled. He kept to himself for a while, but broke the silence.

"I can't believe you won't even check it out yourself."

"That's what he's paid to do," answered Léandre. Unaccustomed to the elites' lifestyle, he dissected the argument, seeking the logic of a different perspective for a moment, but it didn't add up.

"Wouldn't you want to know first-hand if your driver has hit a pedestrian?"

Cold silence.

James added, in an abrasive tone, "One of your most faithful voters could be bleeding to death under the car."

Léandre recognized that hitting a pedestrian, even accidentally, was not a desirable political move. Decades ago, the political career of a Québec Premier had been jeopardized when he drove over and killed a drunk lying in the middle of a road. Yet, he shrugged.

"Bunch of slugs," blasted James, as he stepped out of the car.

"*Tabarnak!*" cursed Léandre to himself. "OK, let's check it out."

The driver heard the limo doors slamming. "*Sacrament!*" he whispered, realizing that the dirty job could not be completed in time. Panicked and cornered, he could only hope they hadn't seen anything. Gambling that they couldn't tell the difference between the ripples made by a body thrown on snow and snow throw on a body, or that the gale would have already erased such subtleties, he tried to save face and started digging Clément out of the snow.

"*Ostie*, you hit somebody! Just what we needed," exclaimed Léandre as he saw the single arm and leg sticking out from the snow. It crossed his mind to bury the rest of the body and run, but he chased the thought away, reassuring himself that he wouldn't have done that even if James hadn't been a witness.

"It's amazing you could find the guy. He's almost completely buried in snow," observed Julien.

"Is he still alive?"

Florent kneeled and took his pulse.

"Yep, but he should be brought to a hospital. It made quite a bang when we hit him. He'd be lucky to have only a few broken bones."

"OK, call an ambulance!" ordered Léandre to the chauffeur. The tone implied that they could just tell them where to find the body, and move on to their other business.

The chauffeur strained to hide his panic. An ambulance would come with the obligatory paperwork and the certain soiling of his driving record. He was deeply relieved when Julien interjected.

"What are you talking about, Léandre? God knows when they'll make it here. On a sunny summer day you can't even rely on these unionized jokers to show up before people die. What do you expect in a snowstorm after an earthquake?"

Réal added, without emotion, "My paralyzed mother died watching the hospital from her living room window, waiting for an ambulance that showed up two hours too late."

Léandre wasn't in the mood to start a debate on the status of health care in the province, nor to be painted as uncompassionate. "You can't move an injured man, you know. You could make his condition worse."

"It's a case of lesser evil," said Réal.

Julien added, "If you let him freeze to death, at least it will be painless when the snow blower grinds and spreads his body parts along with the other dog shit we'll find during spring thaw."

It didn't release the tension.

"Come on! The guy's soaked in alcohol. Even at minus 50, he can't possibly freeze. How about you stay with him until the ambulance shows up?" asked Léandre to Julien.

James was unfazed.

All arguments had been heard. They remained in silence, contemplating the options, exposed to the cold bite of the blizzard seeping through to their bones.

The long streaks of blood on Clément's forehead had coagulated around a clear imprint of the doorway he'd banged during his stormy exit of the last home he'd occupied. However, the growing crimson stains on his clothes evinced profusely bleeding wounds from the car hit.

Léandre decided to defuse the confrontation. He needed James on his side at this time, and had to compromise.

"OK, let's put him on the floor of the *ostie d'*limo and drop him at the nearest *baptême d'*hospital."

Montréal, 1:45 p.m.

Although tried by challenging obstacles along the tortuous, cold, and icy path that led them from hospital to hospital, as if prisoners of a pilgrimage in search of a destination, Jean-Pierre and Audréanne's faith was never shaken; they truly believed in the highest fairness and nobility of human nature, and that someone would eventually recognize their opportune value in this time of crisis.

It didn't matter that this nobility expressed itself by a critical rate of absenteeism at the last hospital where they'd landed late in the afternoon of the previous day. Thanks to staff members upholding personal priorities ahead of professional duties, and to the simultaneous surge of patients from the nearby community adding to those redirected from other hospitals that closed within the last day, the head M.D. had no choice but to enlist Jean-Pierre and Audréanne's assistance. In such circumstances, two lowly interns were worth something, at least for the duration of the crisis. His intent was to use them as a temporary palliative measure in response to the progressive shrinkage of staff on active duty—staff that either left, often without bothering to notify anyone, or who did not report to work.

They were assigned to assist with triage in the emergency ward, within strict constraints. Most importantly, they had explicitly been instructed to work under the supervision of senior staff and prohibited from making final treatment decisions. However, they were often left on their own when the senior personnel were either overwhelmed by the volume of arriving cases, preoccupied by possible shortages of medical supplies, distracted by petty unprofessional arguments, or invested in extended coffee breaks at the cafeteria. As strict as the constraints might have been, they were simply unenforced.

Jean-Pierre and Audréanne thrived in this environment, empowered and elated by the responsibility to diagnose, dispatch, and prescribe without restraint, managing the flow of humanity pouring through the doors of the emergency ward. Like an enormous high-stakes casino in which patients gambled with their injuries as the initial bid, verdicts were dispensed with associated probabilities of recovery, probabilities of errors, probabilities of death.

The diversity and severity of injuries to be treated was phenomenal: contusions, cuts, fractures, tears, ruptures of flesh, organs and bones, attributed to broken glass or fallen objects of miscellaneous sizes; minor to severe burns from home fires or gas explosions; trauma and shock, particularly for those who'd had limbs underpinned for hours under heavy debris; as well as severe frost bite. Not to forget, a few dead on arrival.

However, no single patient made a more singular impression than the one that arrived in a black stretch limousine adorned with small, frozen Québec flags on its hood and wings. The car had barely stopped in front of the entrance to the Emergency, when two large men in dark suits emerged running, carrying a conspicuous, unshaven, unconscious and bloody hobo, trailed by another dark suit capturing the scene on a digital camera and tracking the action as if holding a camcorder.

As soon as the wounded vagrant was dropped on a stretcher, emergency technicians rushed him to an oversized makeshift room that served the gamut of needs, from basic examination to trauma resuscitation, and parked him in front of Jean-Pierre and Audréanne, who immediately tended to him, eager to freely diagnose as their supervisors had not yet returned from the cafeteria—caught in an intense debate on whether the "damn earthquake" would trump the Montréal Canadiens' winning season. Focused on the patient at hand, backs turned away from the open door, they did not see the dark suits approaching.

Digital camera still rolling to capture this stately moment, Léandre gripped Jean-Pierre's shoulder and proclaimed, "We are leaving this unfortunate man in your most capable hands and sincerely hope you'll be able to help him."

Jean-Pierre, recognizing this unmistakable voice, this familiar inflection, turned his head and jumped.

"*Oncle* Léandre?"

"Jean-Pierre?"

Audréanne gazed over. Next to the stunned Québec Prime Minister stood a familiar figure.

"Uncle James?"

"Audréanne?"

Awkwardly, they hugged their respective uncle, pleased to see them but withholding some of their enthusiasm, as an exuberant display of joy would have been incongruous in light of the catastrophic circumstances. The cold stare of dozens of grumpy patients filling the adjacent waiting room, none of them yet sure they were seeing their Prime Minister at this time, was also not conducive to long, warm embraces.

Léandre and James were troubled and uneasy by the discovery that they might be linked by a shared family bond. They both furtively inspected the ring fingers of their nephew/niece and were pleased to establish that no marital vows had been exchanged. Yet, until it could be ascertained whether such a future possibility existed, Léandre and James implicitly felt it might be wise to exercise more restraint and diplomacy in their future exchanges.

"Jean-Pierre, you never told me that you had a famous uncle!" said Audréanne, poorly trying to hide her alarm.

"I was certainly planning to tell you before the wedding, but I didn't think it mattered."

Léandre and James both bit their lips. Creating more distance became urgent. In the hope of achieving this, they reasoned that the tortuous bloodline leading to their niece/nephew provided sufficient emotional distance to prevent undesirable encounters of the "uncles" in the future, but in spite of that self-delusion, they felt the discomfort of an unwarranted Capulet and Montegue relationship.

After witnessing Léandre's repellent display of indifference to human suffering while fishing the tramp out of the snow, James had decided to part ways with him after the impromptu hospital trip, foregoing all the potential benefits that the new partnership offered. That firm intent shaken by the potential kinship, he felt that aborting this professional relationship at this time would be hazardous. This wasn't a matter of ethics, since he wasn't bound to provide non-remunerated expert assistance to anyone. Rather, his concern was that if he abandoned a "soon-to-be uncle-in-law," the news would spread through the family with great speed, leading his ex-wife, mother, and ex-mother-in-law to crash on him like a tsunami wave. Trying to surf such a tidal wave could be suicidal.

Léandre wondered how the press would use the information received from one of the stupefied witnesses, mouth agape in the waiting room. His originally envisioned headlines proclaiming "Laliberté Rescues Citizen from Certain Death" now risked morphing into "Laliberté Puts Members of Extended Family Above National Interests" or "Embezzling Emergency Response

Resources for Personal Use," or other inflamed rhetoric designed to sell newspapers. He attempted to regain control of the story-line.

"It is quite an amazing and unexpected coincidence to find you here, but the national emergency situation requires my immediate attention, and you have a large number of patients awaiting your most important care," he said, pointing to the haggard faces staring from the emergency room. "I urgently need to confer with my strategic operation team at this time, and we will need to use your board room for an emergency meeting."

Having spent all 19 hours of their new jobs in the proximity of the emergency room, and clueless regarding the corporate facilities in place, they consulted the head M.D. on duty, who, starstruck, jumped at the opportunity to lead the prestigious visitors to the director of the hospital. Léandre and James precipitously left the emergency ward, leaving Jean-Pierre and Audréanne bickering about how secrets can destroy relationships, oblivious to patients rattled by the interminable wait, including Clément, who remained unattended on his stretcher, in dire need of medical attention.

Vaudreuil-Dorion, 2:00 p.m.

The first truck in a long row of army vehicles was stopped at the end of the *Taschereau* bridge west of the island. Another, similar column was immobilized by the *Charles-De-Gaulle* bridge, at the easternmost tip of Montréal.

There was irony in the spectacle of federal troops being halted by bridges named for men upheld as antipodal symbols of the resistance against assimilation. West, by a bridge named for the man who, when Québec's minister of public works in 1909, had ordered arrested and imprisoned a journalist who slapped him: Olivar Asselin, a founding member of the *Ligue nationaliste* created to protect the rights of French Canadians in a bicultural and bilingual country in response to the recrudescence of British imperialism. East, by a bridge named after the French President who had visited Montréal as one of the many distinguished guests invited to Expo 67 held in celebration of Canada's 100th birthday, and who caused a political uproar in English Canada by encouraging Québec separatism when he then proclaimed "*Vive le Québec libre*" to an ecstatic crowd gathered in front of Montréal's City Hall.

Collapsed spans, rather than political history in this case, created the impassable hurdles. Further military deployment was frustrated, the columns of vintage trucks at a standstill. The pristine condition of the antique vehicles was a testimony to the time-consuming, conscientious maintenance invested to stretch the resources of a non-combatant army, symptomatic of a military free from international threats and consequently constrained in its budget. However, while this extensive program of metal preservation could keep the wheels turning on pavement, the platoon leaders deemed the trucks devoid of adequate traction and far too heavy to risk crossing on the ice. The mighty Canadian ground troops thus awaited further instructions.

The Department of National Defence Headquarters in Ottawa had the ability to locate within its inventory special portable truss spans, known as Bailey bridges, and dispatch them to the sites. Ground troops were familiar with these light structures, once a year freshly washed, painted, and delivered from hangar to field where well-groomed privates diligently rehearsed choreographed exercises to assemble such bridges in record times during military bases' open houses, mostly for marketing and recruiting purposes. However, headquarters were far less responsive to the immediate needs than during those staged war games. As eager as it was to dispatch one of these bridge-erection sets, the short-staffed command post failed to find a suitable kit available: One Bailey bridge in Ottawa had been damaged during the last training exercise and was temporarily decommissioned awaiting repair of its bent truss chords; one in British Columbia was too far away for immediate deployment; one in Halifax had been borrowed by peacekeepers overseas; one in Québec was unaccountably missing from the warehouse, even though it was shown to exist in the database.

The fruitless search for a functional Bailey bridge was eventually aborted, and headquarters instead brainstormed for solutions to overcome the barriers impeding progress of the ground troops. Alternative deployment of troops by heavy transport helicopters was the preferred solution, but it would have to await the end of the snowstorm. Serving dangerously beyond their recommended safe service life, the Canadian Forces' antediluvian Cormorant search-and-rescue helicopters had a tendency to crash in the best weather conditions. The desuetude of the Department of National Defence's equipment already being the subject of public mockery, it was judged that flying in a snowstorm at the risk of crashing onto a residential area would be politically unsavory at this juncture. Some of the military brass were ready to sacrifice a few soldiers, civilians, and choppers to make a statement on the need for new equipment, but the higher-ranking officers, closer to politicians, refused to endorse this strategy. The regiments were thus grounded, awaiting favorable barometer readings to make airlifts possible.

In the meantime, political imperatives pressured the top commanders for immediate results showcasing the benefits of military interventions for the greater good. Technically, searching for Bailey bridges in a database did contribute to the global goal of assisting the public in distress, but the exploits of bureaucrats staring at computer screens was most unlikely to dazzle taxpayers. The political powers were eager to feed the evening news with footage of troops in the field, showcasing the strong positive impact of Canadian soldiers leading effective emergency-response efforts.

The generals understood well these mission parameters and undertook to stage some rescue operations to appease those at the upper links of the chain of command. Playing art directors, they built on the few opportunities in the surrounding neighborhood that could resemble conditions suffered by distressed citizens on the island, and put their idle manpower to task.

They ordered teams of soldiers to shovel around abandoned vehicles buried in snow, including one that was hibernating in the middle of a field and had possibly not moved in years. They dispatched fleets of properly equipped heavy-armored vehicles to plow a few of the neighborhood streets, careful to select those that had not yet been plowed by the local contractors. They commanded platoons of young recruits in full gear to walk knee-deep in snow fields, advancing in formation, to project an image of resolve battling harsh field conditions.

Some generals even considered pushing down some telephone poles or power lines—even though the local municipalities had not lost usage of these utilities—just for the opportunity to film soldiers as improvised repair crews restoring essential services, but they refrained from undertaking such ambitious deceptions for the time being. This restraint against vandalism for propagandist purposes was only self-imposed out of a concern that modern troops always harbor a few soldiers disrespectful of tradition and willing to serve as moles for the press—despicable traitors violating the unwritten rule of secrecy in exchange for extra compensation to complement their meager stipend.

Without questioning, drilled to live and breathe for the exhilaration of vigorous action, the troops were prompt to execute all tasks that bore a semblance of purpose for the common good, pleased to serve and exercise rather than play cards to kill time in cold trucks.

The resulting tapes were then securely packaged and delivered back to headquarters. Tactical experts would review and edit them and forward the best clips just in time for the evening news, to the delight of information bureaus starving for footage of the disaster.

In some insidious twist of logic, many Canadians parked in front of their televisions that evening and witnessing the stalwart efforts of the Canadian Forces would conclude that the extent of the disaster seemed no worse than the challenges brought on by a good winter storm, and that all stories of extreme pain and suffering reported by the Québec government and media might be exaggerations by separatists again railing against the federal government just to extract as many aid dollars as possible.

Montréal, 2:15 p.m.

Léandre made sure to close the door. The hospital's director was honored to loan his office to the Premier for what seemed to be an urgent confidential strategic meeting. Yet, only he and James were there. Léandre casually surveyed the office to ensure it had no other open door, window, camera, phone line, or other indiscreet active connection that would allow eavesdropping. His faked composure did not fool James, but Léandre's first question suggested a disarray possibly deeper than might have been guessed.

"OK, how do we get out of this *tabarnak de bordel?*"

James was stunned. This was not a desperate cry by a despondent leader, but rather a piercing plea for some expert insight. As if Léandre had assimilated the early morning earthquake engineering primer, had reflected on the significance of the damage observed during the brief reconnaissance trip throughout the deserted city, had considered the poor and incomplete information reaching his office on the actual state of emergency, and had determined that effective decisions were impossible without educated guesses to assess how bad the situation could possibly be.

"You have no idea how deep in shit—"

"Just give it to me. Paint the picture as grossly and explicitly as you wish. Don't try to spare my feelings, I'm a politician, I can take it rough. I don't need you to tell me that it's a disaster—I already know that. What I need to know is the what, where, and why, so that I can figure out the how. Give me the worst-case scenario straight."

James stared for a moment, surprised by the sudden candor, the admitted helplessness, and the apparently genuine plea for an enlightening counsel. If Léandre sincerely wanted the blunt truth, he was more than delighted to oblige.

"There are three parts to your nightmare: Damage assessment, response, and recovery."

Léandre frowned, unclear on the difference between the last two. Attentive, James adapted: "You need to find out how deep in shit the city really is, how to get everybody out of that stinking pile, and how to wash the whole thing squeaky clean such that a few years from now, this mess will just be a bad memory and no tourist will be able to tell that the place just bathed in a mountain of manure."

Léandre's eyebrows relaxed as he nodded, satisfied by this erudite vulgarization.

James pursued.

"The first one is needed to guide the second one, but you must conduct the two in parallel and adjust as new information comes in. You also need to make some assumptions just to get started. Based on what I've seen so far, and experience from past earthquakes, I would guess that about 25% of your infrastructure is entirely out of commission. This includes all sorts of buildings that have suffered damage to their supporting structures and are dangerous to occupy until a professional engineer can perform an evaluation of their integrity and safety—that includes office buildings, shopping malls, schools, hospitals, hotels, condominiums, fire stations, police stations, arenas, and so on.

"With respect to public safety, it is fair to assume that, at first, people will refuse to enter these damaged buildings because they look unsafe, if not downright scary. If fact, for that matter, for a few days, many will refuse to set foot indoors of any building, good or bad, safe or unsafe, just out of an absolute irrational and unsettling fear that all the pillars of strength once held as self-evident perdurable foundations for modern urban life might be an illusion. In the long term though, out of necessity, either due to harsh weather conditions, the desire to retrieve belongings, or the impulse to resume previous occupations and re-establish normalcy, everybody will want to reoccupy buildings—even buildings tethering on the brink of collapse but projecting a false sense of security by the mere fact that they are still standing, and you'll have to prevent people from entering those death traps.

"Professional engineers will soon get organized, or will have to be organized by your government, to perform a rapid inspection of every building in town and to quickly assign them a safety rating. In the past, this safety rating has sometimes consisted of a simple system of red, yellow, or green tags posted at the buildings' entrances. This professional judgment must be rendered in no more than a few minutes per building, so expect the outcome to generally err on the safe side. The yellow tags indicate that there are possible concerns with the buildings' safety and that only limited access is permitted until a more detailed engineering evaluation can be conducted. The red tags are affixed to buildings that are deemed to be severely damaged and unsafe, and indicate that access to the building is prohibited. These red-tagged buildings are likely to be demolished unless satisfactory repairs can be engineered.

"There are not enough engineers in the country to quickly review the yellow- and red-tagged buildings to the level of accuracy required after the first crude rating operations. So expect many of those buildings to be closed for months while awaiting further engineering assessments, or even longer when owners get embroiled in lawsuits to resolve liability tied to insurance compensations—or when they encounter other financial challenges, in some cases simply declaring bankruptcy and abandoning the properties. As for the other damaged buildings, blessed by solvent owners free to act promptly, many will still be demolished as repairs in many instances can be more expensive and take longer than simply rebuilding anew. All of this with a definite impact on the familiar urban landscape, a curse or a blessing depending on the point of view of the remodeling opportunities this provides.

"Now, keep in mind that the green, yellow and red ratings only focus on whether a building can be *safely* occupied, and that this assessment of safety is only made with regards to the integrity of the structural system. As a result, a green-tagged building could still be completely unusable due to damage to its content and equipment. Some will have to deal with a myriad of small annoyances, such as jammed doors due to safe but distorted structural frames, including garage doors in fire stations, derailed elevators, failed mechanical and heating systems, leaking pipes, broken windows, and fractures in the building envelope. Others will have to manage more problematic situations, such as chemical or biological hazards created by spilled and mixed products fallen off shelves, flooded floors due to failure of sprinkler systems, or failure of the equipment essential for conducting their businesses. For example, the undamaged structural frame of a hospital may be pointless if most of the medical equipment is dead as a result of the shaking and banging during the earthquake, or if the medical gas supply lines have ruptured. Likewise, owners of factories littered with destroyed machinery will find little solace in the survival of the green-tagged structural envelope housing that equipment."

Léandre's shoulders had slumped as James depicted the likely condition of the engineered buildings' infrastructure. A positive booster was necessary before describing the equally bleak situation with lifelines.

"On the positive side, wood-framed residential homes generally do not get damaged much by earthquakes, at least not the older ones that have many partitions and small rooms, as opposed to the large open spaces without walls that are fashionable nowadays. Their decorative masonry finishes may get cracked, or completely fall outward, which is inconvenient but not of dramatic consequences for the occupants."

Léandre wondered, "The positive side being that these homes are still usable?"

"Exactly! Provided of course they get electrical power back soon, and do not burn down."

"Burn down? From chimney fires, or unattended candles?"

"Yes, but also from sparks igniting gas leaks as power is restored, if the two utilities do not coordinate their recovery operations. Speaking of utilities, that's your second disaster and possibly your biggest problem. Remember the prolonged power failures that resulted from the ice storm of 1998? Just magnify the problem by an order of magnitude, because this time, your transmission lines and towers are probably all intact, but your transformers are probably damaged beyond repair. Large transformers are extremely expensive, so spare ones are few. There are not many similar and interchangeable units across North America that could be borrowed, either. In addition, many of the computers and control equipment could have been crushed by debris from collapsing equipment stations. The number of weeks or months during which parts of Montréal will be without power will depend on which equipment is damaged, and on whether Hydro Québec has a sufficient number of replacement parts and units to rapidly restore the network."

"A month?" Léandre suddenly saw the "pile of shit" grow into a nasty and nauseating Everest.

"Possibly. It will also depend on the impacts of cascading lifeline failures."

"Cascading lifelines?"

"Lifelines are your key vital networks, those our industrialized society depends upon for its survival, and therefore most important to ensure emergency response and recovery after a natural disaster. These include most fundamentally the power grid, but also the water and waste water distribution pipelines and stations, the communication systems, the liquid fuel and natural gas systems, and all transportation networks, such as highways, railways, waterways and airways. And above the crucial importance of each one of those systems, the co-dependencies between these systems is even more critical, because if you lose one system, you are liable to lose them all, as dominoes toppling each other in a chain reaction, resulting in a cascade of failures. For example, some of the communication systems need power to operate, some back-up generators need water to cool, and some parts of the water-distribution systems rely on electrical pumps. Also, the dispatch of repair crews to damaged areas is hampered by non-operating traffic lights, but more importantly by the challenges in filling up the reservoirs of their trucks because modern gas pumps can't function without electricity. Not to forget that your repair crews need accessible roads to reach their destinations, which can be challenging when bridges are out of commission, when roads are partly blocked by fallen buildings, and, to top it off, covered by 12 inches of snow, which, by the way, is slowly building up to be your third disaster."

Léandre objected. "This is stretching it. A snowstorm is not a disaster. Montréal has seen tons of snowstorms in the past—"

"During which you had crews on active duty to plow the streets. Now, how many of your blue-collar workers do you think reported to work this morning? Given the notorious abysmal productivity of this workforce under normal circumstances, why would their dedication to the city suddenly transcend their personal interests? Most of them are probably at home taking care of their families, busy cleaning up the mess from the earthquake and dealing with acute problems, such as seeking creative ways to generate enough heat to prevent the pipes running in the walls of their house from bursting under the pressure of frozen water, or searching for an open hospital or shelter for their loved ones."

"That's probably true of any organization at this time," ventured Léandre.

"Indeed, finding solutions to the logistic and human problems are your biggest challenges. You can bet that only a few organizations have made some sort of disaster preparedness plans and that in most cases these plans will fail miserably as they are paper plans that have never been exercised or vetted by some reality checks. Expect chaos and you will not be disappointed."

The complex interdependencies depicted by James underscored that the process of recovery seriously needed a catalyst, someone to orchestrate the process, to convert the uncoordinated, random initiatives of disparate stakeholders into a common, integrated master plan that could be executed seamlessly and expedited. Léandre, far from being depressed by the despondency of Québec's largest city and economic engine, heard a calling. Like a crusader about to embark on another holy mission, he was ready to mold his ideals to the cause. He envisioned the government—his government—sternly in control, assuming leadership, providing a beacon of confidence toward restoring stability and ensuring recovery. Empowered by an uncharacteristic surge of pure altruism, his heart impulsively pounded: "That's what the people need; that's what they'll get."

For a moment, Léandre, reinvigorated, was convinced that he could become a changed man, a new man, an unselfish leader who sincerely cared, mustering all the resources of the province to abate the populace's suffering and expedite recovery, depleting the public treasury and borrowing without restraint to reconstruct a safer, grander, more modern and attractive Montréal. The turning point of his life was here, the opportunity to veer towards a new road, where the engine of his government could propel Québec to a new level, pulling all political forces together in a new partnership where bureaucrats, business leaders, union leaders, and politicians of all affiliations would endeavor for the common good, leveraging the goodwill emanating in this time of crisis to build an amazing recovery that would exceed all expectations—to engineer a recovery that would go much beyond mere recovery.

Léandre, at this unique crossroads, elated as a born-again Christian about to proclaim his philosophical rebirth, where a simple turn away from the old paths of partisanship and egocentric politics was possible, nonetheless drove straight through. The pragmatic politician acknowledged the immense opportunities possible at this juncture, and realized that he would actually be more effective if pretending to have become an idealist rather than by actually becoming one. Years of experience developing and honing political skills and acumen could be tapped to achieve substantially more than by wasting time learning how to put the common good first. Léandre felt that the outcome would likely be better, more controllable, and reached more expeditiously, if the process were devoid of naive idealistic ideas, even at the risk of focusing on self-aggrandizing exploits and political agenda rather than common good.

All he needed to do now was to figure out how to play the part with some measure of credibility.

Léandre was as adept as any politician in claiming credit for fortuitous events that would still have happened in spite of his gross ineptitude at imagining any possible way to facilitate their probability of occurring, or even foreseeing their occurrence. However, this time, the challenge in fooling the entire population was significant, both in scale and in complexity. For Léandre, one time-proven strategy had always been to replace current appointees by a new team, bringing renewed hope of greater competency and shielding the top management from the misfortunes of accountability; proxies could always be blamed for all unfortunate events that occurred beyond one's control, and political damage was best controlled by expressing regrets that the high hopes that existed when an agency leader was first appointed were unfulfilled as a result of outcomes of dubious quality. Better to be labeled as a poor judge of character, than being judged to be of poor character.

"James, you seem to have an excellent understanding of the situation. What would you recommend as a plan for recovery?"

James felt he was far from done in painting the bleak picture, and did not expect this sudden shift in Léandre's interest, from situation assessment to recovery. He had interpreted Léandre's long contemplative silence as a pause to better assimilate the severity and reach of the disaster.

"I'm not quite done describing the situation. I don't think you can realistically contemplate recovery without a good sense of the extent of the problem."

"I understand. However, it is becoming clear to me that you have a solid perception of the challenges ahead, and that listening to your presentation, as attentively as I can, will not make me an expert. Having all the data does not enable me to competently sort through it, nor does it endow me with the necessary skills to empower the recovery process. So I might as well immediately hear your views on what the needed recovery plan is. Additional perspectives on the existing situation can always be provided to substantiate your reasoning as you describe the recovery process." James felt far less competent in articulating a recovery plan. The best plans are not improvised, as they require an intimate knowledge of available resources and understanding of jurisdictional responsibilities and accountability.

"A response and recovery plan is something that your *Organisation de sécurité civile du Québec* should have in hand. You probably should seek their counsel in this regard."

Léandre refrained from disclosing specifics about the leadership crisis at the *Organisation,* or from venting his frustration about how Lise Letarte had misled everybody, stalled, and attempted to forcefully make it impossible to operate around her. He banked instead on James's earlier comments about the value of paper plans, betting that this was a prevalent problem not symptomatic of dysfunctional organizations.

"Believe me, don't bet on that plan to bail us out of this mess. I think you can appreciate why."

James nodded while pressing his lips together. He knew that few emergency-response agencies ever account for cascading failures or compounding disasters. Yet, that didn't make him an expert, either, nor did it provide him with the organizational and legal knowledge needed to develop a credible response plan.

"Any recovery plan I may suggest would be pointless, unless it is coordinated with other agencies and emergency responders, so, at best, I can only give you some ideas and examples of things that should be taken into account, with some suggestions of the sequence by which they should be implemented."

"Works for me. Go for it!"

"Can I presume that the command control headquarters for emergency operations where we met this morning is functional?"

"It's a state-of-the-art one that even has an helicopter landing pad, but communications are not fully operational at this time."

James reflected a moment, ordering priorities, sequencing tasks in his mind, trimming the relatively trivial matters from the long list of needs to focus on the key issues that he believed Léandre needed to know and act upon.

"You need to ensure that all of the emergency operations command center functions are operational, with enough fuel to sustain back-up power for three months. Most gasoline-driven back-up generator systems, such as those used in some hospitals, typically have at best 72 hours of fuel in reserve, so you'll need the landing pad for sure. You also need to establish a reliable communication basis for all emergency operations. There are a number of reasons that could explain why parts of the public telecommunication systems have failed. Regular telephone and cell phone switches and hardware are typically resistant to severe vibrations, but this ruggedness is futile if the electronic components are flooded due to ruptured sprinkler heads, or crushed in collapsed buildings, or if antennas fell off the roof of buildings as seismic waves reaching the top of buildings swayed them with the violence of a whiplash. However, whatever the reasons, it is safe to assume it will take weeks to fully restore service. You will have to rely on shortwave radio for general communications. Maybe, if it can be done quickly, you could equip all your key emergency responders with satellite-based cellular phones for private communications."

Léandre already could think of memorable directives to broadcast on shortwave radio, like a World War II general spreading his wisdom for posterity.

"You need to establish an operable refueling base for your snow-plowing equipment; here again, you may need back-up generators to power the gas pumps, and you may need to airlift the first gas supplies. Use security forces to protect what will be a unique refueling station for the short-term, and bribe your security forces with bonuses and a limited supply of free fuel for their personal use to ensure integrity of controlled access to this precious resource."

Léandre thought he probably should also threaten with severe penalties anyone who would illegally use this strategic fuel reserve, pondering whether the stick might work better than the carrot with the most unionized and unscrupulous component of his bureaucratic workforce, who would not see an ethical dilemma in cashing all its perks and still robbing the government—maybe even, at the extreme, operating a black market for fuel.

"Then offer double or triple hourly rates, whatever it takes, to bring back as many snow-plowing operators as you can. Make them focus on the main arteries until the storm stops."

Léandre envisioned a row of trucks plowing René Lévesque Boulevard, himself atop the first truck of the fleet, leading the cavalry to the rescue, as a news clip played repeatedly to symbolize his commandeering control of the situation.

"This will be a slow operation as some of the roads are clogged with debris. So, until all the roads are clear, you need to enlist all available snowmobile owners who wish to volunteer their services to reach stranded individuals and bring them to hospitals and emergency shelters."

A powerful image of hundreds of volunteers, standing next to their snowmobiles, ready to receive a medal from Léandre in honor of their service to the nation in time of dire need could be played in another future newscast as a tribute to the great leader.

"Using this army of snowmobiles, you quickly need to establish which emergency shelters and hospitals have power and can sustain operations, provided you airlift them supplies until the bridges are repaired. You can also use the underground subway system as a temporary shelter, until your network of strategic shelters is operational, but you must provide some sort of security in designated stations."

Léandre shaking hands and offering sympathetic and encouraging words to the temporary displaced population, and promoting his vision of a better and greater reborn Montréal, could be the driving theme and video clip of a future election campaign.

"You need to provide continued credible and detailed information to the population, updated hourly, and broadcast continuously on a selected radio station of your choice."

Léandre-the-idealist envisioned to empower the government-owned Télé-Québec as the logical choice to serve this purpose, but Léandre-the-pragmatic regarded the public television network as an amateurish enterprise, structured to serve its mandate of bland, highbrowed educational and cultural programming and, most importantly for the current purpose, lacking both a news bureau and an integrated network of radio stations. By contrast, the federally owned Radio-Canada, designed to compete head-on with privately owned television networks and unfairly bolstered by immense financial resources, had all the necessary talent and reach, but, for Léandre, using Radio-Canada for this purpose would have been strict heresy, even though the federal agency was deeply infiltrated by separatists at all levels of operations except its upper administration. To overcome this hurdle, Léandre envisioned an emergency bill to immediately nationalize the largest private broadcasting conglomerate headquartered in the province and take over all of its radio stations. Acquiring such control over a large segment of the media would also be particularly convenient for the next referendum campaign.

"Work with Transport Québec to allocate all resources needed to restore access to the island as soon as possible through at least one bridge, by identifying which of the damaged bridges is easiest to repair. Stage subsequent repairs to establish at least one serviceable transportation link along each of the island's cardinal directions. Establish special traffic lanes to ensure privileged bridge access to emergency traffic in the short term."

Imagining all the photo opportunities that would be made possible in a single day by making rapid access to the city possible through dedicated emergency lanes, Léandre felt this was a great idea to optimize the time he would spend visiting Montréal.

"Allocate priority to outbound traffic on those repaired bridges to temporarily relocate the population to other parts of the province until they can safely return to their homes."

Much could be done to emphasize the outstanding hospitality and generosity of Québécois to support their co-patriots in need, a favorite theme of Léandre's discourse.

"Work with Hydro-Québec to ensure their activities are safely coordinated with the gas companies to avoid unfortunate explosions, and to ensure that restoration of service is strategically compatible with plans to restore economic activities. Awaiting the return of power, make massive investment to secure all back-up generator capabilities from around the world, and establish an equitable distribution policy compliant with the priority of restoring economic activities."

Léandre determined that policies that favored the interest of individuals over those of rich multinational corporations would contribute more significantly to a successful referendum and re-election. "Greedy" corporations could always be counted upon to find their own resources to re-open once the consumers returned.

"In the long term, invest in recovery operations that will return the largest number of individuals to some kind of normalcy, such as re-establishing the buses and metro systems, re-opening the banking services, groceries, and other such fundamental services. Offer unlimited no-interest loans to accelerate repair and re-occupation of damaged homes."

Léandre marveled at this completely legal way to purchase votes.

"And in the end, be realistic. Recognize that recovery, as a perfect return to pre-disaster conditions, will never occur. Some will benefit from the disaster, and some will never recover from this disaster, no matter how much effort they invest and support they receive. As such, approach recovery with realistic expectations."

Léandre discerned that James, in spite of his self-deprecating, false modesty, described the plan as only one who'd mastered the topic could, not improvising but rather adapting it from a template developed out of personal conviction over years of observation studying the aftermath of various disasters worldwide. A passionate narrative sustained by the hidden frustration of being an overqualified arm-chair quarterback, spectator to the failings of incompetent leaders. He was ripe to become the proxy.

Léandre ventured, "You have articulated a very clear description of the process that should be undertaken at once. I don't think anybody in my government or in its key agencies has already formulated such a coherent vision of tactical recovery." He paused, staring, attentive to body language.

Fully aware that politicians do not flatter without a purpose, James did not break the silence.

"This level of expertise and qualification is what is needed in this time of crisis." Léandre avoided saying "national crisis" as he usually did, given that he and James did not impart the same meaning to the word.

James correctly guessed what was to follow. He just did not know whether Léandre would beg, suggest, or command.

"James, you have the ability to have a tremendous impact on the lives, and quality of life, of millions at this time. I would like you to seriously consider serving as Chief of Emergency Response."

James was delighted to be recognized for his expertise, but any possible enthusiasm was killed by his ingrained distrust of politicians. He was convinced that Léandre would use him, at best sharing credit for successes, but making him a scapegoat for failures.

"I'm sorry, but I must decline this kind offer. As you know, I am already employed by the Canadian government."

"With all due respect, James, the Canadian government is not calling on your very unique and appropriate expertise at this critical time."

This was not just true now, but had forever been the case. Léandre could read that much from James's sagging eyebrows in response to his remark, and proceeded to take advantage of this weakened defense.

"You are obviously the master of your destiny, and I can't force you to accept, but this is a unique opportunity to put to practice your eminent knowledge."

Léandre could read a re-affirmed resolve. Flattery was the wrong road to take, and he aptly adapted the courtship strategy.

"James, I'll be frank with you. Every day, in the news, armies of political analysts and academic specialists spend time critiquing and destroying me and my government. There they are, self-proclaimed experts left and right, pointing at every action or inaction with the scorn of self-righteousness. Yet, none of these self-centered fat cats have ever accomplished anything for the common good, or, to a far less grand purpose, for the good of anyone else. The academics cash in their fat paychecks and justify their worth by pretending that they contribute to society by educating the next generation of experts, oblivious to their atrocious teaching and general disrespect of others. Pompous egocentric reporters more concerned about their visibility and career use public forums to their advantage, accuse the government of failing to see the wisdom of their proclaimed solutions to all ills of society, and promote impractical solutions that sound sophisticated and erudite. But these academics and reporters are nowhere to be found when it comes time to donate a single day of their lives to benefit a good cause.

"James, there is no shortage of self-proclaimed experts. What I am offering you here is an opportunity to elevate yourself to a position where you can actually implement a solution that will make a difference. I am offering you the opportunity of a lifetime to accomplish something tangible that will make an everlasting impact on society, possibly your greatest professional achievement."

Léandre had struck a sensitive chord. James indeed felt surrounded by self-absorbed prima donnas. Experts at dodging accountability—the antithesis of team players. Their employment fully secured by a powerful union, some of his colleagues were masters at "playing the game" to their personal benefit, to invest the least amount of energy to reap the largest possible rewards.

James loathed the select few at the National Research Council that, on par with academics at all universities, had become experts at developing useless but elegant mathematical formulations, publishing reports that collected dust on library shelves and papers in scientific journals that nobody read, justifying their worth by the volume rather than quality of their writings, and collecting accolades and awards from a network of peers that had produced similar work of no possible tangible impact. He equally despised others who'd mastered the art of deception, strategically serving a few hours a week in enough high-visibility activities to convey an overblown perception of intense engagement in the enterprise, while actually spending the bulk of their time moonlighting, using government resources to supplement their income or investing their time in various pet projects and hobbies.

In a pseudo-collegial environment where salaries and annual increases were doled out per an egalitarian, union-approved formula that took for granted contributions proportional to abilities and assessed employees' worth in terms of years since graduation, a few broke their backs attempting to fulfill the endless obligations and assignments dumped on them, like the dumb horse in *Animal Farm*, while others exuded an utterly abrasive personality sure to fend off any assignments. In this climate that bred self-esteem to excess, James felt choked by the constant posturing of oversized egos and incessant self-serving arguments intended to forever stall any decision that implied accountability.

He was deeply frustrated by the endless, pointless and leaderless sterile meetings and debates that grossly failed to ever reach consensus on any issue, that never led to any effective changes. This was the blessing and the curse of scholarly activities, where a socialist-like valuation scheme resulted in an organization where all accomplishments were equally weighed, where every sophist could squeeze an aura of positive impacts from any inane action and pretend collective benefits from self-serving activities. James was tired of a job where relative values and priorities did not exist, tired of seeing the presumed accomplishments of his lazy colleagues deemed to be of equal benefit to the organization as the blood, sweat and tears of others, tired of that convenient relativism that thrived on the absence of strategic thinking, consensus, or vision. From that perspective, Léandre's proposition was appealing, and possibly a risk worth taking, but not at all cost.

"The challenge may be engaging, but you are asking me to leave a very rewarding and secure position that I love, working for an excellent employer, with outstanding colleagues that I admire, to take on a new position and tackle new challenges, to serve an immediate purpose rich in potential valuable accomplishments that may be appreciated in the short term, but likely forgotten in the long term, and possibly dismissed by your successor. This is a very high-risk endeavor. What's in it for me?"

Léandre knew it was now possible to close the deal. He paused for a moment. Strategically, it was important to give James the impression that his demands were important and worth serious consideration for a moment, even though they were anticipated and the response was ready. Léandre took advantage of this moment, feigning deep reflection on how to answer James's question, to assess whether there was a risk that James could become more popular than him should his recovery plan be successful beyond expectations. Clearly, James would be in the media spotlight every day, possibly for the next year, and would be uniquely positioned to capitalize on a positive-media frenzy. However, Léandre dismissed that possibility—James was harmless, devoid of political ambitions, and much too honest and naive to survive in the political arena.

Léandre sighed to pretend a sympathetic resignation to James's negotiated demands.

"I understand your concern. If you agree, I will appoint you immediately at twice your current salary, and will provide a special provision for a guaranteed pension at two-thirds of that salary should your employment be terminated against your will."

Reading the sparkle in James's eyes in reaction to the financial package, Léandre knew he had wrapped the deal. In his mind, a little bit of the taxpayers' money to advance the march toward nationhood was a nuanced investment, never a squandering of the public treasure.

For James, the opportunity to retire at 133% of his current salary erased his primary concern of shorter-than-desirable employment when Léandre or his successor would have no more use for him—in some pernicious, incentive-laden way, making it even attractive to be fired sooner than later under these circumstances. "Léandre, if you have the power to put that in writing, I am your man."

"What do you mean, James? I don't *have* the power, I *am* the power. *Crisse*, I'll pen the terms of agreement on the back of an envelope, on a napkin, on toilet paper, on the ass of an assistant, whatever works, and my signature will get you the official paperwork in no time. In the meantime, *baptême*, let's move!"

After a vigorous handshake, both men emerged from the room energized. James was elated by the golden retirement package he had secured, aware that serving at the Premier's erratic pleasure was an ephemeral privilege, the demise of political appointees being currency in public life. Léandre was relieved that all the harm done by the loose cannon that led the *Organisation de sécurité civile du Québec* with the efficiency of a potted plant could be mended, if not undone. Stripped of the tactical option to fire her, he nonetheless was confident that he could mold public opinion by implicitly pinning much blame on her, leaking the news that she resigned to save face from her ineptitude at managing the emergency response, and by officially emphasizing the new, capable leadership in place.

Emboldened by his plan and his new appointee, Léandre found Réal, Julien, and Florent—who had spent their time roaming the emergency room, commiserating with the patients over their hardships, lending a sympathetic ear, spreading encouragements, and, as a priority, collecting video testimonials for future use—and bombarded them with directives.

"James here is Québec's Chief of Emergency Response, and he will take over all functions of the *Organisation de sécurité civile du Québec*. Provide all appropriate announcements that James here is our specially appointed 'Recovery Tzar,' who will guide our teams to a prompt recovery process. All our agencies need to report to him, and all private sector industries need to coordinate with our own agencies. Make it clear that if James does not like the information he gets, he will give us the language to legislate their marching orders."

Léandre looked with confidence and expectation toward James, with the glow of a Montréal Canadiens general manager who had snatched a star free agent from the Toronto Maple Leafs.

"And get this guy a written contract. We're moving on before the ink is dry."

Léandre pushed his inner circle to the limo so that a media blitz strategy could be planned in privacy. The objectives would be to show that his "National Government" was fully in charge and to highlight Léandre's foresight and sagacity for having appointed so quickly a top-notch expert who would ensure the fastest possible response and recovery. Their job was to issue as many individual press releases as possible, as quickly as possible. In the meantime, Léandre would focus on planning a nationalism-infused speech for the ten o'clock news.

The accumulated snowfall had now reached 7.5 inches. The meteorological forecast predicted continued snow precipitations at the same rate for the rest of the day.

Ottawa, 2:45 p.m.

Graham, studying the computer monitors in the conference room of Earthquakes Canada, was sure that he couldn't discern from the cryptic graphical symbols any of the evidence that the scientists claimed to see so clearly.

All he wanted to know was why ground-shaking strong enough to produce damage was felt in Ottawa, but not in Québec City or even in the U.S., at the same distance from Montréal. After the "bad soils" theory had been dismissed—all recognizing that poor soils were not unique to Ottawa—obscure issues of fault directionality and "fling" were explained as the likely culprit.

The complex maps were wiped from the screen and replaced by some conceptual illustrations. A short, dashed line drawn across downtown Montréal represented the fault located miles underground, arbitrarily set below Mont Royal. Computer animations schematically showed a slippage of the fault, triggering at the same time a sequence of little "explosions" as a chain reaction propagating from east to west of the fault. Each burst of energy radiated a shock wave that expanded from its epicenter, like a ripple on a pond where a rock was thrown, attenuating with distance, eventually becoming invisible. The speed of each element in the animation was calibrated such that each explosion would only occur after being passed by the wave-fronts coming from the detonations on its right. As a result, the shock waves from all the explosions were not concentric, but slanted to the left, with the crests of the individual shock waves closer to each other on the west side than on the east side. As such, like the supersonic bang of a jet plane, the tight wave-train reached further west than east.

The net result of the simulation was a contour map showing—like isobars—zones within which ground motions were expected to be of equal severity, those colored from orange to red representing the regions of strongest shaking where infrastructure damage was deemed possible. Impressively, the list of cities and villages where such damage had been reported, overlaid on the contour map, provided an exceptional match with the simulation results—suggesting that some "calibration" of the software might have taken place to correct the analysis and present the agency's better face. More importantly, though, all the contours were thin ellipses, showing that the zones of severe ground-shaking stretched east and west—substantially further westward than eastward—without spreading far north and south.

Graham left the agency unsure of the mechanics and physics that sustained all of the science that was presented to him, but, irrespective of the value of the computational models, the maps confirmed that no consequential infrastructure damage was likely to be discovered south of the border. This ensured that the disaster would remain wholly Canadian—Canada's exclusive claim. Graham was convinced that even if only one lousy rotted bridge had collapsed in northern New York or Vermont, preventing a rural road from crossing a tiny creek, pictures of the anemic span would have been plastered all over the U.S. front pages under headlines clamoring the destruction wreaked by the "Northeastern U.S. earthquake." His visit to Earthquakes Canada abated this concern. Nobody would steal Canada's earthquake.

Montréal, 3:00 p.m.

James suddenly stopped, a first foot already in the limo, the other deep in snow. A thought had crossed his mind; one of those intriguing ideas that overpowers all else; one of those eureka moments inspired by the random entanglement of free-flowing strands of knowledge; one of those impulsive calls to action triggered by some mystical karma.

Although never empowered as a manager before, he had long harbored an inner desire to exert leadership. Out of curiosity for this fascinating topic, and succumbing to the barrage of targeted marketing spam, James had amassed a small collection of volumes from various management gurus and self-made millionaires advocating different simple recipes for success, each stretched by the power of creative ghost-writing into a 300-page bestseller. One business leader would preach that incessantly repeating an idea, over and over, louder and louder, with passionate conviction and an aura of confidence, was certain to metamorphose the idea into an accepted truth, even in the face of conflicting data and past history, as the human brain didn't have the resilience to persistently reject dumb ideas. Another guru proclaimed that health, wealth, and power were the deserved reward of those who practiced unbridled self-stroking of their egos and diligently underscored the perceived shortcomings and intellectual inferiority surrounding them, presumably because the chronically low self-esteem genetically-ingrained in humans preconditions their eagerness to join any leader's elitist group of disciples to find acceptance in their scorn of others. A third upheld that knowledge and accomplishments acquired by the osmosis of association were more valuable and faster to accumulate than personal achievements, vindicating that worth was proportional to the extent of superficial friendships, harvested by debasing flattery and ingratiating favors. And so forth. Each imaginable despicable trait or dysfunctional behavior found its exploiter. Each exploiter found its upbeat formula to champion, wrapped in a catchy mantra, glorified as a business leadership model for success, scarily inspired from, molded upon, or endorsed by business tyrants who dangled the perks of a financially rewarding life as signs of intelligence, confusing Darwinian luck with humanity.

James had read tomes of these self-aggrandizing odes to leadership, dreaming of the day when opportunities would arise to put to good use any of those fast-track recipes. In some perverse relapse into a frantic passion stirred by intense brainwashing, burning as a reopened wartime scar, one of those faddish titles had just flashed back in James's mind: *Empower the People*. More a buzz-word than a thesis, the book advocated the idea that great accomplishments are guaranteed when ordinary people are suddenly thrust into situations that require immediate action and empowered to make the right decisions for the greater good of the community—promising a resulting future utopia where, forced to transcend their perceived limitations, and freed from the reign of oppressive debilitating hierarchies and chains of commands, everyone would exhibit distinguished courage and ability, perform brave deeds, and abide by noble moral principles. The fact that the author of that particular book was subsequently sentenced on charges of sexual harassment and embezzlement by his own employees was beside the point in James's mind at the moment. It struck him that, not only did he embody that very concept by virtue of being empowered to lead a process that would, in the end, leave a monumental legacy, but that, more importantly, he had the opportunity to replicate that process by empowering others. He had the power to single-handedly trigger a revolutionary movement by similarly enlisting and empowering ordinary folks. Doing so, he could energize the disaster-recovery process through the cascading effect of thousands of citizens serving with leadership, determined and confident that they too could rise to the occasion and through hard work produce meaningful accomplishments.

"James? Are you OK?" asked Léandre.

He stepped out of the limo and returned to the hospital. Léandre followed, trailing, catching him stopped in the middle of the packed emergency room. Energized, standing tall, he scanned the room to assess how many able bodies could be recruited and empowered. Of course, some were suffering from debilitating injuries that would indefinitely sideline them, but many had what James considered to be minor scratches and cuts that required but a few stitches, or broken non-essential bones that could heal without greatly impairing mobility. Better yet, many were fully able individuals just accompanying loved ones or friends.

"Dear friends, I would like a moment of your attention, please!" announced James to a truly captive audience that was taking root while waiting for the privilege of some public health care, normally dispensed sluggishly and exceptionally so on that day, and did not have anything else to do, anyhow.

"What are you doing?" whispered Léandre.

"Recruiting fresh minds whom I could empower to be leaders helping me implement the recovery plan."

"Here?"

The sight of Léandre ensured a heightened interest. Most in the room had also been there long enough to recognize James, to some degree, from the activity that had taken place in the past hour.

Strangely, now that James had the ear of the crowd, he realized that he did not quite know how to pitch his plan. Anxious to break the awkward heavy silence, he stumbled.

"You have the ability to take, I mean, you can take things in your own hands. Be empowered! Your disaster... the disaster... earthquake... if you want, you can lead through this crisis."

Blank stares.

Léandre, staring wide-eyed at James, was aghast. His new leader was already making a fool of himself.

James realized the urgent need for some coherent, full sentences and tried a different approach. He took a few breaths to calm down and resolved to scrupulously slow down his delivery, pausing after each sentence to mentally construct intelligible linkages before opening his mouth anew. He contemplated all the building blocks of his argument and strung them in a coherent sequence. He then proceeded with the sales pitch at once, afraid of losing his audience's attention if silent for more than a few seconds. Simple, catchy sound bites would have been helpful, but he couldn't think of any.

"I realize that you are all suffering greatly from the terrible disaster that has struck. You are also all waiting for help and relief to come from your government and outside agencies. And in all this turmoil and adversity, you may feel powerless. You may be wondering whether there is anything that you could contribute to help restore things to normalcy. Wondering how you could be empowered to play a significant and active role, to make a difference and accomplish something useful for the benefit of society."

Léandre was not quite reassured, but curious to see where this would lead, and to observe the emerging public oratory skills of his new protégé.

"I think you have all the ability to be leaders in taking responsibility and be builders of this recovery. Each one of you, in his or her mind and heart, has the skills and abilities to be constructive, to be a doer, to be active players instead of passive spectators. You are already displaying, I am sure, many of these skills in your everyday jobs. You only need to tap this creativity that is already manifest in a small and limited way in your daily work, and free it, allow it to express itself on the grander scene of life in this time of national emergency."

James was exhilarated that the abstract but empowering speech kept everyone's attention. He felt it would be powerful to illustrate his point with a few examples, pulling from the everyday experiences of select members of his audience, showing how mundane activities could become enabling opportunities for constructive enterprises.

"For example, you sir, what do you do in your daily job?"

The fat man in a worn pullover, with blood on his arm, proudly answered, "I am a literary critic."

James was stumped. He had no idea how to operationalize his conceptual example in this particular case. He was hoping for an assembly-line worker, who, if empowered to stop the assembly line, could prevent release of a defective car, consequently saving human lives by preventing an accident triggered by the failure of a faulty part. Of the many compelling examples he could recall from *Empower the People*, none dealt with critics. Nor could he fathom how a literary critic could contribute constructively to anything, not to mention disaster response and recovery activities.

Remaining cool, he moved on, "And you, sir?"

A skinny man in a suit, visibly unhurt but accompanying a woman visibly in pain, answered, "A film critic."

"What a coincidence!" joked James trying to regain his footing.

"Actually not," responded a woman with small, bloody scratches all over her body. "Many of us were attending the Joint Conference of the International Literary Critics and the World Film Critics associations at the Congress Center."

Léandre grabbed James's arm and pulled him back toward the limo.

"We must now leave; as you can imagine, our task is enormous. However, I encourage you to reflect on my colleague's inspiring words in finding opportunities over the next few days for playing a leadership and active role in the disaster recovery activities that will affect your lives and that of your colleagues."

As soon as he'd closed the door of the limo, Léandre, containing himself not to explode and to remain cordial in spite of this embarrassing moment, lectured James.

"James, you can assemble any team of experts you wish, and any task force you need. You have my full, unqualified endorsement and I'll vouch for your good work. However, I want you to operate within the existing labor frameworks and rely on those who have the necessary expertise and skills needed for the tasks and services that must be provided by the government."

James understood, and remained silent, acknowledging the embarrassment.

After a brief moment, Léandre busted into laughter.

"And of all things, use doers and shakers. Not critics!"

He slapped James on the back, trying to cheer him up.

"Critics! *Ciboire*! These *tabarnak de* loafers have never accomplished anything in life. They just read and watch like *des ostie de crisse de* couch potatoes."

With tears in his eyes, dispensing bits of sentences between breaths of laughter, Léandre inflected his voice to mimic emotions, like a ham actor.

"They bitch, bitch, and bitch, feeling omnipotent, infatuated by their voice, by their prose, by the wit of their sarcasm. A bunch of frustrated *de sacrament d'enfants de chiennes d'ostie de baptême de* lazy artists who have never had any success, who can't get their own work published or seen, and who grandstand as if they had opinions that mattered, as if creativity and cleverness in destroying the work of others was superior to the sweat and toil to actually create or do something! Aaaah *Saint-ciboire de câlice*, that tops it all. It's so funny! I just can't wait for critics to lead us, to save us all."

Moping, James felt stupid to have fallen for the insipid recipes of a motivational book rigged with cooked-up, idealized examples, worse, to have contributed to enrich a charlatan who might be enjoying retirement in a Caribbean resort on the strength of plush royalties.

Yet, while tortured by Léandre's teasing, it dawned on him that Léandre, as most politicians, would likely publish his memoirs someday. That activity by itself, as was often the case for many politicians, had the potential to pad a cushy retirement. Given that Léandre had delayed his tirades on critics until he reached the privacy of his limousine, James concluded that as much as Léandre despised these "loafers," he was savvy enough to court and flatter them so that his future manuscript would not receive titanic criticisms. No writer, or writer-to-be, would be foolish enough to disparage such an almightily powerful group that could, with the strike of a pen or a lashing tongue, destroy or launch a literary career.

While Léandre was amused by James's somewhat naive expectations of mankind, he remained undeterred in his decision to appoint him as Chief of Emergency Operations, as it still suited his purposes. With that critical, complex task under capable hands, he was now free to focus on the politics of disaster. He fully embraced the "everything is politics" doctrine, and a disaster was no less than an opportunity to create and sway allegiances. In that game, no cards are dealt—they are all conveniently pulled out of sleeves at the opportune moment.

With key operations covered by his aides, and by James, Léandre was free to spend the rest of the day to first write and rehearse his evening address to the nation, and then nap a few hours to look rested, fresh, lucid, and fully in command to the eyes of the world.

Ottawa, 3:30 p.m.

Brendon was daydreaming, imagining an Everest of saved taxpayers' dollars and a Nobel Prize for the invention of a contraption that would harness all the heat and energy generated by hours of intense, relentless brainstorming. In that futuristic fantasy, activities across Parliament Hill alone generated enough raw material to provide central heating for the entire nation and fuel its prosperity to erase the national debt.

Productivity-wise though, Brendon felt that little had been accomplished. His team was still deadlocked arguing on the merits of developing new programs or initiatives beyond those already in place. They all agreed that the frightening rate of death and injuries from this event would negatively impact the psyche of the Canadian public, and that a pro-active major action by the federal government was warranted, purportedly to heal this trauma. Something had to be done—they just couldn't agree what.

Wayne Greenbriar and Shirley Coulthard advocated more compassionate federal policies, showering real dollars on all victims beyond what was currently possible, blowing up the shackles of fiscal restraints and the arbitrary constraints of federal-provincial agreements, and using the government's largesse and infinite money-printing ability to buy a century of voters' allegiance while legally circumventing all electoral or referendum laws that imposed strict spending limits to the dueling parties.

Graham Murdoch and Kaylee Carling supported the status quo, arguing that one can't change the rules of poker after all have looked at their hands. They were adamant that plundering the public treasury to butter up one part of the Canadian constituency would alienate the rest of Canada. Besides, they believed that the electorate, devoid of long-term memory and impulsively driven by superficialities rather than by a grasp of history, just shot from the hip in the voting booth—of fickle allegiance at best over a year, and none beyond that. Instead of burning dollars in a bonfire of futility, they recommended the enactment of a new National Earthquake Vulnerability Elimination Regulation for Modernizing and Retrofitting (NEVERMoRe), committing the Canadian government to upgrading the National Building Code of Canada to integrate the latest leading-edge knowledge into its earthquake-resistant design requirements, to legislate its adoption and enforcement in all jurisdictions, and to require all infrastructure owners to assess their vulnerability and develop risk mitigation plans—a symbolically rich set of measures of no impact on the treasury, burdening industry with paperwork duties and a responsibility to disclose existing liabilities.

Wayne and Shirley objected, concerned that the new program would reek of favoritism, implicitly suggesting a passive acceptance of Québec's destruction, and signal nothing more than an urgency to tighten the level of seismic protection to prevent a similar fate to other beloved provinces that mattered more, such as British Columbia, which straddled major active fault lines. Inevitably, they argued, if such a meritorious program were so important, why hadn't it been implemented earlier?

Exhausted, they sat around the small conference table, contemplating in silence the ideological logjam. Four strong-minded, highly capable individuals that excelled at dispensing strong, well-articulated opinions, yet dunces when it came to listening and valuing the opinions of others.

"Too few had died in earthquakes until now to make this a relevant problem of national security," ventured Graham, testing the tentative excuse on his colleagues.

"That's not a satisfactory answer," replied Wayne. "You either have knowledge or you don't. Either it exists and should have been implemented already, failing an admission of having purposely disregarded this knowledge, or it doesn't exist, in which case one can't proclaim that it will be added to future building codes. It's a flawed strategy leading to the untenable alternatives of being labeled as irresponsible or impractical."

"How many died anyhow in Montreal?" asked Kaylee. "Do we have estimates yet? Should we really worry about this?"

"How many would be enough for you?" asked Shirley.

"I am perfectly comfortable with three million deaths every year," cut in Brendon, stunning his team. He hid a smirk in his mind, remaining impassive as always.

"So what's the big deal?" he continued. "If we were all to live 100 years, then one percent of us would inevitably die every year. There's 300 million of us in North America, so three million of us travel six feet under each year. If we were all to die of the most peaceful, painless, uneventful death, in our sleep, would that make sleeping the most hazardous occupation? Would we then raise billboards with public health announcements warning the population that sleeping is dangerous?"

They all wondered if their chief had gone insane.

"If you've got to die, you've got to die," added Brendon, while pulling from his jacket pocket a few folded pages ripped from a magazine, brought to his attention by a staffer a few hours earlier. He proceeded to read through the list.

"Total number of deaths in the United States each year: 2.5 million persons. Subtotal from diseases alone: 2.3 million, including: 685,089 from heart diseases; 556,902 from cancer; 157,689 from strokes; 126,382 from chronic lower respiratory diseases; 74,219 from diabetes; and 681,150 from other diseases such as HIV, alcohol liver disease, viral hepatitis, anemia, asthma, malnutrition, sudden infant death syndrome, tuberculosis, pregnancy and birth, appendicitis, West Nile virus, anorexia, and salmonella. Interestingly, no one died yet from the bird flu virus or the mad cow disease. In addition, 109,277 have died from various accidents, including: 44,757 from motor vehicle accidents; 11,212 from drug overdoses; 3,676 from motorcycle accidents; 3,369 from fires; 3,004 from choking on objects; 1,588 from falling down stairs; 875 from choking on food; 762 from bicycle accidents; 594 from falling out of bed; 515 from drowning in a pool; 365 from falling off ladders; 332 from bathtub drowning; 103 from slipping on ice; 66 from bee stings; 47 from lightning strikes; 32 from dog attacks; 22 from skydiving; 22 from crushing by human stampedes; 22 from commercial airplane accidents; 3 from playground accidents; 2 from snakebites; 1 from a marine animal attack."

The list sank in absolute silence. They all waited for someone to break the ice.

As Minister of National Defence, emboldened by what he believed to be Brendon's endorsement of his recommendation to dispatch the military in a humanitarian mission to Montréal—unaware of the holy interventions that actually underlay Brendon's decision—Wayne volunteered.

"The point being...?"

"The point being that I won't do policy by death counts," responded Brendon. "Like it or not, we're all going to die someday."

That didn't quite relieve the group.

Taking a political risk to disagree, Wayne said, "Brendon, I'm with you that we shouldn't base our policy decisions on whether or not lots of people died. But only up to a point. I don't mind it that I'll die someday from a heart attack if I've eaten too much ice cream, 'cause I really like ice cream. Likewise, I don't mind engaging in many enjoyable activities that some could consider to be deadly dangerous, like mountain climbing and skiing for example, because I get much pleasure out of it now, and I believe that it is a controlled risk that is worth taking. I'm probably not alone to be hardwired that way, because I think there are still 20% of adults in Canada who smoke, even though the front of each cigarette pack is covered with pictures of black, cancerous lungs and bold letters screaming 'Warning: You will croak in gruesome pain.' However, I'm sure there is no pleasure in being crushed under huge concrete chunks from a collapsed bridge, and if I died that way—or rather if I came close to doing so—I probably would be quite pissed and looking for someone to blame. From that perspective, the government is an easy target that fills the gun sight."

Wayne was pleased to have remained relatively diplomatic and non-confrontational. As a former car dealer, close to the heart of the prairies, confident in his ability to close a deal and in his understanding of what the public wanted, he would have rather told Brendon, "Fuck the numbers! People don't care about numbers. Numbers are what you use to confuse them shitless so that you can sell them a rust bucket on four wheels. Speak from the heart, you callous, constipated prick!" More or less the same thing, in fewer words.

Brendon answered, as if Wayne did not exist. As if the sonic waves on which his comments surfed crossed the room intact to crash and fatally splatter every word on the stone back wall. As if nothing at all had been said by Wayne. As if Wayne were irrelevant, inconsequential, nothing, plainly so.

"There will be no new subsidies or new special programs. Let's first see if the programs in place work, if they can cope with the demands. If they do, it will underscore the foresight and effectiveness of a strong, centrally driven federation in the design of national programs that serve all Canadians. If they fail to be sufficient, there will still be time to enact new emergency measures to respond. If we were instead to do so before the shortcomings of the existing programs become blatantly visible, the public would then assume that we had prior knowledge of their inadequacy and failed to act upon that information prior to the earthquake."

Wayne promptly answered, hoping to find redemption. "These are the tough decisions we expect of a Premier. We're 100% behind you!"

In his mind, Brendon translated that statement into, "You can't cut it, big guy, but I've got to protect my job."

Brendon nurtured no illusions on the allegiance of his cabinet. He knew exactly how many knives were firmly planted in his back, who'd stabbed him in each case, and why. He knew altruism to be rare in public servants, even more so when climbing the upper levels of the hierarchical pyramid.

Recognizing humanity's predisposition to deception and lies, its eagerness to exploit the credulity and fears of others, its unabashed wielding of power to better its own material wealth and prestige, its unashamed taste for destruction and superiority, its conniving, unquenchable ambitions, Brendon harbored no illusions on the permanency of allegiances. Surrounded by circling vultures as a matter of life, he'd seen friends turn into foes and foes into friends, conveniently, without hesitation or moral dilemma, to suit the dictates of career goals or personal vital interests, ready to diminish the accomplishments and magnify the faults of old colleagues turned into new rivals. Disposable friendships, disposable love, disposable loyalties, soiled by the refuse of humanity. Life was just a grand corrida full of matadors and picadores in which one poor bastard bull was afforded the exalted privilege of being repeatedly stabbed.

For the time being, the troops were in line and assuaged. With all tactical matters resolved to the extent they could, Brendon decided to spend the rest of the day drafting his evening address to the nation, and indirectly to the world.

Montréal, 4:00 p.m.

The stacks of colorful plasma screens, receivers with blinking LEDs, and communications systems, surrounded by hundreds of papers, files, reports and emptied boxes scattered on the floor, made the command and control center of the *Organisation de sécurité civile du Québec* feel like an extreme high-tech version of a teenager's room. James wondered how such critical headquarters could have been trashed beyond belief at this time of urgent need. He suspected that the lone technician in charge of operations knew it all, but attempts to pry this kind of information from a seasoned bureaucrat would be futile and likely to jinx their working relationship from the outset. Besides, he was impressed that this good soldier had successfully spent the day repairing the satellite communication system so that the command center now had a lifeline to the world.

Without questioning, he wasted half an hour to push all of the floor's contents into the director's office, which he found too ostentatious to be of any sensible use for the purpose of emergency response. Rather, the clean command center main room would now serve as the temple for a clear mind.

James attempted to remember the steps to the recovery sequence he had improvised in Léandre's presence. Coming to mind at that particular moment as he was drafting the list were: (1) Keep the command center operational, delivering fuel for the generators using the landing pad; (2) Establish a reliable short-wave radio communication network for all emergency operations, while awaiting for key emergency responders to be equipped with satellite-based cellular phones; (3) Enlist snowmobile volunteers as a network to serve hospitals and emergency shelters; (4) Establish airlift operations until bridges are repaired; (5) Regularly feed credible and detailed information to the media; and (6) Restore the public transportation and power lifeline services.

James paused, pen in hand, convinced he had forgotten an important item on that list, when an impromptu visitor casually entered the command center, without knocking, as if confident that years of paying taxes conferred on him partial ownership of the premises. His face lit up upon eye contact with James, as if pleased to have deduced beyond doubt who was the leader of the operations, just from seeing James in a pensive yet domineering stance above a technician doing all the work crouched over a computer screen.

With an assaulting handshake, he introduced himself as the president of the Canadian Union of Public Employees, Local Chapter 301, representing the blue-collar workers employed by the City of Montréal. James now remembered the missing item from his list: (7) An operational and effective snow-plowing force, paying the operators whatever it takes.

The man, even though dressed in a cheap three-piece suit with a faux-silk tie, exuded the demeanor of a biker gang leader, with a cocky self-assurance, intimidating presence, a thick beard, and arms suitable for professional wrestling.

"Léandre has sent me," he said, still gripping James's arm and practically shaking it loose. "He said you will do whatever it takes to put all snow plows on the streets of the City. I can get you all the guys you need to drive the equipment, but I hope you understand that getting them back in the trucks in these extraordinary circumstances will be expensive."

James guessed this was either a personal friend of Léandre's, or that there existed some collusion between the unions and the government as a mechanism to secure votes for the upcoming referendum. Either way, Léandre had definitely relayed to him his earlier comments about the possible necessity for overtime pay at double or triple the regular rate—maybe even extended the courtesy of a helicopter ride to downtown Montréal.

Without James's having a chance to respond, the union representative calculated, "You know, this is much tougher for a guy who wants to take care of his family than regular overtime, or than working on a holiday. A holiday, that's double or triple time, depending on the holiday."

As a resident of Ontario, James never paid income taxes in Québec, and frankly didn't give a damn whether or not the unions wanted to fleece the government in this time of crisis. The political fall-out would rest with those in power in the end.

Besides, James thought, Canadians are already numb to the excesses of unions. In the sweeping pendulum swings of mankind, from the extreme desires of ruthless employers to slave-drive their disposable and impoverished staff to the brink of death, to the radical impulses of overblown individual self-worth and unbounded sense of entitlement pushing towards economic atrophy and irrelevance, the momentum and balance of power was such that an opportunity to screw the system wouldn't be missed by the nation's parallel government.

To bolster his position, the union representative added, "By the way, Léandre said he wants a special event for the media with lots of plows driving down René Lévesque boulevard tomorrow morning, just in time for the early news, with him riding the lead truck. I think we can do that, too, if we can agree on the work terms."

All indications were that the full crew of snow plows would hit the streets within hours, with drivers able to cash a week's worth of pay within a single 12-hour shift.

Ottawa, 4:30 p.m.

Wayne Greenbriar, back from a short meeting with the Department of National Defence's brass, was discouraged by the bleak prospects on the front. To his chagrin, he found the total absence of tangible progress by the armed forces to be a cynical symbol of the paralysis of his own government. Just like an army stopped by a single stubborn collapsed span (and thin ice), he believed the kindness and compassion of the nation to be blocked by a heartless, condescending Premier cloistered within the walls of his ego, stingy to the core, unwilling to unshackle the federal coffers for the greater good.

He had just gotten an earful about the greatness of the Canadian Forces, clamoring for more financial and logistical resources, bragging about their unique ability to restore peace and civilization, and insisting on the urgency of dispatching their Reverse Osmosis Water Purification Units as diligently as possible, to prevent outbreaks of dysentery, cholera, typhoid, diarrhea, and what else—glorifying the clean chloride-laden water freely dispensed by the miracles of modern urban infrastructure as a bulwark against a lethal pandemic, and stressing the imperativeness of plugging the breaches in that fortress. Yet, while listening to those grandiloquent pretenses, Wayne couldn't help remembering his happy childhood winters playfully "eating" a substantial amount of snow, to his mother's despair, without ever falling sick—as if none of the bacteria-causing deadly illnesses could survive Saskatchewan's winters in frozen waters.

Normally a carefree and cheerful politician, gratified by his ability to "play the game" and "work the system" as well as—if not better—than anyone, he was dispirited by the imaginary problems and fallacies created all around to sustain little empires fueled by greed—all on the backs of helpless citizens, like sheep, tamed to the illusion of a benevolent shepherd, about to be sheared naked and herded on to the slaughterhouse.

Not one to meditate long hours on the future of the nation, the disaster reopened wounds inflicted on his national pride by the cupidity of his contemporaries. The blooming promises and pride of his youth when Petro-Canada was founded as a Crown Corporation to give Canadians ownership of their oil, slowly withered as the government divested itself over the years, selling all of its stakes in that national resource—like a banana republic—often to foreign interests. Air Canada, born as another eagle of national pride, lost feathers as it aged and ended plucked of its socialistic national pride in the hands of the private sector. Even the grand-daddy of public corporations, the Canadian National Railways, had landed in private foreign hands. As if no amount of golden national pride could compete with the bold attraction of green dollars, no higher grounds could stop politicians from pimping their maple-leaf body-painted prostitute-country, no civic obligation or pledge of allegiance could prevent hard-core capitalism from decimating all marketplace remnants of Canadian nationalistic fervor. To the point of despair.

In some pernicious twist of logic, in his longing for greater national independence, Wayne started to envy Quebec's sovereignists.

Québec City, 5:00 p.m.

Short-wave radio communications with the Montréal headquarters of the *Organisation de sécurité civile du Québec* were operational, and James's flow of requests was managed by the Québec City district office—the one with the largest staff ready to execute orders. He dispatched detailed instructions on how to deploy a network of responders equipped with satellite-based cellular phones, to enlist snowmobile volunteers, to establish airlift operations, to develop reliable information for the media, and to implement collaborative disaster-recovery strategies with Transport Québec and Hydro Québec.

The district office brimmed with a dozen white-collar bureaucrats freshly minted by the local university, endowed with diplomas, degrees and certificates covering a broad spectrum of qualifications, including expertise in the fields of communications, political science, urban planning, public policy, psychology, social welfare, criminal justice, archeology, philosophy, literature, theology, and sexology, and whose youthful enthusiasm or convenient acquaintances made up for their sometimes gross lack of relevant qualifications.

They were ready to accumulate overtime pay on duty for the nation, serving to the best of their disparate abilities, even though fully aware that they owed their employment to the financial wizardry that justified offering obscenely generous retirement packages to incompetent senior bureaucrats, presumably to replace them by less costly and equally qualified junior ones—it remained voodoo economics to them, mere mortals, particularly considering that salaries and pensions were both part of the government's general budget. To non-wizards, this amounted to switching the sucklings from one nipple of the taxpayers to the other. Nonetheless, with a government exhorted by wise financial advisers to offer such packages, and motivated to sugarcoat the deal from the perspective of an impending referendum, the generosity of the last retirement incentive package had led to an unforeseen exodus of senior employees from the civil service. As a result, some departments lost their entire staff, including the government's financial advisement office, as a testimony to the persuasive power and retirement-planning skills of financial gurus who'd managed to masquerade a heist of the public treasury as legitimate entitlements of deserving senior citizens.

The Québec City office of *Organisation de sécurité civile du Québec* was one such department, abandoned by its entire graying staff, which had to be completely rebuilt with new blood. The new custodians of this critical government mission, freshly implanted after a few training classes and orientation meetings, had barely finished decorating their cubicles when the disaster struck. Projected onto the stage without a rehearsal, they had spent in vain the past 36 hours parsing every document within the confines of the office in search of a response plan that would be more than a thick and elaborate conceptual description of political, administrative, and jurisdictional responsibilities, more than a contact list of long-retired links along a telephone chain, and more than a wishful post-disaster operational plan developed for response to minor localized emergencies and stretched beyond logic for catastrophes with geographically distributed damage and impacts.

Having struck out on all those counts, they were delighted—ecstatic—to be contacted by James, rescued from themselves and showered with valuable guidance from their new leader, taking in all instructions as if drinking straight from a fire hose, with the same resulting mess and lack of effectiveness.

James dispatched orders as he would to a competent staff of seasoned emergency responders on guard in the Québec office, ready to implement on the basis of sound, field-tested judgment. Shielded from reality by a low-fi radio signal that distorted all voices to sound like craggy veterans, he envisioned his every request igniting powerful and immediate stimuli in the minds of gray-haired emergency responders leading to the formulation of an appropriate plan effectively implemented by an energetic set of staffers, whereas an image of frozen deer staring at the headlights of an incoming 18-wheeler would have been more realistic in this case.

Full of energy and of good intentions, the young responders huddled around the radio soaked up all the information and directives they could. After James signed off, they undertook at once to implement the dictates of their new leader, building on the essence of the message but improvising at will with their own new ideas to improve implementation. Working alone or in small teams, they tackled parts of the problem that best suited their professional interests.

As such, in response to James's request to enlist snowmobile volunteers—man and machine—on the island as a network to serve hospitals and emergency shelters, they rather set out to fill trucks with brand new snowmobiles acquired at list price from dealers across the province and formulated a plan to deliver one driverless machine to each designated hospital and emergency shelter on the island, all intended to provide each facility with its own transportation capabilities available around the clock. Although they were hoping that one of the bridges to the island would be back in service soon, they recognized that it might not happen and that an alternative plan was necessary to deliver the snowmobiles to their destinations. Trucks would thus be dispatched to strategic staging areas around the island where their cargo would be discharged. From there, teams of two snowmobiles would drive across solid frozen parts of the St-Lawrence, each team targeting delivery to one of the island's hospitals or shelters. At each destination, one snowmobile would be dropped off, its driver returning to the staging area on the second snowmobile. The plan left it to the short-staffed hospitals and shelters to designate someone to run the errands and fetch the supplies from the staging areas.

Similarly, James's request for airlift operations temporarily morphed into a dispatch order for boats, on account of their greater cargo capacity. Even though this plan was plagued by the inability to unload boats without specialized equipment and by challenges in routing the needed supplies from shore to shelters, hospitals, and other key distribution centers, it remained an option on the table until the mastermind behind this substitution realized that even if icebreakers succeeded in returning the river to a navigable condition by crushing its frozen cover-slab into small floating debris, such an operation would paralyze the snowmobile missions concocted by his colleagues. Undeterred, he focused on developing a strategy to undermine the snowmobile plan as it was currently framed, and to find ways to rally a significant part of the office in support of a revised plan, in which the snowmobile crossings would be replaced by boats ferrying goods, offloaded onto trailers pulled by snowmobiles serving as the distribution network on the island.

The budding emergency responders at the district office, remote from the epicenter and somewhat detached from the intensity of ground truth, also compensated for their inexperience by tapping their special expertise to focus all their efforts and time on problems they perceived to be the most acute priorities in the circumstances.

The communications specialist, on the strength of the dictum that "Knowledge is Power," and a self-proclaimed technology geek, hatched a plan for all emergency responders to be equipped with the latest wireless handheld personal digital assistant device, on which some as-yet-unidentified software could be installed to facilitate inter-agency coordination. She invested her efforts to develop a plan to rapidly acquire the necessary number of devices—by purchases or confiscations in the interest of national security—and to formulate an on-the-job during-crisis training plan to ensure that the key staff of all relevant agencies could most rapidly learn how to operate the tool. The objective was to orchestrate this as a high-profile public relations operation, showcasing Québec as a world center of high technology, daring and bold, confidently deploying state-of-the-art pocket computers loaded with programs created by Québec entrepreneurs to help resolve challenges created by possibly the largest natural disaster in North American history. A continuous barrage of publicity, subliminally patriotic, would be achieved through strategic media coverage of gullible survivors convinced that their rescue would have been impossible without the wireless gadgets and software technology launched by the Québec government.

The urban planning expert concocted an elaborate plan to convert the Métro lines into underground pedestrian highways and bikeways which, as long as the concentration of carbon dioxide in these non-ventilated area remained below toxic levels, would provide Montréalais with sheltered and relatively warmer pathways to various parts of the city until restoration of the transportation system itself, complete with distribution and collection of government-issued helmet-mounted lights at the entrances and exits of each station, respectively. Likewise, all underground parking garages and malls in buildings undamaged by the earthquake were to be requisitioned by the government to serve as safe havens from the outside cold, devoid of essential and sanitary services but providing citizens with a sheltered area to keep warm while awaiting help from friends and families, or to rest for a moment before continuing their journey in the bitter cold. These were to be designated to serve for short-term purposes only, to avoid the risk of creating underground, unpoliced shanty towns, although he recognized that no one knew how long it would be before power would be restored to key parts of the city. Likewise, only malls in which storefronts were secured by steel shutters were to be used, to minimize incidences of looting.

The psychologist and social welfare specialists brainstormed on how to ensure that the critical needs of handicapped and senior citizens would be met. They were particularly concerned about those living outside institutions but barely able to perform routine activities without assistance, likely abandoned to fend on their own against adversity. Reliance on the network of social workers was at best uncertain, as each worker would have to assess how to balance the challenges of personal hardship with those duty dictated by professional ethics—an assessment in which they feared altruism was often short-changed, even when performed by professionals. Furthermore, they anticipated that post-traumatic psychiatric assistance would be acutely needed by a broad spectrum of the general population to cope with various stages of mental distress, from sleep disorders to severe depression and suicidal tendencies.

They concocted an ensemble of ambitious strategies and solutions to these substantial challenges, on the modus operandi that public health was more important than fiscal restraint, in that stopping bleeding of the soul should get priority over preventing a hemorrhage of government money. While complex in their miscellaneous implementation details, all these relied on generous financial incentives and the enlistment, as necessary, of certified experts from other provinces as well as from the United States.

A possible impediment to their plans was an emergency bill unknowingly contemplated by one of their colleagues: The criminal justice expert had envisioned the need for enacting civil emergency measures complementary to current legislation by defining as crimes subject to severe penalties some specific, undesirable activities ranging from price-gouging to the hiring of professionals not certified to work in Québec. This latter prohibition was motivated by years of militancy in unions, fighting the drive of corporations to enhance their competitiveness by lowering their labor costs and keeping salaries in check, partly by attempting to import (from second- or third-world countries or from the former communist bloc) cheap labor and professionals deemed to be equally qualified. In his years working with unions, he had heard all the reasons and excuses, the doom-and-gloom predictions, and the threat of bankruptcies and closures, but had never backed down on the key union demands and positions, and lived to see all the companies who predicted their demise at the negotiation table not only survive, but prosper and continue to amass obscene profits in the end. To him, massive material destruction was simply an opportunity for the construction industry to get out of a slump, tons of injured and sick people were just negotiation leverage for the health sector to eliminate the funding shortfalls it had long decried, and widespread general hardship was a unique chance to enhance the quality of life of the Québécois society across the board by ensuring that all investments remained in the hands of the local, tax-paying citizens.

The archeologist toiled to draft an emergency bill prohibiting the demolition or repair of damaged buildings and infrastructure without special governmental approval—beyond the usual building permit process—to be granted only subsequently to an assessment of each site's "future archeological value," with the ultimate objective of preserving a few select ruins as memorials of the tragic national disaster, each appropriately stuffed with time capsules sealed for the next millennium. He believed that the Olympic Stadium would be a prime candidate for this purpose, with its gargantuan, partially collapsed structure as the perfect symbol of national aspirations broken by the fallibility of mankind—with a particular emphasis on the collapsed phallic tower of the stadium as an allegorical lesson for future civilizations that the priorities of hedonistic societies were askew in relation to their vital long-term survival needs. However, suspecting that the maintenance cost of such a monument kept in a precarious state of near total collapse would by far exceed the already staggering amounts that had been required to keep the structure functional, and recognizing that the valuable land on which the "white elephant" stadium stood would likely be stalked by real estate vultures, he felt there was an urgent need to identify which of the other freshly minted ruins could become national landmarks—much like the skeleton dome of the Hiroshima City Hall which stands as a carefully preserved, permanent reminder of another aspect of mankind's foolishness. Although the proposed emergency bill would slow down recovery to some degree, he was confident it had a good chance to be enacted, given that, in his estimates, the entire operation could be done within a few weeks—meaning months after translating government jargon into realistic assessments—and that all Québécois knew that it was futile to fight the government's will when it came to matters of national pride and symbolism.

The philosopher spent the hours following the disaster contemplating its significance in the perspective of theological fatalism, logical fatalism, incompatibilism, collective responsibility, moral responsibility, moral luck, existentialism, egalitarianism, nihilism, behaviorism, realism, anti-realism, and many more-isms, wondering who among the grand philosophical masters had actually field-tested their theories and beliefs against the harsh reality of a natural disaster. She was fascinated by the opportunities provided by this subject and enthused that the long nights of soul-searching for a Ph.D. dissertation topic might be at last over. In her mind, the multi-dimensional societal failures ensuing from this disaster were unequivocally consequences of rational or irrational, conscious or subconscious, philosophical choices anchored in life-defining decisions made in early life. To be practical about it, she felt that this broad subject could be further narrowed down to an education issue, namely the need to increase the number of mandatory philosophy courses required for graduation with a CEGEP diploma. Since she had been inspired and empowered by James's radioed directives to actually do something in the aftermath of this disaster, she felt that this education reform, and the resulting attuning of the human mind, was the best option to prevent recurrence of such a tragedy. Given that CEGEPs had been created in Québec during the "quiet revolution" in the 1960s as an equitable and accessible network to integrate the final stages of technical and pre-university training under the same roof, as a transitory phase between high school and university, with the simultaneous goal of creating responsible and critical citizens through the teaching of philosophy and literature, she felt the system had progressively strayed from its original mandate over the years by relaxing the rigor of required philosophy courses, under pressure to answer the less noble training requirements pushed by market demands. It was time to revamp the philosophy curricula germane to the CEGEP degree to ensure that future citizens would have the necessary moral tools to make responsible personal choices, translating to a better and more resilient societal environment.

In the little time since he'd joined Québec City's district office of the *Organisation*, the literature expert had typically been sought by his colleagues to proof various texts for compliance with the irrational and capricious grammar of the French language, a task devoid of creativity, which he deeply despised. His love of the language was for its power to arouse ideas and emotions, not for the illogical linguistic minutia and mechanics enshrined centuries ago by the wigged sadists from *l'Académie française*. To render himself unavailable for such mundane tasks, but also to immerse himself in an activity true to his passion, he undertook to develop the rules and regulations for a national literary competition for the best short story commemorating the anniversary of the disaster. As demonstrated by Hollywood in countless movies of dubious quality, disasters are pregnant with inspiring drama and uplifting stories of courage, love, and patriotism, in this case sure to elicit pride in the national resilience and to elicit support by the political intelligentsia. Aptly named to flatter one of the powerful, or to honor a hero yet to be uncovered by the media and turned into some national icon of bravery, such a competition was sure to ignite popular interest, serve as a unique memorial to the national tragedy, and keep the flame of nationalism burning.

The political science and public policy experts, in quickly assessing the potential social costs of recovery and the ability of the province to borrow and repay, focused on developing a roadmap of financial opportunities made possible by this disaster. They believed that while banks and financial institutions were immune to guilt and shame, having never cared for the human suffering ensuing from some of their "best" investment decisions, modern governments ruled by public opinion and political agenda. In tandem, they therefore endeavored to develop a public policy plan and political action plan to shape public opinion in the international arena, to solicit friendly nations to recognize that Québec's recovery was strategically important on the geopolitical map, and to financially contribute to the resurgence of this ally.

They concurred that a first step toward that goal was to flood the streets of Montréal with reporters from all media who, by their nature, would magnify reality to create infotainment drama, focusing on stories of human misery and personal victories in the face of adversity. As experience had shown, countless times before, the narrow window on life provided by television would allow the media to distort reality beyond imagination. Holding captive the minds of those otherwise uninformed, it could convincingly paint a country as in the throes of civil war by focusing on riots spanning the best of three city blocks. Likewise, it could declare a city to be in ruins by showing the same dozen collapsed buildings surrounding stern commentators generically lamenting the horrible state of affairs, propping up their argument by hand-picked testimonials of citizens decrying the overall debilitating impact of the disaster and wailing their despair and despondency as a result of the inadequate general emergency response. Such coverage, beyond boosting TV ratings, would generate worldwide compassion and handsome donations, through religious and secular charity organizations, of goods and services fulfilling all essential immediate post-disaster needs.

They consequently formulated a multi-step strategy anchored on the concept of emergency legislation to establish at once a temporary collection agency that would bypass the federal government, on the fabricated premise that this was necessary to expedite the relief effort and direct the charitable assistance immediately to where it was most needed. This would be the same agency through which the government's own assistance would be channeled, to blur the line between foreign donations and government assistance in the minds of the recipients of such outpourings of love. Special large labels proclaiming "Emergency Disaster Relief Supplies," and listing the contents of the boxes, would be dutifully apposed atop all packages, officially to help sort them by type of goods and purposes, as well as to accidentally conceal as much as possible the logos of donators—with some exceptions. Personal calls would be logged by the Québec's Premier to heads of countries sympathetic to the province's political ambitions, asking them to heed his call for assistance and pledging that their response to his nation's woeful but temporary predicament was a good investment, ensuring tightened future relationships in the event of a hastened independence from Canada—in those instances, the large labels would be affixed with due consideration to not obscure the donators' identity.

The theologist, one of the *Organisation*'s bureaucrats whose expertise was at odds with the demands of the job and who owed his escape from poverty to convenient nepotism, had been sitting alone, mumbling for a while. It had been assumed that he was praying in semi-silence, until he started to progressively raise his voice. As it reached a conversational tone, some stopped in their activities, first intrigued by his impromptu monologue but then shocked by his acerbic utterances.

"...and he will be blamed for all suffering and death, falsely accused of unlashing his wrath upon all unsuspecting humankind, rendering them powerless and destitute, but we know this to be untrue. We know that lies and fear are behind accusations and judgments. Deep down, he does not care, and nor should we. It all doesn't matter. It is but a microscopic quiver of the universe, whose grandeur is undisturbed by our insignificant selves and inconsequential sufferings. The infinite universe, sacred temple of the absolute energy, the absolute love. Timeless limitless absolute love. Sacred! The illuminating power of love, the true energy and single soul that bonds us all."

As the dithyramb crescendoed, from calm, to confident, to assertive, to zealous, to aggressive, to delirious, to a screaming hysteria, the entire staff had no choice but to cease all activities, to suspend all thoughts, bedazzled.

"The infinite love that will spring from the ashes, ruins, fire, and deaths. The love! The sacred love! And in all pain and suffering, lost souls will find themselves anew. In all pain and suffering, lost souls will love themselves anew. And throughout this grand love-making, this colliding warmth of the soul, the spirit, and the body, will emerge procreation, and birth that we welcome in our fold, to embrace and share that imperfect but unique experience of the physical world. The small insignificant world that allows the soul a new experience of love. We welcome the love. WE CELEBRATE THE LOVE. WE CELEBRATE AND EMBRACE THE COMING TIDE OF INTERCOURSE AND FORNICATION AND BIRTHS THAT WILL ARISE FROM THIS DISASTER. WE EMBRACE THIS MASSIVE CREATION AND PROCREATION. WE PRAISE THE PROCREATION!"

Those last words echoed in the heads around the table, as in the expansiveness of a church where a similar embarrassing silence would have weighed. This frantic and impromptu trance from a usually placid spiritual colleague left the group shocked with the induced collective vision of a city-wide fornication spree of souls seeking comfort in trying times, and the ensuing baby-boom henceforth.

On that thought, all suddenly realized that their often ignored and secretly ridiculed colleague, the sexologist, had not yet contributed to the process. Indeed, he sat through the creative intellectual orgy of the past hours curled up in a corner of the room, unimpressed and moping.

Out of misplaced compassion and false guilt, the colleagues suddenly felt compelled to seek his expert opinion on a topic whose possible significance had been lost until now. The communications expert ventured to express the feelings of the group by candidly asking whether he had any particular professional advise to dispense with regards to the theologist's closing thoughts.

The sexologist, disturbed from his sulkiness by the converging tension and surprised by this sudden inquiry, first raised an eyebrow, and paused a moment.

"Oh, yeah...well don't worry about them," he said, sweeping his arm across the lower part of a wall map of the province pinned above him.

Slowly, he stood up, slapped his jeans a couple of times, as if to clear the dust or remove wrinkles, and sashayed towards the exit. As he left the room, he sighed.

"They're all fucked already. They just don't know yet how so fucking screwed they are!"

Québec City, 6:00 p.m.

Lise's list of emergency shelters, still erroneous but partly corrected, scrolled at the bottom of the screen, below a talking head purposely solemn to underline the gravity of the situation. News remained scant on the state of damage and condition of the population on the island. However, the long awaited manna was starting to materialize.

Clips of miscellaneous broken windows and regional damage of limited interest, often shot in bad lighting by amateurs with shaky hands and unaware that their camcorders came with an instructions manual, had played as filler material much beyond their value and could at last be discarded as quality feeds were now available from multiple sources. The six o'clock news would finally start to gratify a public eager for the gory details.

After a long recap of the well-known events of the past two days, intended to build suspense as much as fill time, the news anchor unveiled the long-awaited headlines.

"All indications suggest that the death toll from this earthquake continues to increase. Estimates indicate that approximately 5,000 persons may have died as a result of this earthquake, and over 25,000 may have suffered significant injuries, although we must caution that, due to the challenges created by the limited access to the island, these are only approximate numbers based on the assessments of experts, and extrapolating from known information to date. In the second part of our program, an expert panel will describe how these staggering estimates have been derived, and provide examples from past disasters of the heart-wrenching difficulties that must often be overcome just to find and reach a hospital that is operational.

"In one related dramatic story, an injured homeless person was found today in the streets of Montréal and brought to a hospital by none other than Premier Laliberté to receive emergency care services. The man was found unconscious lying in a roadside snow bank by the Premier as part of an expedition to survey and assess the extent and type of damage to the urban infrastructure."

Images of Léandre at the hospital, opening the door on the passenger side of his official government limo, dragging out the injured man with Florent's help, carrying him to the emergency room while calling for nurses, and depositing him on a stretcher, were described by the news anchor as the acts of a leader who genuinely cared for his people, irrespectively of their wealth or stature. This was news made for television, and basking in the delight of such visual candy, nobody questioned how cameras could so fortuitously catch such an event without some measure of staging.

"Unfortunately, the unidentified homeless person died at the hospital even though he was under the continued attentive care of two medical doctors."

The clip of an interview recorded by the same source was inserted at this particular point, for all viewers to hear the expert opinions of Jean-Pierre and Audréanne.

"The patient arrived at the hospital with many severe contusions and fractures, and significant organ failures," said Jean-Pierre. Audréanne added, "Unfortunately, the severity and compounded nature of his multiple injuries overwhelmed his capacity for recovery, and we are sorry that we lost the patient in spite of our best efforts."

They both hoped that somebody in their family had captured this moment of posterity on a DVD recorder.

Careful not to inject too many personal opinions or display emotions, the news anchor moved on to the next story, treating human tragedy with the same stern apathy as fender-benders and municipal elections, without the enthusiasm and passion reserved for weather forecasts and sports summaries.

"The Canadian Forces already at Montréal's door are fully engaged in the harsh task of assisting in the response and recovery operations."

Reading from a shortened version of the script planted in the Canadian Press newsfeed by political friends of the government, the news anchor served without flinching the platitudes that provided a live soundtrack to the theatrical maneuvers provided by the Department of National Defence.

Awaiting an end to the scarcity of live ground footage, bland propagandist material from all parties would be given equal opportunity to serve their purpose, for the sake of filling the available air time. As had been done for the past 42 hours, talking heads of all allegiances would be paraded to critique, comment, and counterbalance the brainwashing attempts, to generate news in the absence of substance.

However, and fortunately, near the end of the second day since the onset of the disaster, one original news clip, received from a crew on the island, made its way to the studio, allowing all reporters worldwide to save face. This precious footage was scheduled to play last, kept as the *pièce de résistance* to close the information segment with a semblance of journalistic dignity, to leave the spectator with a small dose of journalistic rigor, massaged to provide the usual desirable bias of objectivity. Having crossed onto the eastern tip of the island with snowmobiles—on an ice bridge that seemed thick enough to be worth the gamble—still a long way from its downtown destination, the crew stopped in awe, at the risk of breathing toxic fumes, to document what was becoming an industrial conflagration of chemical plants.

Against a backdrop of fireballs and explosions, a small number of overwhelmed firemen attempted to prevent, as best they could, the spreading of an immense fire burning in intense, unusual colors. Underscoring these images, the anchorman added his own palette of commentary.

"The conflagration in Pointe-Aux-Trembles has melted the industrial landscape into a mass of twisted steel frames and silos engulfed in giant clouds of swirling flames spewing unidentified poisons and toxic fumes into the atmosphere. A handful of courageous firefighting units, in special protective suits with self-contained breathing apparatus, are attempting to subdue the fierceness of the blaze, valiantly working upwind to protect the residences besieged by the advancing flames. Although, seen from the ground, one can only guess at the expanse of the burning footprint, the chief fireman on site has indicated that, unless many more specialist crews are soon dispatched to the front, there are enough fuels and chemicals on site to keep the fire burning for days. Calls have been made to mobilize the many firefighting aircrafts available in the province, but these cannot be used effectively until the cloud cover dissipates, especially considering that indiscriminate use of large volumes of water or chemicals to fight the fire could rapidly transport and spread toxic contamination over a wide area. As a dire potential outcome, the chief fireman predicted that, if winds were to pick up, the fire could advance at a fast pace towards the adjacent residential neighborhoods, which themselves provide all the combustible load necessary to sustain a fire that could spread for weeks unchecked until reaching the edge of the island."

The anchorman painted that doomsday scenario with the same blasé voice used to announce the winning lottery numbers.

Gatineau, 7:30 p.m.

Five bridges stitch together the provinces of Québec and Ontario over the Ottawa River, where the Federal National Capital region precariously spills over from Ottawa to Gatineau, filling the Québec shore with office buildings leased by various government agencies, hugged tight by a cluster of bedroom communities full of civil servants loyal to the federal coffers that hold the funding to their retirement plans. Five ribbons of concrete and steel that, like five crisp fingers, exert a tight grip on the destiny of Gatineau.

Shirley Coulthard drove past the squeaky-clean, modern government buildings and beyond the dilapidated, smelly old paper mill, into the old village, up to an old clapboard house decorated with fake brick veneer, for a secret seance with Stéphane, a gray-haired medium she'd met a few years ago while browsing the occult section of a local bookstore.

Shirley held an unshakable faith in spiritualism and had amassed an impressive collection of antique trumpets, slates, cabinets, and boards all designed to summon and communicate with the spirits. However, when it came to serious dialogue with important historical figures, she depended on channeling through an experienced medium. Given that everybody wanted to pick Elvis's brain, but no one cared to chat with his stableboy or the plumber who unclogged his toilet, the demands of millions of obsessed disciples converged onto a few oversubscribed spirits, victims of their immense contemporary afterlife popularity. Shirley considered channeling as a priority call signaling the highest respect—a convenient way to jump to the front of the line.

Sitting in a meditative pose at opposite ends of a draped table in the semi-dark attic, humming in unison an unintelligible mantra in a mythological, secret dialect, Shirley and her guru sought wisdom from spirits whose earthly knowledge had been enlightened by their transcendental journey to the great unknown.

Shirley had difficulty concentrating, upset that Stéphane had charged her three times his normal fee, alleging an extreme demand on his time over the past two days due to a surge of clients in great distress and urgently needing supernatural communications. She knew that price-gouging for essential staples following natural disasters was a criminal offense, as clearly defined in laws intended to prevent unscrupulous merchants from exploiting a desperate populace crushed by the blow of an extreme event, but she was unsure whether legislation prohibiting such reprehensible profiteering extended to critical occult consultations. In any event, the political roots of the Democratic Canadian Rightist Alliance Party were firmly anchored in a free-market bedrock just as sympathetic to perfectly balanced market forces as to coercive monopolies, and she knew better than to challenge anyone who simply embraced in his practice the supply-demand, capitalistic creed of the party's sponsors.

Shirley's unfocused musings were interrupted by Stéphane's odd, gurgling groans. Like the monotone of an analog television awaiting the start of regular programming, this was his unoriginal way to signal to customers that he had entered a deep trance, and that he invited spirits to take control of his physical body, in symbiosis, for a positive and mutually respectful dialogue. Stéphane also preferred that approach as it dispensed with the need for the theatrics of automatic writing, numbered raps, or levitating tables.

Shirley had her list of favorite deceased idols with whom she entertained close relationships. Contrary to popular trends, hers included no famous religious personas or entertainers, as she believed that neither Jesus nor Elvis possessed the political savvy needed to tutor her in the art of Machiavellian machinations needed to thrive in Ottawa. Her ambitions were all political, her expectations work-related, and her short list of privileged contacts beyond the grave included, bottom to top, her grandfather (an eminent Tory of a century past), Franklin D. Roosevelt, Winston Churchill, and McKenzie King. An all-male list desperately awaiting Margaret Thatcher, Madeleine Korbel Albright, and Angela Merkel, whose remarkable longevity vexed her—she eagerly awaited the death of her contemporary role models to finally have a chance to talk to them. She nonetheless felt a special connection with McKenzie King, himself an addict of seances in his lifetime and renowned for his documented, extensive conversations with dead mentors, including his dog Pat from whom he professed to have learned the values of honor and fidelity—a rivetingly queer admission coming from a bachelor.

Stéphane, careful to never guarantee that he could force anyone to "pick up the phone" when it rang in the afterlife, always made some efforts to satisfy his customers, especially at triple the regular rate. Hence, the King himself (the politician, not the entertainer) took control of his body.

"Shirley, pleased to see you again," said Stéphane, erasing all traces of his French accent.

"Rex?" as his intimate friends and families called him.

"I'm not going to be here long. How can I help you?"

Shirley would have died for a chance to chitchat with the King, but that would have to wait for a few more decades. This expensive long-distance call was to be all business.

"I trust you have seen what has happened to your country for the past two days," she said, as Shirley imagined the afterlife to be a virtual news network of mega-screens monitoring all and every part of the world—as if the best thing to do after one's death was to watch the facetious puerilities of those who remained behind. "Our leaders are at loggerheads with each other and no one seems to care about the compounded suffering engendered by this crisis."

She trusted that the man whose government officially created the notion of "Canadian citizens" in 1947, abolishing the status of "British Subjects," would forever care deeply about the state of the nation.

"It hurts me more than anyone," answered Stéphane, curious to see where this would lead.

"My boss is scheduled to address the nation this evening. I would welcome your counsel on how to appeal to his good senses to serve the nation's higher purposes."

Stéphane basked in pure bliss, savoring every praise, every confidence, and all the love, as if he were the rightful recipient of this adulation. The high school dropout, self-taught in the witchcraft of charlatanism, felt blessed by the inexorable gullibility of mankind—and womankind alike, for he was an equal-opportunity exploiter. Living the fantasy trances of his clients, he sometimes squinted an eye open to witness their ultimate pleasure and satisfaction, almost jealous of their delight in the illusion of a fulfilled desire, envious of their ability to break the chains of reality with reckless abandon. He found vindication and self respect trading in the hard currency of hope and dreams. These were rare gems in a buyers' market in which few alternatives could deliver, and he made it a point of honor to gratify all of his clients' expectations to the best of his abilities—even if, through channeling, it meant answering the pleas of a widow for one more passionate night with her husband. However, he wasn't a political scientist, and his counsel in that field, at best, remained a mix of beatnik philosophy, new age spiritualism, and freethinking improvisations.

"Rex?" asked Shirley, concerned that the long silence implied a loss of communication at the most critical moment, as she was ready to receive the King's gospel.

"Always remember: Insufferable hardships need open arms and compassion, not closed fists and confrontations. Combining our inner strengths and our humanity, we will resolve any crisis. The door is open."

Her heart pulsed like an African drum assaulted by hippies. She repeated the three sentences like a mantra, trying to engrave each syllable in her brain, afraid of the feebleness of her memory.

Stéphane shook violently, released from the grip of a powerful spirit, and collapsed of exhaustion on the table.

Shirley needed no crystal ball to see the future at that point. She sprung up, left a pile of cash on the table next to his slumped body, and rushed to Parliament hill, as if history was on the line.

Stéphane was particularly pleased with his carefully crafted words. As he pocketed the cash and stowed away the seance's paraphernalia, he also memorized the same three sentences, as they would stand prominently in his autobiography—a labor of love spanning the many years of his flamboyant practice and motivated by the conviction that a memoir documenting the foibles and naivete of the political elite was sure to become a bestseller. To add intrigue to that particular passage of the future blockbuster, and further pad his anticipated plush retirement, Stéphane elected to share this information with his wife's brother-in-law, a low-level assistant who happened to work for Léandre Laliberté and to whom he frequently sold such political intelligence in exchange for additional, juicy inside information.

In a city subservient to the federal government, it could be lucrative to be an incognito separatist.

Montréal, 8:30 p.m.

Raging swirls of fluorescent colors assaulted François Laflamme every time he regained consciousness. Terrified by the daggers of fire that pierced in a fury the dense surrounding haze, fondling him with abusive caresses from hell, each time he screamed senselessly through his momentary bursts out of coma, before collapsing anew into silent nightmares. Death kept tormenting him, urging him to loosen his tenuous grip on life, promising a final relief from the excruciating pain that burned inside his lungs and the hallucinatory chemicals that seeped through his brain.

The ambulance's progress was tentative, hampered by the 10 inches of snow that by then blanketed most of the roads on the island. To the driver, all hours were equal and triple the overtime rate—he didn't care how long it took to reach each destination, as each were just points on a map where bodies filled with agony were either collected or deposited. Bodies frozen to death extirpated nearly whole from the debris of collapsed buildings, like the bunch he'd ferried to the morgue earlier in the day, or bodies grossly tattooed with third-degree burns and filled by toxic fumes from chemical fires—all were just payloads to him, as pain conveniently always remained within the carnal envelopes of each suffering victim.

To the paramedics on board, each body was a desperate survivor to generously fill with morphine in the faint hope that competent health professionals could find ways to reassemble the broken parts into a respectful soul. To them, firemen, like François Laflamme, crushed by the wild conflagration in Pointe-Aux-Trembles, were misguided soldiers pushed into a suicidal battle by the lure of heroism, plucked from their stressed, dependent families to defend prevailing civic duties, propped like tin soldiers to face an unstoppable enemy. They had spent the afternoon ferrying to the nearest hospital those partially charred and delirious firemen felled by the combustion forces unleashed at the front.

Dwarfing the oil refinery fire that had burned 30 thousand tons of naphtha unrestrained for five days following the Turkey earthquake of 1999, the Pointe-Aux-Trembles fire was a giant, out-of-control, seething furnace whose engulfing flames generated fierce wind storms by sucking all oxygen at ground level, and polluted the sky with an oppressive black cloud of soot and toxic compounds. Lilliputian firefighters stood no chance facing such an overpowering monster.

The ambulance dropped its cargo of fried, semi-comatose, delirious firemen on the floor of the emergency room with the diligence and compassion of dockworkers unloading crates of vegetables, and drove off without waiting for paperwork, as if leaving a donut shop without picking up a receipt. It had been made clear that, operating under emergency conditions, they could dispense with the mundane bureaucratic formalities of standard procedures, and just rake up mileage on the vehicles as proof of services rendered to settle future payments—prorated to account for the speed constraints imposed by abysmal road conditions.

Unable to cope with the surge of patients, the new arrivals on the floor were eventually dragged to whatever space could be found in the corridors, awaiting the departure of a patient, from successful treatment or death, to provide space in one of the operating rooms or beds. With snow piling up endlessly outside, they did not have the luxury of treating patients in the parking lot, as was often done in warmer climates following major disasters.

Of all the canvas stretchers on the floor, François Laflamme's body was closest to Audréanne. She saw him, but her thoughts were hopelessly scattered, like the patients in the emergency room. Witness to the sorry state of one more hopeless patient in urgent need of surgery, she mechanically prescribed some morphine and stuck the note to one of the bars of the stretcher. She performed the automatism without emotions, as all her passions had been dulled by an assault of questions she couldn't contain and for which she had no answers.

In spite of all the qualities she loved in Jean-Pierre—his ambition and his love of money more than compensating for the fact that he was a bit thick at times—and beyond her delight in the social status of two medical doctors eventually married together, she couldn't fathom the thought of her uncle-in-law being the country's top separatist. She owed her very French first name to her mother, a protective and aggressive parent who had foreseen the imperativeness of having a bilingual child in a city where bilingualism—or the illusion of it as a minimum—was a necessary asset for civil servants to progress unhampered from promotion to promotion within Ottawa's largest employer. Unable to find a space for her daughter in the few available French immersion

schools, she had forced her into the separate French school system, faking a French cultural heritage and using influential connections. Failing an opportunity to bridge the two solitudes, Audréanne forever resented this imposition that had made her a pariah
in the schoolyards, and had insisted on attending McGill for all her
post-secondary education. Jean-Pierre's appeal to her was partly
his charming sweetness, partly his determination to attend an
English university in spite of his substantial deficiencies in master-
ing the language, having grown up in a deep-rooted Francophone
community.

She had envisioned her marriage to Jean-Pierre as one of
convenience, as two dissimilar partners sharing financial interests,
like two parts of the same country. She believed such an arrange-
ment to be advantageous in many ways, as she would never hesitate to dip into Jean-Pierre's savings as she deemed necessary, as
love for her was a one-way street in which she stood at the receiving end. She expected an unconditional devotion, even though she
herself didn't feel bound by love or fidelity, and would never tolerate the disgrace of a divorce she would not have initiated without
crushing her former partner under the weight of a ruinous ali-
mony.

Now, she wondered whether such a wedding was still possible, whether exposure of the distant uncle's political doctrine
would force the couple to discuss sensitive matters that could at
best generate unnecessary tensions, at worst break up their lovely
union. She was anxious at the re-emergence of national allegiance
sentiments that she long repressed, and all the ensuing arguments
about historical grievances and slights, about rights and dues, and
endless unwarranted blame and accusations that she abhorred.
For a moment, she regretted not having picked a more established
boyfriend, 20 to 30 years her senior, well anchored in the English-
Canadian establishment, although she reckoned such a choice also
came with its own emotional baggage and challenges.

Her deep frustrations had no immediate solutions, as a simple, straightforward future that seemed so crisp and clear no longer
existed, drowned in the fog of human deceptions. She was rattled,
deeply confused, and expected the worst.

Yet, all of Audréanne's consuming anxieties were rather
benign compared to those of François Laflamme. For weeks,
François had either had terrifying nightmares or couldn't sleep

altogether. His best friend and colleague barely escaped from a burning building that unpredictably collapsed. Only then, after that close call, did it strike him that while heroes die heroic deaths, they are no less fatal. Death has a certain leveling quality beyond its threshold in that the circumstances to the journey there are inconsequential—once departed, there is no turning back.

Only popping Valium like candy could knock him unconscious enough to erase his nightmarish visions of widows and orphans surrounded by dancing flames. But the medication that drained his anxieties also depleted his resolve to search for a less hazardous job, as decades of training to be a hero weren't easily overridden by a few acute stress reactions and panic attacks, and when the earthquake struck, his call to duty was stronger than the worried appeals to stay that he could read in the tormented but proud eyes of his wife and daughter.

Unfortunately, François would not read love in the beauty of those eyes again. The Valium's benzodiazepines that depressed his central nervous system, mixed with the morphine prescribed by Audréanne and those injected earlier by the paramedics, combined into a cocktail certain to induce fatal respiratory depression. At the onset of hypoventilation, the increased concentration of carbon dioxide and acidity in his blood transformed it into a corrosive poison slowly pumped throughout his entire body. Eventually though, it was his complete failure to breathe, coincidental with his cardiac arrest, that turned out to be most problematic for survival.

François died unattended in a stretcher on the terrazzo floor of a hospital, as if it made any difference.

Toronto, 9:30 p.m.

Norito Sanbiiru was struggling. He had been drafted to Professor Nomiya's earthquake reconnaissance team on the merit of having received the highest grade in English during the university's entrance exams. However, while this distinction reflected his ability to read and successfully regurgitate on paper standard answers to standard English exams questions—or at least his ability to do so at a level above his peers—his verbal aptitude was limited to the standard class drills in which groups of pupils recite without conviction phonetics chained into inane sentences incoherent to most involved in the ritual chanting. He felt that local culture and convenient Japanese translation of all foreign media had sheltered many in his generation from the hardship and inconvenience of having to master a foreign language on top of the other excessive demands of the academic curricula.

The opportunity to state that "John plays with the red ball," something that Sanbiiru could have most competently recited, unfortunately did not materialize. Nor could he understand a word of what the Air Canada representative repeated, each time talking more slowly and loudly, as if increasing the volume of her statements would magically metamorphose meaningless noise into coherent sentences.

Nonetheless, to save face, Sanbiiru informed Professor Nomiya that the airline had no idea what had happened to the 50 boxes of supplies checked by the Japanese team. Professor Nomiya had pretty much accepted this fabricated but plausible scenario, when the Air Canada agent took the initiative to draw a sketch showing a cartoon plane following an arrow from Tokyo to Toronto, and a bunch of suitcases following a different arrow to Vancouver. Sanbiiru understood then that he would have to spend long nights drafting figures and formatting the team report as punishment for having lied to his superior.

Professor Nomiya, helped by his English-Japanese dictionary, asked, "Wen-o Toronto?"

In response, the Air Canada representative doodled a clock whose arms suggested that the team would continue wearing the same clothes for another 17 hours.

Visibly unpleased but calm, he nodded and proceeded with his cohort towards the exit indicated to be nearest to the taxi stand. Lost luggage was more an annoyance than shock. The true shock to the Nomiya team occurred upon the first breath of fresh Canadian winter air as they exited the International Terminal. Toronto, warmer than Montréal as always, was a balmy -20°F, tempered by a virile wind chill factor that pushed the cool air through the fine fabrics worn by the Japanese delegation. They immediately retreated inside the terminal, pondering how one could possibly hail a taxi to the hotel without having to set foot outside.

All of Nomiya's contractual disciples hoped he would elect to return to Japan at once. They were convinced that nowhere in Hokkaido did it ever get that cold, even though most of them had never set foot beyond the southern tip of Japan's northernmost island. But Nomiya was determined to collect valuable information from this disaster, an international one to boot.

Too many times he had been excluded from national disaster reconnaissance activities. Given Japan's exposure to earthquakes, volcanos, typhoons, tsunamis, conflagrations, landslides, industrial mishaps, terrorist attacks, and many others, like a giant department store stocked with every conceivable disaster ready to obliterate Japanese civilization like an amuck Godzilla, his pent-up frustration at being snubbed by the big national disaster reconnaissance teams was considerable. Only once had he been invited to participate in a reconnaissance effort—and only because it required a massive human investment. After the 1995 earthquake that devastated Kobe and its surrounding areas, the Architectural Institute of Japan undertook to survey the extent of damage over the entire city. North to south, the entire city was divided in regular narrow strips a few miles long, each to be surveyed by a different team from the eastern waterfront up to the last street in the westward hills. Not surprisingly, his team was assigned the northernmost such strip, included in the global survey to delimit the geographical extent of damaging earthquake excitations and to ensure completeness of the data collected by the overall expedition, but where all evidence of damage was limited to a few cracks in the stucco of residential constructions, possibly pre-dating the earthquake and due to other causes. It was clear that unless Ultraman himself showed up on his doorstep and hand-delivered him front-row tickets to his private urban demolition derby, his opportunities to frolic knee-deep in damaged Japanese infrastructure searching for discoveries of national significance would forever be impeded.

His self-initiated impulsive travel to Toronto breached all etiquette in a country rigorously respectful of stringent hierarchical protocols, but he knew that by beating the official national delegation by weeks, he could collect perishable data and publish the most comprehensive and earliest Japanese reconnaissance report. If only he could reach the taxis without volunteering for a cryonics treatment.

Scanning the hallways while reflecting on possible solutions, Professor Nomiya spotted a catchy front-page headline hanging from the newspaper stand: "World Expert claims: DND HQ earthquake damage due to improper concrete." He did not need a dictionary to translate "world expert," "earthquake," "damage," and "concrete." Any lingering immense desire to return to Japan and escape the brutal cold died right then. He had just found a way to collect data for his report without having to freeze to death. All he needed was to find this "World Expert" and convince him of the benefit of teaming up with his delegation. The lure of a free trip to Japan to share his research findings and an offer to translate his expert report in Japanese might prove to be sufficient for this purpose, but he was ready to expend some of his university's resources, too, if necessary. A golden partnership—a true win-win situation.

Ordered to purchase the paper and translate its lead article at once, Sanbiiru jumped with delight at the chance to redeem himself.

With an unbridled optimism, Nomiya was convinced that two incomplete, mismatched pieces could be assembled into a coherent, harmonious whole, just like poisonous chloride combines with alkali sodium metal to create the salt prized by countless civilizations, or like dangerously flammable hydrogen links to colorless and odorless oxygen to sustain all life on earth. While Nomiya's conviction was absolute, it remained to be established in the minds of his junior colleagues whether two professors of mismatched expertise, egotistical in the best academic tradition, could marry their debatable, dissimilar strengths and flaws to generate a useful and competent outcome.

Québec City, 10:00 p.m.

Léandre's team had secured the privileged 10 p.m. time slot, the acknowledged prime evening news window for the Québécois audience. They strategically felt that reaching a broader audience would more than overcome giving the Decker team the opportunity to rebut key points of Léandre's address to the nation—they also strongly believed that the Canadian Premier would adhere to his meticulously crafted script; he was rarely known to ad-lib under pressure. Irrespectively, an army of spin-masters was already in post, scattered across the province's editorial rooms and debate forums, ready to highjack all the available time following the address with their respective biased opinions of the evening's outcome. Media coverage was absolute: all national news-able television and radio stations were set to broadcast the event, and the cable and satellite providers had decided to interrupt their specialty programming to ensure all available eyeballs would be captive of one of the news channels.

Almost 48 hours after the ground had shaken, it was assumed, or hoped, that all Montréalais would have been able to find a portable radio, or to congregate with others who had, to join the rest of the Province in this solemn moment. Nonetheless, although the broadcast had an ominous sense of urgency, all understood that it would also serve to project leadership and feed the media archives with one-liners that would be replayed endlessly to promote the sovereignty agenda at the appropriate time. For that reason, it was decided to fly Léandre and his staff back to the capital and deliver the speech directly from the Premier's office, to establish the unequivocal, commanding statesmanship image that the situation required, but also to ensure the high-quality, glitch-free broadcast crucial to assert with authority that the state was in absolute control.

Léandre approached every speech of national strategic significance as a chef about to prepare a classic dish. While the recipe was well known, and a competent execution could be fulfilling, the true master found no contentment in mere execution but rather aimed at surprising beyond expectations; the true art of concocting a delight on the virtue of balancing, on one hand, respect for a timeless, well-tested and successful dogma, and on the other hand, boldness and creativity to invigorate a stale formula.

The *plat du jour* that evening was *Redirecting Blame for an Un-pleasant Situation, with an Appeal to Nationalistic Pride*, a bitter-tasting dish made more palatable by generous sugarcoating.

A red globe alighting on the camera directly facing Léandre provided the needed cue.

"My dear friends. The past two days have been trying to many of you. Some members of our great Québécois family have suffered unduly and have suddenly lost a lot, materially as well as emotionally. To those of you who have suffered such losses, particularly of beloved friends and family, our most sincere sympathies are with you at this time. No one can ever mend the wounds and the shattering pain inflicted by loss of the beloved, but our hearts are open and companionate to your grief and mourning, our shoulders steady for your tears. Rest assured that the Québec government will do everything in its power and capabilities to ease your burden and restore life to economic normalcy with the briefest possible delay."

In a large bowl, copiously rub sympathy until all is wet. Appeal to pride, and spread generously until it adheres to all surfaces (leave the residue in the bottom to provide a basis for other sustaining ingredients).

"Our great nation has encountered adversity in many challenging ways in the past, and through the pride, ingenuity, perseverance, courage and resilience of our citizens, we have always overcome. This time will be no different. I know this without a doubt, because I know the greatness of our people. This hardship is but one more obstacle on our path to self-determination, and Québécois know better than to despair and lose hope. The Québécois way is to rise up to the challenge, confront the problem head-on, bring down the barriers; and move ahead to the most effective recovery, rebuilding with confidence, in full knowledge, such that the past will not be repeated."

Before adding the main ingredients, pour one teaspoon of populist sap, to provide colorful blending opportunities.

"Yesterday, I met *Mademoiselle* Tremblay who suffered unbearable grief through this tragic event. *Mlle* Tremblay's home was effectively destroyed by this earthquake. Her home was built 30 years ago in accordance with the norms of a building code, developed by the Canadian government, that proved to provide insufficient protection. While she was fortunately away from home, working a night shift when the earthquake struck, her brother and father who were visiting for a few days, perished. The place where she worked suffered severe damage and is closed indefinitely. *Mlle* Tremblay lost her family, her belongings, her job, all in a few short seconds. After she candidly shared with me her suffering, in the same breath, she asked me how she could be of service to help her beloved city recover. Her courage is a true inspiration, a testimony of the Québécois' resilience and strength. I promised *Mlle* Tremblay that my government would do everything in its power to ease the suffering of all our compatriots who were so dramatically hurt by this tragedy."

Léandre's aides and advisors knew nobody could ever disprove this alleged encounter, considering there were 35 pages of Tremblays in Montréal's phonebook, and that Léandre presented all information as received first-hand from this fictitious *Mlle* Tremblay.

Add one cup of sifted leadership, and two cups of iced reality, preferably crushed to prevent lumps that will not mix well with the other ingredients. Vigorously stir to a smooth paste; the intended texture is achieved when the paste is easy to swallow—beware that this rough dough could induce some dizziness at this stage, as it is missing some of the final ingredients.

"We have already made great strides in forwarding emergency help to those that can be most immediately reached, in containing hazardous materials released by the earthquake, in preventing access and securing zones around some of the most severely damaged facilities tethering dangerously on the verge of collapse, in establishing access routes to the core of our city to restore basic transportation capabilities, and in marshaling our efforts to undertake the strategic tasks essential to ensure that our infrastructure lifelines and critical facilities can be restored with the highest priority. Yet, at this time, ground access to Montréal is not possible through any bridge. Inspectors from the Ministry of Transportation have been dispatched from across the province to review the structural integrity of all bridges in the metropolitan area, and engineers are assessing means to expeditiously repair the damaged bridges. Damage to the Hydro-Québec network is generally confined to distribution stations and is due to a number of causes, including equipment crushed by collapsed control buildings and failure of transformers and switching equipment as a result of the severe shaking."

Some of these damage assessments presented as facts were substantial speculations, judged credible by Léandre's team based on James's earlier educated guesses, but wrapped into enough weasel words to allow for future elegant corrections.

"Even though the power lines and the rest of the distribution network appears to be intact, progressive restoration of service will be hampered by challenges in securing and shipping replacement parts in these difficult conditions, particularly for the largest transformers. Similar measures are underway to restore other services, such as gas and telephone.

"In all instances, technical support crews from across Québec, as well as from utility companies of other provinces and the Northeastern United States, will be on their way to the city once access to the island is possible, and will help expedite repair of the network—as is always the case following large power outages. To coordinate all aspects of what will be the most complex response and recovery operation ever conducted on the continent, I have created a new position of Chief of Emergency Response that simultaneously overtakes all functions of the *Organisation de sécurité civile du Québec*, and appointed a most capable individual to serve in these functions—as described in more details in a separate communique being distributed to all news agencies. Over the next few days, complete information on all the extensive and complex response and recovery measures that are being enacted as we speak will be shared with the population by the Chief of Emergency Response, directly or through our emergency response units and governments agencies. Your collaboration in ensuring success of those operations is key.

"Yet, while help is forthcoming, past experience following similar disasters worldwide suggests that you should be prepared to be on your own, without water, electricity or other services, for at least 72 hours."

In his morning exposé, James had mentioned this oft-referenced rule of thumb, emphasizing that, while there existed no theoretical basis to support the magic number of 72 hours, it was used to convey the stern message that passively waiting for instantaneous government assistance was unrealistic, and to prompt the population to take initiative and be ready to fend for itself for an extended period. However, Léandre purposely blurred the time line, whereas past experience referred to 72 hours from the initial shock, his speech had just reset the clock to zero, adding an extra two days to the rule of thumb.

"Those with water service are strongly advised to boil any water before consuming it, until further notice. In many instances, for some specific neighborhoods, emergency shelters provided across the city will be the only locations where water and power will be available, together with food and other sheltering service. The list of those shelters has been made available earlier, and will be repeated following this broadcast. If you assess your current situation as unsustainable for the next 72 hours, you should proceed to one of those shelters at once."

Léandre took some creative license to pacify distress and feelings of abandonment, inventing teams that likely were still just embryonic in James's mind.

"In recognition that some of you may need assistance in reaching such safe havens, special teams currently canvassing the city to survey the full extent of damage have been given the additional mandate of providing such assistance whenever appropriate. Feel free to seek assistance should you encounter one of these teams. However, given the enormity and urgency of their primary task, please appreciate that members of these teams cannot provide you with specific assistance to either evaluate the state of damage to your personal home, nor can they provide personalized assistance to restore services or functionality to your dwelling. Other teams of experts will follow with the ability to provide such services. Please respect the need for the precursor teams to expedite their survey and allow them to focus on their immediate duty."

Generously add sugar, selected artificial flavorings and colors.

"Clearly, the magnitude of this disaster could have been greatly mitigated if the federal government had used a small part of the billions of tax dollars it collected in Québec to develop adequate building codes and to train highly capable, proficient, and technically relevant emergency response teams. Instead, these funds were used to further the political agenda of those in power, an agenda at odds with our social and economical interests. In contrition, the federal government will offer financial assistance to those who suffered heavy economical losses, and dispatch its ill-equipped and unprepared army to, at best, protect against looting. This limited aid is the response of a federal government compelled to provide the illusion of compassion and of effective response, a meager return on the financial investment in federalism made by all citizens through their tax dollars. A federal government hoping that a sprinkling of money and labor, all wrapped in a discourse far more generous in words than actions, will hide its incompetence and inability to provide the tangible help that is urgently needed, and will blind us from the failure of its past complacent policies toward Québec and its failure to address the exposure to seismic risk of our nation.

"These mistakes should never be repeated. Never again shall we rely on disinterested federal agencies to quantify the seismic hazards in Québec, to mitigate the seismic risks, and to protect our citizens against existing seismic risks.

"Never again!

"I assure you that when, at last, we will be fully able to control our destiny as a nation, we will instigate the most rigorous building standards and codes to ensure that all future construction will be able to perform at the highest possible level. Furthermore, we will undertake an extensive program of rehabilitation of the critical infrastructure across all regions exposed to significant seismic risk."

Léandre's colleagues noted that enough qualifiers had been planted in the above promises to provide plenty of room to maneuver within the entire political spectrum of resource allocations—in particular, no deadlines or fiscal envelopes were set, providing absolute freedom in designing future policies, all conditional to a successful referendum.

Pour the resulting concoction in an enormous pan, and set to simmer for an undetermined time. Observe throughout the cooking phase and be ready to take out and serve when judged appropriate. Progressively probe for adequate consistency and stir periodically.

"Given our need to focus on the enormous reconstruction task ahead of us, and because our thoughts and attention must be toward those of us most severely affected by this tragic event, it is necessary for my government to postpone to an indeterminate time the currently scheduled referendum on our right to self-determination. As disappointing as it may be, I trust all will share my conviction that such an important decision must be made with a fresh and rested mind, and undistracted by other, more pressing emergencies. However, rest assured that this referendum remains a top priority of my government and will be held as soon as practically feasible within our current term in power, such that a positive endorsement of this societal project can be our mandate to implement in the subsequent term."

Ready to serve. Lay gracefully on a large plate, decorate with a colorful array of vegetables, and savor with a glass of wine.

"Citizens of our nation, Québécois, Québécoise, I bid you all courage facing the adversity of the next few weeks. Rest assured that, together with your own individual or concerted efforts, our government is fully invested in restoring our way of life as its utmost priority, and will spare no effort or cost in this endeavor. Montréal and Québec will be brought back to its phenomenal beauty, as the home of our great nation."

Léandre was delighted with his message and performance. Never one to doubt for a moment his political talents, always arrogantly confident of his superiority, the opposite would have been surprising. However, even though he pictured himself soaring like an eagle above the tree line on a daily basis, the thrill of occasionally reaching for the tallest summits always immersed him in powerfully inebriating levels of dopamine. That it required draining the life of his supporters, crushing detractors and dissidents on this path, and the dictatorial commandeering of an infinite amount of resources, only added to his orgasm.

Ottawa, 10:30 p.m.

The Decker team, attentive and critical of Léandre's speech, had identified many weaknesses and unsubstantiated claims that could be exploited by Brendon. Unfortunately, they also knew that the Prime Minister was set to follow his own script and would not honor Léandre's dithyramb with a rebuttal, no matter how easy and justified it might have been.

To their great despair, they knew that Brendon designed each of his key speeches as if they were a piece of origami, meticulously structured per a pattern of folds unintelligible at the onset, but hopefully resulting in a nice outcome that all could appreciate in the end. As such, ad-libs were perilous and disturbing, like improvisation to the art of origami.

Brendon was thus set to read another dull speech that would rally the unconditional party members, and present an apparently rational, alternative option to those ready to sway their allegiance at a specific conjuncture. This earthquake might have offered such a crossroads.

Broadcasting from the Parliament Hill studio, Canadian flags covering every pixel surrounding the talking head on high-definition monitor, Brendon addressed the population of Québec in English. As usual, this served to remind English Canadians in Québec that they should continue to recognize themselves as part of the Canadian majority and never surrender to the thought of being merely a minority within the anachronism of a French-speaking province. It also signaled that he would not compromise his nature and convictions to serve popular desires.

Brendon despised those countless federal politicians, past or present, who injected snippets of disjointed French into their protracted parliamentary orations, blatantly catering to the evening news and faking a sincere commitment to Canada's linguistic duality, serving the sound bites as a paltry subterfuge to bait suckers into believing the illusionary political construct of the two harmonious founding nations. As such, his message to the French-speaking Québécois majority would be conveyed through the artifice of simultaneous translation.

Besides, Brendon's lamentable French elocution, although rarely heard, provided prime material for impersonators and comics, and he was on a crusade to deprive them of as much of it as possible. Nonetheless, his abundant other personality quirks and demeanor provided French and English Canadian comedians alike with a bountiful supply of twisted opportunities to harvest laughs at his expense, ensuring that they would never starve for as long as he would partake in the follies of political life.

With his usual stern, deadpan style, staring straight at the nation with an intensity that frightened small kids and unnerved their parents, Brendon embarked on his inspirational speech.

Take a large sheet of paper and fold twice to cut the task to size. Keep the decorative printed patterns visible on the outside folded faces, as these insignificant yet colorful designs sometimes matter just as much as substance—if not more.

"My fellow Canadians. As in countless times in our history, a key part of our prosperous nation is suffering from a natural disaster. Many of you in the prairies will remember the terrible floods that struck Manitoba years ago, others will recall droughts, tornados, blizzards that affected your region. This time, and for the first time in Canadian history, a major earthquake has struck a major Canadian urban center, with damage spreading over significant distances. Montreal and Ottawa in particular have suffered grievously."

Brendon's advisors had suggested that blending the small damage felt in Ottawa with the devastation in Montreal would help garner sympathy from across the country, particularly from those parts of the country with antagonistic tendencies toward Québec in those pre-referendum times.

"The hardship that is being suffered by many Canadians is deeply felt, and I wish to offer my deepest sympathy to those that have suffered and continue to suffer through this tragedy. I sincerely feel your sorrow and your pain, with the same empathy felt and shared by your fellow Canadians, whom I know are ready to extend a helping hand, in the purest Canadian tradition.

"Amidst this compassion, we stand with resolve to help implement an expeditious recovery. My government has mobilized and dispatched key units of our experienced military forces, recognized worldwide for the quality of their humanitarian support and ability to provide emergency response assistance and rescue. As one example of how this highly trained national resource can help abate the hardship from this disaster, our Canadian army's unique portable water-purification equipment will be able to provide affected populations with safe drinking water while waiting for the restoration of reliable municipal water treatment services."

Perform all the small folds in rapid sequence, following the patterns established from times immemorial, to establish the core shape and functionality of the origami piece.

"Fortunately, Canada is a large and resourceful country, and those affected by this earthquake will benefit from the resources and capabilities of the entire country, both from the mobilized citizens as well as from the federal government. Our technologically advanced agencies have provided and will continue to provide the necessary support to recover from this disaster and to prevent future recurrence of similar catastrophes.

"The occurrence of devastating earthquakes is extremely rare in Canada, and Earthquakes Canada has done an outstanding job of mapping the regions of the country where such a hazard is most likely to occur, with the development of world-class probabilistic models and leading state-of-the-art science. These seismological maps are at the core of the seismic design provisions of the National Building Code of Canada, a leading model code that has ensured construction of the highest quality across the country for decades, a document copied by many other countries, and that serves as a model for the building codes adopted verbatim by each individual province as part of their responsibility to regulate construction.

"With respect to response and recovery, Public Safety Canada has extensive and state-of-the-art training programs available to its counterpart provincial agencies, and has taken a leadership role to ensure that all Canadians receive the best attention to minimize hardships following a disaster, maximize the number of lives saved, expedite treatment of injuries, and achieve the promptest recovery possible. Many provinces have taken advantage of these services over the years, and will continue to do so.

"Damaging earthquakes are extremely rare, as no lives were ever lost due to earthquakes in Canada until this recent and most unfortunate event. And while we have good reason to believe that another such extreme event is unlikely to occur over the next century, we will nonetheless continue to enhance our level of preparedness to further minimize such future risk. Thankfully, through our unity, and the extensive network of resources and partnerships across this beautiful country of ours, we will, as Canadians, be able to mitigate the impact of such future earthquakes to an extent that smaller countries cannot; we will be able to prevent and possibly eliminate future disasters to an extent that smaller countries cannot; and we will be able to adequately compensate the victims of this natural disaster to an extent that smaller countries cannot."

Brendon stalled for a moment. At this point, inserted in the text of his speech, scrolling unread on the Teleprompter, were a bunch of saccharine pacifistic statements that proclaimed, "Insufferable hardships need open arms and compassion, not closed fists and confrontations. Combining our inner strengths and our humanity, we will resolve any crisis. The door is open."

Clearly, some peacenik had tampered with his speech, likely forging his handwriting in the margins of the manuscript he'd sent for typing. It was laughably naive to expect such an insipid prank to derail a hardened politician with decades of experience in defeating subversive attacks. As discreetly as possible, temper in check, careful not to broadcast his frustration, he pulled his original manuscript from the corner of the desk and flipped to the last page, ready to close with his own words.

Finish with the decorative folds that enrich and add credibility to the final origami. Display for others to admire.

"Citizens of our Canada, I know you are invested with the strongest resolve in facing the catastrophe. Rest assured that our government shares the same resolve to bring the devastated cities back to their former glory, and return our society to its way of life. We will spare no effort, spare no cost, and let no barrier stop us toward these goals. Together, we will recover, because we need to be together to prosper, to grow, and to promote our values and stature as a tolerant and diverse society among the brotherhood of nations."

Brendon's last words rolled into a smirk, unable to conceal his conviction that his speech had dealt a fatal blow to his separatist foes—that history had been written. Delighted by this smashing success, in a giddy spirit, filled by a perverse ecstasy, he strolled across the studio, and in lieu of displaying the glowing smile of satisfaction that burned inside, he dispensed in a dignified way a thumbs-up and affectionate, vigorous slaps on the shoulders to all present. In that mood, had it been a party, he might even have told the few dirty jokes he remembered.

However, as would be later revealed by ratings and polls of television viewers, from 10 p.m. to 11 p.m. Eastern Standard Time, across the country, fewer than 10% of 30- to 50-year-olds watched television at all that night. Ratings for the two speeches were also in the shadow of about two dozen shows in the same time slot from the preceding week, including the ratings for reruns of *I Love Lucy* episodes amongst 50-year-old and older viewers. The same surveys indicated that the 18-30-years-old segment of population preferred instead to play video games while awaiting the deferred broadcast of the MTV Canada Awards; for one short minute, when news of the disaster had become known, MTV Canada had considered canceling the show that was originally scheduled for that night, but quickly came back to their senses after computing how much money they stood to lose. They feigned anger at being forced at the last minute to postpone the start of the awards ceremony till after the two speeches, but knew from the demographics of their audience that its dominant age group would embrace the schedule shift with the bragging pride of night-owls.

Radio auditors, for the most part gathered in shelters across Montréal or having taken refuge wherever they found a helping hand—more fateful listeners, for lack of better things to do—paid close attention to each word of both speeches, waiting for that glimmer of hope in a dark and cold evening. But actions would matter more than words over the next few months for these votes up for grabs.

Québec City, 11:59 p.m.

Réal immediately recognized the familiar phone number that flashed on the screen of his muted cell phone throughout the evening. A call that both parties understood didn't require answering, as some conversations must remain beyond the reach of digital eavesdropping. The call was nothing more than a code, prompting him to call back when alone, on a presumably more secure, anonymous wired line.

Just to be extra cautious, he sat in a private phone booth of the *Château Frontenac* to dial the special number Kaylee Carling had given him years ago, one that rang in a friend's apartment that she only borrowed once in a while to avoid wiretaps.

The warm voice, soft as silk, betrayed the true purpose of the business at hand.

"Hi, Réal. It's been a while."

"It's always a pleasure to rekindle the fire."

They both knew what it implied.

"We need to talk. Our bosses don't have the faintest idea on how to fix this mess."

Réal couldn't agree more. He was particularly offended that Léandre hadn't consulted him before appointing, of all things, an Ontarian to lead the *Organisation de sécurité civile du Québec*. He would have strongly advised against such a misjudgment that, in his opinion, amounted to nothing more than political prostitution of the worst kind: sleeping with the enemy. Besides, it happened so few hours after his own appointment as interim director of the *Organisation* that the capital was surely abuzz with political gossip speculating on his possible fall from grace, his resulting loss of influence, even his political demise. Back-stabbing is rife in political life, but none in the rich collection of knives he carried on his back were more painful than the ones planted by his friends.

"Worse, they're going to screw up everybody in the process. They're both dangerously aloof," added Réal.

Feared or befriended, they both considered their bosses to be leaders of inferior intellect whom they'd supplant in due time—in spite of their continued unconditional support or decades of absolute friendship. Opportunities, conveniences, mutualism, commensalism, amensalism, or parasitism, Réal considered friendship to be a relative currency and an evolving value in a society that calls "best friend" an animal given 20 feet of leash and the freedom to defecate at will during a daily 20-minute, monitored walk.

"Let's meet tomorrow morning in the conference room," suggested Kaylee.

This was code for the suite in Plattsburgh, south of the border, far from the highway and close to the lake, where they sometimes met, a few nights at a time, off the tourist season, checking in separately, incognito, wearing oversized hats and sunglasses as an additional precaution against the odd encounter with an expatriate or with the rare American who cared about Canadian politics enough to recognize cabinet ministers.

The four-hour drive from Québec City was inconvenient, and escaping at a time when Léandre would be heavily leaning on him would require fabricating some clever lies to justify his need to drive alone to Montréal, before banking due south for an undetected detour to Plattsburg, but Réal never missed the rare chances to hook up with Kaylee. Particularly given that she could do things that he'd once thought were physiologically impossible.

Some allegiances are just stronger than others.

Epilogue

Exponential Decays

Eighteen Months Later

Shock, pain, and outrage, were mollified into daze, numbness, and indifference by the dulling continuum of time. Media helping, losses and suffering could hold attention captive for a few months, but no more, as if human nature was wired to favor routine over crisis, like a necessary panacea for coping with the imponderable and uncontrollable risks of life.

After more than a full calendar cycle of normalcy, after 18 utility bills, 18 phone bills, 75 visits to the grocery store, a thousand home cooked meals, lots of fast food, a few good restaurants, visits to the dentist, to the doctor, hundreds of miles of jogging, too much cholesterol, high blood pressure, kids' homework and runny noses, 8,000 miles in crawling traffic, and too few weeks of vacation, whatever social ills which once seemed so urgently in need of fixing became a blurry memory.

The rock-solid popular support urging immediate reforms and fundamental systemic transformations, eroded away under the regular and incessant pounding of daily insignificant crises—as if nobody could muster the stamina to sustain sanity under the continuous and persistent torture of small water droplets repeatedly pounding the forehead, slowly drilling through the thin armor of flesh.

Once phone service had been restored, to most within one month, once the last victim of power-outage was reconnected to the distribution grid, after 9 months, and once the last damaged transportation infrastructure link was re-opened, after 15 months, the instinctive impulse to return to normalcy rendered invisible the many remaining visible scars from the earthquake. Commuters could now drive without pause past piles of debris and condemned buildings awaiting demolition, immune to the symbolic reminders of hardships past—an exponential decay of sensitivity to otherwise unsettling circumstances, as a pernicious effect of disaster recovery.

Landmarks were the exception to the rule, and the collapsed tower of the Olympic Stadium, driven into the ground as a giant stake at one end, and propped by the stadium's fishbowl rim at the other, with loose post-tensioning wires ripped out of concrete, giving a semblance of connection to its former concrete pedestal, was one such unavoidable eyesore that affected all passersby. Emotions ranging from deep sadness to boiling anger were evoked by this gigantic monument to failed engineering, which just couldn't be ignored. Popular agitators seized the issue and provided tribunes to stir these emotions to a boil, wasting countless time and energy in the polemics of whether to obliterate or repair the landmark.

Recognizing the symbolic and political consequences of the decision, the Premier unilaterally cut through the polarized debate and refused to write the last chapter in the love-hate relationship of Québécois with their white elephant. On the edifying advice of friends who happened to lead local engineering and architectural firms, he imposed a four-step compromise that consisted of demolishing the unsalvageable tower as quickly as possible without inducing additional damage to the remaining structure, reconstructing the damaged portions of the stadium bowl, capping the remaining tower stub with some attractive postmodern architectural concept to confer a distinct identity to the repaired structure and avoid any comparison of the new landmark to an emasculated version of its previous incarnation, and finding an ingenious strategy to provide a roof to the remaining bowl—that last part being the most challenging and contentious aspect of the project, as had always been the case throughout the history of the stadium. Beyond the tedious decision-making exercise to converge on a concept agreeable to architectural artistic sensibility, engineering pragmatism, and some measure of fiscal frugality, execution of this nation-building project turned out to be significantly more difficult than anticipated.

Every special interest group weighed in, ramming demand after demand to steer the process in ways that protected or promoted their agendas. The original demolition plans called for controlled explosions to bring down the mast structure in one swoop, but neighborhood groups objected on concerns that it would generate an enormous cloud of dust that would shower them with asbestos (that had been presumably used inside the tower) and toxic chemicals (alleged to have leached from the artificial turf into the base concrete over the years). Environmental groups argued that the materials to be used in the proposed new stadium roof were fabricated using technologies that had an offensively excessive carbon footprint. Conservancy groups alleged that the same roof, in absence of the tall adjacent tower that used to exist, had unusual height and proportions that would confuse and present a hazard to migratory birds listed as endangered species. Even Feng Shui disciples, community planning groups, Raëliens, trade unions, and dozens of recognized associations or obscure lunatic fringe groups felt compelled to partake in the public orgy, even if uninvited to the roundtable.

After due consideration of all options on how to implement the chosen concept and yet please the whims of a myriad of constituencies, it was determined that a systematic pneumatic hammering and deconstruction sequence was the preferred approach to remove the damaged structure. The large-scale equivalent of a pick-and-shovel job, it required construction of massive falseworks to temporarily support the tower throughout this process. As a result, cost estimates tripled from original projections, to the great despair of government officials who had no other option than to move forward.

Yet, all the brick-and-mortar ruptures, steel- and bolt-fractures, concrete-and-rebar failures, belied the flesh-and-blood losses.

One thousand, two hundred and forty seven persons died in this earthquake, and roughly 15,000 were injured. This relatively low number of casualties was attributed to the fact that the earthquake occurred at a time when most were at home. The city's wood-frame residential constructions were racked and twisted, shedding their masonry veneers in the process, but they were able to resist the ground shaking without life-threatening damage. Had the earthquake struck midday of a workday, tens of thousand people would have been crushed to death in the office buildings that suffered severe damage or collapsed, and many more would have been squashed under the collapsed spans of bridges.

Half of the human lives lost were imputed to the cold weather, either as trapped victims frozen to death while awaiting rescue, or as short-lived survivors collapsed under the biting cold when unable to find adequate shelter or health services in the hours and days following the earthquake.

Not tallied in the official statistics, escaping the notice of bean counters but felt everyday by those suffering the sting of debilitating injuries, were the negative impact on the population's health due to the temporary deprivation of health services, or due to the long delays in re-establishing the health care infrastructure to its pre-earthquake conditions—corresponding to a level of service which, by itself, was already argued by many to be below an acceptable minimum standard. All actuarial reports also failed to recognize the long-term public health problems attributable to this earthquake, particularly the emotional distress of the families rendered homeless by the fires that leveled Pointe-Aux-Trembles into a field of charred foundations in neat rows across the scorched earth. Also unaccounted in the numbers was the health loss of the many who contracted acute chronic diseases, and whose symptoms only emerged after tons of chemicals were dispersed in the atmosphere, and for whom years of litigation and studies to link cause and effects would enrich lawyers and scientists alike, rather than the victims.

A year and a half after the disaster, damage and other tangible losses attributed to the earthquake were assessed at $100 billion. Indirect losses, such as disruption to business activities and other impacts on the economy, were estimated at $75 billion. The combined losses amounted to the most expensive disaster in Canadian history. This sizeable bill could only be footed by pooling the resources of diverse donors and creditors. First World countries, who usually contribute generously to help Second or Third World nations recover from disasters, mostly contributed to this recovery by sharing rescue teams and donating some emergency supplies, as those developed countries elected to use restraint and carefully weigh the political implications of forwarding financial aid during the crisis. The perception, reinforced by heated rhetoric, was that, as a matter of national pride, both the provincial and federal governments preferred to suffer in silence rather than risk tarnishing the image of self-reliance and economic strength and stability that they wished to project to the international community.

As such, many were surprised by the multi-billion dollar donation announced by the government of France three days following the disaster, and gratefully accepted by the Québec government, on the "basis of the strong and durable friendship between the two sister nations." This illegitimate intrusion into national politics, thrust onto the public scene with the arrogance of an inducement to prostitution, forced the Canadian government to promptly loosen the strings of its purse and rescind all the fiscally prudent conditions and financial restrictions that had been, years earlier, legislated into the Disaster Financial Assistance Arrangements as safeguards against the largesse of any government tempted to squander the public treasury to purchase political capital.

This sudden opening of the monetary floodgates gave the Québec government an upper hand in claiming that the released funds amounted to no more than a long overdue return of the taxes paid by the province's citizens to federal coffers—dollars that, in other circumstances, would have been available anyhow to spend for the same purposes by a sovereign Québec government free from the yoke of greedy feudal lords.

Sustained bickering between the federal and provincial governments succeeded in hiding from confused observers where true responsibilities and blame lied, but unnecessarily delayed recovery. In spite of the downpour of government assistance, and of other creative financial relief schemes launched to bankroll the recovery process, the extreme hardship afflicting business communities and individual citizens strained the national economy—except for profiteers who prospered immensely, exploiting the misery of their compatriots.

In the first 18 months of the post-earthquake saga, survivors navigated through the turmoil on the winding road of life, driven by the same instincts, impulses, desires, fears, and egos, as if stringing successes and failures together into an amulet to ward off the precarious grip of death on humanity.

James Laroque cashed in his early retirement plan from the National Research Council of Canada, and acted as an expert advisor for the Québec government for 12 months. While he valued the opportunity to have a meaningful impact on the recovery process and policies needed to ensure a more resilient infrastructure against future disasters, he quickly became frustrated with the endless political shenanigans and obstructionism. A public relations firm retained to investigate his marketability concluded from surveys that he had a better than decent chance in the political arena on the strength of name recognition and the positive public perception he garnered from his successful coordination of the recovery process. The data indicated that his electability was greatest in Québec, although it remained high from coast to coast. Untainted by any ideology other than a strong technocratic bias, he was courted by political parties of all allegiances, including Léandre's.

Professor Yago Krapo retired from Saint-Chretistic Technological University and took a permanent visiting professor position at the South Hokkaido Institute of Technology, in Japan, where he could devote his time to research on topics of great interest to no one but himself and his colleague, Professor Nomiya, who delighted in the stellar addition to his department. Their technical paper entitled "Structural damage to reinforced concrete buildings in Ottawa induced by the Montreal earthquake" had been rejected from the first two refereed technical journals to which it was submitted, but they were confident that it would be accepted with glowing reviews in the Disaster Engineering Review Journal, published by South Hokkaido Institute of Technology Press.

Kaylee Carling and Réal Chaput-Vigneault's brilliant stratagems to redress the political mess amounted to naught, as much of her energy was sapped by an unexpected cervical cancer that required her immediate attention and chilled their relationship.

Shirley Coulthard, frustrated by the vagaries of her stressful career, resigned from political life and started a steamy affair with her channeler, as counseled by none other than MacKenzie King's spirit.

Wayne Greenbriar, Graham Murdoch, Florent Racine-Dostie and Julien Léveillé soldiered relentlessly for their respective generals, reveling in the opportunity to shape their nation per diametrically opposed visions, butting heads like rams pumped by an uncontrollable drive to establish dominance.

Brendon and Léandre, like selfish and calculating chess players imbued with passion for the game, filled with hate and respect for a dangerous opponent, yet brashly overconfident in their merciless ability to win, schemed around the clock to ensure their survival at the expense of the other. Both had felt robbed in kindergarten when, each time they excelled at a game, all undeserving participants were declared winners just for the sake of protecting everybody's fragile self esteem—a practice they later construed as the distrustful pedagogical front for a socialistic agenda to kill competitiveness at such a tender age. This time, they were shooting for all the marbles and, eyes on the prize, life didn't exist outside the game.

Their maneuvers were closely watched and harshly critiqued by Richard Turcotte, who became the morning anchorman at a provocative talk radio station within a few days following the earthquake. In the span of six months, his show landed at the top of the ratings, and he managed to get sued for libel by various politicians, and for defamation by various interest groups. This led the Canadian Radio-television and Telecommunications Commission to threaten to revoke the station's license for abuse of its broadcasting privilege by airing offensive and insulting remarks. In a prompt settlement with the commission, Turcotte was fired and the station survived. Turcotte has since been working as a maintenance employee for the City of Montréal, assigned to a snow plowing crew in the winter. In his spare time, he is hosting his own internet-based radio station, and a weblog dedicated to "revealing the truth about our incompetent elected officials and their shameless waste of taxpayer dollars, straight from inside the dragons' lair."

Lise Letarte's touting of her years as director of the *Organisation de sécurité civile du Québec* as a major career achievement won her many interviews. However, wasting the opportunities provided by her inflated curriculum vitae, no job offer ever ensued from these interviews, during which she unabashedly revealed her true personality to prospective employers. Instead, relying on a tried-and-true formula, she was grafted into an emergency planning office in a small municipality where her cousin's husband became mayor, drifting lazy anew on the endless river of public funds.

Misdiagnosed as dead by Jean-Pierre and Audréanne, but reanimated through the relentless dedication of another team of interns who continued to perform cardiopulmonary resuscitation for many more minutes after the two had given up and left to be interviewed in an adjacent room, the homeless Clément remained homeless, with no intention or hope of a career change, and no greater brain damage than before. After being released from the hospital, he moved downtown, where he enjoyed watching the televisions displayed in the large bay windows of department stores. There, he developed a particular interest for the recurring "variety" show that involved snippets of Prime Ministers constantly arguing, and hoped for the stores to someday install outdoor speakers, so that the shows could also be heard by common men like him. Nonetheless, even with only visual entertainment, Clément sensed that something big was happening—he had no sense of the chips being played, but instinctively felt a duty to watch every evening after the stores closed and the sidewalks were deserted.

Jean-Pierre and Audréanne, enriched by their experience following the disaster and devoted to the pursuit of a profligate lifestyle, opened their own private practice, licentiously prescribing pills of all sizes and colors per their good judgment.

The referendum on Québec's sovereignty had been rescheduled to be held approximately 18 months after the earthquake, on an early fall day determined by the scrutiny of a hundred years of meteorological data and statistical analysis to have the highest probability of propitious weather. Data also confirmed lack of past earthquakes or other disasters on that day, although all knew that such statistics weren't designed to forecast catastrophic events.

On the eve of the referendum, polls predicted the voters to be split 50-50 between those who opposed or favored the motion formulated in the referendum question, as evidence that no isolated event, as cataclysmic as it may be, could overcome centuries of political quarrels. The national "sport" was being played intensely, and teams were already planning for numerous recounts to ensure that the last vote from the last ballot box was duly credited, and that the process would be carefully scrutinized and resilient against tampering.

On D-day, with all ballots cast and the polls closed, the whole nation was hypnotized by its television sets, awaiting the implicit instructions to rejoice or despair, depending on their allegiances. All eyeballs across the country were captive to news anchors and computer graphics charting Québec's destiny, except those of Louis Riopelle, whose hermitage in a cabin hidden in the depth of the tundra provided safe haven against politicians, media, and others who refused to recognize his talents.

Breinigsville, PA USA
30 October 2009
226747BV00004B/9/P